Readers love the Seasons of Love series by B.G. Thomas

Spring Affair

"This book is full of pain and hurt, but also hope and elation. It's like coming back to life after a long, hard winter…"

—My Fiction Nook

"This book is very full, and it is the sort of story you want to read when you need to be filled up."

—Prism Book Alliance

Summer Lover

"I highly recommend this to everyone, but especially to those of you that love a good story about finding oneself, sexy stories with a good story to them, broken men, and magick!"

—Good MM Book Reviews

"The story leads us by the hand and reminds all that we are perfectly made and no matter whom we love, the simple act of loving is a miracle in itself and should be treated as such."

—Joyfully Jay

Autumn Changes

"There are so many wonderful elements, from the well-crafted plot to the range of emotions."

—Inked Rainbow Reviews

By B.G. Thomas

All Alone in a Sea of Romance
All Snug
Anything Could Happen
The Beary Best Holiday Party
Ever
Bianca's Plan
The Boy Who Came In From the
Cold
Christmas Cole
Christmas Wish
Derek
Desert Crossing
Grumble Monkey and the
Department Store Elf
Hound Dog and Bean
How Could Love Be Wrong?
It Had to Be You
Just Guys
Men of Steel (Dreamspinner
Anthology)
A More Perfect Union (Multiple
Author Anthology)
Red
Riding Double (Dreamspinner
Anthology)
A Secret Valentine
Soul of the Mummy
Editor: A Taste of Honey
(Dreamspinner Anthology)
Two Tickets to Paradise
(Dreamspinner Anthology)
Until I Found You

GOTHIKA
Bones (Multiple Author
Anthology)
Spirit (Multiple Author
Anthology)

SEASONS OF LOVE
Spring Affair
Summer Lover
Autumn Changes
Winter Heart

Published by DREAMSPINNER PRESS
www.dreamspinnerpress.com

Winter Heart

B.G. Thomas

DREAMSPINNER
PRESS

Published by
DREAMSPINNER PRESS

5032 Capital Circle SW, Suite 2, PMB# 279, Tallahassee, FL 32305-7886 USA
www.dreamspinnerpress.com

Winter Heart
© 2016 B.G. Thomas.

Cover Art
© 2016 Paul Richmond.
http://www.paulrichmondstudio.com
Cover content is for illustrative purposes only and any person depicted on the cover is a model.

ISBN: 978-1-63477-777-3
Digital ISBN: 978-1-63477-778-0
Library of Congress Control Number: 2016913576
Published October 2016
v. 1.0
"Fly" lyrics and music by Bobby Jo Valentine. Copyright © 2011 by Bobby Jo Valentine. Used with permission of the artist.
"Nice Clothes" lyrics and music by Bobby Jo Valentine. Copyright © 2015 by Bobby Jo Valentine. Used with permission of the artist.
"Seasons Changing" lyrics and music by Christine Kane. Copyright © 2009 by Firepink music. All rights reserved. Used by permission of the artist.
"Open Road" lyrics and music © 2003 Heather Thornton. Used with permission of the artist.
"Cauley" words by Cameron Schneberger. © 2015. Used by permission of the artist.
"I Am Grateful for My Spiritual Path" by Malcolm Kane © 2015. Used by permission of the author.

Printed in the United States of America

This paper meets the requirements of
ANSI/NISO Z39.48-1992 (Permanence of Paper).

This is for Andi Byassee.

She has been with me since my very first novel,
and I was so happy because *finally*, someone who "got" me.

She knew when to edit heavy, and when to let me speak in my voice.
I have come to love this woman and count her as a *true* friend,
and to know never, ever to get annoyed when she uses her red pen.

Thank you, Andi, for allowing me to shine!

ACKNOWLEDGMENTS

THANKS TO so many people who helped make this book, and this series happen! Special thanks to….

My husband Raymond (for listening to endless hours of ideas, questions, and wailings while I wrote this book), Elizabeth North (because), Paul Richmond (for inspiration), Lynn West (for the title and fixing *that* chapter), Andi, Tippy, and Katie (for extraordinary edits and making this story so much better!), Noah Willoughby (for insight, research extraordinaire, and for being a voice in the dark), Will Jones (also because), Ross Allen Milam (who has always been the inspiration for *Winter Heart*'s hero and agreed to have his likeness on the cover— such a sweet and sexy man), Brandon Witt (also such a sweet and sexy man—who facilitated Ross being *on* my cover), Elin Gregory (because always, again and again), Cameron Schneberger (for the amazing poem), Brenna (for wonderful edits), Kade Boehme (for all things New York), Ann Kopchik (another wonderful researcher), Nancy Flowers (for the joke—as bad as it was), Masau White (for all things Samoan), Clint Koetting (for camping help and being a caretaker most *extraordinaire* for some ten years now with his lovely wife, Rhi), Thomas Strait (for Steam!) and I *cannot* forget Joanne Papin (she knows why and I know why, and that's what's important) who I miss every *single* day.

And to Christine Kane and Bobby Jo Valentine for letting me use their lyrics in my novel. Words cannot express….

Winter passes and one remembers one's perseverance.

— Yoko Ono

In the depth of winter I finally learned that there was in me an invincible summer.

— Albert Camus

To everything there is a season, and a time to every purpose under the heaven.

— Ecclesiastes 3:1, KJV

CHAPTER ONE

WYATT LOOKED out over the dining room table and thought, *Holy shit, what have I done?*

There was barely any room left, what with the pineapples and bananas and coconuts and oranges (the last of which he wasn't sure really fit the theme, but they looked nice), the big ham and cheese tray (*Oh! Is Asher even eating ham these days?*), and of course the ridiculously huge cake—the centerpiece for the table. It was shaped like a volcano, and Wyatt had baked it and built it up and decorated it himself (mostly). There were little plastic palm trees up its slopes, red icing lava flowing down its sides, and he'd even placed a juice can down inside the top, half-filled with water, just waiting for the dry ice he'd bought so he could make his volcano smoke. Bright and colorful leis hung from the lighting fixture over the table (although he wasn't sure if they were exactly a Samoan tradition or not), along with some silk marijuana versions he'd bought at It's A Beautiful Day in the city.

Nothing too low-key for Wyatt Dolan!

Except he couldn't help but think he'd forgotten something.

I'll have leftovers for days.

What had he been thinking? After all, this was Porch Night, not a dinner party. Everybody would have eaten already.

I should have told them not to eat!

Howard would have been furious if he'd known, especially when Wyatt couldn't really afford to do this these days.

But then, Howard didn't have anything to say about what Wyatt did or didn't do anymore, did he? His lover of nearly eleven years had dumped him two months previously—kicked him out of his life as well as the home they'd made together.

Wyatt shut his eyes tight and fought off the wave of grief that threatened to sweep over him. *No! Not tonight. Tonight is fun. I am going to have fun!* He stood up tall—or as tall as he could at five foot seven—and held his head high, shoulders back. He was Wyatt Dolan, the little bear of the Fabulous Four (so dubbed by himself), and he was a… *superstar*! Short he might be. Chubby too. But he could dazzle. And he was especially dazzling tonight in the gorgeous blue Samoan shirt that Peni had given him. One of Peni's brothers had gotten too heavy for it and passed it on to Wyatt (which made Wyatt feel wonderfully svelte). Everyone would be expecting him to be down and sad, but he would show them! Show them how amazing he really was.

He was determined to, especially tonight, because this was the first Saturday of the month and his turn to host Porch Night; the one evening that he and his friends—the Fabulous Four—vowed never to miss. Barring flood (there hadn't been a flood in Terra's Gate since 1977, and it hadn't been nearly as bad as what had hit Kansas City), earthquake (very unlikely, but not impossible in Missouri), contracts for a special with HBO (but even that had not stopped Asher—the resident soon-to-be-famous member of the FF), or even a zombie apocalypse. And Wyatt had long ago declared that last wasn't an excuse for them to miss showing up either, because wouldn't the four of them show Rick Grimes and crew how to deal with the walking dead with fearsome fabulosity?

Of course, it wouldn't be just the four of them tonight, would it? Where once the rule had been that Porch Night was for only the four of them—no buddies, no visiting relatives, no boyfriends du jour, or even foreign dignitaries—that had somehow changed lately, hadn't it?

And all because Wyatt's three friends, who for years now had been single seemingly forever, had quite suddenly begun to find boyfriends. And not the du jour kind either. One after the other, his buddies, in the space of about nine months, had met and all but married the most perfect men (or at least perfect for them, to paraphrase Grace Jones) imaginable.

Now Wyatt understood how Sloan could get a boyfriend. Sloan was a hell of a catch for any man. Even though Sloan wasn't Wyatt's type (give him a big ol' hairy bear any day), no doubt most men thought Sloan was gorgeous, what with his copper hair, honey-brown eyes, and alabaster skin (with its sprinkling of about a million freckles). Hell, the only reason he'd been single for so long was because he'd been hopelessly in love with Asher, the one gay man on Earth who wouldn't—or couldn't—love him back. At least not in a romantic way. Then—lo and behold—Sloan met Max (a real hunka-cola) and *tout de suite* and easy peasy, the two of them were as googly-eyed for each other as a couple of teenagers.

Well… it hadn't been *quite* that simple.

But it had been awfully sweet.

Unfortunately, when Sloan and Max got together, it had been really rough on Scott. The torch that Sloan had borne for his hopeless infatuation with Asher had been put to final rest after three years when he met and fell in love with Max, but Scott had been hopelessly in love with Sloan for a much longer time (Wyatt suspected for ten years, since Scott first met Sloan in college).

It wasn't that Scott was a bad guy, or even unattractive (although again, not Wyatt's type—he was *way* too skinny). It was just that he lived in a fantasy world of Harlequin Romance love, which wasn't the worst of it. Fantasies aside, Scott was the biggest curmudgeon and pessimist Wyatt had ever met in his whole life.

But then—*slam! bang!*—Scott found a man as well. A truly wonderful man. Scott (of *all* people) had gone to the Heartland Queer Men's Festival (the last place Wyatt would have ever thought he'd go), and through several miracles he had learned to set his stodgy ways aside and met a very, *very* sexy man (but once again a little smooth for Wyatt's taste) named Cedar. Before Sloan's week-long camping trip was over, he'd found true love.

Then came the *biggest* surprise of all.

Asher! *Gods!* Who would have ever thought it? Asher had found love! Asher, who didn't "do" boyfriends. In fact, he rarely did second-night stands. "I can't have a lover, especially a man. I'm going to be famous. Do you think fans want to look up at their favorite hunk on that big silver screen and then picture him fucking a dude?"

So it was a hell of a surprise when Asher started dating a beautiful Samoan man named Peni (only about the sweetest guy Wyatt had ever met). And the cutie had even managed to have a profound effect on Asher's drinking (as in, helping with its reduction).

So now the three of them all had boyfriends, and instead of Porch Night being just the four of them, boyfriends were now apparently invited.

Wyatt supposed he might have been okay with the new turn of events. Except for the fact that he used to be the only one of them who'd *had* a lover (for over a *decade*), and now he was the only single one.

It was like a soap opera come to life!

Like sands through the hourglass....

The wave of grief threatened again.

No. No!

Oh, the irony.

"You don't have to host right now," Sloan had said a few days ago. "Max and I'll be glad to switch with you."

Wyatt rolled his eyes at the suggestion. "How are we going to do that? You hosted *last* month."

"Then just skip a turn. No one will care."

"What will that do? It won't solve anything."

"It'll give you four more months to—" Sloan paused. "—get yourself to feeling right."

Feeling right? Really? Feeling right? Whenever the hell would that be? Wyatt had only shaken his head at that. "No. I might as well take the bull by the balls. Besides, Peni will be coming. He's finally back from Samoa. How can I miss giving him a big welcome-home celebration? It's all planned. I've bought half the stuff already. *No*! I'm hosting."

And then, one more irony.

Wyatt wasn't even hosting Porch Night from *his* porch (not that it was warm enough this December night to use the porch). No, this wasn't even his house. Sloan owned it. Sloan had inherited it from his mother when she died—was that a year ago now? Had that much time passed?

The man who Sloan happened to fall in love with was his next-door neighbor. When said neighbor's wife elected to move to France—

...so are the Days of Our Lives....

—that left Sloan and Max with two houses. Sloan had been reluctant to sell his, even though it was smaller, for the simple fact that it *had* belonged to his mother. What if some buyer came along and did something like plow over her huge, gorgeous garden and replaced it with sod?

But then Howard kicked Wyatt out of their home—the house (a real fixer-upper) they had spent years repairing, remolding, reconstructing, and redecorating into a reflection of the two of them—leaving him no place to live. Kicked him out of their dream home. It had been devastating.

But being homeless had wound up solving a problem for Sloan. It not only gave Wyatt a place to live, but gave Sloan the knowledge that his mother's home would be taken care of, at least for the time being.

Somehow living in Sloan's house, living next door to his best friend, was what had made it all bearable. And it was a relief for Wyatt to have a roof over his head.

But it wasn't *his* roof. It wasn't the house that he had made his home.

Another wave threatened.

I'm alone. I'm going to be alone. Who's going to want me?

He shook himself. No. He couldn't go there. Couldn't be depressed. He had to be *on*.

Goddess, maybe I really shouldn't *have hosted this tonight*....

But it was too late now, wasn't it? Everybody would be arriving soon. At least with all the extra people, they might make a dent in the food. Into the breach!

Wyatt went into the living room and started the CDs he'd burned for tonight. He'd found a bunch of Samoan and Hawaiian music online and then, for fun, thrown in everything from Blondie's "The Tide is High" to Israel "IZ" Kamakawiwo'ole's "Somewhere Over the Rainbow/What a Wonderful World" medley.

He surveyed the table one more time. The only thing *not* there was the cooler of tropical rum punch and the pitcher of the alcohol-free version. Those were in the kitchen where there was a linoleum floor instead of the hardwood of the dining room. Those coolers tended to drip from their little faucets and make quite a mess.

But he *still* couldn't help but think he'd forgotten something.

Then it hit him.

Oh no! A joke!

He didn't have a new joke for tonight! He *had* to have a joke! He always had a joke for Porch Night. At *least* one. Problem was, the only gay ones he'd been able to find lately had been derogatory and homophobic—endless punch lines about fudge packing, AIDS, and rainbow Skittles. He'd hated them. He'd hated the fact that gay men had posted a lot of them.

He needed a joke. How could they have a Porch Night without one of his jokes? Wyatt ran for his laptop and was just booting it up so he could google one when…

The doorbell rang.

Piss!

He stopped, sighed, touched his short spiky hair (hoped it looked okay), and opened the door.

It was Sloan and Max, looking all happy and flush-cheeked and eyes flashing. Frak! It didn't take a genius to realize what they'd been up to before they got here. They were still boinking like rabbits after all these months.

Well.... Well.... Well, good for them! Lucky them. It was good. Someone needed to have sex. *It's not like I'm ever going to have sex again.* Because who would want a fat little bear when they could have someone who looked like these two?

Stop feeling sorry for yourself.

"Tah-low-fa," he said, practicing the Samoan word Peni had taught him. *Talofa*—a greeting, like "hello."

"*Talofa*," Sloan said with a laugh, because he was in on this. And Max? Max gave one of his single macho nods.

Max was such a mystery. Quiet and masculine one minute and all animated the next. Like a friendlier version of bipolar.

"Well, don't just stand there," Wyatt said, opening the screen door and motioning them in. "I mean, it *is* your place."

A car horn honked, and a cream-colored Lexus pulled up in front of the house. That would be Scott and Cedar. They would have been riding their motorcycles if it hadn't been so cold today. It was like they had it timed, getting here at exactly the same time as Sloan and Max. At least Wyatt could count on Asher being late. He did live in the city after all, and…

Except lookee there. Asher's old, battered pickup was pulling over across the street.

Asher and Peni.

Synchronized.

Hail, hail, the gang's all here….

"Come on in, guys," he said. "We're letting the cold in."

CHAPTER TWO

IT MADE Wyatt extraordinarily happy that everyone was impressed with the layout. "Don't forget to get a lei," he announced, pointing to where they hung over the dining room table.

"Oh!" Cedar pumped his fist. "I want one of the ganja ones!"

"Me too," said Scott.

Would wonders never cease? Scott? Wanted one of the marijuana leis? Was it one of the final signs of the apocalypse (that Wyatt didn't believe in)? Wyatt almost giggled.

"I can't believe you did all this," said Asher, and then he answered Wyatt's wonderings by popping a roll of the thinly sliced ham into his mouth before it even reached his plate. He might have been getting curious about his Jewish heritage for the first time since he was a kid, but it didn't look like Asher was converting back to the religion of his grandfather anytime soon. Still, it was sweet to see the way he was watching over Peni. Sweet, lovely Peni with his caramel skin and Superman blue-black hair and the tattoos that Wyatt was dying to see.

Asher turned to his lover. "You know, Peni, you can just sit and rest. I'll load your plate for you."

Peni laughed. "I'm fine and you know it," he declared and then blushed furiously when Asher told him he was far more than fine. He was *delicious*.

"If I was going to have a problem, wouldn't it be *with* sitting?" Peni asked.

"I don't know," Asher said. "I think it should be *me* who would have trouble sitting after last night."

Peni blushed all the more, and there were a few hoots around the table.

"I meant my *pe'a*," Peni said, referring to his new tattoos.

"I know what you meant," Asher said and gave him a sweet kiss. It really was amazing. A side of Asher that Wyatt had never expected to see. Sweet. Kind. Romantic.

"I just can't get over the cake," Peni said, pointing. "I mean, it's even smoking!"

That was because Wyatt had run for the kitchen freezer, taken one of the small chunks he'd chipped off the block of dry ice, and carefully dropped it down into the juice can concealed within the cake.

"It's gorgeous, isn't it?" Sloan said as it smoked away.

"It really is something," said Max. Broad shouldered, a shadow of a beard on his strong jaw, flashing blue eyes, and a hint of chest hair showing at his open collar, he was the one man here tonight Wyatt was attracted to. Wyatt had had more than one fantasy about seeing Max naked, like trying to dodge into the locker room at the local gym where they all worked out. Sloan had forbidden it. And that was even before the two of them hooked up. Now that they were practically married, Wyatt knew he would probably never get a look. And wasn't that one of the first things Howard had taught him? To look?

"Hey, we're men!" Howard had declared on many an occasion. "We *like* to look. You look *all* you want, baby."

"That volcano must have taken you all day," Max continued.

"It really wasn't all that much trouble," Wyatt said, blushing. "I started with an angel food cake pan and then when it was done, did some carving and some sculpting and threw in lots of icing and—*voilà*!"

"Don't let Wyatt fool you," Sloan said. "He's spent like two or three evenings working on it."

"I had to do something in honor of you coming home," Wyatt said, turning to Peni.

"How did you make it smoke like that?" Peni asked.

"Why, magic," Wyatt said. "After all, I *am* a witch."

"You really did outdo yourself," Scott said when he'd circled around the table to Wyatt. He dropped his chin on Wyatt's shoulder. "Asher is going to have to work his ass off to *ever* top this."

"I heard that!" Asher cried, laughing.

Wyatt grinned again. He couldn't help it. He hadn't realized how much he'd needed all the fuss. He was only doing what he loved to do, but it had been a while since he'd been able to show off.

They all filled their plates, and Wyatt reminded them that the cocktails were in the kitchen. "I've got them leaded and lead-free," he said.

"Leaded and lead-free?" Peni asked.

"With and without booze," Wyatt explained.

"You have an alcohol-free version?" Peni asked. "I thought you once told me that gay men are *required* to drink."

Wyatt smiled wistfully. "I'm changing my mind. Plus—" He glanced at Asher. "—you know...."

"Well, I'm certainly imbibing," Cedar said and went right to the cooler in the kitchen. "I love how you decorated it."

It hadn't been a lot of trouble. He'd simply taken a straw mat, wrapped it around the cooler, and tied it on. He would have used a glue gun, but then, the cooler wasn't his.

"Where did you get the tiki goblets?" Scott asked.

"It was an incredible find," Wyatt crowed. "I got them at Michaels, in the city. I was lucky. They were on *clearance*. No one is having luaus this time of year. And they had exactly enough of them." *Seven, not eight*, he thought with a sigh.

"Now you're shocking me," Asher said. "You've always told us we should *never* admit we got something cheap, on sale, or at a garage sale."

Wyatt gave a little shrug. He was looking at all kinds of things differently these days. Watching his money was a big one. With as much as Howard had made, Wyatt had been able to get away with a lot. Without Howard he was wondering how he was going to make ends meet. He was manager of Treasures of Terra, the New Age store where he worked, but it was a small business, and he wasn't paid a fortune. With businesses failing so much these days, it was wonderful that the store was doing as well as it was. He was really thankful that Sloan had refused to take any rent money the last two months.

"I hope you don't think I'm taking advantage," Wyatt had said while Sloan watched him make the cake, even lent a hand with the icing.

"What are you talking about?" Sloan had asked as he slathered chocolate icing where directed.

"That I spent all this money and haven't given you a cent for rent."

"You tried to give us money, Wyatt," Sloan said. "And I said no. We can think about that in the future. The house is paid for. We wanted you to have a chance to get some money in the bank. A cushion."

"I'll make it work," he said. "And Katherine is letting me do readings on my days off for extra money." Katherine was his boss and the owner of Treasures of Terra.

"Readings?" Sloan glanced up. There was some icing on his nose, and Wyatt had to laugh.

"Tarot readings," he answered.

"Did I know you did that?" Sloan looked crossed-eyed down at the end of his nose and then wiped the chocolate away and stuck his finger in his mouth.

"It's been a long time. I did a reading for you one drunken night about five years ago."

"Five years," Sloan said and whistled. "Have we really known each other that long?"

"Ever since my short stint in the call center." Wyatt winced. "*That* didn't last long, did it?"

"Well you did tell a customer to kiss your ass," Sloan said.

"My rosy red ass." Wyatt crossed his arms. "Because she called me a fag! And I told her that I was more man than she was ever going to have and more woman than she would ever be."

"Well, I don't care where you got the goblets," Peni said, drawing Wyatt from his musings. "I love them."

That's when Sebastian the crab began to croon to them from the stereo, letting them know they should take it from him, there was *no* place better than under the sea. That was the perfect time for them to find a place to settle in the living room. Wyatt had brought in a few dining room chairs to make sure everyone had a place to sit, and as he joined them, he looked around the room. Gods…. Lovers paired up all around him. And he was alone.

Yet… was he? Could he really look at all these people and think he was alone?

Wyatt looked from face to face to face, listened to them as they chatted, and the warmth surged into almost overwhelming love. He really was lucky. As hard as things had been these past months—how lonely he'd been lying in that bed by himself night after night and week after week—how much worse would it have been without these friends?

"Asher," said Max. "Any word on *Drunks*?"

Which was the movie Asher was doing for HBO. Imagine. HBO. Asher had gone from a small stage in Kansas City to a movie for HBO. Wyatt had always insisted they would all be famous one day, and Asher, at least, was on his way.

"I think it's scheduled for November," Asher said.

"*November*?" cried Wyatt. "*Next* November?"

"Well, this November did pass last month," Asher replied.

"But that's a year away! We have to wait that long?"

"Wyatt, we've barely begun shooting."

But... "But the play wasn't even two hours long! How long does it take to make a movie?"

Asher chuckled. "We've got about two weeks under our belts and another three more weeks to go, and that's because they've added a couple of flashback scenes that take place outside of the hotel where the play took place."

"They've added scenes?" asked Sloan.

Asher nodded. "Yes. That's pretty normal for a movie. Did you know the *play* version of *Steel Magnolias* is set strictly in the beauty shop?"

Wyatt nodded. "I saw it at the Pegasus Theatre. It was pretty cool. Half the women were played by men in drag!"

"Movies are able to add all kinds of stuff. They almost always do since they don't have the constraints of what can be done onstage. And then there'll probably be pickups. After that there is a host of stuff that happens. Editing. Music. Promotion. I'm excited we're only having to wait that long."

"But a *year*!" Wyatt whined. He couldn't help it. Somehow he thought it all went so much faster. Then a new thought. "How did you manage to get home this weekend if you're still shooting?"

"I told Spencer I wanted the weekend off, and he didn't even blink."

"Oh," Wyatt said. "You're on a first name basis with him now?"

Spencer—Spencer Morrison, the actor—was the big name who was making *Drunks* into a movie and possibly only one of the biggest stars in Hollywood these days.

"I wanted to be here for Peni." Asher hugged his lover close. "I didn't tell Spencer that—he thinks it's something else."

Something else? Did they not know Asher was gay? Wyatt thought Asher was out of the closet. He'd slept with about a million men—it wasn't like he'd been discreet. People would find out.

"I wanted to fly from Samoa right to Los Angeles," Peni said. "But my family wouldn't hear of it."

"No, I don't suppose they would," Max said. "You can't blame them. That's the way it *should* be."

That's the way it should *be*, Wyatt thought. But it wasn't like that for everybody.

Which made it all the more painful that Howard was out of his life. Howard was—had been—his entire life. His family. Howard had rescued him when his blood family had rejected him.

Only to abandon me.

He bit down on his lower lip. *No.* No pain tonight.

"But the advance buzz for *Drunks* is already good," Asher was saying. "People are talking. They might pick it up for a series."

"Really?" asked Scott. "This is the play you did a few months ago at the Pegasus?"

Asher nodded.

"How can they make it into a series? Wasn't the story pretty much told?"

"Yeah. But they like the characters a lot. They want to explore the idea of what happens next."

"Whoa." Scott grinned. "It only proves that anything can happen."

Wyatt grinned back. Amazing. *Scott.* The pessimist. Talking like anything could happen. Then, mind bouncing as usual and unable to resist—he was Wyatt Dolan after all—he asked, "So tell me, Asher. Have you seen Spencer Morrison naked?"

"Wyatt!" said Max. "How was he supposed to do that?"

Asher shook his head and then, bless his heart, blushed. Had Wyatt ever seen Asher blush? "No. But I *could* have. He sure offered."

Wyatt's mouth fell open.

"He tried to get me in bed."

Wait. What? What had Asher just said? "Spencer Morrison?" Wyatt exclaimed. "Spencer-*fucking*-Morrison?"

Asher nodded.

"You know, they say he's going to get nominated for an Oscar this year," Scott interjected, apparently unaffected by Asher's bombshell. "For *Crosshairs.*"

Wyatt shook his head, held up a hand. "You know I was mostly kidding, right? About the naked part?"

Asher grinned. "No, you weren't. You were hoping I got a look at him in a dressing room or something…."

Wyatt bit his lip. Well. It was true.

"Well, I was standing next to him, taking a piss if you must know, and I could have looked—"

"And you *didn't?*" Wyatt said, his voice a squeak. "You didn't even peek? You could have seen Spencer-fucking-Morrison's dick and you didn't look? Oh—My—Gods! *Sacrilege.* Hand over your gay card! *Now.*"

Asher looked over at Peni and placed a hand on his knee. "There is only one penis I want to see these days, Wyatt."

Peni smiled like a high-school girl. "Oh, Asher." They kissed.

I don't believe this! I have fallen asleep and woken back up in the twilight zone.

"You know I wouldn't have minded," Peni said. "I mean, if you'd peeked? After all, I certainly don't want you to have to give up your gay card."

Asher laughed. "Well… I might have caught a glimpse…."

Wyatt jumped to his feet, nearly spilling his plate of food. "And? *And?*"

"I honestly didn't get a good look. But he was sure trying to show it to me."

Wyatt shook his head violently, held his hands up high, and then clasped them to his chest. "Okay. *Wait.* I am *trying* to picture this." And he could. He could! Standing next to Spencer-*fucking*-Morrison—only the next Matthew McConaughey or Bradley Cooper. "You are telling me that *Spencer* Morrison was wagging his cock at you—"

Asher laughed and gave a shrug.

"—and you *didn't* look?"

"It was kind of pathetic, really."

"His *cock?*" The world was coming to an end. "Spencer Morrison's cock is pathetic?" It couldn't be. It—could—not—*be!*

"No," said Asher. "Not his cock. *Him.* So full of himself. Thinking all he had to do was show me his cock and I'd be on my knees. Trying to seduce me that way. As if I couldn't resist him."

Wyatt shook his head. If Spencer Morrison had waved his cock at him, he would have been on his knees in a flash. Of course, it had been a long time since he'd been on his knees. Sometimes he wondered if he ever would again. Then sometimes he wasn't sure he wanted to.

"I don't even know why you care," Asher said. "He's not your type. Way too skinny, isn't he?"

Wyatt opened his eyes wide. "Doesn't matter. That was *celebrity* dick, Asher. You *never* miss a chance to look at *celebrity* dick."

Everybody started to laugh.

"You know, I used to feel that way," Scott said. "But now Cedar…. Well, I don't need to see anybody else's either."

Wyatt put his hands on his hips. He was feeling a real fit coming on. "No! No-no-no-no-no!" He shook his head again.

"I *would* look," Cedar said.

"Cedar!" Scott glowered at his lover.

This only caused more laughter around the room.

"Anyway," Asher said. "When I wouldn't look, he took another tactic. He came right into my trailer one day and all but grabbed my ass. I told him I belonged to Peter Wagner—"

Only one of the richest gay men in the country—hell, richest men in the country period—and a producer on *Drunks* as well.

"—and he let go of me so fast you would have thought he'd grabbed a hornet's nest. Started apologizing like crazy. It was all I could do not to laugh at him. It's part of what got me here this weekend. He didn't object for one second when I mentioned I was flying home. Of course, he thinks it was to be with Peter Wagner."

"I won't tell him if you don't," Wyatt said and tried to let it sink in. Spencer Morrison was gay. And tried to show Asher his cock. Surely it would have been okay to look! Wyatt had an entire collection of celebrity nudes on his computer. Hundreds (thousands?) of pictures. But not *one* of Spencer Morrison. Shirtless, sure, but not even a butt shot. Howard wouldn't have cared if Wyatt looked. Howard wouldn't have cared if Wyatt blew him. Howard would have called him crazy for not doing so. Would have pushed Wyatt out of the way if he'd been there.

Then Wyatt noticed the way Asher was looking at Peni and the way Peni was looking back. Gods… in love. They were so in love. Had Howard *ever* looked at him that way?

Yes. He could remember Howard holding every door open for him, taking him to dinner, buying him single red roses. And making love to him like no one ever had before. It had been so much more than the fumbling, awkward sex he'd had with boys in high school. Boys who would call him faggot at school but happily ask him to their houses for a sleepover and an exchange of mutual blowjobs on weekends. Mutual if he was lucky, that was. Usually it meant him blowing them. And Wyatt, desperate for any human contact, accepted it.

Howard didn't deny him anything but his ass and treated him so differently from those boys….

But even in the beginning, Howard had made it clear he could *never* be monogamous.

That had broken Wyatt's heart. It had. It really had. Hard to remember that kid he used to be. The dreamer. The romantic. Looking for a knight in shining armor. Yet now it came back clearly. The ache at the idea that Howard wanted other men. How could he practically cut

Wyatt's steak for him but want other men at the same time? The first night that Howard told him they wouldn't be monogamous, he'd gone and taken a shower. Taken a shower to muffle the sound. So Howard wouldn't know. Taken a shower and bawled. Then Howard came home the next day with flowers, and Wyatt had been lost, totally unable to resist him. He'd decided "fuck it." If he couldn't have the Disney fairy tale, he'd have the next best thing.

Howard convinced him that not only were other men no threat to the two of them, but there was nothing wrong with Wyatt being with other men as well. Even on his own. He encouraged it.

How had that happened?

"You're young," Howard had told him. "You need to sow your wild oats, Wyatt! *Try* things. Try different men. Experience life. I mean, don't you ever want to try topping?"

And he had, hadn't he? He had found the sexual adventures to be fun. He'd decided that maybe Howard was right—it was stupid to think he could have a Harlequin Romance life (his mother had read those his whole life, and he'd snuck dozens of them late at night). But those stories weren't real.

But…

But now, looking at his friends? Had he been right? Did they have it? Did they have everything Wyatt's boyhood heart had ever wanted? Did Harlequin love really exist after all?

"And in a week or so," Peni said, breaking Wyatt from his thoughts, "I'll fly out to be with him."

Even though the two of you will only be there a week or so? Wyatt wondered.

"We know it will only be a week or so," Asher said as if reading Wyatt's thoughts. "But that's a week we'll have together. And besides… come on… *Hollywood.* I want to show him around."

Everyone agreed that was just splendid, and Wyatt managed a smile. Good for him. Good for *them.*

It didn't make the ache go away, though.

And then…

…as Wyatt looked around the room, he had a sudden thought.

It seemed crazy, but…

When had the trouble really begun with Howard?

Why… why, it had been *the* month that Sloan met Max.

And as the sparks between the two of them turned into a fire and then true love, the fights had begun to turn serious between Wyatt and Howard.

He would never forget when Howard had ignored their veto rule—the ability they each had to nix a partner's potential playmate. Wyatt had told Howard in no uncertain terms that he didn't want him having sex with Chuck (Upchuck) Mueske, a complete gnome, and Howard told him he didn't care—he was going to anyway. He wound up not doing anything, but not before Wyatt had a complete fit and stormed out.

Next, when Scott met Cedar out at Camp during the annual Heartland Queer Men's Festival (an event that Wyatt loved and Scott had always mocked!), things only got worse. *Way* worse. He and Howard had a huge fight that time—their worst ever. It seemed Howard had practically raped some kid, and word was, he hadn't worn a condom (not that a condom would have made it okay). The kid—a sweet airhead named Blue—came to admit his part in what happened. And after Wyatt and Howard had their roof-raising fight, Wyatt accepted Howard's story. That the incident had been a role-playing game that had gone wrong. That Howard hadn't realized he'd taken things too far....

Then, finally, Asher had found love.

Asher—who Wyatt figured would *never* settle down—fell in love with Peni, and *suddenly* Wyatt was the only one single.

How had that happened?

Well! It had happened when Wyatt had gotten off work early one day and picked up some Nilgiri chicken korma and samosas on the way home to surprise Howard and found his lover in the middle of a bareback party—fucking some guy bent over their coffee table (they'd picked it up for a steal in a little antique shop on one of their trips) while he, Howard, was getting fucked by a man with one of the biggest cocks Wyatt had ever seen (and he'd seen some huge cocks).

Howard.

Who did *not* get fucked.

When Wyatt got (understandably) angry—started shouting about it—Howard kicked him out. Broke up with him! Told him he was tired of Wyatt's shit. Slapped him! Howard had never hit him. Close once or twice, maybe (he'd seen it in Howard's eyes), but never hit him.

And now for the first time in years, *he* was single and his friends—every one of them without a lover in all the time he'd known them—were all quite suddenly and happily deep in wedded bliss.

What if…

What if there were something… cosmic going on? What *if* the gods only had so much wedded bliss to go around? What if him being in a relationship had somehow… blocked his friends from doing the same? What if their finding love meant some cosmic balance had shifted, and now *he* had to be alone?

Maybe this was some weight he needed to bear so his friends could be happy?

Would he ever have someone again? Would he ever have what they had? Was Howard right? That no one would ever want him?

Gods.

Please….

No.

The group began to whoop and holler, startling Wyatt out of his thoughts.

"I'm not stripping!" cried Peni.

"No," agreed Asher. "He most assuredly is not!"

"But I do want you to see…," Peni said.

See? See what?

"Be back in a flash."

"I can't wait," Cedar was saying. "I bet he looks amazing."

"He does," Asher said with a sweet smile.

"I just can't imagine the pain," said Scott. "I looked it up on Google and found some articles that made me downright queasy."

"I'll bet they don't come close to describing how bad it really was." For a moment Asher's face went grim. "I don't know how he did it. *I* could barely make it."

Oh gods, thought Wyatt. Did they mean…?

And to confirm Wyatt's wonderings, Peni came back, jeans replaced by a sarong. No. A lava-lava. That is what Samoans called the colorful piece of cloth tied around Peni's waist. It flowed around him as he walked and there was no way you could help but see the tattoos.

The pe'a.

Magnificent.

Unreal.

Almost otherworldly.

The elaborate tattoos were nothing like what Wyatt had drawn all over Peni's legs and lower buttocks with a Sharpie last Halloween.

Nothing.

Wyatt was quite simply in awe at the sight. Nothing could have prepared him for what he saw.

The pe'a began at Peni's knees and rose up his body to his waist and higher, covering every inch of skin with black and line and pattern. Wyatt's marker art had stopped at the waist, but Peni's Samoan art did not. In front it did, with a sort of checkerboard just below his belly button and said navel filled with a square of black. But then, in an upward fan pattern, the tattoos swept high on his sides and over his entire lower back. There were great plains of solid ink and then dozens of radiating lines— some straight, some jagged—dots, tiny squares, and daggers spread out like a palm leaf. Peni lifted his lava-lava high, concealing only his groin, to reveal more lines radiating out across his buttocks, some that met at the top of his cleft, which was filled in with even more black.

He was beautiful.

Wyatt couldn't speak. For a long moment, the only sounds around the room were the intakes of deep breaths and quiet gasps. As Wyatt stood there drinking in the beauty of Peni and his pe'a, he found himself feeling… spiritual.

None of this work had been done with a tattoo gun. Oh no. This ink had been inlaid deep into Peni's flesh by tools made of fish bone and boar's tusk. Tools carved into tiny, jagged, razor-sharp combs that were then dipped into the ink and tapped or even pounded in with a mallet. When Peni went to Samoa a couple of months ago to get his tattoos, Scott had called Wyatt, all but freaking out. He'd read what Peni was going to be doing—or having done to him—and sent Wyatt the links he'd found. Reading them had made him squeamish, even dizzy. Looking at the expansive artwork today, Wyatt could only rub at his teddy-bear tattoo on his upper arm and be embarrassed about what a big deal he'd made while getting it. His had taken an hour. Asher—and the online articles—said Peni's had taken days. Long twelve-hour days. And if Peni had stopped the *tufuga ta tatau*—the tattoo artist—before it was all done, he would have brought shame on himself and his family for the rest of his life.

Again, Wyatt could only stare in wonder.

"W-well?" Peni asked.

Around him, Wyatt's friends each opened and closed their mouths, at first not speaking. It seemed that the tattoos—the pe'a—had affected them all. They looked at Peni. They looked at each other. They looked at Asher.

Asher nodded once. "I know, right?"

Wyatt reached out, almost touched Peni's skin, then jerked his hand back. "It's… it's like holy ground."

Peni smiled, and his big black eyes turned wet. "Thank you, Wyatt."

Then Wyatt was crying and that "thank you" somehow broke the spell that had fallen over the group and they all began to speak.

THEY CHATTED more quietly after that, though. None of the robust hilarity that often ensued on Porch Night.

They updated each other as usual.

Scott and Cedar talked about how they were going to visit Cedar's mother, the famous rock star Cyan Carrington, for Christmas. She still hadn't met Scott and wanted to, and Scott was as nervous as fuck about meeting her. Wyatt was agog. "Wow! You're going to meet Cyan Carrington! You know she wrote 'Dark Witch,' right? And 'Night Birds'? I mean… whoa! And her new one playing all the time: 'Stuck out on the open road, I don't know which way I'm supposed to go….'"

He stopped, hearing the voice of Howard in his head shouting, *"Don't give up your day job!"* every time he sang. *"You sound like a cat in heat!"*

"Why do you think I'm so damned nervous?" Scott cried.

Sloan talked about how he might be flying out to New Hampshire for a few months to open another call center and how he didn't like the idea of being away from Max for so long. Max didn't like the idea either. They hadn't even been together a year, but the opportunity was incredible.

Asher told a few tales of Hollywood and what it was like to film a movie. Peni talked about all those weeks he spent recovering from getting his pe'a and how different island life was. But it had allowed him to find out even more about his heritage.

There were polite but cautious inquires as to how Wyatt was getting along.

Then, while Wyatt went to refresh several cocktails, Peni followed him into the kitchen and asked for a couple himself.

"I thought you didn't drink," Wyatt said.

"Not really. Especially after that drunken night when we all went to The Male Box." Peni rolled his eyes. "But I think I would like one tonight. Experience what you made. The 'lead-free' version is pretty good."

"Well, as long as you understand the lead-*in* version packs a little more punch, no pun intended. So be careful."

"I will."

"And Asher? He's drinking?"

"We're experimenting. We had a glass of wine with our dinner last week. It went just fine. He drank it slow and told me he couldn't remember actually *enjoying* a glass more. So I thought we could try one of these." He pointed at the decorated cooler.

"Okay." Wyatt nodded. Poured the fruity cocktails into the plastic tiki goblets, stopped about midway, and asked if perhaps he could half-and-half them with the nonalcoholic version. Peni thought that might be a good idea. Then just as he was about to hand them over, Peni was suddenly hugging him—holding him—in his arms. It felt so good. To just be hugged. Even by a friend. Maybe especially by a friend.

"Thank you, Wyatt," Peni whispered into his ear.

He was taken aback. *Thank you? For what?* "For what?" he asked aloud.

"For being *you*. I love you so much. I thought of you…."

"Th-thought of me?"

"When I was getting my pe'a. Sometimes." Peni got a faraway look on his face. "The pain…." He trembled. "It took me to this other… plane. I don't know how to explain it. There were times that I sort of… rose out of it. Like I wasn't in my body. Like I was… not drunk exactly. I don't know how to explain it. Strange thoughts would come. One time I was thinking of Tangaloa—the highest Samoan god—and then…. Well. I heard you. I heard your voice in my head—talking about your Lord and Lady and the Queer Ones. And that day, *you* were what got me through it all."

"Wow." Wyatt didn't know what to say. What did you say to that?

Peni pulled back. "When you said my pe'a was holy ground, I knew you understood. Maybe more than Asher—and I know he gets it."

Wyatt sucked in a breath and for some reason felt like crying.

"It reminded me of something. The other day I was thinking about us. You and me. About the paths we've chosen to walk. The not-Christian paths. And suddenly I remembered something. Don't *you* have a holy day coming? Isn't it really soon?"

Wyatt sighed. Felt that deep ache again. "Yule," he replied, remembering years of celebrating with Howard. And circles of friends, standing—hand in hand—celebrating the defeat of darkness and the triumphant return of light. "The Winter Solstice."

"What are you going to do this year? I mean… since…."

Since he wasn't with Howard anymore.

"I don't know," Wyatt said. "I guess I'll skip it. Just celebrate Christmas with the guys. It's not like Asher celebrates Chanukah, right?"

"But it seems wrong," Peni replied. Then something happened in his dark eyes. A determination. "Come here." He took Wyatt's hand in his own, ignoring the drinks, and led him back to the living room. "Hey, guys. I want to ask you something important."

They all stopped talking and turned, curiosity clear on their faces.

"What is it, baby?" Asher said.

Peni looked at Wyatt. "When is Yule?"

"I…." What? "It's in a couple weeks. On a Sunday."

Peni turned back to the group. "Yule is in two weeks. Big deal from what I understand for our friend here. And Wyatt doesn't have anyone to celebrate with. I think I'm going to. *No*. I *know* I'm going to. Does anyone want to join me? Join *us*?"

Wyatt almost gasped. What? What was Peni saying?

"Yeah," said Cedar immediately. "I'm game." He looked at his lover. "Scott?"

Scott smiled. "Sure. Why not? You mean like a circle, right? Like we did at Camp? I'd love to."

Wyatt's mouth almost fell open.

"You know you can count on me," Asher added, further astonishing Wyatt. Asher and Scott? In circle? Sloan he might have imagined but….

"I think that sounds fantastic," Sloan said.

Max, ever-practical Max, nodded. "I'm willing. It'll be educational. To see another spiritual approach to this time of year."

"Seriously?" Wyatt asked.

He looked around the room, and they were all nodding. Including friends that had—at least at one time—called what he did "witchy-woo-woo." Of course, one of those people had been Scott, and now he might as well be witchy-woo-woo himself. These friends. They had all changed so much. It wasn't just their love lives. It had been a year of transformation for all of them. And now? Now they were willing to celebrate a pagan ritual with him.

The tears came back to his eyes. "You guys…. You won't think it's too weird?"

"Not me!" proclaimed Scott. "Not after some of the things I saw this past summer."

"And I dig it big-time," added Cedar.

"I'm excited," said Peni. "I mean *really* excited."

"Oh gosh," Wyatt whispered, a tear threatening to roll down his cheek.

"Does it have to be Sunday?" Asher asked. "If we did it Saturday, I could fly in that morning and then go back to Los Angeles on Sunday."

"No!" Wyatt smiled. "Saturday is fine. We mostly do that anyway. Celebrate on the Saturday closest to."

"That works great," said Peni.

Everyone agreed. Wyatt couldn't believe it. The tears were building. *No! No tears.* He had to fight them. This was wonderful. A time of joy! And then! Inspiration struck! The night would be complete!

"Hey," Wyatt cried. "I got a joke."

Would wonders never cease, no one moaned!

"What do you call a bear with no teeth?"

Everyone shook their heads. Apparently no one had any idea, although he was sure someone would have guessed.

"A gummy bear!" he exclaimed.

There were groans. And a few giggles.

It wasn't a very good joke. But considering the circumstances, it wasn't bad at all.

CHAPTER THREE

KEVIN OWENS sat up in bed the minute the alarm clock went off, neither hitting the slumber button nor even considering going back to sleep. He was awake. Time for the day to begin.

Not that he had anything to do.

He stood up, scratched his underwear-clad balls, stretched, heard his back pop. It felt good.

He turned and looked out the window, seeing the silhouette of the New York City skyline. He never tired of it. He loved the city. Loved the old familiar buildings—was proud of the new. He loved the people. And that often reminded him of a line from one of his favorite books…

…to be in the midst of the whirl and rush of humanity, to share its life, its change, its death….

But to call Kevin a city boy would be wrong. He loved the country as well, and this morning—already—he was hearing the call of the Land. He'd been hearing it, *feeling it*, for a week. At least.

He could see it all in his mind's eye. The sun on the lake, and the great blue herons flying over it. Feel the grass beneath his bare feet, the sun on his skin, the soil sifting through his fingers as he weeded Hesperides Garden. Smell the earth and growing things. Almost hear the cicadas and the wind in the trees. He couldn't remember if there had been a time the call had come so early. He wasn't going to go to Camp for another seven months.

Of course, at this time of year Camp Sanctuary wouldn't look anything like he was used to. Not anything like what his senses remembered. He'd only been there once when it wasn't lush and green, and that had been for a memorial service for a dear friend late one fall a few years back. The trees hadn't been thoroughly bare—with some red and orange and more brown leaves stubbornly hanging on—but wow, quite a difference. And that had been in November. What would it look like now?

There wouldn't be anyone there now. Except for the caretakers, he would most likely be alone if he heeded the call and headed down there.

Then again, he was usually alone anyway, so that wouldn't make all that much difference. And it wasn't like he couldn't just jump in his truck and leave. What was keeping him?

But why? Why this feeling? Why this urge? He wasn't even sure Camp would be open this time of year. Would they have the water turned on for the shower house, what with the very real possibility of the pipes freezing and bursting?

Kevin closed his eyes, breathed in deep, let it out slowly.

Shower. Coffee. Check the calendar and make sure he didn't have to be anywhere today.

But he knew he didn't. He always knew. He was too conscientious for anything else.

So….

He left his bedroom, crossed the living room to the counter that separated it from the small but efficient kitchen, and booted up his laptop.

Everything was white. He liked that. White walls, white carpet, white kitchen with white appliances. Only the furniture was dark to hide dirt. Because that was sensible—and if Kevin was anything, he was sensible. Black suede couch, black chairs, black end and coffee tables. And he had plants, of course: the big Ficus, the huge angel wing begonia, and a few ferns. Somehow they made him feel like he could breathe easier.

The prints on the walls were his only concession to color (along with the plants), and they had black frames. All of them were photographs he had taken himself. Several came from Camp, including a gorgeous (to him) picture of a nearly-full moon in a sunny sky. Maybe they weren't masterpieces, but he liked them. Other people did too. Cauley and Theresa and one or two others. His few friends.

Friends were all he had right now. He definitely wasn't dating anyone. Or pursuing any one-night stands. He hadn't been with a man in over a year. That was okay. Sometimes (a lot of the time) it was lonely. But nothing compared to being left alone after a night of passion with a stranger he might never see again—almost never did see again. The sex wasn't worth it. The aloneness he felt after those men left was often worse than what he'd felt before they arrived.

While his computer booted up, Kevin went into the kitchen, opened a cabinet, and pulled out a bag of coffee beans he'd gotten from Sweetleaf, a funky Queens coffee minichain. He ground them, put them in his coffee maker, and started it up. He'd used a french press for a short while; it made the best coffee—his friend "Poof" from Festival had taught him that. But it created such a mess. Kevin didn't like messes.

The coffee was brewing, and the aroma was already waking his senses.

By then his computer was wide awake, and a quick glance at his calendar—which he could have checked on his phone with one of the apps he'd created, but he needed to turn on the computer anyway—showed him that he was right. Nothing for today. Gym, of course. That was marked in. It was legs day. But no business. Good.

He knew he should call his ex—Cauley wasn't doing very well lately. He'd find out if he should drop by. Cauley's mother said the visits helped. He hoped so. If a few hours here and there did as much as she claimed it did, who was he not to help? He had the time after all.

Shower.

He loved his bathroom. It was big, and he was a big man. Big tub and a shower with multiple showerheads and some of the only other color in his whole condo—stone tiles of tan and umber and beige on the walls and floor. And the large staghorn fern, of course. He stepped out of his Calvin Klein underwear (red, he liked red—he didn't stick with white and black when it came to clothing) and started the shower, flossed while he waited for the water to heat (it wouldn't take long), and left brushing for after the coffee. When the water was steamy hot, he got in, shifted the water to the massage setting, and reveled in it.

The pulsing woke Kevin the rest of the way, made him feel so good and vital and alive. He even considered jerking off. But no. Nothing sexual on a whim, not even masturbation. He wasn't even truly horny. And the coffee would be ready.

So he soaped up, shampooed, shaved the strip of beard down the middle of his chin (which gave him an almost muttonchop look), rinsed, dried himself with thick towels. Macy's Hotel Collection MicroCotton—expensive, but he didn't consider them an indulgence. They soaked up the water and didn't feel wet afterward and besides, they felt *good*.

Kevin had a code of sorts when it came to money. In some ways he indulged—he could, after all—and in some ways he didn't. The money Google had offered—too much to refuse—had made him quite comfortable. But this was New York, and he'd spent nearly three quarters of a million on his condo—a good chunk of his money. But that was an investment, and property values didn't go down in New York City.

Still, why buy a Tommy Hilfiger flannel shirt at seventy dollars that looked *just* like one from Walmart, which cost less than twenty-five? A brand name meant *nothing* to him unless it also meant quality. Better that money could go to something like Children's International instead, where it would help. A brand itself meant nothing to him personally. But those Macy's towels? He liked them for what they were and not "who." *Um, um, good.*

After Kevin dried, he padded back to the kitchen without dressing because he liked being naked. Being naked felt better even than Macy's towels. It felt good to let his dick sway. He liked the sensation when he sat down on his suede couch and his balls settled first, and he liked his bare feet on the carpet. He liked being naked at Camp as well, loved the sun on his skin and the grass under his feet, and he didn't give a shit that most men who saw him whispered about his big balls and his below-average-sized cock. They hadn't seen how big he got when he was hard after all (only one man at Camp ever had), and what mattered more in the end? And it wasn't like he was small when he was soft for God's sake. He just didn't flop from knee to knee like Bruce "Rat Bastard" Douglas, for instance. But then, who did have a bigger cock than Bruce? Kevin had wondered more than once what you could even do with something so large!

The coffee was ready and filled the condo with its heady rich scent, and he poured it into one of his big mugs and went back to his computer to check e-mails. There were two stools next to the counter—mahogany with suede upholstery that felt good on his bare ass (and his balls; oh yes, his balls), and he always felt one should appreciate life's little pleasures. One of his favorite authors, Malcolm Kane, had helped him learn that.

Most of the subject lines for his e-mails showed they were junk, and he deleted them quickly without opening them. Oh, look, the country of Monterosia owed him two hundred million dollars—delete. "Obama Is Killing Our Country!"—delete. "Cialis and Viagra Cheap from Canada!"—delete. "You Qualify For A $500 Gift Card from Best Buy"—delete. He could delete a lot of his Facebook notifications too, but he opened anything from the comedian who called himself "God" because those postings were always good.

Today he read several he enjoyed: "Just because you can't figure out how ancient civilizations built stuff doesn't mean they got help from aliens" made him laugh out loud because he always thought those von Däniken theories were bullshit. A Cheesus Christ cheese grater. And finally (and he loved this one), "Hi, I'm God. All religions got it wrong. Let's start over. Just be cool to one another. The End."

That really said it all, didn't it?

Kevin smiled. Poured more coffee. Sipped cautiously.

Knew that *he* had got it right.

Life was good.

Wait. What was this? An e-mail from BigSir75@aol.com?

Big Sir? From Heartland Queer Men's Festival?

Weird. To be thinking about the Land and then get an e-mail from Big Sir. What the hell could he possibly want?

He almost deleted the e-mail—Big Sir was far from his favorite attendee—but then that tickle happened. The one Kevin had learned to pay attention to. That little tingle that started at the base of his skull and shivered out over his scalp. His curiosity was captured now, and if he was wrong, he was wrong. But if he was right….

Kevin had learned to trust the tickles.

He opened the e-mail.

Hey Dude!

This is Big Sir also known as Howard. Not sure which you would remember me by.

I just wanted u to know I am free! I have finally dumped my loser lovers ass! I know you would not even think of getting with me while I was with Little Bear, but now i can tell u that it is no longer a worry. He is out of my life.

So I was wondering if you would want to get together sometime? We could have a LOT of fun I can tell! You are so freaking HAWT and I KNOW the sparks have been flying between us but you wouldn't be with me while I was with Little Bear. I might be in New York next week. Could we hook up? You and me! Would be most hot.

Ok. Looking forward to hearing from you.

Howard aka Big Sir!

Kevin could scarcely believe his eyes. *Howard* (he had never been willing to actually call the man "Big Sir") wanted to get together with him? Howard from *Festival*? Howard thought there were sparks flying between them? How in the world had he ever gotten that idea?

Kevin shuddered. He couldn't stand to be around the guy. He'd never liked the way Howard stared at him, flirted with him in the shower

("Want to wash each other's backs?"), and acted in ways that the jerk obviously thought were sexy.

Kevin shook his head and hit the delete button. He wasn't even going to dignify the e-mail with a response.

Sex with Howard?

He grimaced.

It wasn't that he thought Howard was physically gross. He liked guys with some padding. But what was ugly about Howard was his heart. There was something in his eyes, something… dark. And he didn't like the way he treated his lover—well, apparently now his *ex*-lover.

And on the tail of that came…

So Wyatt is single now?

Well damn! He had never expected the two of them to split up. They seemed forever married. At least, that was the way Wyatt appeared to feel about Howard. He was always looking at the man as if he was so in love it almost hurt. And somehow Kevin figured that was how it had always worked. With Wyatt loving Howard desperately, and Howard hurting Wyatt. He was pretty sure Howard had been fucking around behind Wyatt's back. That's what Lorax, another Festival brother, had told him a few years back.

"It's pathetic is what it is," Lorax—who bore a striking resemblance to the Dr. Seuss character—had said one night in his cabin.

"But how can he cheat if the two of them have an open relationship?" Kevin had asked.

Lorax had looked at Kevin in wide-eyed surprise. "You speak!"

Kevin shrugged and hoped that Lorax hadn't noticed him blush by the glow of the strings of Christmas lights that were their only illumination that evening. This was Queer Men's Festival after all, and get-togethers should be festive.

"That's the most I've heard you say all week, Hodor."

Which was an exaggeration, surely. Kevin didn't like to talk all that much and had gratefully accepted his Faerie name—his nickname—which allowed him a way to speak as little as possible.

Lorax gave a shrug of his own and then explained. "You're more naïve than I thought a man your age could be, especially one who comes to Festival every summer. It's cheating if Big Sir isn't following the rules they made. An open relationship doesn't necessarily mean a free-for-all, unless that's what a couple negotiates. Most nonmonogamous people have rules. Like veto power."

Kevin had just looked at him, unsure of what that meant.

"Like, if you and I were a couple and you were hot for someone, and I wasn't comfortable with you fucking that guy, or I just didn't like him, I could veto you playing with him. Well, I know flat out that Little Bear said he'd vetoed someone I happened to know Howard was fucking."

Kevin had only been able to shake his head in barely contained disgust and sympathy. It broke his heart that anyone could treat Wyatt that way. "It's why I could never do an open relationship," Kevin had said then in another uncharacteristic rush of words. "If someone—

(like Wyatt, sweet, adorable Little Bear)

—wants to be with me, then he has to be with only me."

"People make mistakes, though," Lorax said. "You couldn't forgive a mistake?"

A stab of pain pierced his heart then. "I've forgiven." He leaned back on the bed he was sitting on. "But in my experience, once a cheater, always a cheater." Even if there were other things involved.

And God! Why was Wyatt *with* that asshole? *How* could he love that man?

If Wyatt were mine….

How could he stay with a man who cheated on him so many times? Who didn't honor him? Didn't love him? A man who cared so little for his welfare? A man who was a complete and total ass.

Wasn't there some story going around about how Howard had practically raped some kid—young man? What better reason for Wyatt to dump the asshole. But he hadn't. And now the sweet little guy was probably devastated that Howard had left him. Getting out from under Howard's control was the best thing that could have happened to him, but somehow Kevin knew Wyatt was probably sitting around grieving, tearing at his hair and clothes.

Sad. Really sad.

Wyatt was so sweet and sexy: short, rounded just the way Kevin liked (padded), with a lightly hairy chest, adorable round plump butt, and the darkest eyes—puppy-dog eyes. How often Kevin thought it would be fun to cuddle with Wyatt in a hammock under a shady tree or on a blanket on the beach. But Wyatt would have wanted more than cuddling, and Kevin didn't get involved with married guys, even if they were in an open relationship. It always felt wrong to *him*. Plus he didn't want to take a chance that he would start feeling something for Wyatt. Not when Kevin couldn't have anything more. Sexual intimacy did that to him. He couldn't help it. More than once he'd felt a bond with some one-night stand, which was part of what made him feel so alone when they went their way after sex. He guessed he was an old-fashioned type of guy. He'd heard gays pontificate on sexuality and how it was castrating gay male nature to assimilate into straight culture's ideas on what sexuality should be. That free-for-all sex was a gay man's right and a big "fuck you" to anyone who said men couldn't have sex with other men. But please! How was *not* sticking his dick in every ass that presented itself castrating himself?

So okay, that made him old-fashioned. Sex was special to him. It was the ultimate intimacy. He couldn't do that with just anyone. And anytime he broke that rule, he wound up regretting it.

His mind went back to Howard's e-mail. So the SOB had broken up with Wyatt?

Wyatt was single now?

Hmmmm....

Kevin felt a little rush. Wyatt. Single. Wow. Next year's Festival might be nice. Especially if Wyatt didn't get back with Howard in the meantime. That thought bothered Kevin. Because Wyatt could do so much better than Howard. Getting back with Howard was a horrible idea. He needed to be completely away from that man.

Hmm....

So Wyatt was single.

Kevin smiled.

Because he found the idea of a single Wyatt appealing.

WHEN HE called Cauley, it was Lois—Cauley's mother—who answered.

"Oh Kevin, I'm so glad it's you."

Kevin's heart tripped in alarm. "Is Cauley all right?"

Lois paused. "No, Kevin. He's not. It's not *bad*… but it's not good."

Shit. "Do you want me to come by?"

"Oh, could you? Would you? I could make lunch—if Cauley will eat, that is."

Not eating again? "That bad?" he asked aloud. *God.*

"Soup," Lois said. "Cauley will eat my soup. He likes the tortilla the best, but he can't always keep that down."

Shit. That wasn't good.

"What time? Can I bring something?"

"Why not right around noon? I like to keep him on schedule, you know? I think that's important."

She was keeping him on schedule? "Are you staying with him?" he asked, concerned even more.

"I—yes. Been here a few days. Thought I would stay at least a week."

A week. "Okay."

"And bring him some flowers? Nothing much, okay? Don't make a big deal. But he loves them so. They make him feel better. Even a single daisy."

"No problem, Lois. I'll find something."

"You're a dear."

A dear. Really. And she used to hate him. But that was a long time ago now. Back when she thought he was the one who made her only son sick.

Kevin dressed after that—black jeans and a heavy red plaid shirt (Cauley had always liked him in flannel, he'd had a thing for lumberjack types), and his high-tops. Checked his reflection quickly, fixed his hair a bit. Finally, filling a travel mug with the last of his coffee, he headed out the door. He took the elevator down to the garage and climbed into his Ford F-150 (big and also white) and headed for Club Fitness on Broadway. A workout always cleared his mind and made him feel good, and he wanted to be feeling good when he faced his ex.

His workout went well; he liked the gym a lot. It was the best gym he'd tried in Astoria—which included Blink, NYSC, and Synergy—with several floors and plenty of machines, free weights, and cardio equipment. There was even a boxing ring, although he never used it, and two men's locker rooms, which included a Jacuzzi, steam room, and sauna. He liked the juice bar as well, and especially the rooftop, which was open in the summer. And since it was close to the gay bars, it was one of the more gay-friendly gyms as well. It was nice to know he didn't have to worry about some straight guy starting trouble (although he did have to fend off a grope more than once in a while in the Jacuzzi).

CAULEY LIVED in Rosebank on Staten Island, near the Verrazano Bridge—which was only about a forty-minute drive from Long Island City, where Kevin lived—and he got there just before noon. He'd visited a couple of places on the way: picked up his dry-cleaning, dropped off his DVD at a Redbox (a Joe Hill movie; it wasn't all that good but he thought Daniel Radcliffe was adorable), and then stopped at a flower stand and bought a big bright sunflower he thought Cauley would like. He suspected, though, that it was something else he'd grabbed that would bring his ex more joy.

The house was small; Cauley's Aunt Karen had left it to him, which was good because with his health, he couldn't have managed anything bigger. They'd even converted the little dining room in the back of the house into a bedroom and put safety bars in the first-floor bathroom (Kevin had done a lot of the work) so Cauley wouldn't have to try to manage the stairs on bad days.

Lois answered the door, looking radiant dressed in one of her colorful dresses (that always reminded him of something Stevie Nicks or Cyan Carrington would wear) and ornamented with big pieces of jewelry. She wore lavender African violets in her silver hair. It was a nice touch.

"Oh, Kevin. I'm so glad you're here. Please come in. Let me take that." She pointed to the sunflower. "Cauley's in the living room, watching his TV as usual. I wish you'd try and get him out of the house. He needs some fresh air."

"You don't think maybe it's a little cold?" Kevin asked.

She shrugged. "We could bundle him up good." Lois looked away, and Kevin could see she was gathering strength to go on—it *must* have been a bad day. "I mean, we have to be real. He isn't going to live forever…."

"None of us are," he replied gently.

She sighed. "Go on now. He's waiting."

And as soon as he saw his ex, it was clear that Cauley was indeed having a bad day.

It hadn't been two weeks since he saw Cauley last, but he looked like he'd aged ten years. Which was bad because he already looked years older than his actual thirty-five. His cheeks were hollow, his skin pale and jaundiced at the same time (if that was even possible), and his blue eyes all but washed of color. He hardly looked like the man who, with a contingent of demonstrators, somehow infiltrated a wedding for an infamous antigay city official at St. Peter's Church—only the oldest Roman Catholic church in New York State—leapt up in the middle of the service, and started shouting, "We're here, we're queer, and we have the right to get married too!" And oh, the chaos that had ensued! Plus getting arrested and needing bail to get out.

And when Kevin had shown up? Cauley had refused to leave without his compatriots.

As well-off as Kevin had become, he still couldn't bail out seventeen people.

Luckily in the end—finally—he hadn't needed to. He had, however, had to pay for Cauley's lawyer to make sure he didn't spend a long time in jail.

No. He didn't "have" to, but ex-lovers or not, he couldn't let Cauley stay there. Especially when he'd only gotten his diagnosis the week before.

Part of why he'd done such an insane thing in the first place. Cauley had been thrilled he'd made the news.

"And not just Fox," Cauley had exclaimed. "*Real* networks as well! We did it!"

At least Cauley was dressed—that was good—and sitting on the flower-patterned, burnt orange couch (a sure sign of Cauley's Aunt Karen's seventies decorating) watching TV.

He went to Cauley and motioned for him to stay seated when he tried to stand. Kevin bent, hugged him carefully, and kissed him lightly on the mouth. There was a new lesion on his neck, but it was low, and if he buttoned his shirt, he could hide it. Kevin knew Cauley was happy about that.

"I like the goatee thing you've got going there," Kevin said, touching Cauley's face.

"Ain't no big thing. I had to do something to fill in my face." There was a short silence and then he added, "Thanks for coming, Kev."

"No problem." He grinned. "Got you something."

"He sure did," Lois said, coming into the room and placing the flower in its vase on the coffee table.

"To the side, Mom. That's right in front of *Supernatural*!"

Kevin moved it for him, and Cauley watched the television screen. Kevin sat next to him, but he had no idea what was going on.

"I'd do John Winchester in a New York second," Cauley said, pointing to the older man on the screen and not one of the show's two young heroes.

Lois put her hands on her hips. "Cauley!" She huffed and walked out of the room, calling, "Lunch in ten minutes," over her shoulder.

"Isn't that Jeffrey Dean Morgan?" Kevin asked.

Cauley nodded. "It is. I'm impressed you knew that."

"Yeah," Kevin agreed. "He's hot all right. He gave me sexy shivers in *The Watchmen*."

"You always liked the bears, didn't you?" Cauley asked. "Whatever did you see in me?"

"Silly man," Kevin said, and when his old lover turned to him with a question in his (washed-out) eyes, Kevin tapped Cauley's chest with a finger. "Your heart, Cauley. It's gold."

Cauley shook his head and looked back at the men on the TV. "Then why couldn't I keep you?"

But they both knew why, so Kevin didn't answer.

"I would like to think you liked my sweet little ass a little bit."

Kevin laughed and assured him that he had.

"'Course there isn't much back there these days, is there?"

Kevin chose not to answer that one either. After all, what was there to say?

A few minutes later Lois came into the room to let them know lunch was ready. So Kevin helped Cauley stand; he accepted it but refused the hand on his elbow. "I can walk," he said proudly—almost defiantly.

"Of course you can," Kevin said.

Lunch was in the kitchen since the dining room was now a bedroom. The quarters were tight but not impossible, and they sat at the old gray laminate table with chrome edges that had been there for fifty years. Lunch was soup (of course), a white bean soup (with plenty of pieces of ham) that Lois reported she had made herself. It was delicious, and even Cauley finished—or nearly did—his bowl.

"Good job," Lois cried as if he were six years old, and Kevin was afraid Cauley would make a caustic comment, but he didn't. Thank God. That was good. But a quick look made Kevin think that maybe Cauley was too tired to even scowl these days, and he couldn't help but wonder how much time Cauley had left. He decided to bring out his surprise.

"Got you something else," he said.

"Oh?" Cauley asked, mild curiosity on his gaunt face.

So Kevin went to the door and dug the bag out of his deep coat pocket and brought the Dove chocolates back—dark chocolate, Cauley's favorite.

Cauley grinned like a kid.

Lois only smiled, with no threats that they weren't good for him, and opened the bag. They all had a few—Cauley chomping noisily on his. And so what? After all, he was eating.

And that was good.

CHAPTER FOUR

THE COUCH and chairs had been pushed back against the walls, the giant rag rug rolled up and pushed under the dining room table. There were candles everywhere, most notably in a circle on the floor. In the middle of the circle sat a small table with a green tablecloth, his athame—a ceremonial blade about eight inches long—a chalice, his wand, a small plate filled with Christmas sugar cookies, and a little statue of a pair of nude wrestlers (Wyatt would explain that later). With greenery arranged outside the circle, it was all really quite lovely in the soft warm glow of the many candles, and Wyatt was pleased. He'd only mentioned that he wished he had some evergreen boughs, and his friends had all showed up bearing a few branches each. They had brought just enough to complete the circle. He didn't know if they knew it, but the gesture was incredibly magickal. With a *k*.

Wyatt's friends were all there, and their presence and the setup made Wyatt so happy he thought he would cry. He *was* happy. Happier than he'd been in weeks.

He couldn't resist a little joke.

"Thank you all for coming," he said. "You don't know what this means to me. We'll be ready to begin as soon as you all take off your clothes." And then made a move to unbutton his shirt.

There followed a gasp and a few mutterings, and as he looked around the room, he couldn't help but be amused at the surprise and even shock on his friends' faces (especially Peni's). Then, just as Cedar and Scott exchanged a look, shrugged, and started to unbuckle their belts, Wyatt laughed and held up his hands. "Just kidding."

The others laughed too, and Cedar gave a half shrug and said, "Well, skyclad is the thing in a lot of circles. A lot of us do it naked at Men's Festival."

"True," Wyatt said. "But I *warn* people so they could choose whether they want to come do something like that. Which is only polite. And most of you aren't pagan." He glanced at Peni. "I reserve stuff like that."

"I'm not even sure what we're doing here tonight, Wyatt," Max said.

Wyatt nodded. "Well, I thought I'd explain that."

So he had them sit down and relax. He had bottles of water—no cocktails tonight, at least not until after. This was a time to be clearheaded.

Wyatt looked at his friends, all here, and a small rush passed through him. The only person who hadn't come was his boss, Katherine. He'd invited her. But in the end she, more than he, decided that tonight needed to be a Queer evening. And as queer as she felt she was, tonight called for sacred *Male*-spirit.

Wyatt looked at his friends again and saw them looking back—their faces attentive, their expressions curious. His heart jumped again. This was happening. He felt like crying but fought the urge. For now at least.

This was happening!

Wyatt cleared his throat. "I'll start by giving everybody a little explanation of what tonight is all about and what we're going to be doing. So you'll know what's going on."

"I appreciate that," Sloan said.

Max nodded.

So did Peni. "And I'm really excited."

Wyatt took a deep drink from his water bottle, suddenly twice as nervous. He cleared his throat again. "Okay. First of all… Yule. It's also called the Winter Solstice, and it is the longest night of the year and the shortest day. Some call it the 'dark night of the soul.' In some traditions, Yule is the time that the Goddess takes on her role as the Great Mother and gives birth to the new Sun King. But I prefer to honor the story of the battle of the Oak King and the Holly King."

Wyatt's heart was pounding—and for more than one reason. He loved this story, but there was also the fear that his friends would think what he was saying was silly. But no. They were all listening. He could see it in their eyes. No one was making fun. Not even Scott.

He took a breath. "There are a number of versions of the story of the Holly King and the Oak King, but my favorite goes something like this. There are two times of the year—the Winter Solstice, or Yule, and the Summer Solstice—when these two, these… *cosmic* rulers, meet in battle. And what they're fighting for is supremacy of the Wheel of the Year. At Yuletide, it is the Oak King who wins, and his victory ushers in the end of long nights and the lengthening of the days. But then once the Summer Solstice arrives, they do battle again, and the Holly King wins. And the days begin to shorten and the nights to dominate the year.

"Sometimes I've even been in rituals where two men act out the fight between the Holly King and the Oak King."

"Hey!" cried Cedar. "Scott and I can do that!" He turned to Scott and waggled his eyebrows. "Wanna…?"

At Scott's uncomfortable look, Wyatt broke back in. "No!" He laughed. "Not the kind of thing we want to do inside with candles and breakables." He pointed to the statue of the wrestling men on the table in the center of the circle. "This sculpture of Hercules and Diomedes will represent the Kings tonight."

Cedar got a funny expression on his face and Wyatt was sure he was going to say something. A joke? But no. It looked like he had changed his mind. Thank goodness. Wyatt was already nervous enough.

He cleared his throat and continued.

"Okay. So the first thing I'll do is cast the Circle. It's simply… well, declaring sacred space for us to do our work." He nodded. "Some people believe it's about protection. That when the magick is being worked, it attracts the attention of all kinds of forces, some good and some not so good. For that reason we never step out of the Circle once we begin. Go potty first in other words. And I'll try to keep it short."

There was some general chuckling.

"Then I'll call the four directions, the powers of the Watchtowers of the four compass points. They also represent the four elements. North, fire…. No. I mean, earth. God, I'm nervous!"

"It's okay," said Scott. "We're all here for you."

Wyatt smiled at his friend. He liked the new Scott.

"Thanks." He laughed. "Okay. Whew! North—fire. Earth! Earth!"

"It really is okay, Wyatt," Max said. "Take your time."

Wyatt nodded. Gulped. "North—*earth*. East—air. South—fire. And west—water. Traditionally four different people call the directions. But that isn't necessary tonight. I'll do it."

Then, surprising Wyatt once more. "I'll take a direction if you want," Cedar said. He grinned. "I don't mind. I did water at Festival this summer."

"Wait," Peni cried. "I'd like to join too. And may I do water?" He smiled happily. "You'll have to tell me what to do."

Wyatt's mouth dropped open. "I—I'd love—"

"Then do you want me to take north?" Cedar asked. "Since I've called a direction before? Show people how? That's the first Watchtower to be called, right? North?"

"I…. Yes. First, that is. North is. And… and you can be too. First, that is. If you really mean it."

"Sure, I mean it!" Cedar nodded enthusiastically. "I'm already thinking of what to say."

"I'll take south then," Asher said, and Wyatt could only goggle at him. *What?*

"South is fire, right? Isn't that what you said?"

Wyatt nodded.

"Well, my people are pretty fiery, right?"

"Your…," Wyatt stammered. "Your people?"

Asher shrugged. And was that a blush? It was hard to tell in the warm glow of the candles but it *looked* like…

"I'm not ready to give up honey-baked ham just yet, but… yeah. Maybe."

Whoa!

"So we need someone for east," Cedar said. He turned to his lover. "Scott?"

"I…. Ah…." Scott visibly gulped. "I'm… not sure if I'm quite ready for that."

"You sure?" Cedar touched Scott's cheek.

Scott nodded and this time, candlelight or not, Wyatt did see a blush spread out over his face.

"Okay, baby," Cedar replied and pulled him close.

"Ah…." Sloan cleared his throat. "I suppose I can."

Wyatt smiled. This was all too unbelievable. "I don't want you to do anything you're not comfortable with."

Sloan gave one of his half shrugs. "Your ways have never bothered me before. I even went to that camp with you that day, forever ago. Tell me what to do?"

Another rush spread over Wyatt. Love. It was a nice change. He took a deep breath. "Think of the things that remind you of your element." He nodded at Sloan. "Like a tornado or a hurricane or even a cool breeze on a hot day. Or the first breath a baby takes."

Sloan's eyes widened. "Really? A baby's breath? So it doesn't have to be 'godly' powerful stuff?"

Wyatt sighed a long happy sigh. "A baby's first breath is pretty powerful stuff!"

"Wow," Sloan said and sat down. "I need to think a minute."

Was this going to be too much for his friends? "You guys really don't have to do this."

"I think we do," Asher said. "Really."

Unbelievable.

Magick.

It took Wyatt a moment to compose himself. This was all so... so much.

Finally, Wyatt nodded again. "Okay, then." Next step. "After the four Quarters are called, then the next thing usually done in Ritual is to call on the Lord and the Lady. The two creative forces of nature that make everything. But tonight we are going to call on the Queer Ones."

"Queer Ones?" Peni asked.

"Yes," Wyatt replied. "That other force that has been around for all recorded history and before. The force that draws members of the same sex together. Gods and animals and myth."

"Yes!" Peni cried. "I can get that!" Wyatt could see he, almost more than any of the others, was getting quite excited by all of this.

"It's another reason why Yule is one of my two favorite times of the year. There's something kind of... what's the word, Max? Homo-rotic?"

Max smiled and nodded. "Homoerotic."

"Yeah," Wyatt agreed. "Something homoerotic about these two big male forces of nature wrestling for dominance."

"And howdy!" Cedar said with a grin and another eyebrow waggle. He indicated the little sculpture of Hercules and Diomedes. "One of them sure has a nice grip on the base of the other guy's cock, doesn't he?" He laughed. "And it looks like it's giving Mr. Gripper a hard-on too!"

Wyatt couldn't help but laugh. It did look *just* like one of them had an erection. He'd always thought so. Surprisingly, he found himself blushing.

"So when you had two guys acting this out, did they do that?" It was Cedar asking, of course.

"What?" Wyatt asked.

"Grip each other's cocks like that?"

"That would be a rare thing," Wyatt said. "It's usually acted out by straight men anyway."

"But what about when it's gay men?" Cedar pressed.

"It all depends." Wyatt looked away.

And in one very... special Circle he and Howard had been in, they *had* acted out the fight that ended when the Oak King won—the Oak

King being Howard, naturally. It would have been ridiculous-looking any other way. It had ended with Howard fucking him over the altar in front of the other attendees. It had been humiliating at first, being taken that way while the others stared. He hadn't been expecting Howard to take it that far. But then… something happened. Everything had turned sexual after that. The other men in the ritual were masturbating and then having sex as well. It had startled the hell out of him. But rather than allowing himself to be embarrassed, Wyatt had chosen to go with the flow. Or with his hormones anyway. He pushed away the idea that the sex between him and Howard *needed* to be romantic and private. Switched it off in his mind.

In a way it had been freeing. When Howard had first urged him into sexual situations with others, his response had been halfhearted—a way to please (and keep) Howard. But when it had been in the context of a religious rite? Somehow that was when Wyatt finally let go and really did whatever Howard urged him to do. After all, wasn't the Goddess supposed to say, "For behold, all acts of love and pleasure are my rituals"?

It had also been when his and Howard's sexual escapades had truly begun. Or at least his own. Howard's had apparently begun long before then—just without the virtue of Wyatt knowing about it.

"Wyatt?" Cedar asked again, louder, breaking him from his thoughts.

"Huh?"

"I think I just might have Scott talked into it."

Wyatt looked at his blushing friend.

"No," he said. "No wrestling. Not tonight. Breakables. Candles."

"Sure," Asher said. "Burning the house down would be a bad way to end the evening."

"And no nudity, right?" asked Cedar.

Wyatt had to laugh once again. Coming from anyone else, he would have thought they were trying to make this sexual. It was not something he was prepared for in the least. The wounds were still very fresh with Howard. But no. As sexually free as Cedar was, Wyatt knew he wasn't suggesting some repeat of that night Howard had taken him over the altar. Not the way Cedar was bonding with Scott. Cedar was just a naked kind of guy.

"No, not this time," he answered.

He could see from their expressions that Max wasn't the only one who was relieved. But then he got yet another little surprise.

"You know, I was kind of expecting to show off," Peni said. "Would you mind if I just wore a sarong?"

Wyatt raised his brows in surprise and then nodded. "Sure. Whatever any of you want."

Peni looked at Asher, who nodded, and then they excused themselves.

"What are they up to?" Max said.

"I can't imagine," said Wyatt, because he really couldn't. Show off? What did that mean?

"You know I wasn't trying to turn this into some kind of orgy, right?" Cedar asked.

Yes, he did know that. Wyatt told him so. And hadn't he just been thinking that—a thought confirmed when Cedar put his arm around Scott's waist and pulled him tight against him.

"I was just wanting to respect your path, and I knew a lot of rituals were done in the nude."

"Some," Wyatt responded. "But not all by any means. I doubt even the majority. Remember that Men's Festival is hardly the 'real world.' And when we did Ritual, most of us weren't naked. I appreciate it, Cedar. But just the fact that you're all here tonight means the world to me. That you are respecting my beliefs."

"Well, Wyatt," Asher said, coming into the room holding Peni's hand, "I'm starting to learn respect."

They all turned to see Peni and Asher standing there, both wearing gorgeous sarongs tied around their waists. They were folded in half lengthwise so that instead of hanging nearly to the floor, they came down to midthigh, showing off their muscular physiques and—of course—Peni's magnificent Samoan tattoos. The lovers looked like two gods standing there in the light of the candles.

"Wow," said Sloan.

"Wow, indeed," said Max.

Yes, thought Wyatt. Wow. Because even though they'd seen Peni's pe'a before, here, tonight, they were magnificent.

"Oh, what the hell," said Max. "I can wear one of those. Actually they look pretty comfortable. You have any more of those sarong-thingies, Wyatt?"

Sarong-thingies? Really? Mr. College-Teacher Max Turner just said *sarong-thingies*? Wyatt laughed. "Do I?" Did he have any sarongs? Even after Howard took half of them, he still had a million. "Come on!"

So he took them upstairs and showed them the big green tub he had and left them to it. They could pick out whatever they wanted. He didn't care.

Then halfway down the stairs, something hit him. Yes! If even Max was willing to shed his comfortable ways and wear a sarong, that meant *he* could skip his jeans and T-shirt (even if it did have a silhouette on the front of a witch on a broomstick with a rainbow flowing out the back instead of billowing smoke, *and* the words Ride With Pride, on it).

He wouldn't go naked—he couldn't do that. But he could....

While Max and Sloan went through the tub, he dashed back up the stairs, went to the closet in his magick room, and found his special outfit. The one he'd made himself. It wasn't perfect, but to misquote Grace Jones once again, it was perfect for him.

The outfit consisted of two sarongs that he had batiked himself in a class at Festival several years ago. (Gods, was it going on five already?) The two sarongs had started out white. He'd dyed them gold and brown. Then he'd used the batik technique to apply wax in a bear pattern over and over on the fabric. Once that was done, he'd dyed the sarongs black, and where the wax crackled, it left wonderful tiny lines of black to come through. Once they were dry, they were washed in hot water, which melted the wax away and left a completely unique set of sarongs. Then he gave them to Zebra the Baker (who also sewed wonderful quilts) to turn one of the sarongs into a jacket and—*voilà*—Wyatt had his own magickal robes!

And he could wear the outfit tonight! He could be all flowy and lovely tonight. He quickly shed his clothes, swept into his homemade garments, and found his bear-claw necklace, and he was ready!

Watch out, McDonalds!

Wyatt stepped out into the hallway just in time to finally get a quick flash of Max's butt and, as lovely as it was, to not really care. That's not what tonight was about. You'd seen one perfect ass, you'd seen them all.

Wait!

Had he just said that?

Wyatt shook his head and dashed past the crimson Max—*Oh, relax, Max. How many men have seen you naked in the locker room at the gym?*—and down the stairs, garments flowing about him like, well, magick!

CHAPTER FIVE

IT WAS a colder night than expected, but there was no talking Cauley out of joining them, and really, who were they to say no? It got him out of the house. And at least it was his own backyard.

That night there were three of them: Kevin, Cauley, and Theresa—the woman Kevin jokingly referred to as his "voice."

They were sitting around the black, bowl-shaped fire pit Kevin had bought for Cauley for his birthday (which ironically resembled a cauldron quite a bit) on patio chairs pulled as close as they could without burning themselves.

Cauley was especially bundled up, and his mother had made quite a fuss about it too. Flannel shirt, two sweaters (one of them Kevin's, and Cauley would have looked ridiculously small in it if there hadn't been layers beneath it), heavy gloves, and a hat that made him look like a skinny Cossack. And that wasn't counting the blankets. He'd complained, but only a little bit. Kevin knew it was just for show.

"So how come there's only three of us?" Theresa asked. She was wearing a thick sweater and had pulled off her hat, and the big fluffy snowflakes that had begun to fall moments before looked like down feathers caught in her very blonde hair.

At least the snow wasn't falling hard. The weather report was only calling for a few inches at most. It was interesting to watch it sizzle midair over the fire pit and never reach the ground.

"What do you mean?" Kevin asked. "Only three?"

"Don't we need a fourth?" she asked, blue eyes flashing. She brushed the snow off her head and pulled on her thick fuchsia knit hat. "Weren't the chicks in that movie looking for a fourth?"

"Oh hell, Theresa." He shook his head. "This isn't *The Craft*. And it's nothing like that. And I'm not a witch."

"Then what are you? I mean, I've never really gotten that."

"Me either," said Cauley from the depths of his hat and blankets.

Kevin looked over at Cauley and huffed a quiet half laugh. The comment was just part of why they hadn't worked out. He'd begged Cauley to go to Camp with him years back, and Cauley had just said, "Yuck. Bugs. Spiders." Shook his head and then told Kevin that he didn't have the shoes to go camping. "And I refuse to use a Johnny-on-the-Spot!"

"I guess," Kevin continued, turning back to Theresa, "if you had to pigeonhole me, I'd say I was pagan, or neo-pagan—"

"Neo what?" Theresa asked.

"—but I don't like either of those terms. I don't *want* to be pigeonholed. I *don't* want to pick a 'god.' I think they're all the same and that each of us finds God in their own way. For my mom it was Jesus. For someone else it might be Buddha. I had a friend once who prayed to Baldur for me. And do you know Parya? At work? Have you noticed she has a little statue of Ganesha on her desk?"

"Oh, yeah," Theresa said.

"Well that's not just for decoration. Did you ever notice she keeps a few M&Ms or Lifesavers or something in that itty-bitty dish in front of it? It's an offering."

"Okay." Theresa smiled. "I knew that was way too small to be a candy dish!" She laughed.

"It's all the same, you know?" Kevin nodded. "All spokes of a wheel leading to the same place."

"Damn," Theresa replied. "That's the most I think I've ever heard you say all at once since you introduced me to your apps that made us all so damned comfortable."

Kevin ignored her. "Let's just say my religion is nature. I don't like to label it. But nothing makes me feel closer to… God, if that's the word you want to use, than nature."

"Which is why I never understood why he likes New York so much," said Cauley.

A slow smile crept over Kevin's face. "And where did I meet you?"

Their eyes met over the flames, and Cauley returned his smile. "Central Park."

"Exactly."

"If you boys tell me you met cruising and had sex in the bushes, I don't know if I'll be grossed out or turned on," Theresa said. "You told me you met at a picnic."

"We did," Kevin replied. "Our mutual friend Mark was having a birthday party, and we were both invited, and from the minute I saw Cauley, I couldn't keep my eyes off him."

"Which makes *no* sense because he likes bears." Cauley let out a long sigh that sent several snowflakes puffing away from his face.

Kevin sighed as well. He'd hoped the story might make Cauley smile.

Apparently Theresa noticed, and always knowing what to do (it was she who made his apps something that Google wanted so badly), steered the conversation back to why they were gathered together that night. "Okay, then, if we aren't here to cast a spell, then what are we here for?" she asked.

Kevin took a deep breath. "To take notice. To take a moment. This is a very special time of year."

"I know my nephews and nieces certainly think so," Theresa said. "You should hear the not-so-subtle hints of all they want for Christmas."

"But this is far older than that," Kevin replied. "I'm talking about Winter Solstice. We're doing this a night early. But that's okay. It's real close. The real event takes place at 10:49 tomorrow night. But that doesn't lend itself well for us. That's pretty late for Cauley here—"

Who let out a scoffing huff even though they all knew (including Cauley) that it was true.

"—and Theresa, *you* have to be at work Monday morning. So I decided that tonight would be good enough. It's pretty common for people to celebrate on the closest Saturday to a Solstice or Equinox. So tonight we'll go ahead and take notice that we are on the threshold of the longest night of the year. Starting Monday, the days lengthen and call for summer to arrive once again, and surely there is something very powerful about that."

He looked at Cauley, eyes hooded in darkness, and could read nothing. Fire and shadow played with his face and obscured Kevin's ability to read the expressions of the man he had known and loved for years. Then he turned to Theresa, whose eyes were filled with the flames of the fire pit and whose very posture showed that she was far more serious than she let on. She was biting her lower lip, and she looked alive, and Kevin knew he'd been wise to not only ask her to sell to the world what he could not, but to ask her here tonight.

He loved her.

He loved Cauley.

There were few he dared to love, despite the fact that his heart wanted him to give it away. These two knew him and respected him like no one else, even though he was so quiet and private and rarely shared much of himself (and when he did share, it was a baring of the soul that left him ultimately exhausted). He treasured these two. And tonight he didn't need to face such an important event as Yule on his own.

"I believe," Kevin said, "that there is power tonight. Power *tomorrow* night. Power always. But I can't believe that there is no significance to a night that so many cultures have taken notice of. The Romans had a festival called Saturnalia on the winter solstice, where they brought branches of evergreen trees to decorate their homes. They exchanged gifts. All businesses were closed. The Persians held this time as sacred, as the time of the birth of their sun god, Mithras. In Sweden this time of year was sacred to the Lucina, the Shining One, and like all the others, it was a celebration of the return of the light. On Yule itself, bonfires were lit to honor Odin and Thor.

"We don't have a bonfire, but we have this instead." He waved gently at the fire pit with an upraised hand. "And I think it takes little imagination to see those ancient times in our mind's eye."

Now he could see that Cauley was listening. His shadowed eyes were hard to see, but they were focused in Kevin's direction.

"After this weekend, the nights will begin to shorten, and the days will grow longer and longer as the earth moves around the sun. Just think about it! Earliest man noticed that the sun's path across the sky changed. People today think they were ignorant, but they noted that the length of daylight changed and the location of the sunrise and sunset shifted in a habitual way throughout the year. Those 'ignorant' people built monuments like Machu Picchu and Stonehenge or the Great Pyramid of Giza to follow the sun.

"Today we use science, and we can see the earth from space. Now we know that the solstice is caused by the tilt of Earth on its axis…."

"Huh?" asked Cauley.

"Because Earth doesn't orbit upright," Theresa said.

Kevin nodded enthusiastically. "It's tilted on its axis by 23.5 degrees. And as we go around the sun, the Northern and Southern Hemispheres trade places in getting the largest amount of direct sunlight. And this very weekend our hemisphere is leaning farthest away from the sun for the year. Until the Summer Solstice, called Litha, when we experience the longest day and then continue around the sun, with the days growing shorter and winter returning."

"But that's just science," Cauley replied stubbornly. "It's not religion."

"My religion is nature," Kevin said again, unable to keep the wonder from his voice, the smile from his face.

"This all sounds very leapish to me. That's what it is, right? You got this from that Malcolm guy? Your guru?"

Kevin rolled his eyes in his mind. "Leapish" is what Theresa called it? "Malcolm guy"? "Leapish" from the book *Leap and the Net Will Appear!* and "Malcolm guy" meaning Malcolm Kane, the author.

"You've never been the same since we went to see him speak," Theresa said.

"That's not true. And please don't call him my guru again. It really annoys me."

Cauley gave a little groan from beneath his blanket, and Kevin winced. Cauley had much worse things to say about Malcolm Kane.

"What I love so much about him is he is saying what I've somehow known my whole life. Things that were bouncing around in my head, but I had never known how to say them out loud. *He* put it all into words for me."

Theresa nodded. "I know. I'm sorry. I don't mean to tease. Apology accepted?"

"Of course," Kevin said and smiled.

And when he turned to look, he saw that Cauley's eyes were still in shadow… but there was a spark as well that was more than a reflection of the fire.

"So what do you want us to do?" she asked.

WYATT TOOK a deep breath. His friends stood around him in a circle, holding hands. He reached down and took his blade—his athame—from the small table in the center of the circle (he'd found it in the basement, and it had been perfect for tonight's altar) and raised it high over his head.

He took a deep breath, tried to calm his nervous heart. This was sacred. *This* is *sacred*, he thought. He cleared his throat and took another breath. And began: "Tonight, my friends, is the festival of Yule. Tonight we celebrate the darkest night of the year. We are in the midst of frozen winter, and the rose is asleep beneath the snow. But take heart! For even in this deep darkness, we are on the eve of the night the sun is once again reborn. A spark of light comes to life and promises us that spring is coming again, light returns to the world, and new life. Just as the candles burn brightly around us, so soon will the sun."

Wyatt turned slowly to the north, athame now pointed before him. "I now draw the sacred Circle." He continued to turn, drawing an imaginary (but no less meaningful) border around them all. "Let no man leave its boundaries until our Ritual is done."

When he had come around to the direction where he started, he nodded and then placed the blade back on the altar.

"And now we call to the Watchtowers, asking them if they will, if it pleases them, join us tonight." He looked at Cedar and nodded once.

Cedar was already standing at the north side of the circle, and he turned and faced outward. "Spirits of the North," he called out. "We ask you this evening to attend our Circle. Element of Earth. Element waiting to be awakened on this Solstice. Element of soil under and between our toes. Dust that makes our bodies and to which we will return. Come to us!"

Cedar swiveled back around on his heel like a soldier, eyes flashing. Wyatt's heart sped up. Perfect. His words were *perfect*!

He turned to Sloan, wished that his friend could have gone last, gotten more hints on what to do. He looked so nervous. It was clear that Asher and Peni had reasons to claim the directions they'd claimed. But Sloan? Of course, except for Cedar, none of them really knew what they were doing. And was there anyone here that really knew what to do?

"Sloan?" he said.

Sloan bit his lip. And then he turned around, facing the east, and, voice quivering ever so slightly, said, "Spirits of the East, we call to you this evening and ask that you join the Circle. Element of Air." He went quiet for a seemingly endless moment, and then he continued, voice going stronger as he went. "First breath that a baby takes. Breath that my mother believed God breathed into Adam. Gentle wind that brings to me and the whole neighborhood the scent of the hyacinths from her garden. Breeze that plays the music of her chimes that she loved so much. Please join us!"

The words took *Wyatt's* breath away. They were even more perfect than Cedar's. So personal. So powerful. Exactly what this Circle, any circle, *needed*. And when Sloan turned around, there were tears in his eyes, and he smiled at Wyatt and Wyatt's heart filled with love. *I love you*, he mouthed to his friend, and smiled when the silent words were returned.

He looked to Asher, gave him a single nod.

Asher returned the nod, smiled a gentle smile, and visibly swallowed. He turned to the south and after a brief pause, let his voice ring out. "Spirits of the South, we call out to you and ask that you join us tonight. Element of Fire. Element of our souls. Fire that flames across the branches of that ancient bush, but does not burn it. Flame of the burning coals that the seraphim touched to Isaiah's lips and took away his iniquity and forgave his sins. Pillar of fire that led the Israelites out of captivity in Egypt. We invite you to join us."

Wyatt's eyes had gone wide, his heart beating faster. Asher's words…. Again! Perfect! He had made this personal as well. He had known. Tears welled up in Wyatt's eyes. How had Asher known?

He took a deep breath and turned to Peni. Had Cedar's eyes been flashing? There was that and more in Peni's black eyes. A virtual storm. Once more Wyatt could scarcely breathe. There was power here. The hair on his arms was standing up. He thought he could almost smell the ozone. Was he the only one? Was he just imagining it? Could anyone doubt that the Spirits of the Watchtowers were arriving?

Peni turned slowly to the west, his movement graceful, his lava-lava (now hanging to his ankles again) swirling around him and revealing his pe'a, and once more Wyatt felt that power in the room as it cranked up another notch. What Peni had gone through to get those black marks of deep-set ink…. Yes! There was magick there!

"Spirits of the West," Peni cried. "We call to you tonight and ask you to join us, *o ou uso*—my brothers—in this Circle. Element of Water. Element of our blood, seed of our loins, *To Sua*—water exists within. Of the seas and fresh water that *Tangaloa-fa'a-tutupu-nu'u* brought forth from the Rock. Tilafaiga and Taema swam through you to bring the basket full of tattooing tools to Samoa. Please, oh Spirits, join us tonight."

There were tears running down Wyatt's face by the time Peni turned. Not in his wildest fantasies had he imagined that anything like this would or could happen tonight. This was wonderful.

This was true friendship.

That his friends would not only do this for him tonight, but join with all their hearts.

Wyatt opened his mouth, closed it, and tried again to no avail. There was so much emotion.

He took another breath and let it out slowly… and began again.

"Thank you, my brothers, for your special gift. I have no doubt that the Spirits of the Elements are here with us tonight, helping us work our magick. I *feel* them.

"Tonight is the time for looking forward, for moving forward, for calling forth what will come and manifest all that we wish to come. The Solstice is when the Oak King challenges the Holly King to rule the world and his half of the year. Should he win, he will bring new life and challenge us to grow."

Wyatt took his wand in hand—one he had carved himself from a hawthorn branch from Camp Sanctuary—raised it straight up over his head, and closed his eyes. "Ground yourselves, my friends. Close your eyes. Imagine that you are a tree, your body the trunk, your arm the branches, and your feet sinking like roots into the ground. Imagine that they are roots. Feel them extend down, down, down…."

Wyatt could see it in his mind's eye. He could feel his feet, feel them rooting, growing, reaching downward.

"We are pulling energy up from the earth, pulling in the power of the earth, letting it nourish us and fill us. Feel it in your feet, feel it running up and flowing into your body—the trunk, your legs, your thighs, your cocks, your ass, your torso, your chest, your heart. This is ours to take. A gift of the Mother. Let it run up into your face—"

Wyatt could *feel* it!

"—and up your arms and into your fingers—"

He could feel the energy, and his skin tingled and even his fingers felt hot. He let all of that rise up through the wand.

"—and now out! Let it rise up above you into the air and into the night sky! And let it rise and rise and rise until finally, it slows and falls like gentle rain onto your heads and your body and down into the earth again, a continuing cycle. Taking and giving and receiving and giving again…."

And Wyatt could feel that too. He'd felt it before. But there was something different about *this* time. It had never felt so wondrous, not even at Men's Festival in a Circle of a hundred men.

He waited. Rode with the feeling. Let it fill his heart with gladness. Finally opened his eyes.

"My brothers," he said, "we are grounded and ready to work our magick."

CHAPTER SIX

"I'M GOING to guide us in a simple meditation," Kevin told his friends.

"A meditation?" Cauley asked. "No magic? I mean, I was hoping for some magic."

Kevin shook his head. "No magic. Except for the magic that is always there around us."

"Oh," Cauley said. "I was hoping for…." His voice faded away.

"For what?" Kevin asked, and then quite suddenly knew.

"Nothing," Cauley replied quietly, lowering his head, his face totally lost in shadow now.

"Cauley," Kevin said, his voice barely above a whisper. God. Was Cauley hoping for some kind of magical healing ritual? If so, it was certainly nothing he knew how to do.

He got up from his chair and went to one knee, ignoring the melting snow. Reaching out, he took Cauley's gloved hand in his own. "I don't know how to work magic. Not really. Nothing more than any of us."

Cauley lifted his face and, *God*, in the light from the flames his face looked almost like a death mask. "Why did this have to happen to me?"

Kevin had no idea how to answer. Did anyone? His mother had asked the same kind of question when his father had an affair on her.

"Why, Kevin? Why? Why did he do it? Was it me?"

He hadn't known what to say to her then, and he had no idea what to say to Cauley now. But that look on his old lover's face begged him to say something.

"I… I don't know, my sweet friend—"

"*Friend*," Cauley whispered.

"I don't know why *any*thing happens. Not really. I know that I believe what my Wiccan friends say at Festival. That we all come from the… well, they say the Goddess. And to her we will return. It's a circle. None of us will live forever." He looked up into the falling snow and Cauley followed his example. The big flakes fell on their faces, and when they looked at each other again, Cauley's eyelashes looked like downy feathers. In seconds they melted away into tiny drops, catching the firelight like crystals.

"We are all the same," Kevin said. "Us. The snow. The fire. We're made up of stars. We've been around forever, and we return to that energy, and we come back again and again. I believe that."

"Will I come back?"

In some form, thought Kevin.

"I think it would make me happy if I came back as a snowflake and I could fall on your face."

Kevin's heart swelled with both love and sorrow at those words, and he couldn't help but lean forward and kiss Cauley on the mouth. He kissed him hard. Fully. Nothing chaste about it. He wanted Cauley to feel the love he would always have for him.

When he sat back, Cauley gasped. "Oh, Kevin." A tear rolled down his cheek. "Thank you for that."

Kevin swallowed hard, nodded.

"So let's get on with your meditation," Cauley said with a little laugh.

"You got it," Kevin said. "And I have one little ritual planned as well."

"There we go!" Cauley exclaimed. "I knew we could get something in there!"

So Kevin returned to his chair, caught Theresa's eyes (she had been so quiet), brushed away the little snow that had accumulated on his seat (this close to the heat of the fire it was like they were in a protective bubble), and sat down. "All right, then. Everyone close their eyes."

Theresa did as bid, and through the flickering of the flames, he could see Cauley had as well.

"Now. I want you to imagine that you are standing. You turn away from the fire, and you walk into the dark. Feel it all around you. But wait! Surprise. It's not cold. If anything, it's *nothing*. Just very comfortable. *Perfect*...."

"Then… there ahead of you… you see a door. It's red. There is a single light on that door and you go to it and open it. You are not afraid. You know there is something good inside waiting for you. And yes! To your surprise you are looking out at a beautiful summer day and you are surrounded by a field of red zinnias."

He was using part of the Queer God Ritual from Men's Festival, but modifying it for his own use. Making it simpler. That ritual could go on for a long time, and he had an idea that Cauley was good for *maybe* a half hour more out here. Maybe less.

"See them? Can you see the zinnias?"

"Yes," said Theresa. "I—I can…."

"I think so," Cauley said. "Yes. Me too…. May I pick one?"

"Yes," Kevin said. "Pick as many as you want."

"Just one," whispered Cauley.

"Now we are going to walk through the field. We don't hurt them. They almost seem to part for us. And as we walk, we see something ahead. The red… it's ending. They seem to be getting taller. Oranger. And yes! It's poppies!"

"Like in *The Wizard of Oz*," Cauley said with delight.

"But these aren't deadly. They don't want us to go to sleep. They fill us with their orange. Orange light. Orange life. And just like the zinnias, they part for us…."

"I'm picking one of these too," Cauley said.

"Me too," Theresa said. "I love poppies."

"And look guys! Up ahead." Kevin could see it all as well. A field that went forever. But…

"…but up ahead the flowers are changing again. Yellow! It's yellow sunflowers. All different shapes and sizes. And yellow. See them?" He could. "*Feel* them…."

"So beautiful," said Theresa. "Warm."

"Yes," Kevin agreed. "So warm. Like heat on sore muscles. Or warm water on tired feet."

"Warm," Cauley said in a voice Kevin could barely hear. "Picking one…."

"And we're walking… walking…."

"I think it's changing again," said Cauley.

"Yes. It is. Can you see what it is?"

"Green," Cauley said. "It's green! Right? Green?"

"Yes," said Kevin. "Green, lush ferns."

"And those flowers you gave me for my birthday last year," Cauley said, excitement in his voice. "Bells of Ireland or something like that!"

Kevin smiled. Yes. *Moluccella laevis*. He could see them too. Tall stalks covered in bell-shaped green flowers. One of his favorites, and one day he would live somewhere where he could have an actual garden and grow them himself.

"Yes," Kevin agreed aloud. "Bells of Ireland. And they radiate life. Green life. Filling us with their growing energy."

"Picking just a tip," Cauley said. "A small one. I'm making a bouquet."

The thought made Kevin smile again.

"We walk. We keep walking. It is a wonderful day. The walking is easy—"

"Flowers parting," said Cauley.

"—and we don't get tired. And up ahead…."

"They're changing," said Cauley.

"Blue," said Theresa.

"Blue," repeated Kevin. "Big, huge hydrangeas. Some as big as your head."

"Ooooh…," said Cauley.

"They feel cool," said Kevin. "Can you feel it? Can you feel the cool?"

"Soothing," said Theresa.

"Soothing," echoed Cauley.

"We are walking through a field of hydrangea bushes. Weaving through on a tiny path. And any hurts we have? Any pains? Why, the coolness of the hydrangeas are taking them away."

"*Soothing*," Cauley said again. A whisper.

"And now the bushes seem to be shrinking. Getting smaller. Making way for… indigo. Indigo irises. Stunning, gorgeous irises. So many. Everywhere!"

Kevin was totally lost in the vision he had created for them now. He was there. There completely. He could see Cauley standing to his left, looking strong and healthy like he had on that first day they met in Central Park. He was glowing. Surrounded by a golden aura. Kevin looked to his right, and there was Theresa, looking resplendent. Like a fairy queen. Or a goddess.

He sighed. And moved on. "We keep going," he said. "Keep walking and look…. There. Just up ahead of us. Shrinking again. And this time for purple violets. Violets as far as we can see."

Gorgeous.

"But this time, instead of going on, we lay down. We lay right down in the violets. And they are like a warm blanket. A thick blanket. We lay down on our backs." Kevin could see, now deep in a near hypnotized state. Drifting along…. "And they fluff up around us, and we look up into a beautiful sunny sky. The sky so very blue, with only a puff of pure white cloud, and the light of the sun is so warm, so golden. And the violets. They fill us with their purple power."

"Queer power," Cauley said quietly, the awe clear in his voice.

The words surprised Kevin. Purple *was* the queer color. Had been for thousands of years. Gay men had identified each other by wearing amethyst. But how had Cauley known that?

There really was a kind of magic in the world, he thought.

Kevin all but whispered, "Now my friends—"

A piece of wood popped in the fire pit.

Now is the hard part!

Or at least potentially.

"—this is where we're going to do a little bit of work. It might sound hard, but it's worth it. I want you to use your imagination. I want you to think of something that happened this past year that no longer has a place in your life. Something you are *done* with. Over. See it in your mind, floating over you. Picture it. Picture it blocking your view of the lovely sky."

Kevin allowed himself to do what he asked of them. Wouldn't let himself wonder what Cauley might be seeing.

He saw too much time in an office where he no longer worked day to day. He saw a city that, even though he loved it, kept him from the Land that he loved so much. He let a furtive night in an apartment with a man whose name he didn't know flash there as well—a night that had made him feel so empty afterward, and the memory of an orgasm that wasn't even very good.

"Now let the sun blaze through it," he said aloud. "Let the new-coming sun burn it away. Let it banish those images, those thoughts. Let them burn away with the old year."

He imagined it. The sunlight poured right through the visions in his mind like a bright light through a piece of celluloid. It got brighter and brighter yet didn't burn his eyes. It only shone through and through and through and then the pictures were… gone.

After a long moment, he said, "Now picture something you want. Something missing in your life. Something you want to come *into* your life in this New Year. See it…. See it before your eyes… and pull it into your arms."

And here was the joke—he'd come up with this idea and gotten his friends to go along with it, and he wasn't even sure what it was that he himself wanted.

But then to his surprise…

Kevin saw words floating before him, dark against the glowing screen of his laptop…

I just wanted u to know I am free! I have finally dumped my loser lovers ass!

And the echo of a thought…

So Wyatt was single now?

And another image—a sweet, short little man, rounded just the way Kevin liked (padded), with a lightly hairy chest, adorable round little butt (oh! Such a sweet little round butt!), and the darkest eyes, puppy eyes. Saw them cuddled on a blanket on the beach at Camp Sanctuary. Almost felt lips against his own, full and soft and so sweet. Heard his laughter—Wyatt's laughter.

Kevin let out a gasp.

CHAPTER SEVEN

"THE HOLLY King and the Oak King are battling, my friends," cried Wyatt. "See them! *Feel* the energy—the forces of nature that radiate from them! Not destructive. No. This is not evil. This is *not* war. This is *change*. This is Creative Force. Feel it hit you in waves."

Wyatt could. His skin was crawling with it. He could scarcely breathe from the power of it. He couldn't remember feeling anything like this in Ritual before. Surely he had. But this was *amazing*!

"Now feel it *fill* you," he continued, his voice trembling. "Feel it penetrate you in waves. Into you and through you and out of you…."

It was powerful. Something very powerful was happening. Was he doing this? Or was it all just in his mind? Some flight of fancy?

It couldn't be, though, could it? Because if what happened during Ritual was only in his imagination, if he thought that his religious practices were just some kind of flight of fancy, he would have given up this spiritual path years ago.

Like he'd given up growing his own vegetables. Or the remake of *Battlestar Galactica*, a show he'd liked for about a year and then he'd gotten bored with (especially with a woman playing Starbuck!). Or knitting (or trying to). Or making his own soap and trying to sell it at Camp Sanctuary (but then after one weekend at Midwest Pagan Festival, sitting at his table day after day instead of being able to run around and do what he wanted, he was cured of that for good).

No…. This was real! His spiritual path was real. What he was experiencing right now was *real*!

Keep talking. Stop *thinking*! Go with this. *Use* this! *Go on!*

"Let this energy wash away all from last year that brought you hurt," he said, voice growing with his determination. "Let it wash away the things that brought you pain, brought you discouragement, made you cry."

Wyatt wondered only for one tiny second what the others might be thinking of. Then shook it away. That was not what he needed to be thinking about. That was *their* magick. *This* was his own. His own pain, and of course all of his pain was Howard.

The fights. The screaming. The insults. A man that he loved—*laughing* at him, telling him that the only reason anyone liked him at all was because he was with Howard. How everyone liked *Howard*, not him. He was only a silly little homo. An annoying little bone-smoker. How often had Howard said things like that? Things that Wyatt had *believed*. Believed to his core.

"The only reason you get laid is because of me. I tell them they have *to have sex with you if they want me."*

Except of course that wasn't entirely true, was it? Howard had "let" people have sex with him when Wyatt wasn't there.

Then—in one brief flash—he *saw* the word "FAGGOT" scratched across the right quarter panel of his beloved Mini Coop.

Another image. A horrible night at Camp where he and Howard fought over something a dear friend had told him—that Howard had supposedly raped a young fellow festival attendee named Blue. How impossible that had seemed. It was like watching a scene from a movie. He saw his anger at Scott for telling him such *lies*! He felt that deep knowledge that it wasn't a lie. Saw Howard convincing him that it was all just a role-playing game gone wrong—and saw himself choosing to believe it despite the fact that he somehow knew Howard wasn't telling the truth.

And worse, a vision of coming home early with a bag of Nilgiri chicken korma and samosas and seeing Howard fucking some stranger bent over their coffee table while he—*Howard!*—was taking a huge cock up his own ass. Howard. Who didn't *get* fucked…

…at least not by Wyatt.

The pain was so huge and gigantic that it almost took Wyatt out of the magick. Out of the moment. Out of the ritual. Out of all that was happening on this powerful night. It was only grabbing the cliff's edge by his fingernails—nails that almost tore away from his fingertips—and focusing all of his will—

(*you will not fall!*)

—that allowed him to stay. To stay in the moment.

With reserves he didn't know he owned, he opened his mouth and let the words flow.

"The waves of energy," he managed, "are wearing the pain away. The hurts and pain and imagined failures are nothing but dust. They are blowing away. It is past. It isn't *real*. There is only the *now*. Yesterday does not exist. Yesterday's *pain* does not exist. There is only the perfect love and perfect trust of this Circle. The perfect love and trust that we have, brothers, friends—the *Fab*-ulous Four!"

And somehow it was working. For a moment, at least, the images faded and crumbled and blew away in a strong breeze. Pictures of Howard sailed away into forevers, gone. He let his shouts fade away. Let Howard's *if-only-you-were-more*s slip into nothing but quiet echoes and then die away completely. Saw only his four best friends. Sloan (of course) and Scott and Asher. His four friends and more. Max. Cedar. Peni.

In that moment he was very suddenly nearly rocked off his feet by the love he felt.

People did love *him*. Wyatt. They loved him, and their love had nothing to do with Howard. Most of his friends didn't even like Howard. Hell! Did any of them like him? How many times had they told him that Howard wasn't worthy of his love? *Worthy!*

Right then—*in* that moment—he finally knew they *meant* what they'd said. What they had told him weren't words designed to make him feel better.

Tears began to run down Wyatt's face.

So much love! Enough love to allow him to face anything. He wasn't alone!

And that gave him enough strength to finish what he had begun.

"Now," he called out in a clear and strong voice, "as this new year begins, as the sun rises, as the Oak King wins—can you feel him win? Can you hear him call out in triumph? Can you hear the Holly King concede?—see something new! Imagine what you want this year to bring. What is it you want? What is it you *need*?"

And unbidden: *Someone to love me. Someone to cherish me. Who loves me just as I am. Someone who won't tell me that I'd be better if I was only more of what he thinks I should be! Someone I can care for and who will care for me, love me....*

The strength of the desire, the depths of it, surprised Wyatt. It wasn't at all what he'd planned to wish for and try to manifest tonight. He'd been simply wanting to be able to afford to get by. To, for once, not owe anyone anything.

Finish the Ritual! You're leaving everyone hanging.

"See whatever it is…! See it. *Welcome* it. *Embrace* it. Know that it is real."

Love.

Gods, it was love.

More than anything, he wanted love. Real love. Someone who loved him like these six friends. And *more*.

Love.

And then quite suddenly, to Wyatt's complete and total surprise, an image filled his mind. Wyatt. Sitting in the shade of the branches of a tree. Sitting with Scott. It was at Camp Sanctuary. He could *hear* the breeze in the leaves and feel the dirt under his bare toes. And now... the sound of gravel crunching under tires. A big white pickup truck coming out of a tunnel of trees and pulling up in front of Wyatt. And a big man with barely tamed muttonchops stepping *out* of that truck.

The man, who Wyatt had known for years but with whom he had rarely exchanged words—how could he when that man rarely said more than one *single* word?—walked up to him. Stood over him. His big hazel eyes were shining. Shining with want—

(he wants to register for Men's Festival)

—and...

...something more?

He reached out and placed his big manly hands on Wyatt's shoulders. Then bent his head down, down, and... *gods*! Kissed him! He could almost feel the lips against his own, full and soft, and so sweet.

Gods. The man was...

Wyatt let out a gasp.

CHAPTER EIGHT

KEVIN'S EYES snapped open.

He was back at the fire, his friends Cauley and Theresa to his left and right, and the snow was still falling—they were frosted with snow—and there was no Wyatt. No sweet Wyatt kissing him.

"Wow!" cried Theresa, her eyes wide open.

Cauley didn't say anything. But there was something in his eyes. His Cossack hat was pushed back enough that the light from the fire—dying though it was—now illuminated his face.

Kevin gulped.

Wow, indeed.

They sat for what seemed forever, and then the chill hit Kevin and he knew he had to get Cauley inside. *Finish this....*

He took a deep breath.

"And so now let us end our little ritual," he said. "On Monday the days will begin to lengthen, bit by bit. Soon, instead of deep dark filling every morning, the new sun will slowly brighten the sky in the east and chase the darkness away. Soon we will wake with the light and perhaps even climb into our beds before the last of the light has vanished in the west. Summer is coming!"

He stood.

"Summer is coming."

"I wish it would get here," Cauley said. He let out a strange little laugh. "'Cause I am fucking freezing!"

Theresa laughed too, and Kevin couldn't help but join in.

The moment was gone. The "magic" done. And the feeling of soft lips on his own just a strange memory.

With that thought he helped Cauley to his feet and brushed him off and, with Theresa, helped him inside. She gave them both a big hug, declined any hot chocolate that Lois tried to push on her, and left. And after forcing just a bit on Cauley, Kevin helped him undress and get into bed and then lay down next to him, lending his old love his warmth.

Cauley sighed. Cuddled closer. Kevin gave him a hug.

"I so wish I hadn't fucked up," Cauley said quietly.

"Shhhh…."

"And you are so lonely, Kevin. That's what makes it worse. Worse than *me* being lonely."

Kevin's brows came together in a knot. Where had that come from? "Cauley, I'm fine. I'm not lonely."

"Yes, you are. I see it in your eyes. The way you look off into nowhere. And I hate myself that I can't take that away."

Kevin pulled back just enough to look down into Cauley's eyes. "Please don't hate yourself," he said. "Ever. It hurts to think that you hate yourself. You are a wonderful man, Cauley."

His ex sighed again, and then after a very long pause, he said, "Promise me you will find someone?"

Kevin rolled his eyes. "I don't *need* to find anyone." *Because I just can't go through anything like that again*, he thought and tried not to feel even that occasional twinge of anger toward Cauley that he had not quite exorcised from his heart. "I'm fine. I'm happy."

Cauley sighed again. Then: "Read to me?" Cauley asked, his voice foggy.

"Read to you?" Kevin rested his upper weight on one elbow and looked down into Cauley's face. "Read what?"

"I have that book you gave me. That book of essays by Emertson." He pointed over Kevin's shoulder.

Emerson, Kevin mentally corrected him. *Ralph Waldo Emerson*. "Have you tried to read it?"

"Tried," Cauley said and yawned. "It's easier to understand when you read it to me."

So Kevin got up and grabbed the book and then quickly scrambled under the covers again. He paged through the book, found an essay he liked, and began to read,

We have a great deal more kindness than is ever spoken. Maugre all the selfishness that chills like east winds the world, the whole human family is bathed with an element of love like a fine ether. How many persons we meet in houses, whom we scarcely speak to, whom yet we honor, and who honor us! How many we see in the street, or sit with in church, whom, though silently, we warmly rejoice to be with! Read the language of these wandering eye-beams. The heart knoweth.

He'd read for perhaps ten minutes when Cauley began to softly snore. Then Kevin kissed his troubled brow, which had relaxed at least somewhat in sleep, and carefully climbed from the bed.

Lois had already gone upstairs.

Kevin microwaved Cauley's leftover hot chocolate and drank it in a few quick swallows and then let himself out into the snowy night. He stood for a moment. Watched the snow. Especially in the bright glow around the street lights. It looked magic. After a long moment, he climbed into his F-150 and headed home.

And thought of a cute little bear. Couldn't help it. Remembered what those lips, which had never touched his own, felt like.

Wyatt, he thought.

The images left as he drove. The snow was falling thickly now. There would be more than a couple inches. The road demanded his attention now.

But in dreams that night, Kevin saw those big brown eyes again....

WYATT'S EYES snapped open.

He was back at his living room, his friends Sloan and Scott and Asher and Max and Cedar and Peni all around him.

And there was no big man holding him, kissing him.

"Wow!" cried Peni, his eyes wide and electric.

There were murmurs of agreement and nods, and Wyatt couldn't believe all that had happened. From their expressions, they meant it. Had their experiences been anything like his own?

And what *had* happened to him?

Something that had never happened before, that was for sure!

"That was frigging awesome," Cedar said. He laughed, and then they all joined him.

Awesome indeed.

Then, as Wyatt saw their expectant expressions, he knew. *End this.* It was time to close the Circle.

Somehow he found the words.

"And so the Oak King has won. The Holly King submits and awaits his turn at the Summer Solstice. Our magick is done. The old is done. The new is coming. The new is *here*. Forming and manifesting even if we can't yet see it. Rest in that knowledge. And let us thank the Guardians of the Watchtowers and release them from the duties they graciously performed for us tonight. Cedar?"

Cedar nodded, stepped forward, and turned around to face the north. "Thank you, Elements of Earth, for your presence tonight. Stay if you wish, depart if you must. Thank you for your blessings."

Then Sloan, wide-eyed and clearly not realizing his duties for the night were not done (oops!), managed to stumble through his thanks to the Spirits of the Air and the East.

Asher, always an actor, blustered through his quite well, and then Peni, full of excitement, finished with aplomb.

"Thank you, Elements of Water and Ocean and Sea!" Peni cried. "Thank you, Element of blood, and cum—"

That surprised Wyatt, and he almost laughed. Bless you, Peni, for being brave enough to shout that!

"—and thank you *To Sua*—water exists within. Thank you *Tangaloa-fa'a-tutupu-nu'u* and spirits of Tilafaiga and Taema and Samoa. Stay if you wish, depart if you must. Thank you for your blessings."

He turned back to face the group, his face flushed and glowing.

Wyatt felt the power of this night return.

"Thank you, oh Holly King and Oak King," he called out. "Thank you for your presence. Thank you for eternally turning the Wheel of the Year. Stay if you wish, depart if you must. Thank you for your blessings."

Wyatt raised his wand over his head, turned full circle, then placed it on his altar. Finally he picked up his athame. He faced the north and then made an upward, cutting motion. "The Circle is open, yet ever unbroken," he declared. "Its power flows with us and through us always. Merry meet, merry part, and merry meet again. Blessed be!"

"Blessed be," chorused both Cedar and Scott, who were in the know.

"Blessed be," echoed his friends.

Blessed be indeed.

Wyatt staggered. Almost fell.

Sloan was there in an instant and led him to the couch, sat him down.

"You okay?" his friend asked.

"More than okay," Wyatt said in awe, skin still crawling with something wondrous, like St. Elmo's fire.

And the ghost feeling of soft lips.

Soft lips that had never touched his own.

Where had that image come from? *Him* of all people! Had he ever spared the man much serious thought? Except that he had always considered the man sexy? But why would he, *he*, appear in Wyatt's thoughts tonight?

Wyatt shook his head and smiled. "Time for wine and cakes," he said.

"All right," exclaimed Cedar.

Wyatt tried to stand and found he couldn't.

"We'll do it," Asher said. "You just sit."

"It's all on the dining room table," Wyatt managed.

Sloan sat with him, and Peni pulled a hassock next to him and sat on it and began to jabber excitedly. Wyatt couldn't help but smile at his enthusiasm. There was laughter from the dining room and the pops of wine bottles, and then he was being offered a glass and a sugar cookie.

"Is that what you meant by cakes?" Asher asked.

Wyatt nodded.

"Is it all right that I gave you one from your altar instead of the package on the dining room table?"

Wyatt nodded again, words hard to form. He took it and broke it and handed the other half to Asher and the look in his friend's eyes showed that he understood the gesture. Wyatt ate his half in two or three bites. He was quite suddenly ravenous. A moment later Asher handed him another and Wyatt ate it almost as quickly.

He was starting to come down from the high of the Ritual and beginning already to take on the high of the wine.

He still couldn't talk. He was too amazed.

Those lips....

Finally he joined the conversation, which was mostly congratulations from his friends. Words of encouragement. Compliments. But at the same time, to his joy, they seemed to be excited by the events of the evening. Most were sharing their experiences, sharing what they'd hoped to banish from their lives and what they hoped to draw in. Even practical Max appeared to have enjoyed the Ritual.

Someone to cherish me, thought Wyatt. That had been his wish. Someone who would love him for who he was. Someone he could take care of and who would give him caring and love as well.

He was finally able to stop thinking about the tall man in his mind's eye and focus on his companions instead. They didn't stay long. A half hour or so. Then the group began to break up. Max wanted to check on his son. Sloan seemed eager to join his lover. Wyatt could feel the sexual energy crackling between the pair. And Peni was all but crawling all over

Asher. Cedar was eyeing Scott with lust as well. Wyatt knew what they would be doing tonight.

And later, alone in his bed, he found he didn't resent them and what they had.

In fact, he didn't even have the energy to masturbate.

He slipped off into dreams, not feeling alone at all.

In those dreams he saw hazel eyes looking down at him.

Felt those lips.

And let the man's name—the only name he knew—slip from his own.

Hodor ....

CHAPTER NINE

CHRISTMAS WAS quiet, but nice. Wyatt spent a big part of the day binge-watching *Friends* on Sloan's Netflix account. He'd stumbled on the show a few days before, not realizing it was available, and had watched the first episode—"The One Where Monica Gets a New Roommate"—on a lark. He'd never watched it before and decided to see what all the fuss was about. Just to see why so many people loved it. He seemed to remember the six cast members had gotten a million dollars apiece per episode toward the end.

Wyatt wound up staying up just past midnight, having watched eight episodes that first night. They made him laugh. He needed to laugh. It was strangely better than beating off, and didn't make him feel lonely when he was done.

Tonight he had just started watching a Christmas episode, "The One with Phoebe's Dad"—second season, third?—when the doorbell rang. He looked at the front door in surprise—Phoebe was just commenting about the size of Ugly Naked Guy's Christmas balls—then shrugged and got up to see who it was.

It was none other than Logan, Max's son, and Logan's boyfriend Devin. And imagine! Fourteen (or was he fifteen now? Wasn't he fifteen?) and had a boyfriend! A boyfriend his parents knew about. And the boyfriend's parents knew about Logan. It was like something out of *The Twilight Zone*. Quite a different story than Wyatt's own.

They were both dressed up in their Christmas finery, most notably long hats—Logan's red and Devin's green—with a big white poof ball at the tips and huge, ridiculous pointed elf ears to either side.

Then to Wyatt's surprise, they began to sing.

Deck the hall with boughs of holly, Fa la la la la la la la la.
'Tis the season to be jolly, Fa la la la la la la la la.
Don we now our gaaaaay apparel, Fa la la la la la la la la.
Troll the ancient Christmas carol, Fa la la la la la la la laaaaaaaa!

"Merry Christmas, Uncle Wyatt," Logan said, a big smile spread over his cute face.

Uncle Wyatt?

"And a Happy New Year," Devin added.

Wyatt grinned and couldn't help the tears that touched his eyes. If anyone had ever come to him with Christmas carols before, he couldn't remember when.

"Thank you, boys," he cried. "Do you want to come in? I can make you hot chocolate. It'll be instant, but—"

"Nope!" Logan said cheerfully. "That's not why we're here. Get your coat, Uncle Wyatt. You're coming to our house for dinner!"

Wyatt gaped at the pair. "But your...." Did he say "dads"? He gulped. "But your dad and Sloan helped me celebrate on Saturday."

"And you are *not* eating alone tonight!" Logan stated with an authority that could not be argued.

"I... I...." Wyatt didn't know what to say.

So therefore he said the only thing he could.

"Can you give me a minute to put on some gay apparel?"

Logan and Devin burst into laughter. "Yeah, we can do that. You have five minutes."

Wyatt spread his fingers over his chest. "Me? You expect *me* to be ready in five minutes?"

"Four and three-quarters minutes now," Logan stated firmly.

Wyatt looked at them, horrified, and told them to get inside. "Hurry!" And with that he dashed up the stairs.

When he got to his room he opened drawers and threw things hither and yon. He knew he had something he could wear. Was sure of it. Howard couldn't have taken it because he would have never fit into it.

Just when he was about to give up... "Eureka!" he shouted, pulled off his oversized nightshirt and pulled on the T-shirt instead. He scrambled into bright red jeans he'd found at a thrift store, then green socks, and finally his red high-tops. Then it was back down the steps just as the boys were calling out, "Five, four, three, two, *one!*"

They took one look at him and once more exploded into laughter.

"That's perfect," Devin said.

Wyatt grinned. The shirt said it all. "Merry Elfin' X-Mas!"

"It's elfin' perfect," said Logan.

"YOU KNOW you didn't have to do this," Wyatt said as Max helped him out of his coat and then got a good laugh at Wyatt's shirt himself.

"Nonsense," Max said and chuckled again. "We've got plenty. There was no sense in you being alone."

That almost made Wyatt cry.

The house was lovely. They'd put up a big tree—live, but plantable of course. Max was as green as they came and explained that he liked having a living, breathing tree in the house and was excited about the idea of planting it as soon as he could. As for the rest of the decorations, it was all very gay with only a nod to the traditions. Wyatt decided he could have hardly done better. Lots of huge purple and blue and silver ribbons everywhere. No crèches. Not even an angel on the top of the tree, but some kind of bird instead. Max was more Buddhist than anything; Sloan had no real religious feelings one way or the other. Wyatt suspected all the decorating was more for Logan than anything else. That and habit. He'd read in some Gallup poll recently that only about 50 percent of the people who celebrated Christmas did so for any religious reasons. The rest just celebrated because that's what you did—like setting off fireworks on the Fourth of July or decorating and hiding eggs on Easter.

Dinner was a huge turkey with stuffing and all the trimmings, all the traditional side dishes—including mashed potatoes and gravy, green bean casserole, yams, Waldorf salad, and not one, but three pies. Wyatt was simply grateful that the turkey wasn't tofu (Max was about two steps to the side of being vegetarian). That and to have been invited in the first place. He hadn't realized how much he didn't want to be alone today until the boys showed up at his door, or even more, until he was sitting at this table. It didn't even bother him that he was the only single person there (well, not too much). It all came with a comprehension that he'd been secretly (secret even from himself) dreading spending the day in his big empty house filled with echoes of Christmases past.

Howard celebrated Christmas big-time, although Wyatt was the one who wound up putting up and taking down the considerable decorations. Except for the outside lights of course. Howard took joyful charge of that. Plus Wyatt was afraid to stand on a chair to change a light bulb in a ceiling fixture (which naturally had been one more thing Howard made fun of him for).

But at least Howard's celebrations drowned out the earlier echoes—
Wyatt's family Christmases. They'd been even bigger than Howard's—
without Santa Claus or anything to do with the big man in red—and
included lots of Baptist church services.

Wyatt could remember just exactly when Christmas had stopped
being fun and turned into something almost scary. It was when his father
had the accident—one that could have killed him. An *eerie* accident. One
that convinced his father that God had given him a second chance and
that he should turn away from his wicked life and rejoice in Jesus.

This had all been early in Wyatt's childhood. Right before he went
into first grade, in fact. His father denounced the existence of Saint Nick
(along with all those heathen, idol-worshiping Catholics' false gods)
and made it a point to teach Wyatt the *true* meaning of Christmas. That
Saint Nicholas was something pagan and evil. Wyatt's little sister Wendy
hadn't had a real chance to believe in the jolly old elf even that long.

The Dolan household had Nativity sets all over the place—
every room, every nook and cranny. There was even a night-light in
the bathroom with the Christmas star shining down on the silhouette
of a manger (Wyatt had found it nearly impossible to take a bath and
especially pee when he was little, wondering if the baby Jesus could see
him from his manger).

There were still presents to be sure, but it was clear that it was in
honor of the wise men who brought the Christ Child gold, frankincense,
and myrrh—and not for some profane celebratory ritual.

When Wyatt was in fourth grade and realized that the three kings
didn't come to Jesus in the stable, but later, he'd almost said something to
his father. But even at ten years of age he'd figured out that discretion was
the better part of valor—especially when it came to his father's religious
conversion. He certainly didn't point out that the visitors weren't kings
at all, that there weren't necessarily three of them, and that "wise men"
almost certainly meant astrologers. That would only have been more
trouble than he wanted to deal with.

It had sparked an interest, though. At ten he was already intrigued
by things not-Christian. Things just a little less scary than tales of kings
and pharaohs slaughtering babies. Or the beheading of John the Baptist.
Or the story of God taking Ezekiel and dropping him off in a valley
filled with human bones that rose up, tendons and muscles reforming,
as a zombie army. He'd read about Jonah being swallowed by a whale
as well. He wouldn't even go swimming at the lake that whole summer.

And those plagues! Frogs and locusts and flies and angels of death and killing poor little baby lambs and painting their blood on thresholds!

But the worst of all was that whole concept of eating the body of Christ and drinking his blood.

No. The worst of all was the idea he was going to hell because of something Adam and Eve did six thousand years ago, and it was only through Jesus's gruesome death on the cross that he could be saved.

Even at ten he kept wondering about what seemed like contradictions in the Bible and how his father seemed to pick and choose what was evil and what wasn't. For instance, what about the dreams that warned Joseph to take Jesus and flee to Egypt? And what about those pesky wise men—*astrologers*? Astrology was something that was not tolerated in the Dolan home. His father even crossed out the horoscope in the newspaper with a big black magic marker (which bled through and often made doing the crossword puzzle impossible).

If astrology was evil, as his father claimed, how had it led the wise men to Jesus? And if God hated fortune-telling, then why would God create people who were able to do such things? And what about the commandment that said, "You shall have no other gods before Me"? If, as Wyatt had been taught, there was only one god, then how could there be any other gods before or after? And what about God being "a jealous God"? Again—it seemed to imply there were other gods as well!

He'd had so many questions but found the minute he asked them, he was punished and told he was a sinner that needed to pray for forgiveness.

"Wyatt, you okay?"

Wyatt gave a little start and turned to see that Logan was looking at him curiously. He cleared this throat. "Yeah. Just got lost in thought there."

"Was it a bad thought?" Logan asked quietly.

"I…. No. Just…." Wyatt sighed. "Just distracting."

Then to his surprise, Logan squeezed his knee. "If you need to talk, let me know."

The gesture touched Wyatt. This young man, not much more than a boy, was offering to be an ear. It was incredibly sweet. This "boy" was going to make a fine man.

"Thanks," Wyatt replied.

Then from Wyatt's left: "Would you pass the mashed potatoes?" Sloan asked.

Wyatt nodded, forced a smile, and passed.

After dinner, Wyatt had two pieces of pie—cherry and chocolate pecan—and they watched *A Christmas Story*. It was nice to be in a room full of laughter. There was eggnog too. With whiskey. Then, just as he was getting ready to leave, Sloan told him he needed to wait.

"One more thing." Sloan reached under the tree and pulled out a purple-and-silver-wrapped flat box. He smiled and handed it over. "Happy Yule," he said.

Wyatt's eyes went wide. "Sloan! I thought we'd all agreed to the Secret Santa thing." Which was true. Wyatt had gotten Asher's name and found a lovely tallit—a Jewish prayer shawl—and hoped it was the right choice. The jury was still out on the religious heritage thing. They were supposed to get together on Sunday to exchange gifts.

Sloan smirked. "Come on, buddy. You're my best friend! Open it."

Wyatt bit his lower lip and swallowed hard. *You're my best friend.* He fought the tears and turned the box over and tore the paper off. He saw it was a shirt box and lifted the lid. Inside was a turquoise T-shirt. Wyatt pulled it out only to see there were two. "Sloan!"

Max chuckled. "*Look* at them."

Wyatt unfolded the first one to see the words I Like My Men Beary Hairy. He let out a joyful laugh. "Oh guys! This is a riot!"

"Look at the other one," Logan cried excitedly.

Wyatt grinned and pulled out the second shirt. This one had the classic picture of Uncle Sam pointing at the viewer. Only what he was saying was decidedly not his classic words. "I Want You To Pull My Finger," he was saying. Wyatt burst into laughter. "Oh my gods! This is hilarious!" He jumped up, pulled off his Christmas shirt—not caring in the least to be bare-chested and chubby-bellied in front of his friends—and pulled the Uncle Sam shirt on. It fit perfectly. "I love it!" He dashed out of the room to the sound of his chuckling friends and went into the bathroom to check his reflection. And yes. Perfect. He loved it. Loved both the shirts, and ran back to tell his friends just how much he loved them. Both the shirts and all four of his Christmas companions.

"Thank you," he all but shouted and fiercely hugged everyone.

They even sent him off with a piece of the eggnog pie!

And when Wyatt went home, he found the big house was just a little less lonely.

Yes, he was the only one there. But instead of seeming like a mausoleum, it felt like a home. It was almost like the ghost of Sloan's mother—who had always been so kind to him—was still there.

"Gods, I hope not!" he exclaimed. Because how many times had he walked around the house naked and sat on the couch and jerked off to stories on porn sites?

Well, he hoped she averted her eyes.

CHAPTER TEN

WYATT WASN'T home a half hour when his cell phone rang. When he saw who was calling, he froze. It was one of his sister's two annual phone calls. He took a deep breath before he answered it. "Feliz Navidad," he said cheerfully.

"Merry Christmas to you too, big brother."

"Thank you, little sister." He closed his eyes. The familiar conglomerate of emotions were swirling through him: love, hurt, loyalty, shame…. It was always this way.

"And how are you doing today?" she asked. Her voice was cheerful—as usual. Seemingly genuine. And despite everything, he believed she *was* being authentic. They'd been nearly inseparable as kids, and surely that was what really mattered. Not what came later.

"I'm pretty good," he answered, deciding to tell her how he felt in this moment, and not the general feelings that had ruled over him the last few months. "Just got back from Sloan's house. He and Max had me over for Christmas dinner. You should see the T-shirts they got me." Which she wouldn't approve of, but what the shit.

"You mean your… Howard didn't make his big dinner this year?"

There it was. Already. But at least she'd said his name. It was more than his parents had done—when they still spoke to him. They. Meaning her. His mother. His father hadn't spoken to him in, what? Ten years? When his old man had said he'd been right all along. That Wyatt's evil ways had led him to hellfire. To homosexuality. And worse. Thinking that he could find love with another man.

(*"And you're never going to last! Two faggots can't make a home. It takes a man and a woman. He that made them at the beginning made them male and female. For this cause shall a man leave father and mother, and shall cleave to his wife: and the twain shall be one flesh. A man and a woman. A man brings home the bread and the woman takes care of the nest. How can two men—two sodomites—make a nest?"*)

Might as well get it over with. Get it done.

"I'm—" His throat locked up. *Shit.* It wasn't going to be that easy. *Deep breath.* "I'm… I'm not with Howard anymore," he managed and found himself once more wrestling his grief back down into its place deep inside that room he'd made for it.

Wyatt heard a small intake of breath from the other end of the phone. He didn't know if he really heard it or if it was just his imagination.

"I…. Wyatt, I…." Then a moment of quiet. Because what was she supposed to say? She was sorry? Because she wouldn't be, would she? She wouldn't be *allowed* to be. But then she surprised him. "Wyatt, I'm so sorry. Are you okay? How long has it been?"

"A couple of months," he said, his voice miraculously not trembling. "He left me." *Kicked me out is what he did.*

"Why didn't you call?"

Why hadn't he called? *Really?*

"And hear you say, 'Well maybe now you can find a nice lady and settle down and have a family'?"

"Oh, Wyatt." She sighed. "Like *that's* ever going to happen." Long pause while Wyatt tried to figure out what to say to that. Then just before he could: "Although nothing's impossible through our Lord."

"Oh really, Wendy?" Wyatt laughed. It wasn't a feel-good laugh. How many nights had he cried himself to sleep begging God to make him straight? Hundreds? And when He hadn't done what Wyatt had prayed for, it was the final straw. It was what made him finished with his family's God forever. "Don't even think it." *After all, you knew I was gay before I did.* Which wasn't entirely true. She was just the first to say it out loud.

Another sigh. Then she asked, "So is Sloan your new b-boyfriend?"

B-boyfriend? She could hardly say it. And she was the one who had thought it was so cool to have a gay brother. And could she be his best "person" if he got married? And wouldn't it be *hil*-arious when their parents found out? "You're supposed to carry on the family name," she had said.

As it turned out, it hadn't been *hil*-arious at all. Wyatt had always known that. It was part of why it had taken him as long as it had to admit to himself he was gay.

"Sloan is just a friend." Well, hardly *just* a friend. "He's my best friend in the world."

"I'm glad to hear that," she said. "We all need best friends. What did that movie say that Mom liked so much? In a cold world, you need your friends to keep you warm? Or something like that?"

The Big Chill. Except his mother only watched it when his father was out of town and couldn't walk in on her. She wasn't quite old enough to have been a teenager in the sixties. But her older sisters were, and they had played the music on their record players when she was little. She'd lived the sixties vicariously through them.

"*The Big Chill,*" he said aloud. Then asked about her husband—*the bastard*—and her kids.

"Oh, goodness, Mary! She just got straight As. Can you believe it? A child of *mine*? Miss C Average Wendy Dolan? And my kid is making straight As?"

"That's nice, Wendy."

She sighed. "And then there's Norman Jr. He's in and out of trouble. Second grade and a terror. Sometimes I don't know what we're going to do with him."

"You'll think of something." She was born to be a mom, if not a wife. And why wasn't she mentioning her husband? "And Norman Sr.?"

"Ummm… Norman is Norman, you know? His job at the dam is stressful. There was so much rain last year, and the lake was higher than it had been in years. It's calmed down a little with winter, but you know…."

Wyatt didn't know. Didn't have a clue. He'd toured the dam, of course. What with Mountain Home, where he went to school, being so close to one of the biggest lakes in the country, there was no way to avoid school field trips there. Plus the fact that the little town where he grew up was so close he could walk to it. But what the workers actually did there had always been sort of a mystery to him. So no, he didn't know what Norman did. Then there was the fact that he'd never met the man.

He hadn't met her kids either. And he figured he probably never would.

"He's leading the men's prayer group on Thursdays, and he's applied to be a deacon. I'm sure he'll get it. I can't imagine them turning him down."

"That's nice," Wyatt said, not thinking so in the least. The only thing he could think of that sounded worse than being a deacon in the Baptist church he was raised in was maybe being the guy who drove that truck that vacuum-sucked the shit out of the porta potties at Camp.

"He really likes it, Wyatt. He says it gives his life purpose. Oh, and now he's doing outreach at the prison in Calico Rock. He goes once a week and leads a prayer group there too. He says it's a wonderful thing to help those men turn from their criminal ways and seek the Lord."

Wyatt shifted from one foot to the other and found himself thinking about eggnog and whiskey. Was he tipsy enough to listen to any more of this? He went to the kitchen to see what he had to drink. "I…." Wyatt coughed. "I would imagine that adds to his stress, though." He looked around the kitchen. Oh, thank the gods. Some tequila was on the floor next to the stove. But what did he have to drink it with?

"I think it *relieves* his stress actually," Wendy said.

"All that soul-saving," Wyatt managed without choking. He didn't have anything in the refrigerator that would go with tequila. Certainly not milk or the eggnog. Did the eggnog have whiskey? He didn't think so. Did he have any Country Time lemonade?

"Yes," Wendy said, and then there was a long pause.

Yes? Yes, what? He couldn't remember what he'd asked her.

Wyatt found a couple of single packets of Crystal Light pink lemonade. It would have to do. In the meantime he opened the bottle and took a slug of the tequila. He winced, shuddered. *Gods! Blech!* He coughed. Shuddered again. Cleared his throat. Began to make a glass of the Crystal Light. Tried to build up the courage to ask *the* question.

Thankfully Wendy took that out of his hands. "Momma and Daddy came over for Christmas dinner."

"Wow," Wyatt said. "You guys didn't go over there?"

"Ahh…. No, Wyatt. Not this year. Mom helped, but Daddy…. Well…."

Well what? Wyatt wondered.

"Daddy's been a little… *funny* lately."

"Funny?" Wyatt asked. The last thing he had ever considered his father to be was funny.

"Well, they think he had a little stroke."

Wyatt jerked. Almost knocked his glass over. "Wh-what?"

"A *little* one," Wendy said quickly.

Wyatt's heart was rushing. "A little one?"

"Yeah. He…. Well, the other day he got up and almost fell over. He said everything was… tilted. He was having trouble walking. And he was having a little trouble talking. Slurring his words, you know? Mom wanted to take him to the hospital, but he wasn't having any truck with that. Until he did fall, that is, and we insisted. They couldn't find anything at first, but then they thought he might have had a very minor stroke."

Wyatt found he could hardly move. Strokes. Were they ever minor?

"His doctor said he should have gone to the hospital right away because there are drugs they can give you to help, but it's got to be in the first three or four hours. But as Daddy said, I don't know what good that would have done since they weren't even sure he *had* one."

Wyatt shook himself. "Is—is he okay now?" He reached for the tequila and added a good bit to his glass, put the bottle down and took a hefty drink before stirring. It was a mistake and he began to cough. *Whoa! Strong!*

"Anyway, that's why they came to our place. Norman was a little mad at first. Until Momma said she'd already bought the turkey and everything so he didn't need to buy anything. I just ran to Damview and picked up everything from her place. We didn't have to buy anything except some Stove Top. You know Norman likes that better than the homemade stuff."

Wyatt didn't know that either and thought it sounded crazy. How could *anyone* like that boxed shit when they could have his momma's stuffing?

He quite suddenly found himself missing that stuffing, even though he did a fairly good knock-off. He'd even made a change or two through the years: sage from Sloan's mother's garden and a can of black olives, chopped up real fine.

Howard had loved it, anyway.

And what the fuck was he doing thinking about black olives?

"H-how did he act?" Wyatt asked her suddenly. Gods. Why was his heart doing that little dance?

Unbidden he saw his father—clearly, as if he were right there—standing over him. Tall. Hair and thick mustache going gray. Those intense blue eyes—like they were chipped from a glacier. And how that mouth could smile… or frown. You didn't want to see the frown.

"He seemed fine, though he got tired fast. He wanted to help drain the turkey—you know he always does that for Mamma—but with Norman here, there was no sense in that."

"No. Of course not." Wyatt took another drink of his pseudo cocktail—drank it slower this time. But it was a big drink.

"I think we can all breathe a deep sigh of relief," Wendy said in seeming conclusion. "God is taking care of things. He always does." But why didn't she sound like she believed what she was saying? "At least now Daddy will pay attention. Dr. Shelvy insisted that he get to the hospital immediately if any symptoms reoccur. Counseled us all on what to watch for. Gave us literature and everything."

"That…." Wyatt's voice caught. Dammit! "Th-that's good."

"He'll be fine, Wyatt. I'm sure he will be. Trust in Jesus."

Trust in Jesus? Had she *really* said that? She wanted *him* to trust in *Jesus*?

Wendy was blind and deaf and who knew what else. She would never learn. Never. Never see him for who he was. Chose not to.

And now the tears wanted to come.

Fuck that!

Wyatt picked up the bottle again and took a swallow. He shuddered but didn't cough. It didn't stop the tears, though. At least these were caused by the booze, he told himself.

"What?" Wendy called out.

What?

"*Yes. I'm on the phone. Yes.*"

Wait. She wasn't talking to him.

And then she was. "Look, Wyatt. I need to go." And, "*Yes, it's my brother.*"

Wyatt closed his eyes and leaned heavily against the kitchen counter.

"Wyatt, I'm sorry. I have to cut this short. Merry Christmas, big brother."

Wyatt sighed, forced back his body's traitorous desire to cry. "And a Happy New Year, little sister."

"Yes, Wyatt. And that too." Then, with no preamble, she hung up.

Wyatt stood there a long time without moving. Then he made a second cocktail with the last of the Crystal Light and took the full glass and the one he'd already drunk half of and went back to the living room.

He watched "The One with Phoebe's Dad," and let the six people he was getting to know sweep him away. Who knew? Maybe Chandler and Joey would finally get it on. That would be hot!

That night he *didn't* dream about Howard.

THE PHONE call stunned Kevin and yet didn't surprise him. Somehow he'd been waiting for the news all week and didn't even know why. Cauley looked well enough at Christmas dinner the night before, and yet….

He rocked on his feet and leaned heavily on the kitchen counter.

"God, Lois," he said.

"I—I know."

"I can't believe it." But he could. He just didn't want to.

"At least he was at home," Lois said. "I found him on the couch. I guess he got up after I went to bed. He was watching TV. That's not a bad way to go, is it?"

"No," Kevin somehow said. His heart felt like it was made of lead. "It's a good way. He loved to watch that old TV." He fought the tears. He couldn't cry. Wouldn't.

Kevin turned and walked to the big glass sliding doors that let out onto his balcony and offered him his beloved view of the New York City skyline. The city that never sleeps. The Capital of the World. The city with over eight million people.

Now minus one.

Suddenly those tall buildings he loved so much seemed ready to fall down on him, smother him.

God. He needed to sit down.

"Kevin? Did I lose you?"

He sat carefully on the big black couch. "No. I'm here."

"They came and got… got his—" Her voice cracked. "It's gone. They took him—it—away." There was a stifled sob. She was not the kind of woman who would let anyone see her weak, not even at a time like this.

He needed something to do. "Lois, do you want me to come over?"

"No," she said quickly. "My sister is here. My brother is practically on a plane right now. I'll be fine." Pause. "What about you?"

"Fine," he managed. "Do you know what's next?"

"Not exactly. Exactly when, that is. He had it all planned. To the very last i dotted and t crossed. No funeral—by his request. But there will be a memorial service. Just figuring out when that will be. He wanted you to say something…. Well, read something. He made sure I told you that."

"Of course," Kevin said and wiped his face. "Anything."

"He knew how much you hated talking in front of people."

"Anything," he said again.

"But he also told me to tell you that you didn't have to."

"You know I will," he said and sighed heavily.

Gone. Cauley was gone. No more flowers. No more *Supernatural*. Kevin was quite suddenly sure that *he* would never, *ever* watch another episode.

"He's being cremated of course. Said there was no way he wanted people to see him in a coffin looking like…."

"Yes," Kevin broke in—so she wouldn't have to say it.

"…*see me lying there like a fucking concentration camp victim*" came the echo of Cauley's voice. "I couldn't stand that, Kevin! I couldn't rest! It's too humiliating. Too horrible to even think of. I want there to be pictures. When I was young and hot and sexy. I'd have you put some of my nudes out, but the old relatives wouldn't be well for that, would they?"

"No," Kevin had said.

"I suppose not even the one with me in my jockstrap? The one where my dick looks simply enormous?"

Kevin had just shaken his head. "Your Aunt Anne would faint."

Cauley had laughed at that! "Oh wouldn't that almost make it worth it?"

Kevin had laughed too. He couldn't help it. It might just be worth it.

"No," Cauley continued. "But I *did* ask Tam down at The Back Door if he'd do something…."

The Back Door had been Cauley's favorite bar.

"He said that would be fine. After my memorial service, all the queers could head on down there, and he said you could put out any kind of pictures I wanted. There would be discounts on the cocktails for anyone showing a program that proved they'd been at my service. Isn't that great?"

Kevin had told him that would be great indeed.

"Extra incentive to go, right?"

"Are *you* going to be okay, Kevin?" That was Lois. She had come downstairs to make her son breakfast and found him dead on the couch and she was asking Kevin if *he* was okay?

(*"And you are so lonely. That's what makes it worse. Worse than me being lonely."*

"Cauley, I'm fine. I'm not lonely."

"Yes you are. I see it in your eyes….")

"I'm… okay," Kevin assured her. He had almost said he was fine, but he wasn't fine.

"Kevin, dear… do *you* need anything?"

"No." He shook his head—as if she could see him. Thank God she couldn't. "Not right now. But promise me you'll call *me* if *I* can do anything."

"I will. And I am sure there will be. But as far as the service and all that… like I said… he had—" Then her voice caught again, and so Kevin finished for her.

"All the i's dotted and the t's crossed."

"Yes. Yes, exactly."

"You'll need help with the house," he said.

"No," Lois replied firmly. "He even did that. All I really have to do is make phone calls."

And there would be money to do it all. Kevin had taught him to take care of his money. With what his aunt had left him, there would be enough. Especially since there was no coffin, no burial, no plot.

Another pause. Finally she said, "I have to go now, Kevin. A lot of phone calls to make. You were at the top of a long list."

"Do you need me to help with that?" Looking for something to… to *do*.

"No. It gives me something to do. I really need that right now, you know?"

He did.

"O-okay. I'm hanging up now."

"All right, Lois." He wiped at his face again. "Good-bye."

"Good-bye," she replied. And then, just as he was putting his cell phone down on the coffee table—sure that she'd hung up—her voice came again. "He loved you, Kevin. I suspect more than he did me."

It was a stab to the heart. He put the phone back to his ear. "Nonsense, Lois. You were his mother."

"And a man shall leave his mother," she quoted. "That's the way it's supposed to be. If we loved our mothers more than our husbands, we would never leave our family home to start one of our own."

"I—I suppose."

Then she hung up. He only knew by a soft little beep from the phone.

Kevin sat down. Sat for a long, long time. Staring. Staring. And now the damned tears wouldn't come. He figured he'd already done the equivalent of that a long time ago. In some ways he'd just been numb for months since. But now? Now he felt even number. Was that even a word?

Gone.

And the world really did seem emptier.

Theresa.

Her name and her face filled his mind, and he knew he would—needed to—call her. No need to wait. She wasn't working today. She had a long holiday weekend.

So he called. In no time she was on her way. And in not much longer than that she was there, bottle of whisky in hand.

They got shit-faced.

CHAPTER ELEVEN

IT WAS the second day of the year, and luckily Treasures of Terra wasn't nearly as busy as Wyatt had feared it might be. A lot of people tended to hit the store right at the beginning of every January—resolutions or some such thing—looking to somehow "fix" their life so that the new year would be better than the last. They usually sold about a million tarot decks for instance. And there was all the crap involved with returns and gift cards, the anticipation of which had prepared him for throngs of people. But so far that hadn't been the case. Just little rushes here and there instead. He'd even had a chance to run to Café Namasté for a vegetarian lunch with Sloan and Max.

"I'm not complaining," said Kitty, one of his coworkers. She was cute in that way that straight boys liked, and from what she said, she never had problems finding a date. At least a first one. If she got started on astrology too soon, though, a lot of guys thought she was too weird, and that was that. Too bad, Wyatt often thought. She was one of the best he'd ever encountered at drawing up a chart. Pretty damned good at tarot readings as well.

Wyatt wasn't complaining either. He'd gotten a lecture that morning from Katherine, his boss, and he didn't know whether to be pissed about it or cry. Dealing with a bunch of customers just wasn't on his bucket list for the day. "It does make the day go by *way* faster, though," Wyatt said. And lately, he wanted the days to go by fast. Wanted as much time to flow away as possible. Wasn't time supposed to heal all wounds? Well, he had some doozies. And they were still bleeding, and he couldn't get over how many times the grief would sneak up on him. He'd always thought that he and Howard would be doddering old men together.

That wasn't happening.

Yes, right now he just wanted time to pass. Get past some of these holidays. It was the holidays that were the hardest. Samhain was gone and Thanksgiving, thank the gods. Yule and Christmas. And then New Year's without someone to kiss. His friends had insisted he go to the big party at The Male Box, and he'd dreaded that countdown, the first without Howard kissing him in so many years.

He'd had a little moment about a month ago. At The Male Box (he sure wasn't going to The Watering Hole!). He'd had a few drinks with a hot bear—gotten groped by him on the dance floor, followed him into the bathroom and stood next to him at the trough and wow, the guy had told him he had a nice cock. He'd been amazed because Howard had told him that its small size was another reason Howard had to have sex with other men. This stranger liked his cock, and Wyatt had gotten all scared/ excited at the possibility of having sex for the first time in months, the first time since he was single. Sex for the first time without Howard in his life. But then about fifteen minutes before closing, the guy vanished. And no matter how hard Wyatt tried, he couldn't grasp and hold on to that I'm-not-alone-when-I-have-these-guys-as-my-friends feeling.

"Oh no," said Kitty, breaking into his thoughts. "It's Other Person Lady…."

Wyatt's head snapped in the direction she was looking, and gods, it was true. It *was* Other Person Lady. One of the kooks that came into the store every now and again. And he hated to use the word "kooks." He knew he was a kook to many people, and Katherine—the owner of the store—had reminded him that "kooks" were their customers. But what else did you call a lady like this…?

And by then she was at the desk. Wyatt had no idea just what age she was. It was hard to say. She was incredibly thin, couldn't have topped five foot four, and had a huge wild mane of hair that had turned almost completely gray and silver. Her skin tone was olive, but her racial background could have been almost anything. Her eyes were a silver-blue that might have been natural or affected by something like cataracts. And while her skin was not teenager fresh and tight, there were only a few lines on her face. She was dressed in layers of skirts and shawls of every color and description, with no apparent eye to whether they clashed or not.

"Bear Boy!" She was very excited. "Utnapishtim here told me to tell you something."

Utnapishtim was the name of the "Other Person" that she frequently spoke to. No one else could see Utnapishtim, of course. But then Wyatt did have to be fair. He did believe there were stranger things in heaven and earth than even he could dream of.

She looked to her right and began to nod. "Yes, yes… I'll tell him." She turned back. "Utnapishtim says for you to buy the *green* candles and not the purple ones." Her head suddenly swiveled with alarming speed to the right. "Fine! *Forest* green! I don't think they have more than one kind of green candle! Brown if you can't get green. They will help you *float*."

Float?

Then she looked back at Wyatt, rolling her eyes. "He says that *forest* green candles are best." She put simply tons of emphasis on the word "forest," then continued. "He also wants you to know that you will be a prince one day. *Arrrgh*!" Her head snapped back to the right. "That doesn't make any sense! Why would he be a *princess*?"

Kitty giggled. "I can think of all *kinds* of reasons."

With a huge dramatic sigh, Other Person Lady put an elbow on the counter and rested her chin in her upturned palm. "He wants me to tell you that you will be a princess one day. Soon even. Maybe in the next couple of months."

Princess? Wyatt tried not to giggle himself. He could see himself wearing a tiara. In fact, he had one.

"But you'll be cut first. *Biiiiiiiiiig* cut."

"I—I see," Wyatt said. He glanced to the empty place beside her. Nodded carefully, then looked back. "Tell him thank you."

"He's not deaf, you know."

Wyatt gulped and then addressed the empty space. "Thank you, Ut-naps-ism—"

"*Utnapishtim*," she cried.

Wyatt only nodded. He wasn't going to try to pronounce the word.

"*Oot*-nah-*pish*-tim." She stared at Wyatt.

He cleared this throat and nodded to her "friend" once more. "Thank you, Oot-tah-pish-tim."

The lady smiled beatifically. "Close. No cigar—but close." She spared a look to her invisible companion. "He'll get it. Took me a while, so don't get your kilt in a wad."

Then speaking to Wyatt again: "Do you have the new Infinity Tarot deck?"

Now that was something Wyatt could help her with, and he quickly started tapping at his computer. He was having trouble finding it. At last he discovered why. "Sorry, Other…." He caught himself. "Sorry, ma'am, it hasn't been released yet."

"*Sugartit*!" She slumped. Paused. Lit up again. "How about the Advaitarot?"

"Now that sounds familiar!" Wyatt pecked away again at his keyboard. "Yup, let me show you."

And so it went.

But it was late afternoon when the day took a decided turn downward.

He was busy holding court with Kitty when it came.

A voice. One that he hadn't heard in weeks.

"Wyatt?"

He froze—jerked up straight first, *then* froze. Kitty's eyes were wide. She looked at him, and her expression told Wyatt what he needed to know.

Howard.

Gods…. Howard. Wh-why is he here?

Wyatt had to force himself to turn and look, look up and up, and yes—it was Howard. Standing over him like he had a thousand times before—except…. His face.

Wyatt felt like he had quite suddenly turned to lead. His stomach heavier.

The look on Howard's face….

His eyes were red. He'd been crying. Howard? Crying?

Wyatt's throat seized up, and he couldn't breathe.

What? What was it?

He wants me back came a voice in the dark, a voice trying desperately to shove away the thousand and one other possibilities he felt looming over him like ragged cliffs. *He's decided he can't live without me. Say it, Howard! Fucking say it. Oh gods, gods, gods please—*

"W-Wyatt…. Wyatt… I…." And now there were tears running freely down his face. "I've got it."

"Got what?" Wyatt asked, his voice barely above a squeak.

My P!nk concert DVD. Yes! Wyatt hadn't been able to find it, no matter where he looked, and finally figured Howard had taken it. He loved that concert! He'd been wanting to watch it. Watch P!nk on that trapeze thing flipping and flying over the audience—

"Wyatt… I've got *it*!" Howard said with a grunt.

Got what, goddammit? Got wha….

And then Wyatt knew.

Knew.

With total and crystal clarity, knew what "it" was, and all he wanted Howard to do was just… shut… up.

Gods, please. Don't say it. Please not—

Howard trembled, his voice hitched, and then he said the words. "I've got HIV, Wyatt. My God. I've got HIV…."

The rush of dizziness that swept over Wyatt was almost enough to make him fall to the floor. If he hadn't had the counter to grab hold of, he would have. Out of the corner of his eye, he saw Kitty dashing off. The room, everything around him, had come into sudden, unbelievable focus, and there were customers all around—some staring—and Howard had called him a silly little faggot so many times and somehow, somehow, somehow Wyatt forced himself to stand up straight. He would *not* be a "silly little faggot"! He. Would. Not. Faint.

Won't faint. Won't *faint. Will. Not. Faint.*

Howard wiped his face with his shirt sleeve. "Darrin came to me. Told me he'd tested positive."

He looked down at Wyatt, and Wyatt felt *tiny*. Like an ant. "Who's Darrin?" he asked and wondered if Howard could hear him. Howard was so high above him—and his own voice sounded so far away, even to him.

"He's the guy who—" Howard looked away, then back. "—fucked me."

The one who was fucking you when I got home? Wyatt wondered. The image came back in 70mm. The guy bent over the coffee table (the table they'd found for a steal on one of their trips) and Howard fucking him hard while a big muscular bodybuilder with a gigantic cock fucked Howard. Howard! Who did *not* get fucked!

"No," said Howard, shaking his head. "Not him." Said it as if he had seen the film playing on the movie screen inside Wyatt's head.

Not him?

Then that hit Wyatt too.

More than one man had fucked Howard?

Of course.

Of course there'd been more than one.

"He told me I should go get tested, so I went to the clinic in the city, and they tested me and called me in today for my results and…." The tears began again. "They think you should come in right away. They told me to tell you. That you needed to." He wiped his face again. "Go right away."

And if Katherine had not suddenly appeared at his side and placed a strong hand on Wyatt's shoulder, Wyatt very well might have fainted dead away right then.

CHAPTER TWELVE

WYATT WAS numb for most of the trip. And terrified. When he wasn't too numb to feel anything at all.

Howard was HIV positive.

Wyatt gave Katherine an animal-caught-in-headlights look and tried with all his might not to cry. There had been a lot of tears in the last few months…. They'd been a gift from the man he had loved with all his heart. And now this?

Wyatt looked out the windshield, trying to calculate how much longer it would take to get to the city. Where were they? And then he saw it. The Kansas City skyline. Fifteen minutes now?

Then he went numb again. It had been like that since Katherine herded him into her van—the one with Treasures of Terra painted on the side—and drove them out of town. Sometimes a minute seemed to take two hours to go by, and then a half hour was gone in a flash.

I've got it too. I have to. How could I not? Why else would they want him to come in right away?

"You don't know you have it," Katherine said as if reading his mind—and who knew, maybe she could?

Oh, look! They had somehow entered the city, and he'd lost a chunk of time again. They'd be there in minutes, thank the gods… and yet the thought made him want to vomit. Again. Katherine had already had to pull over once so he could puke by the side of the road.

She placed a hand on his knee and squeezed lightly. "It's going to be okay," she said.

"How can you know that?" he asked, voice trembling.

"Whatever the outcome, Little Bear," she said, using the endearment only certain people used, "it's going to be okay."

Wyatt saw the sincerity in her crystal-blue eyes. She believed it. But how could it be okay? He knew the real world. When they tested him and told him his result, then nothing would be the same again. He'd be a pariah. He had eyes. He *saw*. He knew what happened the second someone admitted they were poz. Did those guys ever get a hit on their Growlr app? Their Craigslist ad? No. They certainly didn't have a chance at finding a lover. He had already been convinced he'd be forever single. But now that he had HIV?

He felt his stomach rise again but fought it back down. They were on a busy city street in a center lane, and Katherine couldn't just pull over, and he couldn't upchuck in her car!

Calm. Calm down.

Wyatt closed his eyes. Tried to imagine the green grass of Camp Sanctuary. Or the path through the trees he loved so much—the one that reminded him of being in church, but a church that didn't hate him for who and what he was.

...my religion is nature came a voice in his head, he knew not from where.

This is it, he told himself. *Enjoy these last hours. These last moments of knowing you're just Wyatt, and not poz-Wyatt.*

Except it was worse, wasn't it? It would be two weeks before he actually *knew*. How was he supposed to wait that long? How was he supposed to sleep? Fuck. How was he supposed to be awake? Eat? Work? Do any-fucking-thing?

They had to drive around to the back of the building. The three spaces right in front had been made into handicapped parking since he'd been here last—what? The beginning of August? Since Howard had fucked that kid bareback? *That* had almost been the ending of them right then. And if he had only been willing to admit it, it might have been him that had broken up with Howard instead of the way it turned out. Getting dumped. Thrown out.

Why did I forgive him... again? Why did I believe anything that man said? Why didn't I have the guts to tell him I was done?

How many times had he asked himself that since that July day?

The problem was, he hadn't been *brave* enough to leave Howard. All those years of Howard telling him that if he left he'd never find anyone again. That Wyatt would be alone. He'd believed Howard too.

"Who would put up with you?" Howard had asked him on so many occasions. *"The only reason anyone puts up with you now is because you're with me!"*

Quite suddenly the thought made Wyatt surprisingly angry. *My friends "put up with me"! They did a Yule ritual with me! And it was fucking amazing. Better than any ritual you and I ever did!*

Howard's voice came again: *"The only reason anyone puts up with you now is because you're with me!"*

But then something happened. A new voice surfaced.

Not true!

It sounded familiar, but he wasn't sure just whose voice it was.

Not true, not true, not true. My friends love me! They love me.

Gods. That voice! Was it *his* voice?

"Wyatt?"

He jumped.

It was Katherine. "We need to go in now, Little Bear."

He looked around him. They'd parked. When had they done that? Wyatt nodded, and damn it, the tears were back.

Katherine came around and opened that door, and gods, he was feeling like a "silly little faggot" *again*. He wished that "new voice" would just take control of his feet, but when it didn't, he figured he would just have to do this for himself. *Prove* he was no silly little faggot. He somehow got out of the car and marched to the back door of the clinic. But by the time he got there, his resolve was gone. He let Katherine put her arm around his shoulder and lead him inside, down the hall, into the elevator, and up. The doors opened silently, and a dread fell over Wyatt like he had never felt before.

But Katherine was there, thank the gods, arm still around him, and they crossed the lobby and went through the doors of the clinic and up to the counter. In some part of his mind, Wyatt noticed that the place looked different than the last time he was here. And the sign….

The sign! It didn't say *Free* Health Clinic anymore.

"Do I have to pay now?" Wyatt moaned.

The pretty African American nurse—at least he thought she was a nurse—asked him why he was there.

"They told me to!" Wyatt cried.

"*Who* told you, sir?"

Katherine leaned over the counter slightly. "His ex was here a few hours ago. He received a positive result on his HIV test. He was told that he should have his sexual contacts come in—"

Sexual contacts, Wyatt thought. *Not husband. I'm a "sexual contact."*

"—to get tested right away."

"Oh," said the nurse. "Your name, sir?"

"Wyatt Dolan," Katherine supplied.

The nurse nodded, then pulled out a sheet of paper. "Yes. Yes, I have it right here." She looked up. "You got here fast. I'm glad."

Yes, he got here fast. Katherine had taken care of that. Luckily the store had been slow, and she put Melrose in charge and got Wyatt into the car before he could find a way out of it. Katherine knew—told him so—that there was no way he could have driven himself. In truth, the relief was enormous when she said she would take him. Gigantic. *Huge.* And he might have chickened out. Now how could he?

It wasn't like he could call his friends. Asher and Peni were in California. Scott was involved with some big legal thing—had been getting more and more recognition at the law firm where he worked and getting more and more responsibility. From what Wyatt understood, he was actually *in* court today. And Cedar had a brand-new job, was in his first ninety days and needed to have perfect attendance. Sloan was at work—something terribly important was happening today; he'd been talking about it for days. Max would be in classes.

"Would you please sign in, Mr. Dolan?"

The nurse gave him a clipboard, and he wrote his first name down. The form didn't ask for a last, yet somehow it felt like he was signing his life away. He did it blindly. The nurse had to tell him to add his birth date and the last four numbers of his social.

"If you sit, we'll call you shortly," she said and gave him a cheerful smile.

Katherine helped him to a seat against a wall under posters asking, "Have You Been Tested?" and, "HIV. It's No Longer a Death Sentence."

"Oh, gods, Katherine. This is it. This is *it*!"

"Is what, Wyatt, sweetie?" She petted his back.

"The very beginning of the very last two weeks where I don't live in the land of knowing I'm HIV…." And there he stopped. He couldn't say that last word.

Positive.

"*Wyatt*. You do not *know* you're HIV positive," Katherine said firmly.

"But in two weeks I will!" Tears. Fuck it! More tears. How many tears could a human body hold?

Katherine shook her head. "My Little Bear. Two weeks from now doesn't exist. And right now we don't know anything. Stop claiming a fate that might not be yours. Let's just wait."

"Will you go in with me?" he asked. "I'm so fucking afraid of needles." Which had made getting a tattoo almost impossible—would have been impossible if his friends hadn't all been there holding his hand and the tattoo artist hadn't been a big hunky bear.

"I will if they let me. But Wyatt, dear, I don't think they're going to allow that."

"But *Katherine…*," he whined, "I'm *scared*!"

"Wyatt?"

Wyatt jumped again and turned in the direction of the voice. A man was standing in a doorway. He was maybe sixty, with stylish black-and-antique-gold glasses.

Gay. Thank the Queer Ones, Wyatt thought. He raised his hand. "Here!" He winced. Why did he say that? He wasn't in grade school!

"Why don't you come this way, Wyatt?" the man said, motioning.

Somehow Wyatt stood up and then asked, "Can my friend come with me?" He turned pleading eyes on the stranger and then Katherine and back again. His biggest puppy-dog expression ever.

The man shook his head. "I'm so sorry. It's completely against policy."

"*Please…*?" Wyatt begged. He looked at Katherine helplessly. Then back at the man. "Can't you just this once? Please?"

A look of total sympathy came over the man's face. "I am so sorry, dear," he said. "I just can't do it."

Wyatt felt a hand on his shoulder, and Katherine was beside him, eyes focused deeply into his. "You'll be fine, Little Bear. I *will* be with you. Right here. If you need to, just picture my hand in yours. I am *right* here."

It was only that and the sympathetic look on the man's face that did it—allowed him to uproot his feet from the floor and begin walking. Had the guy been some kind of asshole, Wyatt would have fled. He went through the open door, and once more a hand came down on his shoulder, gently but firmly guiding him down the long hall that lay ahead. They turned left at the first corner and toward an open door. "Right in here, Wyatt."

The room was small but nice and bright. Sunshine-yellow walls, no examining table—which Wyatt thought might be a mistake as far as he was concerned. He liked to lie down when he was getting his blood drawn. In case he fainted. He had before.

"My name is Geoff, by the way," the man said and held out a hand for Wyatt to shake.

Wyatt almost didn't take it—this was the guy who was going to harpoon him, after all—but he did, and thankfully it settled him. Strong enough to comfort, but not to hurt. Howard's handshakes were crushing.

"I really am sorry your friend couldn't come back with you," Geoff was saying. "The testing is completely confidential. If you choose to tell her your results afterward, that's entirely up to you."

"Why don't you have a table?" Wyatt snapped, ignoring the comment.

"Why would you need a table?"

Wyatt told him.

"Oh," Geoff said. "But you're not getting a blood draw."

"I'm not?" Wyatt looked at him in complete surprise. "Don't you need to get my blood for the test? How can you test me without blood?"

Geoff smiled and patted Wyatt's knee. "Because all I need to do is prick your finger. We're doing a rapid HIV test today. Normally we don't on Fridays, but in this case we thought it best to find out right away. If anything, to reduce your anxiety. I imagine you're quite distressed right now. I know I would be."

"You don't have to draw my blood?" An immense wave of relief fell over Wyatt. It was like a comforting blanket. For some reason it made him want to cry. And the man really did seem nice.

"Nope. Just a tiny little prick on the end of your finger and that's it. I won't promise you won't feel it at all, but the needle is very small these days, and I'm pretty damned good if I say so myself. It'll be over and done in a jiffy."

Wyatt nodded. Or tried to. He was still going to have to get poked. But then it hadn't been so bad at the Gay Pride celebrations where he had his done annually. Of course, during those Howard had been sitting at another table within eyeshot.

Another immensity hit him. The full meaning of what Geoff had said previously. *Rapid testing?* "I'm—I'm not going to have to wait two weeks?"

Geoff shook his head, smiling again. It was such a nice smile. A good smile to have with a job like this. Wyatt wondered how many times the man had had to tell someone they had HIV.

"O-okay…," Wyatt managed.

Then another image came to his mind.

Peni's pe'a. The vastness of his Samoan tattoos, spanning nearly half his body. The fact that it had been done with razor-sharp tools of bone and tusk, pounding deep into Peni's thighs and legs and back and ass, relentlessly, hour after hour, day after day.

And he had the fucking gall to worry about one teeny tiny little pricked finger?

I'm not Peni!

No you're not, came that voice again. *You are Wyatt Dolan. And you are Little Bear!*

Somehow, that inner voice did it. And when, on the very tail of that voice, Geoff asked him if he was ready, he held his hand out sure and strong and—damn—barely shaking.

He did look away, though. "Warn me? So I won't jump?"

"Sure," said Geoff. Then he did something to Wyatt's finger, wiped it with something cool, and sort of—touched it?—and then to Wyatt's surprise said, "Okay. Done. Can you hold this against your finger?"

"What?" Wyatt asked and realized Geoff was pressing a piece of cotton against his finger and then was doing something with a little piece of something. Wyatt wasn't looking too closely, but Geoff was doing something else with a tiny, tiny little test tube (that didn't show blood, thank gods). He placed it to the side and set a timer.

Geoff then explained that the rapid test was 99 percent effective and these days just as sure as the two-week-long wait. That the test detected HIV antibodies and not the virus itself. In other words, the body began making antibodies to try and kill off HIV, and that is what they would be looking for. Those antibodies and not the virus itself. And that HIV died within seconds of hitting the air, and that's why ejaculating inside the body was dangerous and getting semen on you was okay. "That's the old saying, cum *on* me and not *in* me," Geoff said.

Wyatt nodded. He'd probably known that. Been told that, surely. Right now he wasn't in the right mind to remember any-fucking-thing.

"Now I have to ask you a bunch of questions. Sorry. All these questions they need to know to track statistics and so on. But it will help the time go by fast. Funny how twenty minutes flies when you're having fun and drags like hell when you're not."

"And this *ain't* fun," Wyatt said sarcastically.

Again the gentle smile. "No. I don't imagine it is."

Then Geoff started asking all kinds of questions. Whether he'd had oral sex—"Hell yes," he said and blushed. Giving or receiving and yes and yes. Anal sex, giving or receiving. Only receiving as far as the last year was concerned. "Howard never let me top him—"

The image of Howard and those two men flashed 70mm once again in his mind.

"—and I lose my hard-on half the time if I try and top anyone while I wear a condom." So Howard didn't wear condoms when he topped Wyatt? And the answer was, of course, "no," because it never occurred to Wyatt that Howard played without wearing them with others.

The picture came back—Howard, *Howard*, getting fucked. Bareback!

"He always used rubbers while I was there. With the other guys."

Again, that image.

No! Stop! Stop looking! He shook his head to banish the vision.

"You okay, Wyatt?"

Wyatt sighed. "As okay as I can be." *Knowing that I am about to find out I am HIV+.*

"You don't know you have it" came the echo of Katherine's voice. He felt her hand. Reached out with his thoughts and *felt* it, just as she'd told him to do. *"It's going to be okay. Whatever the outcome, Little Bear. It's going to be okay."*

But how could she know that?

It couldn't be okay to hear those words, "I'm so sorry, Wyatt. You have HIV. Now this is what we do next…." He'd die. He'd freak out. Geoff was going to be so sorry he hadn't let Katherine come!

There were more questions. A lot of them had to do, over and over again, with how many sex partners he'd had—

"None! Not since Howard left!"

—and if Geoff had asked if he'd had sex with someone besides Howard *over* three months ago, then Wyatt might have been able to say more than one. Howard would have seen to that. Hell, the last time they went to Cactus Canyon—was that September?—he'd had sex with at least four other guys (and gods knew how many Howard had been with, thinking retrospectively).

The questions about if and how often he'd had any vaginal sex made Wyatt laugh. "How about none. Ever. Never-*ever*. Mr. Gold Star Gay, here."

Geoff laughed. "Me too."

Geoff also wanted to know if he'd ever been incarcerated or gotten a tattoo—

"Wait! Why am I asking *you* that?"

Wyatt laughed. "No! I have! Look." He bared his upper arm and showed Geoff the teddy bear, about five inches tall. "It was supposed to say something too, but my friends rightly talked me out of it. If the artist hadn't been such a hunk and my friends hadn't taken shifts holding my hand, I wouldn't have been able to do it."

—and if he'd ever exchanged sexual favors for sex—

"Oh, *please.*" Wyatt rolled his eyes. "Who would pay *me* for sex?"

(*"The only reason you get laid is because of me. I tell them they* have *to have sex with you if they want me."*)

"I don't know." Geoff actually blushed. "I think you're pretty darned cute."

That shocked Wyatt into silence. He couldn't remember when someone had said he was cute. Wait! The tattoo artist had flirted with him. Wyatt had just chalked that up to the big guy trying to calm him down.

—and if he'd ever used IV drugs or had sex with any known IV drug users.

And finally there had been the questions about how much risk he thought he'd taken in the last twelve months on a scale of one to ten, with one being the lowest and ten being the highest, in doing something sexually that could have allowed him to contract HIV, or scarier, that he might "test positive today"?

It was just as the timer went *bing.*

That had almost brought the tears back. "Ten, I guess," he said and moaned.

"Well, Wyatt. I can tell you right now that you are—"

"*Nooooooo...,*" Wyatt cried and dropped his face into his palms. He moaned long and hard and actually began to rock in his seat. *Positive!* He *knew* it! Geoff had said the words. He was positive! What was he going to do?

"Wyatt!" Geoff all but shouted, making Wyatt flinch back and drop his hands.

"Wyatt. What's wrong? Aren't you happy? This is great news!"

"That I'm *positive*?" Wyatt asked incredulously.

Geoff gawked at him. "Sweetheart! I didn't say positive. I *said* negative. You're HIV negative."

Wyatt looked at the man, stunned.

The room took on a tremendous quiet.

A celestial mute button had silenced the world.

Time stopped.

Then: "Wyatt? Did you hear me?" Geoff was smiling.

Time decided to start moving again.

"Wh-what?"

Geoff nodded. "Yes, Wyatt. Now I do recommend you get tested again in about one month. From what you said you had sex with your ex about two months ago?"

He had to think. Hard. The world was going all wonky again. Howard had dumped him right at the end of September?

Yes. Of course it was. September 29th. A Monday. He would never forget it. He said the date aloud.

Geoff checked a calendar. "So, wait. End of September? That means all of October and November and December. Wyatt. That's three months. Honey!" He clapped. He actually clapped. "That makes you free and clear."

Wyatt gaped at him. "Wh-what?"

A wave of dizziness came over him.

"R-really?"

Then for a second he thought the man might kiss him.

"Wyatt, the HIV antibodies usually show up in about three to four weeks. But to be safe we say ninety days. It's been more than ninety days."

"I—I don't believe it!" Wyatt cried.

Geoff nodded vigorously. "You know, my little man, I honestly cannot tell you when was the last time I so joyously gave somebody that news."

Wyatt leapt to his feet and threw himself into Geoff's arms and— *godsdammit!*—started to cry again.

But of course this time the tears were of joy.

THE JOURNEY home was much better than the drive into the city.

Katherine asked him if he wanted to stop at The Male Box for a celebratory drink first, or even The Watering Hole (he was far too worried that Howard might be at the second), but Wyatt didn't want that. After crying in her arms in the waiting room—

"Ah, my Little Bear, didn't I tell you? Didn't I tell you that you didn't *know* you had it?"

—all he wanted to do was go home. Even if it was his new home.

She dropped him off, and he watched her go—insisted she go on even though she wanted to wait until he'd gone inside—and then stared at the house. Suddenly it didn't seem so awful a place. Even welcoming. Like it was telling him to come on inside and it would keep him warm, just as warm as friends could.

It was nice.

But that wasn't completely true.

He wanted to see his *friends*.

So he went directly next door instead and rang the bell, and when Sloan answered the door—Max or even Logan, or hell, Devin would have been okay—Wyatt was so skyrocketing happy that it *was* Sloan that he threw himself into his best friend's arms and buried his face in his shoulder and just... *held* him.

Wyatt didn't cry. He thought he would. He thought for sure he would. Hadn't he cried a mammoth amount lately? But somehow he didn't. And when they finally separated—a bit, not much—he looked into his friend's dark, honey-colored eyes and said...

"I don't have it."

Sloan hunched closer, and for half a second he thought *Sloan* was going to kiss him, and then he saw puzzlement in those eyes.

"It?" Sloan asked.

"HIV," Wyatt exalted. Funny the way that word sounded. Like an alleluia.

And Wyatt told him. Right there. In the threshold of Sloan and Max's home, neither in nor out, and then Max was there and so was Logan and they led him inside and he started telling it all again from the beginning and Sloan was calling Scott and when Scott got there with Cedar he told it again.

They called Asher too. He actually answered his cell phone. He was on a break and he "Hee-hawed!" in great shouts and said he would call Peni right away.

Somehow it had all come out all right. After one horrid, awful thing happening after another for months, finally something had turned out right.

CHAPTER THIRTEEN

WYATT GOT the phone call the next morning.

He almost didn't answer it. He was taking a wondrously hot shower—the shower at the home he and Howard had made had something wrong they hadn't fixed yet, and it had near zero water pressure. This one, on the other hand, felt so good he didn't want it to stop.

But then…

Something told him to go ahead and answer. And as his cell *was* resting right there on the top ledge of the sliding shower doors, he could. He stepped out of the direct spray and grabbed it and saw it was his sister.

What was Wendy doing calling at this time in the morning on a Saturday?

Especially when it wasn't his birthday or Christmas?

"Hey, Wendy," he answered.

"Oh thank the Lord I didn't have to leave a message," Wendy said, a desperate sound to her voice. Desperate and something else. There was a strange sort of sound—a strangled sound?—on her end. Crying?

Wyatt stood upright.

"Wendy? What's wrong?"

"Wyatt…." And yes. A sob. Quiet. "It's Daddy."

A shiver went through him, despite the heat of the water and the steam swirling around him. "What about Daddy."

He's dead….

"Wyatt. You know… I told you… they think he had a little… little stroke before Christmas?"

Wyatt nodded. Then realizing she couldn't see him—*thank the gods*!—said, "Yes."

"Well, he's had another one."

"Another little stroke?"

"B-bad one, b-big brother. *R-really* bad. They're trying to figure out *how* bad."

"*Fuck*," Wyatt said before he could help it. "Is he in a coma?"

"He w-woke up this morning…. But it's *bad*, Wyatt. The whole left side of his body…. He's in ICU. He…. Well, he can talk, thank Jesus. But it's hard to understand him. And he can't do shiiii… anything with that side of his body."

Crap. Crap, crap, crap….

"He wants to see you."

Wyatt froze.

What?

"What?" he asked aloud.

"He wants to see you."

"*Me?*" Incredulous.

"He told Momma and he told me. He wants to see you."

Lick a witch, thought Wyatt. "M-me?"

"Yes, Wyatt."

"*Why?*" See his father? He hadn't seen the fucker in ten years. More!

"Don't ask why! He wants to see you. This could be it. You two finally making peace."

"*Us* making peace," Wyatt exclaimed, still standing there in the tub, the shower pounding down at his feet, the steam swirling around him. Stood there, hearing, *seeing*, his father screaming at him in his mind's eye, *feeling* the smack on his face that knocked him to the ground. "*Us?*"

"Wyatt…. This is *serious*." And he could tell Wendy was crying. "The doctors are telling us to prepare, that he might not come out of the hospital."

Wyatt stepped back until he could lean against the shower wall.

"Will you come?"

He didn't answer.

Maybe if he didn't, she'd hang up. He wouldn't have to answer.

Come? She wanted him to go home? To see his father?

Had he woken up in the fucking twilight zone?

"Wyatt?"

"Yes," he blurted. "I'll come."

Fuck. Why had he said that?

"I'll call you back in a few minutes."

It was time to get out of the shower.

So he hung up, and then he let himself slip to the bottom of the tub and leaned forward and let the water fall on his head until it started to turn cold. Then he got out and dried and looked at himself in the mirror.

"Now what?" he asked.

NOW WHAT turned out to be that he needed to get down to Damview, Arkansas, and soon. So he called Katherine, and of course she was understanding. Told him to take as much time as he needed.

"You need to get one of your friends to go down with you," Katherine said. She couldn't. Taking him to the city for an HIV test was one thing, but both of them couldn't be away from the store for days. Or more.

But looking in that mirror again, he knew the truth. There was no way that any of the Fabulous Four—gods, had he really given their little group such a silly name?—could go with him.

"I can't even ask," he told himself aloud.

And he didn't.

He made some calls while he packed. When he told Sloan, his friend was stumbling over his words. There was no way he could go with Wyatt. Not for several days. Not knowing when he would even be coming back. The terribly important thing he was doing at work turned out to be that someone was flying in from someplace or other—he should have paid more attention but, holy shit, Wyatt had other things on his mind—to be trained to open the new call center. Sloan wouldn't have to go away after all. But with that happening, he couldn't very well up and head off to Arkansas the guy's first week.

"It's okay," Wyatt told him. "I wasn't asking." He was feeling strangely strong at the moment, unsure just where the strength was coming from, and figuring he better not wonder too much. He might panic.

"No! It's not okay," Sloan told him. "Look. I'll find a way. Shelia can do it."

Wyatt let out a bark of laughter. "Shelia! *Riiiiight*! Your enemy?"

"She's not my enemy," Sloan said. But of course she was, and letting her take over Sloan's new project would ruin everything Sloan had been working toward the last year. It would thrill the woman.

"You shouldn't have to make the trip alone. You're my best friend, Wyatt. I mean, jeez. And how many hours' drive is it to Arkansas? And what about snow? And we don't have any today, but you never know when it could start."

"It's about seven hours," Wyatt said. Stifled a sigh. No guilt. He would not make Sloan feel any guilt.

Something clicked in Wyatt's mind then.

Best friend.

That went both ways, didn't it? Best friends didn't only mean trying to do anything to help him no matter what. No. Best friends also meant not *letting* someone help you, certainly *not*, if it was going to hurt them (and Sloan taking off a week from work when things were finally, *finally* really going his way would hurt him).

"I need to do this by myself anyway," Wyatt said calmly, assuring his friend. "I mean, come on, how would I explain you? You think *they* won't think you're my boyfriend?"

"Max will come with us."

Wyatt laughed. "And really throw homo in their faces?" Wyatt shook his head. "I'll be okay, Sloan. I promise."

Sloan wasn't sure, but he finally acquiesced.

"I just wish I had a GPS," Wyatt confessed. It had been a long time since he'd been home, and even though Cactus Canyon was most of the way to Damview, he never remembered how he and Howard got there.

"Sweet pea," Sloan said. "You've got a cell phone. You've got a GPS. I will just about guarantee it."

"Huh?" Wyatt pulled the phone away from his ear and looked at it (as if he could tell if what Sloan was saying might be true from looking at his friend's profile picture). He put it back to his ear and laughed. "I'll look."

"Stop by if you need to," Sloan said. "I can show you real quick."

"Sure," Wyatt said, intending to do no such thing.

They talked for a few more minutes while Wyatt debated if he could bring even one of his T-shirts, gay or otherwise. Certainly nothing "witchy-woo-woo," as Scott would say—or *used* to say. The unwanted image of his father standing over him, Wyatt wiping his mouth and seeing blood, came to mind. He shuddered.

Then they were signing off, and Wyatt was asking one favor. "Would you tell the guys?"

"I…. Sure, Wyatt. You aren't going to ask anyone else to go with you?"

"No," he said firmly.

Because he couldn't. Asher and Peni hadn't gotten home from Hollywood in the last twenty-four hours, and Wyatt thought they'd be there at least a week. And gods! He couldn't imagine Asher and his father meeting! And Scott's big court case wasn't finished. Bringing Cedar would be a disaster. He might punch Wyatt's father—even in a hospital bed. And old Daddy wouldn't be able to resist saying something about Cedar's fauxhawk.

No.

He was going alone.

And quite suddenly something from *The Hobbit* came to his mind. Or was it *The Fellowship of the Ring*? He thought the latter. Hadn't Sean Astin used the line in the movie?

Something about how it was a dangerous business walking out your door. That once you took one step onto the road there was no knowing where you'd be swept off to.

Yet for some reason, it didn't scare him.

It made him excited. Yes, he was going alone. No Samwise Gamgee at his side. Or Peregrin Took or Meriadoc Brandybuck. A *fab*-ulous foursome if there ever was one.

Didn't Frodo make it on his own at the end? If you didn't count Gollum that was…. He couldn't remember exactly.

So he sat and checked his cell phone, and after a moment he had to laugh. It did have a GPS. A little bit of fiddling and he even figured out how to use it.

And less than two hours after his sister called him, Wyatt was on the road, not allowing himself one moment to wonder where he was about to be swept off to.

CHAPTER FOURTEEN

THE DRIVE wasn't so bad. At least that's what Wyatt kept telling himself. He found he sort of wished that the GPS didn't have a female voice, one that sounded oddly British—but not.

Didn't these things come with men's voices?

Wouldn't it be hot to have one that sounded like Brad Pitt? Gooseflesh flashed up his arms. Or Chris Hemsworth? Oh, yeah! Sounding all Thor-ish. Shouting from his cell phone, "You! What realm is this? Elfheim, Niflheim?" Wyatt waggled his eyebrows at no one. *Wyattheim?*

Or Matthew McConaughey. Hugh Grant, maybe? Even if *he* did sound British—because there was nothing actually *wrong* with sounding British at all. In fact he found the accent kind of sexy. And his GPS did sound a little British. Something anyway. Not *quite* British. It was just… *different*. And if he was going to go with the United Kingdom, then how about Ian McKellen? Of course, he was really old….

Or Darth Vader! Not sexy so much as just fucking cool. He could hear it now! Like when he'd ignored his little electronic guide a while back and had to turn around? His GPS would have said something like, "I find your lack of faith… *disturbing*. Make a U-turn and go back…."

Wyatt laughed at that and hoped he would remember to tell Sloan about it.

No! Wait. He had it. Spencer Morrison! Spencer-*fucking*-Morrison. Spencer who showed his cock to Asher! Gods, his voice was *soooooo* frigging sexy.

He still couldn't imagine why Asher hadn't looked, even if he was in love with Peni. Wyatt didn't care if Peni had the most beautiful cock on the planet! But then Wyatt loved celebrity nudes and had spent an hour one night freeze-framing *Terminator 2* dozens of times trying to get that shot of Robert Patrick's hanging balls during the scene where he first comes back through time.

It was with these kinds of thoughts that Wyatt passed the time as he took 71 going south, and then 44 east to Springfield. It was gratifying how he recognized where he was going—the familiarity of the way. He was surprised how much he actually remembered.

He decided to fill up on gas at the Kum & Go while he was there—or the "Jerk & Squirt" as he and Howard had never tired of calling it. He was delighted to find all kinds of merchandise that he hadn't seen before. He bought a big mug and a baseball-style cap and even T-shirts. Four, for each of the Fabulous Four. He considered getting them for Peni, Cedar, and Max—but the total had already come (or Kum?) to a pretty outrageous amount, and he just couldn't afford it. He couldn't afford what he was spending already, but after all, Sloan hadn't charged him anything for rent yet. Which only made him start feeling guilty again. Hey! The gift of a shirt would be nice, then. A thanks. And wouldn't the four of them all look *fab-ulous* out together at The Male Box in their matching shirts? If Asher would wear his now that he was about to become a famous movie star, that was.

And there was music to help eat the miles. The luau/Samoan discs he'd made for Peni's welcome-home party were just a taste of what Wyatt liked to do. He made all kinds of music collections, and of course he'd put together one with all of his favorite P!nk songs. P!nk was his hero. If he were a girl, he would *be* P!nk. How often had he stood on the big California-king-sized bed when Howard was at work (or wherever), shampoo bottle in his hand for a mic, singing his heart out to a crowd only he could see while the songs boomed out of the stereo? Especially when he was belting out his anthem, "Perfect." The version with the F-bomb, because, as he had argued many times, he thought it was more powerful. He hit the Repeat button a half-dozen times on the last twenty minutes to Springfield.

He had nothing to hold for a mic today, plus he needed to keep both hands on the wheel, but that didn't keep him from singing all about how he should raise his glass if he was wrong, but fuck you Howard, because if he was wrong, it was, as P!nk proclaimed, in all the right ways….

He sang "Raise Your Glass" over and over until his throat hurt and he finally had to stop.

He played her songs because they made him feel good. "Empowered" was the word that Scott would have used these days.

But he was also pressing the Skip button quite a bit. He just couldn't listen to "I Don't Believe You"—the song about having a lover say they didn't love you anymore. Or "Please Don't Leave Me." And worst of all "Who Knew?" *Oh gods, gods, gods*—that one hurt too much. Because who knew when Howard said he would be there forever… that he would leave? Or make *him* leave. Who knew?

Nope. That song was right out.

It was the happy music, played loud, that helped him feel a little less lonely. The loneliness had been terrible. Ten years of being with someone and then suddenly being on his own was terrible. No matter what Howard had been, at least he'd been around. He had friends whose lovers seemed to be away more than they were actually beside the man they professed to love. At least Howard had spent time with him. Lots of time. They'd spent so much time together. It was part of what made being single so hard. He was so very, very single now. He found he even missed the mean Howard. The one that laughed at him. The one that told him that he only had friends because he was with Howard and people liked Howard. And that if the two of them ever split up, Wyatt would be alone forever.

Truth was, Wyatt had come to believe it.

And he was listening to those echoes that even P!nk could not drown out when he was struck once more by an idea that had been sneaking up on him more and more often of late.

What if there really *was* some kind of cosmic "love" balance that ruled over the Universe? He could almost picture it in his mind. Out in space, an immense pair of cosmic scales, shimmering blue-white, resting in the constellation of Libra. What *if* the gods had made these scales, a balance that only allowed so much love? What if him being with Howard for all those years had somehow kept his friends from getting love of their own? What if that balance had shifted in his friends' favor, and now there wasn't enough love left for him? What if there really was only so much wedded bliss to be divvied up? What if there wasn't love left for him?

And then…. *Gods*. Had he ever really had Howard's love in the first place? He had thought so. Those first years with Howard had been a fairy tale equal to any that Cinderella or Sleeping Beauty or Snow White had ever known!

Why, it was the reason why he'd held on to his relationship with Howard when things began to sour.

Wyatt winced at that last. "Sour." There hadn't been too many times when he'd been willing to admit to that, to give that word substance. To utter it.

"Sour," he whispered while P!nk sang "Who Knew?" Who knew that love wouldn't last forever?

It was with thoughts like those that he was pulled down into a whirlpool of memories….

CHAPTER FIFTEEN

WHEN WYATT'S little car had broken down in Kansas City eleven years before—and he'd been surprised the piece of shit had made it that far—he had no idea what to do. He had no idea what was wrong with his ancient Camry, but the horrible grinding noise and the black smoke that came out from under the hood told him it had to be bad. Wyatt didn't know much about cars, but he did know that black smoke wasn't supposed to come out from under the hood.

He managed to pull over and dropped his forehead against the steering wheel and just cried. His face still hurt where his father had struck him seven—eight?—hours ago? He could feel with his tongue where his teeth had cut the inside of his cheek.

Wyatt was freaking out. What was he going to do? It was dark. It had to be after ten o'clock. He didn't know anyone in Kansas City. His friend Barry (one of the few) had run away to Los Angeles a few years before, and when Wyatt had jumped in his car and left his home, it was with some crazy idea of trying to get to California to find him.

That wasn't going to happen now.

So he'd somehow gotten ahold of himself and climbed out of his car and spotted a bar across the street. The Watering Hole, the sign said. Why the fuck not? If they checked his ID, they'd throw him out; he was only eighteen. But maybe they would let him have a Coke. Although it was certainly not money he should be spending.

It wasn't until he got inside that he was struck by the fact that he had somehow—through some cosmic joke or accident or maybe miracle—walked into a gay bar. His eyes had popped, and he gawked in wonder at the sight, his mouth fallen open as if his jaw had come unhinged.

The rainbow beer signs with their flickering neon lights—he knew what the rainbow colors meant.

The posters on the walls of "half-nekkid" cowboys. Cowboys weren't really the kind of guys that put lead in his pencil, but Jesus bald-headed Christ. Those jeans were so low he could see their pubic hair!

Oh—my—God! Look over there! Two guys kissed while something baseballish happened on the big flat-screen TV—right there in front of the whole world!

And finally the bartender, wearing impossibly tight jeans and a ripped tank top, who stretched (making muscles pop and revealing sexy hairy armpits) and then sidled up to Wyatt's end of the bar and asked him what he would like to have (and even though Wyatt was small-town naïve, he couldn't help but hear the innuendo *dripping* from that question).

There hadn't been one word about an ID.

Of course, all he'd asked for was a Coke. A Diet Coke.

The bartender leaned on the bar, an actual toothpick sticking out of his mouth, and looked at Wyatt with heavy-lidded eyes. "You sure you don't want something in that, sugar bear?" Wyatt could see a hairy chest at the low neck of the wifebeater. It looked soft. He wanted to touch it.

"I...." Don't *say you're not old enough*, a wise inner voice advised. "I can't really afford it."

A brow shot up, and the bartender gave Wyatt a suspicious look. "Can you afford the Coke?"

"Oh! Oh, y-yes!" Wyatt pulled some singles and a couple of fives out of his pocket. His on-hand cash. He had more hidden in his car (his piece-of-shit car). He'd stopped at an ATM and cleared out as much cash as he could from his account, but it would only let him take out so much per day. He'd hit it again tomorrow.

The bartender nodded, reached out with a finger, and touched the end of Wyatt's nose playfully. "You are just adorable as hell. Tell you what. The first one's on me. What would you like to drink?"

Wyatt gulped. He had no idea. The only time he'd had anything was with this one boy who wanted blow jobs but always had to sneak alcohol from his parents' stash to give himself the nerve to go through with it.

Say something! Anything!

"Rum and Coke?"

"You got it, sugar bear." The bartender stepped away.

A drink? I'm having a drink? He hadn't even had anything to eat! Would this be a big mistake? It didn't take much to get him drunk, and he really didn't like how it made him feel. Except that sometimes it made the world hurt less.

The bartender was back and asked if he wanted a lime.

"I don't know?" Wyatt asked more than said.

"We'll leave it out, then," said the bartender. "I'm Buck. What's yours?" He held out his hand.

Wyatt took it and told him his name.

"Like Earp?"

Wyatt rolled his eyes. "Yeah. I know. Dad wanted me to be a man's man."

Buck's eyes twinkled. "*Are* you a man's man, Wyatt?"

He blushed furiously. "I guess I am," he admitted and blushed all the more.

"Good. What do you do?"

Do?

"I worked in a grocery store before I came here."

Buck chuckled. "That's not quite what I meant, but okay. Where you from?"

Now he was blushing again. Did he tell the guy Damview? He'd laugh. "Mountain Home," he lied. Because it wasn't too bad a lie. Damview was fourteen miles from Mountain Home, where he'd gone to school. Of course the road had so many twists and turns it took at least twenty-five minutes to drive at least, *if* you were lucky and some old person wasn't putting along in front of you.

"Never heard of it," Buck said. "Where's—"

"Hey, Buck!" shouted a man from the other end of the bar. "You serving today?"

"Ah, kiss my ass," Buck cried. He winked at Wyatt. "I'll be back."

Which left Wyatt alone with no idea what to do. He looked around. The baseball game was right out. He'd rather match socks. Match socks while watching *Late Night with Conan O'Brien*.

So what to do? Get a book out of the car to read?

Maybe take a drink of his rum and Coke? Probably. So he did, and he choked—*Crap!* How much rum was in this?—and hoped Buck hadn't noticed. He wasn't sure, but he thought Buck might be flirting with him. And something told him Buck was a whole lot different than the high school boys he'd fooled around with. *Too bad you're so thin*, thought Wyatt. Buck had all that pretty, soft-looking chest hair, but he was *sooooooo* skinny. He was still hot, but gods, wouldn't he be even hotter with a bit of belly?

Wyatt looked around the room again and near the entrance spotted what looked like little piles of magazines. He went and checked and found what looked like some kind of combination of a newspaper and a magazine. Several of them. With names like *KC Gay Times. Gay newspapers?* Why, one even had a sexy, husky, hairy guy on the cover. "Bear Bust" it read. What the hell was that?

He grabbed one of each of the little newspaper things and took them back to his seat, leafed through them, sipped at his cocktail, and became amazed.

It seemed there was all kinds of gay stuff in this city! Had he fallen into paradise? He trembled. Scared. Delighted. Stunned. Bars. Drag shows. Advertisements for bath houses in St. Louis—*sexy* advertisements! He'd read about places like that online. So they were real! Imagine…. And bear busts. Holy crap! They were for guys like him. Hairy guys. Chubby guys. He'd heard about bears when he was on the Internet too. But to think. The guys he *really* liked, the ones that really turned him on—never the high school football star with his tiny waist and all muscles but men like Mr. Carson, the shop room teacher, older, big and burly, and *hairy*— the ones he'd masturbated thinking about late at night. They were right here in this city! And they were *advertising*!

He'd died and gone to the Summerlands!

"How's that drink coming along?" Buck asked him, making him jump.

It was only about half-gone. Wyatt had been very busy reading his magazines. "I'm okay for now. Give me a little bit." What he wanted was something to eat. All he'd had since he left Damview was a dollar cheeseburger from McDonalds, and he was starving. He already felt buzzed.

"You have anything to eat here?" he asked.

"There's popcorn," Buck answered and cocked a thumb in the direction of a small movie-theater-style popcorn maker near the door.

Wyatt all but ran to it, filled one of the cardboard rectangular bowls provided, and made his way back to his stool, eating as he went. He finished it in seconds. He couldn't slow down.

"You're hungry, aren't you?"

Wyatt turned to see a big man sitting a couple of stools down. Really big. When had he gotten here? He was seated, so Wyatt couldn't be sure, but he looked like he was probably at least six foot. He was bald, but it was sexy, and he had a fairly thick beard that was shaved down to the jaw line. Like that bartender, he was wearing a wifebeater, and it did nothing to hide his huge hairy chest, and unlike Buck, this guy had a nice sexy belly.

Wow, Wyatt thought. *He's fucking hot!*

The man studied him with sexy dark eyes. Like he was waiting for something.

Oh! He hadn't answered the man's question. *Shit!* And embarrassed, he simply shrugged in response.

The big man sighed. He looked to be at least thirty, a good twelve years Wyatt's senior. "And you can't really afford anything, can you?"

Wyatt shrugged again.

"What were you going to use to buy something if Buck had told you they *did* have food?"

Wyatt paused. Shrugged once more.

The man shook his head. "Tell you what. I was about to order a pizza—"

Wyatt's mouth immediately began to salivate.

"—so how about if I share?"

Wyatt could only sit there in surprise. "I… I don't want to take your dinner!"

He laughed. "That's okay, baby bear. I wouldn't have offered if I didn't mean it."

Wyatt didn't know what to say. It was charity. His father had always told him not to take charity. But his dad said all kinds of crazy shit. Like God made Eve out of Adam's rib! And Wyatt was hungry. *Really* hungry. He gave a single nod.

The man moved a seat closer. "What's your name, baby bear?"

Wyatt shivered. Gods. Was this happening to him? This was like something right out of one of Wyatt's wet dreams.

"Wyatt," he replied.

Now he's going to say, "Like Earp?"

But he didn't. Instead he said, "Well, I'm Howard," and held out his hand. Wyatt's all but vanished in Howard's callused and considerably bigger one. Wyatt trembled again. Felt his penis shifting in his jeans.

"Nice to meet you, Wyatt. Now what do you like on your pizza?"

"I like pepperoni," Wyatt said quietly. "And sausage."

"Didn't hear you," the man said.

Apparently the lady belting out, "I'm a red-necked woman," from the jukebox had drowned him out. Wyatt gulped. "I like pepperoni and sausage," more loudly this time.

Howard laughed. "I bet *you* do! How about some mushrooms?" He arched an eyebrow suggestively.

Wow. This guy was *really* flirting with him. Right here in public! And he was so *hot*.

"Whatever you want," Wyatt replied.

Howard leaned in close and in a husky voice said, "What I *want* is for you to take your shirt off. That'll pay for your pizza and at *least* one more rum and Coke."

Wyatt shivered. God. Wyatt looked down at the table. Take his shirt off? Right here in the bar? He turned his face back up and looked shyly at the big man.

"I'm kidding," Howard said and then leaned closer. "Mostly."

"You—you really want me to take my shirt off right here?" Wyatt said, his voice almost a squeak. Thank goodness the song had faded, and the new one was a little quieter.

"Why not?" The response was almost a growl. He pointed over Wyatt's shoulder.

Wyatt turned and saw that the two guys who had been watching the muted baseball game were now kissing without the incentive of anything happening on the screen. And both had taken their shirts off. When had they done that?

And as if to encourage him, the song on the jukebox had shifted to one about how no shirt and no shoes were no problem at all for him.

"I will if you will," Howard said.

God. He wanted to see Howard's chest. He wanted to see his belly.

"O-okay," Wyatt said bashfully, his heart pounding. And pulled his shirt off over his head.

Howard made a sighing sound and got close again and said, "Oh, my. *Soooo* nice."

Me? thought Wyatt incredulously.

Howard liked his chest? And told Wyatt he liked his tummy too. A lot. Asked politely if he could touch. And, trembling, Wyatt had given permission.

The touching had been so gentle. Not at all what he expected from the big man. His fingers raked slowly through the hair on Wyatt's chest—"So soft," Howard whispered—and his nipples went as hard as two little pebbles as Howard's fingertips brushed them. His cock grew even harder. He could feel it leaking in his underwear.

And when Howard whipped off his wifebeater and offered to let Wyatt touch him, Wyatt did so with shaking hands. Gods. So sexy. Howard was sweating a little too. Not a lot. *Just* a little. The wetness was sexy as hell. And he could smell him too. It wasn't acrid or gross. Just man. All man. Like the boys in the locker room right after PE class. Fresh.

But this was manlier. Not boy at all.

The pizza came, and it was huge, and Wyatt all but fell upon it. Howard only laughed and encouraged him to eat all he wanted.

They talked. They talked and talked and talked. Wyatt told him about how his day had started and where it had gone, the violence, throwing as many of his worldly possessions as he could into his Camry and then driving away. The last sight, his mother, hysterical, in his rearview mirror—and wondering if he would ever see her again. He started to cry at the end of his story, and Howard shifted his chair around—they'd moved to a table by then (getting a scowl from Buck in the process)—and then he was holding Wyatt against that big soft chest. Soft, but hard underneath. There were muscles of steel under that padding and Wyatt had gotten hard *again*, even while he cried. Somewhere along the line, he let his hand drop to Howard's belly, and it was so sexy he thought he might shoot off in his pants.

But he didn't.

They had more drinks, Howard drinking small pitchers of beer—no glass—and plying Wyatt with all the rum and Cokes he wanted. Even buying some shots called Cock Sucking Cowboys, and boy, hadn't that been funny? And they were so good! Wyatt had protested at first, said he was getting drunk and could he just have some water, and that's when Howard said it. "We're not allowed…."

"Allowed?" Wyatt asked.

"We're gay," Howard said. "Boring nonalcoholic stuff is not allowed. Gay men are *required* to drink alcohol. Besides, you know about water—right?"

Wyatt said he didn't.

"Fish fuck in it," Howard replied and then shuddered.

Wyatt laughed. More than he should have probably, but by now he was drunk.

Then, since he'd already told Howard just what his father had found in his room and the full extent of why he'd been kicked out of his home, he shyly asked if Howard would like a tarot reading. Howard said that he would.

So Wyatt went to his piece-of-shit car and got his deck—thank the gods he'd had his favorite deck in his car or who knew what fate might have befallen it—and brought it back and read Howard's cards. Howard had been intrigued by it all. Said the layout wasn't at all what he was used to.

Wyatt had looked up, surprised.

"You know about that?" he'd asked.

Howard nodded. "The usual layout is called a Celtic Cross, right?"

"Yes!" Wyatt said, thrilled that the man knew.

"There's a placement for your past, your future, above, and below, and I forget the rest."

"Yes!" Wyatt nodded happily.

"But the way you're laying the cards down. It seems… random. And you don't reverse any of the cards. They're all right-side up…."

Wyatt grinned. Howard really *did* know about the tarot! "Well… there was this big fair in town once," Wyatt said. "And I went into the gypsy tent—at least the lady was pretending to be a gypsy. She was doing the standard layout and something kind of funny happened. She saw I knew a little about the cards, and she stopped and looked at me and then swept them all up—I thought I'd pissed her off at first—and then she said, 'You have the eye, don't you?' Well! I didn't know what to say, and I sorta shrugged—you know?"

Howard nodded encouragingly.

"And then she just started putting the cards down wherever, and sometimes she would say a card meant what I've read they meant and sometimes she would say something different. *Totally* different. And she told me that was what *I* needed to do! To say whatever popped into my head. She told me something horrible was going to happen, but not to worry. That I would go on a journey, and I would find my way. And gods…. Howard. Do you think she meant today? It was certainly fucking horrible! And I took a journey…."

"Maybe I can help you find your way," Howard said. And his voice was so gentle, but strong and warm, and he reached out and took Wyatt's cheek in his big rough hand.

Wyatt was stunned. He didn't know what to say.

Pulling his hand back—Wyatt hadn't wanted him to stop touching like that—Howard said, "What does my reading say about tonight?"

"Tonight?" Wyatt looked down at the cards spread out in several rows before them.

Howard nodded. "Does it say if I am going home alone tonight?"

Wyatt had to fight to keep his mouth from falling open.

"I—I…." He looked back down at the last two cards he'd placed on the table. That was the Page of Cups. A young man. Usually a bit effeminate. *Is that me?* And the Knight of Swords was *right* next to it. Brave. Strong. Was that Howard?

He looked back up at Howard, suddenly afraid.

Howard reached out again and this time laid a hand gently on Wyatt's. "Not trying to scare you. But you don't have any place to stay. If you want, I can make you a place on my couch."

Wyatt felt his eyes well up with tears.

"Tomorrow I can look at your car. I'm pretty good with them. Maybe I can fix it."

"Gosh," Wyatt managed. His voice caught. No more words would come out.

"Is that a yes?"

Wyatt paused. Then wondered why. True, he didn't know this man. True, the guy could be taking him home to rape and kill him. But hell. What was he going to do? Sleep in the car? And tomorrow?

"I—I don't know how to thank you."

"Finish the reading," Howard said gently. Wyatt could hear him because there was a ballad playing. He recognized this one. Shania Twain's "From This Moment." For some reason his heart started to pound.

Wyatt turned another card over.

The Ace of Cups.

He gasped.

He looked up.

Howard was watching him with those dark eyes. Wyatt's heart trip-hammered.

"Well?" Howard asked him.

"A-Ace of C-Cups," Wyatt stuttered.

Howard smiled. Did he know what it meant?

"Cups are emotions," Wyatt got out somehow. "Aces are new beginnings…."

Howard smiled. "I like the sound of that."

Wyatt swallowed hard.

And he went home with Howard.

He didn't sleep on the couch.

WYATT DIDN'T know sex could be like it was that night. Drunken fumblings with mostly straight boys (or at least boys who wouldn't consider that they might be gay) and porn hadn't prepared him for a gay man making love to him.

And the surprises started before then. The apartment was huge. Beautiful. There were several plaques on the wall over the couch. A Pan, a Green Man, and a lovely triskelion. Three different pagan symbols. Could it be...? Or did Howard have them simply because they were considered cool these days?

He looked up at Howard, who was at least six feet tall, questions in his eyes. "Are you...?" Then he stopped. He couldn't say it. For some reason "gay" was easier. But pagan? Wiccan? He'd never met anyone who was actually pagan before. Sure there had been a couple girls at school who wore black and painted their faces pale and used black lipstick and tons of mascara and *said* they were witches. But they were more into the movie *The Craft* than anything real. Could Howard.... "You know the cards," he said. "And you have these plaques. Is it just because you like them or...?"

Howard smiled and turned around and there between his shoulder blades was a pentacle tattoo the size of a saucer. How in the world had he missed that?

"So you're... pagan?" There! He'd said it.

"It's the closest thing I've found to what I believe."

"I've never met anyone who believes the way I do," Wyatt said.

"So you've never done Ritual *with* anyone?" Howard asked him.

Wyatt shook his head. Found he was trembling again.

"Do you want to see my altar?"

Wyatt managed only a nod.

Of course it was in his bedroom. A bedroom with the biggest bed Wyatt had ever seen.

Howard went to a corner to what looked like an army locker up on one end. It was draped with a silk cloth. On top were several glass pillar candles—which Howard lit—and a statue of a dancing satyr. It was naked, one hoof raised high, playing the panpipes. It sat on top of a wooden box. Howard pointed at it. "My deck is in there. But I'm a pretty shitty reader. I can't do anything without consulting the book for every single card." He opened a long slender box that lay in front of it, took out a stick of incense, lit it from the candle, and placed it in its place on the wooden burner. Without turning he said, "I could take you to a ritual if you wanted. With all men. All *gay* men."

"What?" Wyatt gawked at him. "There are gay rituals?"

Howard chuckled. It was more of a rumble. Wyatt got goose bumps.

Howard made one of his little growls again, and Wyatt shivered delightfully. "And sometime we go skyclad."

Wyatt, who had of course read Scott Cunningham's and Starhawk's books on the Craft, knew what *that* meant. "Oh. I don't think I could be naked in front of a bunch of guys. Especially *gay* guys." He blushed *again*. He'd hated taking showers in gym class. To just *stand* around naked in front of other gay men? No way. They might laugh.

"And camping!" Howard exclaimed as if he hadn't heard what Wyatt had said. "You would love Men's Festival."

"Men's Festival?" What in the world was that?

Howard nodded. "Heartland Queer Men's Festival. It's at the end of July. Anywhere from a hundred to a hundred and fifty gay men, out in the woods for close to two weeks. It's great. It's like this big gay brotherhood. We do this big Queer God Ritual one night—"

Wyatt's mouth fell open. "Queer god ritual…?"

"—and there's a talent show. One day we usually have a big group mud bath. There's an auction and there's food and swimming in the lake and—" He arched his eyebrows. "—and *skinny*-dipping."

There was that naked thing again. "I don't know." The skinny-dipping he'd done at home was late at night, and it had been dark. "I just don't think I could get naked in front of people."

Howard reached out and cupped Wyatt's cheek like he had in the bar. Gazed into his eyes. They stood for what seemed like forever.

And then Howard kissed him.

Wyatt had never been kissed before. Not by a boy. And certainly not by a man. His knees turned to water, and he almost fell. Howard's strong arms kept that from happening.

And then came the sex. The loving. Slowly undressing. Kisses, gentle kisses and surprising nips of teeth on his collarbone and nipples and… other places. Howard wasn't afraid to suck Wyatt's cock either. No fumblings. No teeth. Wyatt arched up off the bed and clutched at the sheets and came all too soon. He wanted to cry. "I'm so sorry. I couldn't help it."

Howard looked down at him and wiped his mouth. "It's okay. I wanted it. Your cum is as sweet as cream with sugar."

Wyatt blushed for what felt like the millionth time.

Then Howard raised Wyatt's legs high and back, so his own cock, only half-erect now after his orgasm, was in his face. And then Howard did it. What would become his favorite thing. He lowered his mouth into the cleft of Wyatt's cheeks and began to lick. Rimmed him. Wyatt shouted and cried out and even sobbed. He couldn't believe what was happening. He was stunned. He was lost in feelings and pleasure, and when Howard lowered his legs again and reached into a drawer and pulled out a condom, Wyatt knew what was next. But Howard looked so *huge*!

He looked at Howard in fear.

"I'll be as gentle as I can," Howard said.

"Is it going to hurt?" Wyatt asked.

"Yes," Howard answered. "At first. But that's part of it, my little bear." It was the first time Howard ever said *my* little bear. "But it gets better. If you can just hold on with me. And I promise, if it doesn't get better, then I'll stop."

So Wyatt nodded. How could he deny this man who had been so kind to him, and then given him such pleasure, anything?

And it hurt. It hurt badly, no matter how much Howard had prepared him. He felt like he was being impaled. Torn apart. But Howard did go slow. So slow. And whispered calming "shhhhhs." Encouraged him. Told him he could do it.

Finally, just as he was about to shout, "Please stop," that he just couldn't… the pleasure finally came. Howard was right. Like nothing he could have imagined. Like nothing his own exploratory fingers had ever prepared him for.

It was magick.

Afterward, as they lay together, Howard holding him close, he whispered something that almost made Wyatt cry.

"You have *no* reason to worry about being naked. You're beautiful…."

Wyatt never left.

Not for eleven years.

CHAPTER SIXTEEN

THE MEMORIAL was nice. Cauley's mother was there, of course, and his aunt Anne and his uncle Percy—her family. And (Kevin couldn't keep all the names straight) a couple more aunts from Cauley's father's side. There were also about a half-dozen cousins, and Kevin couldn't help but wonder if Cauley would have been surprised by how much family had come.

"They're not here for me," Cauley would have said (Kevin could almost hear him). "Most of them were done with me when I led that flash mob singing 'One of Us' in St. Patrick's Cathedral. I loved it, though. You should have seen the faces when we got to the God being a 'slob like one of us' part."

Kevin hadn't been there, but it had caused quite a little splash in the news.

In the end Kevin figured it didn't make a difference why everyone was really here today. Maybe they'd learn something. Learn something about the man who was now lost to them.

Thank God, Theresa was there. Plus a dozen or so of Cauley's friends. It made Kevin mad that there weren't more. At one time Cauley was a pretty damned popular guy, what with all of his activism. There were a lot of people who considered him a hero in the community. Kevin could only hope that there were people who would show up at the get-together at The Back Door. Maybe they were just too uncomfortable with anything even resembling a funeral or religious ceremony.

Cauley had chosen a minister from a local MMC—the church dedicated to outreach to the gay, lesbian, bisexual, and transgender community—to run his memorial. She wasn't a Catholic priest, and just the fact that she was female upset Cauley's uncle Percy. But somehow Kevin wouldn't have been surprised to find out that was part of why Cauley chose her. Percy had written Cauley many times over the years trying to get him to turn away from his sinful ways and embrace Jesus.

The thing was, Cauley did believe—*had* believed—in Jesus. He'd just come to think that Jesus didn't have any trouble with him being queer. He used to joke that Jesus was probably gay himself, "What with him hanging out with all those dudes? And the fact that he wasn't giving the prostitute who hung out with them the old in-and-out. And wasn't John supposed to be the 'Beloved Disciple'? Have you looked at the two of them on that painting *The Last Supper*? I mean... come on!"

The service, if it could be called that, wasn't particularly religious, but the prayers and opening and closing scriptures—the program referred to them as 1 Corinthians 15:50-51, Romans 8:35-39, and John 14:1-3—helped with any feather ruffling his family may have experienced.

Kevin was just grateful that Cauley had such an iron-clad living will. That Lois hadn't been able to counter Cauley's wish to be cremated, and she hadn't been able to make today's service some kind of Catholic High Mass. Kevin didn't *think* she would have, but Catholic guilt was big, and Kevin wouldn't have been surprised either.

"I love that verse about how persecution or nakedness can't separate us from God," Theresa whispered out of the corner of her mouth. "Do both those words make you think of Cauley, or not?"

Kevin was grateful for the little slur. It made him chuckle, and he desperately needed to laugh. He just kept it very quiet. He wouldn't have been surprised to find that Cauley had picked that particular biblical reading.

He'd planned everything else. Including the fact that he'd wanted Kevin to do a reading. Cauley hadn't specified what. Just a note that said, "Anything, Kevin. Please?"

Why, Cauley? When you know how much I hate getting up in front of people? To prove I love you? You know I did. Do. Always will.

He chose a short part of Ralph Waldo Emerson's essay "Nominalist and Realist." He thought Cauley would like it.

When it came his time, he walked up to the front of that small room and went to the podium, took a deep breath, and began.

It is the secret of the world that all things subsist and do not die, but only retire a little from sight and afterwards return again. Nothing is dead; men feign themselves dead, and endure mock funerals and mournful obituaries, and there they stand looking out of the window, sound and well, in some new strange disguise.

He swallowed hard. Paused, then closed the little piece of paper and finished from memory.

Jesus is not dead; he is very well alive; nor John, nor Paul, nor Mahomet, nor Aristotle; at times we believe we have seen them all, and could easily tell the names under which they go.

It was short, but he almost didn't make it through. When he was done, he didn't wait or look to see what people thought but quickly went back to his seat. But when he dared glance at Theresa, sitting there beside him, he saw tears on her cheeks, and she laid her hand on his and squeezed ever so gently and gave him a tiny nod.

Then she, and Kevin, looked back to the platform.

A handsome young man, perhaps twenty-five at most, was now standing there. He began to speak. "Cauley came to one of my very first readings about three years ago. I saw him in the audience and I noticed that he never stopped *looking* at me the whole time I read. It was like he was looking *into* my head. I couldn't tell if he was cruising me or not."

The gay people in the room laughed, sharing the knowledge, perhaps, that it was entirely possible. Some of the cousins did as well. Kevin couldn't tell about the aunts and uncles, but the one scowl he could see across the aisle indicated at least one uncle didn't appreciate the comment.

Fuck you, Kevin thought.

"After the reading, he bought my little book—if you could call that photocopied and folded in half and stapled thing a book—and asked for me to autograph it. I did. I signed it, 'For He who looks into me.' I think he liked that. We talked a bit, and he didn't make a single pass at me, and I realized he really *did* like my poetry. He told me I would be famous one day and then bought a second copy to sell on eBay for a million dollars."

He rolled his eyes, and there was more chuckling.

"Yeah…. After, I'd get e-mails from him every now and then. He came to several of my readings… and then just sort of stopped. I guess he just got too sick.

"Anyway, he asked me if someone could read one of my poems at his memorial, and I told him *I* would do that. Promised him in fact. And so here I am today. It's not one he ever heard or read. I hope he won't mind." He closed his eyes and then opened them and looked out over the room, up somewhere toward the ceiling, maybe farther away. "Cauley, I still haven't become famous. Sorry you didn't get to sell my book on eBay. But I wrote this just for you."

He closed his eyes again. They seemed to be closed forever. But then, just as a few people looked as if they might be getting restless, he opened them again and began,

> I prefer to remember you on Halloween,
> 2013. The multicolored ruffles of rayon
> and sequins you hastily hot glued before
> the party. How that dress flowed in the dry
> October air. How it brushed against every
> guest as you shuffled through that crowded
> apartment. If it weren't for the crown of
> fruit on your head, I'd have guessed a sea
> anemone before guessing Carmen
> Miranda. I remember you used real fruit
> too, you goof. I remember the fruit flies
> orbiting your head that night as we smoked
> on the fire escape. At the end of the night
> you let the drunk guests fight over your
> headpiece. 'No one should walk home hungry' is
> what you said. How that dress flowed in
> the dry October air. I remember the walk
> home, you insisted on keeping the gold
> heels on. I remember the walk home, a
> man in no costume tried to pick a fight
> with us. He just pointed at you and
> shrieked: 'LUCIFER LUCIFER LUCIFER.'
> I remember you click-clacked right up to
> his face and gave him the last overripe
> banana glued to your head. You smiled and
> said, 'I get cranky when I'm hungry too, sweetie.'
> The stranger was speechless. Then you
> skipped off, barely visible in the sliver of
> moonlight. That's how I choose to
> remember you.

The poem left Kevin speechless—although he had smiled once or twice, couldn't help it. He remembered that costume. He remembered that party. He remembered that dress and how much it had embarrassed Kevin (for some damned reason—they weren't even a couple anymore) and excited him too—filled him with joy, even turned him on a little bit. That night had been *so* Cauley—had been exactly what he had loved so much about him. Kevin liked to be quiet. He liked to almost fade away into a crowd. But he *loved* to be *with* people who could never hope to disappear. It was almost like he lived vicariously through them—but that wasn't quite right. Because he liked to be seen *with* Cauley. He had been so proud of his lover. Not only for all he had done for the community, but for being the little shining beacon that he had been. Dazzling!

The only costume that Cauley concocted that might have been crazier was when he insisted on using green food coloring on his skin and even his face when he dressed up as Elphaba from *Wicked*. Oh, had that been crazy getting off.

The night that Cauley wore that outrageous Carmen Miranda outfit had been the first Halloween that they hadn't been a couple in eight years. Kevin had sort of suspected Cauley had gone all out to make Kevin… what? Jealous? Sorry that they weren't together anymore? Who knew exactly why with Cauley? At first he'd wondered if the poet— what was his name? He glanced down at the program—*James* had been his date, especially the way Cauley had hung on his arm. It seemed so unbelievable because he had total disdain for "twinks," and while James wasn't exactly chicken, at the time he couldn't have been much older than twenty-one or twenty-two. When Kevin saw James in a corner kissing someone else and Cauley sailing past him with not a care in the world, Kevin realized that they weren't an item at all. Stupidly, he'd felt relief. Why?

He'd made sure to drive Theresa home that night and therefore hadn't been at that now famous incident where Cauley had "click-clacked" right up to the Lucifer-shouter and given him the banana. Until this moment he'd assumed it was apocryphal. But now? Maybe not. He liked to think it was true—but again, who knew with Cauley?

Before he realized it, his eyes were filling with tears, and when he turned to Theresa, he saw her cheeks were wet, and he knew he loved her. Amazing that she had made him rich and also become such a good and dear friend. Thank God for her. He wouldn't have made it through this day without her.

It all ended with Handel's "Hallelujah Chorus." Cauley's way of saying that his family should be happy that he was in some better place?

It was perfect. Because Kevin did believe that. Really did believe that everyone was made of energy—energy that had been around forever and came back again and again. In some form or other....

(*"I think it would make me happy if I came back as a snowflake and I could fall on your face."*)

The echo came up from somewhere deep and shocked Kevin into silence after that. He couldn't talk. Didn't. He didn't speak a word. He knew he should say something to Lois, but he quite suddenly knew he *couldn't*. Not and still maintain his quiet composure—not and still be Kevin Owens. He might have been able to say "Hodor" if he thought anyone would have gotten it. Somehow he didn't think Cauley's family watched *Game of Thrones* or read the books. Besides, that was his Men's Festival name.

So instead he took Theresa's hand and they made fleet feet over to The Back Door. Sure enough, Tam, the owner, had put up a good dozen pictures of Cauley when he was "young and hot and sexy." The one where he was wearing a jockstrap—the one where his dick looked simply enormous. A photograph of him in the tiniest shorts imaginable. Some in drag—including Elphaba and Carmen Miranda (thank God). Several nudes. And everyone agreed he'd been a very sexy man.

Cauley would have been happy.

He got to be the center of attention one more time.

Kevin got shit-faced.

CHAPTER SEVENTEEN

ABOUT TEN miles down from the junction of 60 and 5 was the tiny town of Ava. Sitting at a red light, Wyatt—on some crazy impulse—almost headed to Cactus Canyon. It had always struck him as ironic that a gay men's nudist camp was only an hour from where he'd grown up. If he'd only known. But they probably wouldn't have let him in. And he wasn't even sure it was around before he was exiled from Damview.

Wyatt often wondered if his father knew about the camp. There had been protests through the years. Someone had even bought a pig farm and put it just upstream so the pig shit—only the vilest farm animal shit on the face of the earth—would come down and foul out the camp, driving the heathens and sodomites out. Except it went to court, and miracle of miracles, the good guys—and for once that meant the *gay* guys—won. Since then there hadn't been much trouble.

Wyatt had never understood why the town had gotten its panties in a bunch anyway. All those gay men spent a *lot* of money in the town by purchasing everything from gas to tons of stuff from the weird, almost alternate dimension, version of a Walmart. That was revenue. Why would they complain about that? He would have thought they'd be thrilled. The town was tiny! Three thousand people. And it wasn't like the men were parading around naked, dicks swinging, *in* town. They were sodomites, not dumb shits.

He wouldn't have been surprised if his father had not only known about Cactus Canyon, but had been one of the protestors. Of course, Wyatt had no way of knowing. The one trip he and Howard had taken where they actually saw people with signs, he'd ducked. He didn't want the first time he saw his old man in years to be on their way to just the kind of place his father probably envisioned him in—some modern-day Sodom and Gomorrah.

But today was January the third. Cactus Canyon was closed. There was the smell of snow biting the air, although none had fallen yet. Thank the gods. He was making remarkably good time. The last thing he wanted to do was drive in the snow.

He listened to a Stephen King novella on audio, and that killed lots of time. *The Body*, the one that the movie *Stand By Me* was based on, and when it got near the end and Chris, the narrator's best friend, scared the bad kids off with the gun, he suddenly couldn't remember if that was the way the movie had ended or not. Hadn't it been Gordie, played by the kid who went on to be Wesley Crusher on *Star Trek: The Next Generation*, who threatened the bullies with the gun in the movie? Or had he only said, "Bite my big one"? Not for the life of him could Wyatt remember.

And right at the end there was a line that froze Wyatt and made him gasp.

"Love has teeth; they bite; the wounds never close. No word, no combination of words can close those love bites."

A shiver of anticipatory dread passed over Wyatt in a wave.

It was a feeling he had to ignore.

Or he would turn around right then and head home.

HIGHWAY 5 took him south to Midway, and then he knew... knew he was close. *Very* close. Close to Damview, the tiny town—population 706—where he was raised.

And what a fucking name for a town! *Damview*! It *really*, truly *was* the name of the town. Because it looked out over the dam, the old codgers would say, nodding and smiling in their sunken-cheeked way. Isn't it a lovely name?

"Well," Wyatt had wanted to say. "What's wrong with Lakeview? Right there across the dam?"

Of course, *it* was already taken!

Also, there were the jokes. Just like the ones in that National Lampoon movie.

"Hey," the kids would say. "We're the damned kids who live in the damned town of Damview! There's not a damned thing to do here except go to Bull Shoals Lake and swim."

And there really wasn't a damned thing for them to do either, except as residents of the local town they had stickers on their cars and didn't have to pay the prices the tourists had to pay. They knew the places to sneak to as well. To smoke pot and skinny dip. It's where Wyatt saw a naked boy for the first time—as well as he *had* been able to see with

nothing but the light of a quarter moon. It was also where he gave his first
blow job. Which had been wonderful until the next day when said boy
made fun of him at school and called him a faggot.

Faggot.

How many years had that word followed him until it became what
Howard called him—

Silly little faggot!

—and then was scratched on his beloved Mini Coop.

Gods, that had hurt.

He'd never found out who did it either. Figured it was one of his
customers. He'd even had the horrid suspicion that it was someone from
work, but who? Sometimes he would look around the store, look at the
coworkers he thought of as friends, and wonder: *Was it him? Or her? Was
it Melrose? Or Kitty? Surely it couldn't have been Kitty. Kitty likes me....*
Or did she? He had gotten the manager position over her, and she had
certainly wanted the job pretty badly when Buddy, the previous manager,
left. Left because he wanted a job with benefits and a future. Except what
the shit had Buddy done since leaving Treasures of Terra? *Not* shit.

But speculating about who at work might have scratched up his car
was dangerous thinking. Thinking that Wyatt couldn't let himself do. He
had to work with those people.

He *had* to believe it was someone else.

Oh, and hadn't Howard been furious? Howard—who hadn't helped
him pay one dime on his car. Who hadn't helped him fix it. That had
been Cedar, who had all kinds of talents. And the door hadn't looked the
same—not showroom—but it looked better than FAGGOT.

Wyatt had kept to himself how much that word—*faggot*—had hurt
him. Hadn't told his best friends. He'd even blown it off when Scott
saw it. "Kind of fun, isn't it?" he'd said. "Kind of like what happened to
Brian's Jeep on *Queer as Fuck....*"

Except he hadn't thought it was the least bit fun.

Faggot!

Scratched into the paint.

He had paid for that car. Had worked his ass off at a part-time job as
well as his manager job at Treasures of Terra to be able to make the down
payment. If it hadn't been for Men's Festival, he wasn't sure he would
ever have told anyone what it had done to him.

But again.

Dangerous thinking.

Then quite suddenly he was passing the sign.

Damview—Pop. 706

More kids went to his high school these days (which was in Mountain Home; Damview was too small to have its own high school) than people lived in the entire town where he grew up.

Minutes.

He was just minutes away.

His mother was expecting him. He'd called home from Midway.

Wyatt almost drove right past the turnoff, but that would have been stupid. Where would he go? Back to Terra's Gate? Another seven hours?

Wyatt turned his car in and passed the little itty-bitty police station and then took another left, which curved to the right, and there it was.

Home.

Or what used to be home.

It had barely changed. It even had those tacky tree-trunk pillars he had loved as a little kid—the sawed-off branches had been great for his GI Joes—and then come to loathe as a teenager. The driveway was full. Three cars—none of which he recognized—so he parked on the street. There was a sidewalk now, lo and behold, and he wondered when that had happened.

Wyatt was just climbing out of the car when the front door of the house flew open and his mother rushed out onto the front porch. He froze.

Mom.

He hadn't seen her in nearly eleven years. From here she looked like she hadn't changed one bit.

He tried to move. Tried to say something. But he couldn't. He couldn't move.

And so she did.

She was a big woman, and she came across the lawn like some cruise ship plowing through the ocean, arms outstretched and crying out his name. "Wyatt! Baby!"

He broke.

Wyatt tore around the car to meet her halfway and was almost knocked from his feet when they met in a great crash of flesh. She threw her arms around him, crushed him to her ample bosom, and burst into tears.

There was a yapping sound, like a small dog, but Wyatt was so encased in her big arms that he couldn't see anything but her dark blue blouse.

And he didn't want to move. This from his mother—it had been the last thing he'd expected. He wanted to start crying *again*, and suddenly realized he *was* crying.

Then it was his sister: "Mom! You're going to smother him. Let me have my turn."

The grip relaxed and his mother started to let go, but then she surged forward and crushed him tight again. Thank goodness he'd gotten a chance to take a breath.

Finally, with his sister's apparent help, she let go of him enough to hold him at arm's length. She shook her head, and gods, she didn't look the same after all. Her face… it seemed… bloated. There were lines around her eyes and mouth that he didn't remember, and gray in her shoulder-length blonde hair that he certainly hadn't seen before.

Of course, it had been a long time….

"You look wonderful, baby," she said, voice cracking.

"You too, Mom." And really it wasn't a total lie. Just a little white one.

His sister cleared her voice, and he turned and she was the one that really shocked him. The last time he'd seen her, she was fifteen. The Wendy who stood before him today was a woman.

She was bigger. Nearly as heavy as their mother. Her cheeks pudgy and her breasts startlingly large. But the weight suited her. And her dark eyes twinkled, and she had let her beautiful dark brown hair grow, and damn, she was lovely. She took his breath away.

Her nose crinkled and she laughed and said, "Well?" and held out her arms.

Wyatt went to her then, amazed that this was happening.

What had he expected?

Certainly not this.

It was nearly impossible to believe.

At last the hugs were done, and when they got inside, he was hit by the smell of cooking food. "It's your favorite," his mother was saying.

His mouth was watering. "You mean…?"

She grinned and quite suddenly looked ten (or eleven) years younger. "Chicken-fried steak, mashed potatoes, and fried green tomatoes."

"Oh my…." He stopped. Had almost said "gods" and didn't even try to abbreviate it. "God" would have been just as bad as far as the Dolans were concerned. Even that was considered taking the Lord's name in vain.

"Wait until you see what she made for dessert," Wendy said.

"Shouldn't we be going to see Daddy?" he asked. "You made it sound like I needed to rush. Do we have time to eat?"

His mother nodded. "He has this procedure they're doing, and then he'll be eating and the nurse told us we didn't need to show up until after six. That will give us a few hours. Visiting hours are over at nine."

They sat down at the kitchen table. The same table. With its gray faux-marble top and chrome sides. The salt and pepper shakers were different. But the little wooden lazy Susan in the middle was the same one he could remember from as far back as he'd been on this earth.

"Where are your kids, Wendy?" Wyatt asked while his mother got things out of frying pans and the oven. He'd never met Mary and Norman Jr. The idea of seeing them was very exciting.

His mother placed a platter of gorgeous chicken-fried steaks on the table, and Wendy got a funny look on her face, but it vanished in a second. Had he imagined it? "They're with their father," she said. "He thought it would be best if we had time to catch up, you know?" But she didn't look him in the eye with that last part. Somehow he thought maybe she wasn't being entirely truthful.

It was then that, out of nowhere, he heard the high-pitched barking again. He'd forgotten about that, almost thought he'd imagined it. He looked under the table to see that a little Chihuahua had grabbed the cuff of his jeans and begun to shake its head.

"Joseph!" his mother shouted and scooped the tiny dog up in her arms. "Sorry, Wyatt. His bark really is worse than his bite—"

"She says that," Wendy broke in, "because he's never bit her!"

Joseph snarled, eyes nearly popping out of his head. Wyatt laughed anyway, despite the fact that it looked as if at any second the dog could launch itself out of her arms and into his face. But he knew just the way to a dog's heart.

He picked up his fork and cut off a piece of meat (because his mother's chicken-fried steak had always been tender enough to cut with a fork) and then pierced it and held it out to the snarling dog. Joseph sniffed it for all of 1/100th of a second and then scarfed it down.

And Joseph and Wyatt were friends for life.

CHAPTER EIGHTEEN

THE DRIVE to the hospital seemed almost as long as the one from Terra's Gate to Damview. Hells, longer than the one from Treasures of Terra to the health clinic to get tested—and had that only been days ago? It seemed like years. Wait! Only yesterday? How could that be?

Wyatt's stomach was tied in such knots that he felt his favorite meal might come springing from his stomach like one of those trick snakes from a bogus can of mixed nuts.

He kept the meal down somehow.

Mountain Home had grown. There were all kinds of businesses that he didn't remember being there before. The town seemed to have doubled in size. He didn't remember the Home Depot or the Lowe's, and there was actually a Petco. It seemed like civilization had arrived in this part of the world.

The hospital was beautiful. Things really *had* changed since he'd left, and he said so.

"No," his mother told him. "This is how the hospital looked when you still were here."

He guessed that he just hadn't had the need to visit the hospital then. Thank goodness.

So they went through the big glass doors of the hospital, and Wyatt found he was breaking into a cold sweat and dinner really was dying to be tasted a second time. Yeah, right. And how would that look? "Hey, Dad," after eleven years, followed by, "Blaarrggh!"

He might have laughed if he wasn't actually ready to puke.

They made their way to the ICU—and it was all painted *pink*! He couldn't help but think of the line from *Steel Magnolias*: "That sanctuary looks like it's been hosed down with Pepto-Bismol." They checked in with a nurse, and then before he even realized it, they were told they could go in.

Wyatt found he couldn't move. He was paralyzed. A chubby Grecian statue. Medusa had turned him into stone. How was he supposed to go in there? How was he supposed to face his father?

"Come on, honey," his mother said, reaching out and touching his arm. "He *wants* to see you."

But somehow Wyatt wasn't sure. It was something in her eyes. What was it? Was it what he was feeling? Was it fear in her eyes?

No, he didn't want to go in.

But he did anyway.

At first he couldn't quite take in what he was seeing. He gasped in shock. The man in the bed was huge. Bigger than his mother by at least a hundred pounds, and his father had always been thin. He was almost completely bald (which Wyatt imagined was possible as his father's hair had been receding back in the day). But how could he have changed this much? It was deep shock that made him step back, unable to say a word.

"Honey?"

Wyatt jumped and spun around. It was his mother. "Come on," she said and walked past the bed and beyond the curtain to the other side of the room.

Then it hit him. The man wasn't his father.

Of course it wasn't.

There was a second bed even though he hadn't expected that in the ICU. And in that bed was his father. No doubt. He was sitting up in bed, and gods, the left side of his face had an actual noticeable sag. He was older, no doubt, grayer, his hair had receded (but not like the man in the other bed), and he still had the mustache (although it was now a silver color)—but it *was* him. Wyatt almost turned and ran.

The old man struggled to sit up straighter, and Wyatt's mother rushed to help him. "Look, Charles... it's—"

He swung his right arm to stop her, and she visibly flinched.

"Wyatt," he said. "Is that you?"

Except it didn't sound like that, and Wyatt wasn't sure how he'd understood him. It was more like "Waaay-ah, ith tha ooo?"

"Y-yes, Charles," said his mother. "It's Wyatt. He came like you asked him."

"Wayyy-ayt...."

Again Wyatt wanted to run. This was like something out of a horror movie. Somehow, he didn't. "Daddy? I'm here...."

This time his father let his wife help him sit a little straighter, and then she used the control on the bed to raise him even more.

"Son?"

Wyatt trembled. He'd called him son?

"You're here…."

"Yes, Daddy…." Tears. They wanted to come. And Wyatt wasn't sure he could stop them. Son! His father had called him son!

"My *son*. It *is* you. You came. Thank the Lord God. You got here in time. I prayed, Wyatt. I prayed you would get here before it's too late." At least that's what Wyatt thought he said.

Wyatt took a step.

"Wyatt (Way-at). Your sister tells me that you aren't with that man anymore…."

Wyatt nodded. Took a step. "No, Daddy. I'm not."

His father gave a single nod. "That's good." *Thasth gud.*

It *wasn't* good, but at this point, why the fuck not? Wyatt took another step. "Yes, Daddy. I'm not with Howard anymore."

His father seemed to hiss at the mere mention of Howard's name. Then he took a deep shuddering breath and said, "Thank Jesus. I've prayed and prayed that you would escape that man…. For years I've prayed."

Escape? How had his father known there had been any reason for him to escape? He'd never told Wendy about their problems. But hell, the old man was actually talking to him. Did it matter?

"Yes, Daddy," he said. "I escaped." If being kicked out was escaping. If he had wanted to "escape" or not.

His father motioned him toward the bed. Were those tears in his eyes? Wyatt took another step.

"And the Satan stuff?"

That one took Wyatt a little longer to figure out. The slurring of his father's speech was hard enough to understand. It was horrifying as well. To see the big, strong man in this state. But stroke or no stroke, this one—*Satan stuff*—he couldn't let go by.

"It's not Satan stuff, Daddy. I don't even believe in—"

This time his father did hiss, long and drawn out, cutting Wyatt off. "It *is*! That witchcraft stuff. Fortune-telling cards. Candles. *All* of it. Those people deceive you. Tell you it's all nature. But where do you think they get their powers, son? It has to *come* from somewhere."

Son. He'd called him son!

"They get their powers from *Satan*."

"Daddy, it's not—"

Wyatt's mother turned and fixed him with a pleading stare. *Please*, those eyes said. *Just let him say whatever he wants.*

So Wyatt said nothing.

"I called you here to save you, son. Come to me. Before it's too late."

Wyatt did. He stood close enough that his father could reach out and grab his arm in his still-strong right hand. Wyatt winced at the clawlike grasp.

"Kneel, son. Ask for forgiveness."

Wyatt started. Forgiveness? *You want* me *to ask for forgiveness?*

His father nodded. "Yes. Ask the Lord God Almighty. Ask Him to forgive you of your sins. Kneel and ask Jesus into your heart. Ask Him to be your savior."

Wyatt could barely believe what he was hearing.

"Tell Him you want Him to save you from Satan. That you have turned your back on worshipping the cloven-hoofed one. We can be a family again."

Wyatt's eyes went wide. Cloven-hoofed one? This is why his father had wanted him to come? Not to condemn him. Or not—and Wyatt had only secretly hoped for this—to ask Wyatt's forgiveness. But to ask him to become a Christian? His father thought he was a Satan worshipper? He didn't even believe in Satan!

But his father wanted them to be a family again. It was almost too much to believe.

Could he do that for his father? At least tell him he'd turned away from Satan? After all, hadn't he? It was years and years and years ago—when he stopped believing in the devil. But if it might help somehow? This *was* his father after all. And from what the nurse had said, there wasn't much hope he would leave the hospital.

But then...

"Tell Him you are no longer a sodomite and fornicator. Tell Him you renounce your faggotry!"

And there was that word.

Faggotry.

Faggot.

Silly little faggot.

"*FAGGOT*" scratched into the red paint of the Mini Coop.

All the times he'd been called faggot by the kids at school.

By the boys he'd blown. By boys who had blown *him*! *Eagerly* sucked him.

His father shouting, "Two faggots can't make a home. It takes a man and a woman."

The word that had been hurled at him on the street, even in Kansas City.

The signs that had said God Hates Fags when Fred Phelps and his Westboro Baptist group had protested Gay Pride one year. A *Baptist* church. Baptist like his father!

And quite suddenly Wyatt couldn't do it.

He shook his head.

"No, Daddy. I can't. I can't ask to be forgiven because I don't have *any*thing that I need to ask forgiveness *for*."

His father's eyes went wide, flashing.

"I don't even believe in Satan!"

Wyatt's mother turned to him again. "Wyatt!"

Wyatt shook his head again. "And just because I'm not with Howard anymore doesn't mean that I'm *not* still a *faggot*! I *am* a faggot. I've always been a faggot, and I always *will* be a faggot, *and* I *like* being a faggot!"

"Wyatt!" his mother cried. "Please!"

He felt his sister at his side. "Please, Wyatt. Just do whatever he wants and—"

"No!" He looked at his sister in a way that made her step back. "I *won't*."

"Wyatt…," she whispered. "He wants you back in the family."

"I don't care!" He spun back on the horrid old man in the bed. "I've been doing fine without you, old man!" The words flew from him and he wasn't even sure from where. It started with the word faggotry and then seemed to explode from out of him. "I have family that loves me. *Just* the way I am. I'm gay, and I was *born* that way, and that means *you* helped. It was your *gay* sperm that made me this way."

His father's eyes flew wide. He began to shake. His face turned red.

"Enough!" And even though it came out as *enuff*, it was still with a power that stopped Wyatt's words. "*Enough*. Get out, sinner! Get out, thou evil one! Never cast your shadow on me again. I turn my back on you! I dust off the dirt from my feet. I disown you!"

"Charles," Wyatt's mother cried. "Please!"

"Wh-what's going on over there?" came a trembling voice from the other side of the curtain.

Wyatt's father swung at his wife and caught the side of her face and sent her stumbling back, and the memory of Wyatt's father hitting *him* that long-ago day, even the very copper taste of blood in his mouth, came back so strongly that now Wyatt's eyes were blazing.

He leapt forward and shouted, "Listen, you old bastard! You touch her again and I don't care that you're on your fucking death bed, I'll beat the *shit* out of you!"

"Nurse!" came the disembodied voice again. "*Nurse!*"

"You are a vile, *evil* old man! That lightning should have killed you. I wish it had!"

"Wyatt!" chorused his mother and sister.

His father drew back, a grimace on his face, threw up his arm in front of him. "Get out of here! I know you not! I have no son!"

A nurse ran in. "What's going on?" she cried.

"Fine!" Wyatt growled. "And *I* have no father!"

Wyatt dashed out of the room, past the nurse, and into the hall. He crashed into a wall and bounced off of it and nearly fell. His mind and heart were a tornado of emotions, and for a moment he thought he would black out. But the anger rose again, and dammit—tears! No! He would *not* cry, and that very thought made him all the angrier. For eleven years he'd lived with the echo of the day his father had kicked him out of his home. For years he'd wondered if he would ever see his family again. And this was it? This was what finally happened?

Well fuck him! Wyatt's mind screamed. "Fuck him!" he exclaimed.

"*You,*" squawked the nurse, now in the hall. "I've called security! Get out of here!"

"Yeah," Wyatt shouted back. "And *fuck* you *too.*"

He turned and fled.

Love does have teeth, he thought. *And all too often the wounds never close.*

IT WASN'T until Wyatt got outside that he realized he had nowhere to go.

They'd come to the hospital in Wendy's car.

He could take a cab back, he thought. It would cost more than he could afford, but.... Wait. He slapped his pockets. He didn't have his keys! He had automatically, even after over a decade, put them on the little table next to the front door like everyone did in the Dolan household. So even if he took a taxi, how would he get in the house?

The extra key.... He was willing to bet anything that it was still under the little rock that said "Welcome" by the front door. Dolan traditions were deep and steady. Like hating faggots.

But what if the key wasn't there?

He slumped against a car and then, sighing, looked for his sister's. Sure enough, it *was* unlocked. Who from Damview locked their cars? Hell, he wouldn't be surprised if the house was unlocked. He opened the car door and sat down, legs outside, and waited.

It wasn't a long wait.

The sound of a clearing throat caught him, and he looked up to see his mother and sister there, faces ashen. They nodded, and he pulled his legs inside. Then they joined him, and it wasn't until they were halfway back to the house that they told him his father had been sedated.

He didn't say anything. What was there to say?

"He didn't mean it," his mother said. "It's the stroke. He isn't right. You're still his son. You will always be a part of this family."

"Have I been a part of it for the past eleven years?" he snapped, and then (almost) regretted it.

They drove the rest of the way in silence, and as soon as they got there, as soon as they went inside—the door wasn't locked, of course—he grabbed his suitcase and turned to leave.

"Wyatt, no!" His mother blocked his way. "Please. *Please* don't go." He saw she was about to cry, and that made him want to cry and he couldn't. He couldn't!

"He told me to go," Wyatt said.

"And what he doesn't know won't hurt him," his mother said.

"Wh-what?" he asked.

"I don't care what he said. You're home. I haven't seen you in so long, baby. You can't go. Please stay. I made Oreo ice-cream cake. Your favorite."

He trembled. The tears threatened again. "Mamma," he whispered.

And then he was in her arms again, and gods, Wendy's too. And even little Joseph was barking and wanting to be a part of it.

So he let himself be led to the table, the dining room one this time, and he sat and his mother brought him a huge piece of her homemade ice-cream cake—layers of crumbled Oreo cookies and vanilla ice cream, topped with Cool Whip and chocolate syrup. There was no way he could eat it all.

But he did.

He did, and he pretended that all was well.

He told his mother about his friends. He told her about Sloan and how they'd met at the call center where he'd worked. He told her about Asher and how he was going to be a movie star and that he was making a movie with Spencer Morrison (but he didn't tell her the name of the movie or that Spencer-fucking-Morrison had tried to show Asher his cock). And he told her about Scott and how Scott worked for a big law firm and that Scott didn't used to believe in God or anything, but after going on a "men's retreat" with Wyatt, he had changed his mind (and he didn't tell her what kind of retreat it was or that her version of God wasn't the one that Scott was starting to believe in). Finally he told her that he was the manager of a store that was respected all over the country, and she beamed with pride (and he didn't tell her what kind of store).

In other words, he edited his life.

She made hot chocolate while he talked, real hot chocolate, not the instant kind.

And after a while, he saw it in her eyes. Saw it in those eyes that had always shone with her love, but were never, ever naïve. Saw that she knew he was leaving things out. She didn't stop him, though. She really didn't want to know.

Strangely, that was all right.

She told him she was sorry that Howard had kicked him out and that he had lost his house, but she was so happy he had such good friends to take care of him.

Sometime after that she was yawning, and so was he. He realized he was almost catastrophically exhausted and needed to go to bed. She told him he could stay in his old room, that she had it all ready for him. But after he kissed her good night, he saw that it wasn't his room. Not anymore. There was nothing of him there. His poster of Cyan Carrington was gone. He would never have imagined as a boy that one day he would be friends with Cedar Carrington—her son! The poster of the dragon was gone too, and the one of Ian McKellen as Gandalf.

Instead there was the famous poster—in a tacky, cheap gold frame—with the poem "Footprints in the Sand" and the bare foot impressions on a beach.

And a painting of Jesus standing at the door and knocking.

Everything was moved around, and his bedspread, the dark blue one with stars all over it, was gone, and there was a gingham one instead. His desk was gone too, replaced by a sewing machine, and he saw there was a folded ironing board behind the door.

He had basically been erased.

Could he sleep here?

He didn't know if he could.

But in the end, he did.

He lay in the bed and looked up at the ceiling, and he finally found something that was the same. The cracks. The one in the corner that reminded him of the head of a buffalo. The one that ran right through the middle and branched twice and had always made him think of a river. Maybe one he could take to get away from the tiny town of Damview.

He was looking at those cracks when he finally drifted off to sleep.

There were only a few nightmares.

HE LEFT, despite his mother's protests, the next morning.

Wyatt couldn't stay. He knew that.

Plus he was making his mother lie, and when she said she didn't care, and that what Wyatt's father didn't know wasn't a lie, Wyatt reminded her of the sin of omission.

"I have to go, Mamma."

"Can't you stay until Wendy gets here?"

"Will she have the kids?"

His mother's silence answered his question. It also confirmed his suspicions. Norman, Wendy's husband, wouldn't allow it.

"He's just like your father," his mother whispered. And then it quite suddenly occurred to him that so was Howard. Big and bold and cruel.

Wow, Wendy, he thought. *What they say is true. We grow up and marry our father, don't we?*

So he took his one bag, and he held his mother tight, and then he left. She made him take the leftover chicken-fried steak, along with gravy and mashed potatoes and the remains of the fried green tomatoes, even though they wouldn't be nearly as good microwaved. She would have sent him with ice-cream cake too, but there would have been no way to keep it from melting on the long trip back home. His real home now.

He did have a piece before he left, even though she offered to make him a big breakfast with eggs and fried potatoes and pancakes.

No. He couldn't. It might tempt him to stay.

And he couldn't.

Not in this place where he had been erased.

She stood and watched him go, holding Joseph close. For security, Wyatt imagined.

He didn't cry until he got to Ava.

He pulled over and he bawled. He cried and cried and cried until there were simply no tears left.

He thought of where he had been—not only in the last eleven or so hours, but the last eleven years. He thought of the man who had rescued him, only to hurt him over and over and over again—and why? Why had Howard done the things he'd done over the last five years or so? How could a man who had been so fundamentally good turn so… so evil? Or had he always been that way? Had he tricked Wyatt? Had he made him believe in some character that Howard had created and maintained for over five years?

(*"The only reason you get laid is because of me. I tell them they* have *to have sex with you if they want me."*)

He thought of Howard walking into the store, eyes red and swollen, and telling him, "I've got it…." A day that seemed so long ago but in reality was only two. How he wasn't even sure what had happened to Howard. Katherine was rushing him out the door and into her van, and he couldn't remember if he'd said anything to Howard after that.

He thought of the day he came home from depositing his check at the bank and saw his father sitting at the kitchen table with Wyatt's Scott Cunningham books and several of his tarot decks, his eyes blazing with fire. How his stomach had dropped, his heart stopped, and how he had literally nearly peed his pants.

About the slap.

Wiping away blood.

Driving and seeing his mother in his rearview mirror and wondering if he'd ever see her again.

The phone call where his father had told him that two men couldn't make a nest. Two sodomites. Faggots.

He considered the long drive ahead of him and how surprised Katherine would be to see him returning to work…

…and wondering if it was Kitty or Melrose or one of his other coworkers who scratched the word "faggot" on his car door.

He thought of all that and more, for what else did he have to do, sitting in that parking lot in the tiny town of Ava?

Wyatt thought of those things and knew he just wasn't ready to face the world. Face anything. Anyone.

Not even his best friends. His wonderful, well-meaning, loving friends—all of them with lovers and perfect little worlds of their own.

He had to get away.

Someplace safe.

And then he did something purely on impulse.

He called Camp Sanctuary.

Gryphon, one of the caretakers of the land, answered on the first ring. It surprised Wyatt until he realized that it was off-season and he probably didn't have a lot to do this time of year.

"Hey, Gryphon. It's Wyatt."

"Hello, Wyatt," he exclaimed, sounding as if Wyatt's call had made not only his day but maybe even his month. "How are you?"

Those five words and already Wyatt knew this was right. "Well," Wyatt replied. "That's what I called you about. I guess I'm not doing too well."

"What's wrong?" came the question—fast and full of concern.

Someplace safe, Wyatt thought.

"I need to come to Camp. I know you're probably closed… but, Gryphon… I need to get away. I need someplace safe. The world…. Oh, gods, Gryphon. It… I don't know if you heard, but Howard left me. And my dad just had a stroke. And then he disowned me… again. And—"

"Say no more, Wyatt. You're welcome."

"I—I am?"

"Yes. I'll put you down for North Three. The cabin with the wood-burning stove."

"Th-that would be p-perfect," Wyatt said, feeling a warm blanket of gratitude settling over him. "That would be wonderful. I just have to get away for a little while. Be alone. All alone. I won't even bother you. You will hardly know I'm there."

"I'll make sure to have some wood ready for you."

Wyatt's mouth fell open. He thought he'd buy some firewood somewhere on the way. "You don't have to do that."

"Nonsense," Gryphon said. "No problem for our favorite little bear."

Favorite little bear?

"Especially with all you've done for Camp Sanctuary. Helping so much with the big Memorial Day celebration each year." It was the weekend that was the big fund-raiser for the camp. Just last year the land mortgage had finally been paid off—and five years early.

"I really haven't done that much," Wyatt said. He'd only helped.

"When will you be here?"

"Well… tomorrow sometime?" It was pretty spontaneous, but the more he went with it, the more he knew it was right.

Someplace safe.

Because love can have teeth and right now it felt as if the wounds would never close.

He needed someplace healing.

What better place than Camp Sanctuary?

And the fact that Camp was basically closed would mean alone time.

"You got it. How long?"

How long? "A few days?" Wyatt said.

Would that give him time to stop home and pack? He would need food. And he wouldn't necessarily want to do much cooking while he was there, even though there was a good cooking stove on the cabin's front porch.

"However long you want, I just needed to know how much wood to have for you."

"Gryphon, you don't need to—"

"So you're trying to talk me out of it?"

Wyatt shut his mouth. That would be stupid, wouldn't it?

"Thank you, Gryphon."

"You shouldn't need a lot," Gryphon said by way of an answer. "I checked the forecast, and there's a call for snow, but only a couple of inches.

Snow might be nice, he thought.

"Okay," Wyatt said. "Thanks."

"Then I'll see you—tomorrow?"

"Sure," Wyatt said. He grinned. Despite everything, suddenly he felt a sense of hope.

"All right! Now Saffron needs me."

Saffron was his wife of untold years.

"Okay," Wyatt said again. "See you soon."

They hung up, and despite the fact that he had many miles to go before he was home, it was with just a little less sense of dread.

He popped his P!nk CD out and listened to the radio. He found a station that was playing songs he'd never heard of. Nice songs. Soothing ones for the most part, with only a few of them being sad. Each one seemed more amazing than the last. New Age songs, he thought. Songs his father would have called Satanic, probably. And right here in the middle of Bible country.

Who would have thought?

He was listening to one that suddenly grabbed his attention when the sound began to crackle out. Beautiful. But gods…. So tragic! A song about a son not being loved. The lyrics called to him.

When they stop fighting and turn out the lights
I pretend that I'm already sleeping
After the violence alone in the silence
Just me and the secret I'm keeping
My dad tells me I'm not worth anything
And I've almost admitted defeat…

Wyatt moaned. The radio crackled again. No! He didn't want to lose the song! He had to hear the rest of it. It was about him. And his father. He had to hear where the song was going, and there was no place to pull over.

…but in my dreams I can fly
And I soar and my feet touch the sky
And it seems I can go
Anywhere if I try
And the world's not so dark
When the clouds make it white
If there's no hope, tell me why
In my dreams I can fly.

Wyatt sighed. Listened as the chorus repeated and then was lost in static.

That song….

The timing.

The lyrics hurt.

But somehow, they filled him with hope.

And he didn't even know who the singer was.

But that's what Google was for, right?

Wyatt smiled.

Somehow, he *was* feeling hope.

Somehow he was feeling he just might be ready to fly.

CHAPTER NINETEEN

CAULEY LEFT Kevin everything but the house. That he left to SAFE, an organization that provided housing for those with HIV/AIDS, mental disabilities, and substance abuse problems.

Perfect.

Even in the end, Cauley gave to the community.

But everything else Cauley gave to him.

It had shocked him. Surely his mother should have been the one.

But as Kevin sat in the basement looking at all of Cauley's things—at his very life—he knew. What would Lois have done with all of this? There were albums (vinyl) and CDs, videotapes, boxes and boxes and boxes of magazines and clippings, yearbooks, photo albums and loose photographs (including most of those that had been on display at The Back Door—Tam kept the one of Cauley in the jock and put it on the wall behind the bar), costumes and dresses, awards presented to him by the gay community and even one from the mayor, and, inevitably, porn galore. Porn that would have aged Lois by ten years.

"What am I going to do with all of this, Theresa?"

His friend was sitting on a plastic milk crate filled with albums across from him and only shrugged in response.

Kevin had no place to put any of it for one thing. He could put it into storage… but for what? And where? Why? So it could molder and disintegrate—Cauley's life forgotten?

So once more Cauley had left it to him.

"Goddammit!" Kevin cried and dropped his face into his upturned palms.

He felt a hand on his shoulder. Theresa of course. She gave it a squeeze.

"You could have a big yard sale," she said. "Get rid of everything that isn't something personal. Like his photo albums…."

"In January?" Kevin asked, looking up at her. "Who has a yard sale in January?"

"Surely they have estate sales in January," she said. "People don't die only during the summer." She winced. "Sorry, sweetheart. I didn't mean it to sound like that." She sat down next to him. "Boy, and I'm supposed to be brilliant with words."

Kevin sighed. "You are."

She put an arm around him.

"Why did he do this to me?"

"Who else?" she replied. "Who else could he trust to go through all of this stuff?"

All of this stuff. They'd already been at it for hours.

"Why the money?" he asked, throwing his hands up. "I don't need it."

She nodded. "There was a surprising amount of it, though. I couldn't believe how much."

But Kevin, who had helped set up Cauley's savings accounts and funds and stocks, had known it would be something like what the will had revealed. He'd been impressed nevertheless. Cauley had kept up with the deposits after they broke up, and he had little head for money. He'd *had* little head for money.

Fuck!

They broke for lunch—Lois made them grilled cheese sandwiches and soup. That brought up memories, more memories, and they ate mostly in silence. Lois had surprised them by showing up to help with the upstairs, packing up linens and towels and such. She told Kevin she'd wait to pack the clothes.

"In case there's something you want."

Like anything Cauley had worn would fit Kevin!

"You never know. Sometimes it helps to keep one or two things. I still have Cauley's father's bathrobe and his favorite sweater."

So Kevin promised he'd make time to look. It was a chore he dreaded more than all the pieces of paper in the basement that represented Cauley's life.

After lunch he and Theresa went back to it and worked late, stopping only to order a pizza. Their main thrust was separating out anything personal. Photographs and such. Things that no one would want if Kevin chose to have an estate sale—and it was sounding better and better.

"I could give the money from the sale to the same charity Cauley left the house," he said aloud and without preamble.

"Yes. That would be perfect," Theresa replied without missing a beat.

It was only while driving home that evening—after Theresa declined to stop and get a drink with him somewhere (which was just as well since he'd done more than his share of drinking in the last week)—that he was hit with an idea.

He'd read an article recently about some archivist who was putting together a collection of gay history. Kevin couldn't remember all the details, but he thought if he looked he could find the article again. What was Cauley if he wasn't gay history? Hell! They might even want some of his outrageous costumes!

The idea gave him a profound sense of relief.

Perfect. It was perfect.

Let future historians have a field day.

But by the time he got home, the relief was replaced by a numbing depression. And a strange panic. The buildings—tall and towering, the very ones he loved so much—had begun to feel threatening lately. As if they might reach down and grab him. Or fall on him.

Going inside didn't help.

Going up to his condo didn't help.

That only came with a conviction that his building would collapse into the streets below while he was sleeping. That he'd wake up to the sight of brick and mortar and concrete and of falling… falling… falling.

It was enough to keep him awake and feeling sick.

It was all too much! He couldn't do this. He had to get away! The fucking estate sale would just have to wait. There wasn't anyone from SAFE even scheduled to come out to see the place for weeks.

Then he felt it.

Felt what he'd been feeling on and off for the last couple of months.

The call of the Land.

His safe place.

The place where he didn't even have to talk. Where he could be the silent giant who had nothing to say to anyone except "Hodor."

The thought of Camp grew so strongly in his mind that once again it was almost like he was there. He could almost feel the hot sun on his skin and the soft grass beneath his bare feet, smell the green growing things, hear the *ooo-eee-ooo-eee* of the cicadas, see the sunflowers that covered the earthen dam, the fields and fields of blackberries that grew out past the main camping area (he could almost taste them) as well as the great blue herons flying over him as he floated on a rubber mattress on the lake (and how they always and every time made him think of pterodactyls).

It won't look like that, though, he reminded himself. *It's winter here and it's winter there*. Camp Sanctuary wasn't even a twenty-four-hour drive away. It was near Kansas City, not Key West. And even though it seemed that way at times—like some magickal place out of time and space—Sanctuary wasn't Brigadoon, or K'un-L'un, or Shambhala or Shangri-La for that matter. It would be cold. The trees would be bare. The lake was probably at least partially frozen. It might even be snowing.

And he'd be all by himself. Gryphon and Saffron would be there, of course. They were the caretakers of the land and lived there year-round in a small little cabin. But none of Kevin's friends would be there. Not Lorax or Bobcat, not Domi Dearest or Knotty Scottie, or Cedar and his new boyfriend Roman (he hoped that was working out), or Dolce and Gabbana, or Hound Dog and Bean....

...or Wyatt....

Kevin started, surprised at Little Bear's sudden appearance in his thoughts.

Why not stop and see how he was doing?

It wasn't like he couldn't divert off the road for an afternoon. Wyatt lived close to Camp if he remembered right. No. He was sure of it. He could stop and see how Wyatt was doing. Kevin was sure it wasn't well. Getting rid of Howard was the best thing that could have happened to the little bear, but Kevin knew—*knew*—that Wyatt was in pain. For some crazy reason, Wyatt loved Howard. And who knew, maybe Howard was different when the two of them first met—people change. *He* knew that, considering what had happened with Cauley. It had been hard for Kevin to break things off with him. Maybe Howard had changed and Wyatt had the same trouble that he had.

Maybe relationships weren't supposed to last.

Wouldn't it be nice to see Wyatt, though? Take him out for coffee? *No!*

He needed to leave Wyatt alone. The last thing Wyatt needed was some guy he hardly knew showing up unannounced on his doorstep. And it was his own damned fault that Wyatt didn't know him better, what with him hiding behind the Hodor persona.

"And besides," he said aloud, "I need to be alone." If he went to see Wyatt, he'd be tempted to flirt with the adorable little guy. Knowing Wyatt, he'd go for it too. He knew Wyatt was attracted to him. At least he had been one drunken night. And there had been times when he'd seen Wyatt looking at him in a certain way: across the dining hall, sitting around Domi Dearest's camp drinking cocktails, swimming in the lake or sunbathing on the beach, that time they did the mud ritual….

Kevin smiled. Then without even thinking about it, he walked to his bedroom to one of the prints he'd decided weren't for public consumption. The mud ritual. That summer that was simply perfect, and he and more than a dozen others had all gotten naked and climbed down into the big muddy pond to the south of the camper's circle. They'd all been laughing and carrying on and helping each other get even muddier—slathering on each other. He wasn't the least bit surprised when Wyatt had started something by piling mud on top of his own head. He'd sculpted a big thick sculpture—without the benefit of being able to see what he was doing—and then he'd plucked a bunch of black-eyed Susans and clover and Queen Anne's lace and stuck them down into his creation, and it was so funny and cute, but somehow beautiful as well. Kevin wanted a picture, and it wasn't until he was climbing out of the pond that he had realized he was getting hard.

"I know," said *somebody*. Kevin couldn't remember who. "Fucking *hawt*!" Kevin saw the guy was looking at his semierection. "Hey, Hodor…. You're a grower and not a show-er, aren't you?"

The comment had pissed Kevin off, and he'd turned his back on the skinny little man so he could take some photographs (after wiping his muddy hands through the grass, of course). No one was concerned. There was an unspoken law at Men's Festival. Pictures were private, and no one had to be worried that the photographs would be seen by anyone that wasn't a part of the tribe.

"All those hot bodies," the guy was saying. Naked Ned. It was Naked Ned. Kevin remembered that now. One of the few downright creeps who came to Festival each year. "Make sure you don't get the fat guy with the flowers on his head."

Kevin had turned on him then, willing with all his might for his hand *not* to clench into a fist. Naked Ned stepped back, eyes wide. "S-sorry," he'd muttered.

Now Kevin stood looking at that photograph, and there to the right was Wyatt, looking his way, hand over his crotch, smiling shyly up at him. God. So *damned* cute. And he was the only one covering his penis. Kevin had always thought Wyatt had a nice penis. And Wyatt was like him. It might not look all that big when it was soft, but Kevin had seen his bear with a hard-on once in the shower and….

No! Stop it! For God's sake! Wyatt was *not* "his" bear. And Wyatt wasn't even going to be at Camp. *You're not going to stop by and visit him either.* It was better that there wouldn't be anyone at Camp. He needed to get away to be *alone.* Get away from the sudden claustrophobic feeling the city was giving him. Camp would be perfect. He wouldn't even have to say much.

The idea hit him as so perfect and with such urgency that he realized this wasn't just pretend. It was the tickle. And he knew not to ignore that strange little tickle at the base of his skull. The one that then rippled outward and over his scalp. He needed to go with his instinct. He wanted to go to Camp. He could barely wait as he booted up his laptop to get the phone number for Sanctuary. He was surprised at how his heart pounded. His heart never pounded!

Kevin found the number and dialed it into his cell phone and waited a seeming century for an answer—and truth be told it really only rang two or three times before the voice came from the other end of the line.

"Camp Sanctuary, this is Gryphon speaking."

"Gryphon," Kevin cried, then forced himself to calm down. "This is Kevin Owens."

There was a pause. Then: "Okay...."

Kevin laughed. Of course. He wouldn't have a clue who Kevin Owens was. "Hodor. This is Hodor."

"Oh!" came the reply and an answering laugh. "Hey! How're you doing?"

Kevin took a deep breath. "To tell you the truth, not so good. I.... Things have been rough, and I'm finding I just need to get away. And for some reason, Camp has been calling to me for weeks." He felt funny using that phrase. *Calling to me.* But hell, Gryphon hung out with all kinds of people who professed to be psychics and channelers and reincarnations and high priests and priestesses. Surely Gryphon heard such ideas all the time. "I know Camp is probably closed," he continued in a rush, "but is there any way you would let me come stay for a few days? I won't be any problem."

There was another laugh on the other end of the phone. "Wow. You won't believe this, but you're the second person to ask me that today."

Someone else had called? Shit. He hoped it wasn't Howard.

"I see," Kevin said.

"You're welcome to come stay, Hodor. The problem is that he's reserved North Three, the only cabin with heat."

Kevin's shoulders slumped. *Shit.*

And he had so wanted to go to Camp. It had seemed like a life preserver he needed in a turbulent ocean.

"You know, I could go check in the basement of Main Hall. I think there might be a couple of space heaters in there. As long as they don't blow the breaker, you could stay in North One. We just reinsulated it, and I think you'd keep warm enough if you wore the right clothes."

"Really?" Kevin asked. His heart was pounding again.

"The seven-day weather forecast is only calling for a couple inches of snow and temperatures in the thirties. It won't be toasty. But you won't freeze."

"That's fine," Kevin said quickly. "I'll dress warm. I just want to be on the Land. You know?"

"Yes, I do, my friend. Why do you think me and Saffron have been living here for so many years? I understand completely."

Kevin nodded, feeling good for the first time in a week—feeling a premonition of hope.

"Of course, you won't have any way to cook…."

"Can I use the camp grill? Or no. I have a little hibachi. I'll bring that."

"Perfect."

"Oh, Gryphon. Thank you." Kevin was smiling. It felt good on his face.

"Sorry that you can't share North Three. But Wyatt's called and asked for the same thing you have. He wants to be alone too. Guess he's got a lot on his plate."

Kevin froze. *Wait. What?* What had Gryphon just said? *Wyatt?* The coincidence was too much! "Did…. Did you say Wyatt?" Did Gryphon just say Wyatt?

"Yeah. He's another of you Men's Festers. He goes by the camp name Little—"

"Bear," Kevin finished, his heart now in overdrive. "*Little Bear's* going to be there?"

Kevin closed his eyes. He was shaking.

And he remembered a kiss.

Of course the kiss hadn't been real. But still.

"Yes. But like I said, he's wanting solitude. I don't think he's going to want company—"

"That's fine," Kevin said, his voice trembling. Remembered sitting around the fire pit on Yule and the feeling of lips on his.

Crazy…. This is crazy…!

He could see Wyatt in his mind's eye. So cute and sexy, short (the top of his head came to about Kevin's collarbone), wonderfully plump (padded), a hairy chest (but not too hairy), that sweet plump butt (that he always stared at when Wyatt shed his sarong and waded into the lake), and of course his big dark puppy-dog eyes.

"Well, when do you think you'll be here?" Gryphon asked.

Gryphon's question banished Kevin's vision, and he paused to answer. Sanctuary was about eighteen hours away if he drove straight through. If he left now…. No. He was too tired. He needed a good night's sleep. He took a deep breath. Willed himself calm. "I can be there day after tomorrow," he replied.

"Okay. I've got you marked down. That should put you here before the snow. And you know, if you do want some company, Saff and I could have you over to our cabin for dinner one night."

"I'll think about it," he said. "Right now all I want is to be by myself."

Or was that true? Quite suddenly Wyatt was filling his thoughts again. He found he was buzzing, had butterflies in his stomach, felt like he wanted to giggle.

What are you doing? You called because you wanted to be alone. You wanted to get away. What the hell are you doing thinking about Wyatt like this?

And Wyatt wants to be alone. He doesn't want to see me.

Yes. But if he's walking around, I can always say hello.

"I'll see you Tuesday," Kevin said.

"Tuesday it is," Gryphon replied.

Kevin signed off and *knew* he couldn't even consider going to bed. *Pack. I have to pack!* So that's what he did. He had to really think about how he was going to pack. It wouldn't be the same as camping for the summer. No. He needed to be warm. Staying warm was the last thing he needed at the end of July in Kansas! He had no need for his tent or his canopy or any of that. But bedding he would need. Sleeping bag. Extra blankets. Other stuff. On a whim he threw his autographed copy of *Leap and the Net Will Appear!* into his duffle bag. Theresa would have said it was foolish to take it on the road, but he liked the idea of taking a bit of Malcolm to the land that was so special to him. The book had helped him through tough times— helped him break up with Cauley, something that he had so needed to do. Cauley had forever hated the book and author—said that it had ruined their lives. But it wasn't a book that had done that. No….

Then Kevin went down to the basement and his storage unit, and even though he'd spent a long day going through "stuff," he knew he couldn't hope to sleep until he'd sorted through all his camping gear to find everything he might need. Luckily he had Pack, one of the very apps he'd invented, to help him remember anything important he might need. On a whim, and a silly whispered feeling, he went ahead and brought his Coleman lanterns even though the cabins had electricity. It wasn't like he didn't have room in his Hulk-sized truck....

It would be so different going to Camp and not sleeping in a tent. He'd never slept in one of the cabins, although he'd been in some of them for little parties and such.

And the one time he'd had sex with someone from Festival, which had been a total mistake. Kevin had been nothing but a one-night stand, and the next morning the guy was treating him like a red-headed stepchild. Kevin had almost left Festival and gone home.

But no, he loved that land. *The* Land. And it was the Land that he was going for. Not a cute little guy who needed to be just as alone as he did. He had no clue why he'd been so affected by the news that Wyatt would be there.

Just because he'd harbored a little crush maybe....

I do not have a crush on Wyatt!

"You have *such* a crush on him!" That had been Domi Dearest, one of his favorite people from Festival. And a man who was *happy* that Kevin didn't want to talk all the time. Didn't Stepper and Gentle Ben do more than enough talking?

"Hodor," had been his quiet response that day, like all days. Hodor. *His* Faerie name. The one that someone had given him because he so rarely spoke. Kevin had seized on it and even enjoyed it. "Hodor" was a perfect way *not* to have to say anything.

Domi had just rolled his eyes. "Don't even *try* to deny it. Do you think I'm an *idiot*? I *see* it. The way you *look* at him."

Kevin hadn't said anything then, just held out a glass when Greg, bartender extraordinaire at the Domi Dearest campsite, asked if anyone wanted refills.

And when he was leaving, Domi leaned in and said, "Wyatt could do a lot worse than you. Maybe you should steal him away. I can't *stand* Big Sir. He is such a *fucker*."

Kevin hadn't said anything to that either.

And he needed to stop thinking about Wyatt. Wyatt was going to Camp to get his head together. For solitude. So was he.

It could be fun.

Fun? You aren't going to Camp for "fun." You wanted to get away.

Nice, then. It could be nice.

And if he *did* see Wyatt, what was wrong with that?

Which only sent his heart racing again.

Be careful, Kevin…. He's just broken up with a man he's been with for years. Howard—and he grimaced at the name—*is probably part of what he wants to get away* from.

The last thing Wyatt needs is my company, he thought.

And I'm going to Camp to get away from everything. To get away from people and decisions and responsibility and hurtful memories. Not to be with *people.*

But that doesn't mean if I see him wandering around I can't invite him over—if he needs to talk. It would only be polite.

When he got to bed an hour or so later, it was with such a feeling of anticipation that he was sure he would never get to sleep. But sleep did come. And it was the best rest he'd had in weeks.

CHAPTER TWENTY

FOR SOME reason Wyatt didn't tell anyone he was back in Terra's Gate, not even Sloan. He pulled up into the driveway—all the way to the back where he most probably wouldn't be seen—instead of parking on the street like he usually did and began packing for his trip. He didn't call work either. Katherine expected him to be gone several days. Why call her? Why give her more drama? Hadn't he been responsible for enough of that lately?

No. Going to Sanctuary without telling anyone would make his trip even more… special. What did the nun call it in *The Sound of Music* when Maria needed to be alone? Seclusion. Yes, that was it. He would be in *seclusion*.

So he packed. Then, once again, Howard ruined his mood.

Packing sucked.

Wyatt had spent years making sure that he—they—had everything they could ever possibly need for their camping trips. Everything had been in tubs and a stacking plastic set of drawers. From the everyday stuff like bedding, air mattresses, Off! mosquito spray, and tarps to all the more unusual things that made people admire his campsite: fun party lights to decorate the camp, immensely long extension cords to reach the cabin down the hill so they could have power, camp chairs that had little side tables for food and drinks, a collapsible bar, a solar charger for cell phones, bear flags and garden statues, a terrific collection of music, and more. But when they had to split it between them, it ruined everything. Not only was he missing some summer necessities, he'd also lost some treasures. Nothing he would need for his winter sojourn, but big ugly reminders of what he *didn't* have anymore.

No! I won't let him ruin this! I won't.

But it was true. Howard had ruined everything. He had ruined Wyatt's dreams. He had taken away the home that Wyatt had spent so many years making *just* perfect—or close to. They had been nearly there. And gods, what was next summer at HQMF going to be like when he was camping in their old tent and Howard had the pop-up camper that had sprung right out of Wyatt's dreams?

There he went! Thinking of Howard ruining everything—*again*.

He refused.

So he packed, and he made a list of the necessities he would need the next day. He checked the cabinets, and he made a few meals. His chicken salad, some boiled eggs, some hamburger patties—he would use the stove on the cabin's porch for at least one dinner and to heat water for instant oatmeal and stuff like that. He'd pick up a loaf of bread and sandwich meat and chips and such at the Walmart that was twenty minutes or so from Camp. He had a cooler, although it was a small one, and—Hey!—a tiny little microwave, smaller than a toaster oven. That would work. He wouldn't need to heat water on the wood stove.

He got online and bought some e-books for his reader, a Stephen King novel and some romances. He made sure to grab his dog-eared copy of *Eat, Pray, Love* and a few other standbys—Scott Cunningham for sure. Christopher Penczak's *Sons of the Goddess*. And Starhawk's *The Spiral Dance*.

And his bearskin. That was one thing he would have actually fought Howard for—tooth and claw. Thankfully Howard didn't even want it. It was important to Wyatt. For many reasons, one of them knowing that the bear hadn't been hunted down and killed. It had been a beloved performing bear from some old traveling small-time circus. The owner wanted to keep his bear around. Then he died, and sometime after that the circus had gone out of business, and Wyatt had been in the right place at the right time and gotten the skin for a steal.

After Wyatt had done all the packing he really could, he decided to sit and watch *Friends*. He laughed, and for a while that chased the shadows away. He even slept decently.

The next morning Wyatt packed his Mini Coop and headed out early. He wanted to get settled.

Walmart went uneventfully, and he got a bright idea and bought some boneless chicken wings from the deli, all cooked already and so good they didn't even need to be heated up. For some reason Howard had always hated them, and so it was one more thing that Wyatt could do at Camp that wouldn't be Wyatt and Howard. It would be just Wyatt.

It was weird making the final leg of the journey. He was used to all the green. He was used to the tunnel of overreaching branches that campers always had to drive though in that last few hundred feet before pulling into Camp. Of course, there was no green. Just branches that looked skeletal and gave him little shivers. He drove past Iggy, or Yggdrasil, the name that someone in the founding years of Camp Sanctuary had given to the huge, eighty-foot-tall tree that grew just past the front gate. It too looked dead, although Wyatt knew it was only sleeping.

Wyatt drove up the steep hill to the secondary level of Camp, where he could register and check in with Gryphon. He'd no sooner climbed out of his car when the very man he was looking for came out of the dining hall, a building off to Wyatt's right, and strode up and gave him a big hug. He was an older man of indeterminate age who looked to Wyatt like he could be anywhere from forty to sixty—it was hard to tell. He was thin, but fit, with many lines on his face but no sagging skin, and with no gray in his brown hair but plenty in his well-trimmed beard. "Wyatt! Merry meet! It's so good to see you."

Wyatt hugged back and let himself sink into the warm embrace. Gryphon gave good hugs, and right now Wyatt needed one. Especially if he was going to withdraw even from Sanctuary's caretakers and go into "seclusion."

"Let's get you settled," Gryphon declared and went right to the car to help Wyatt unpack. With the caretaker's aid, it was an easy two trips to the third cabin heading up the north trail from the buildings that made up the hive central of Camp Sanctuary. The kitchen/dining hall, the Main Hall (where most meetings and such were held), and the shower house. Wyatt had had many a midnight shower there with friends. Again, he was struck by how different Camp looked without its green foliage. Gray, quiet, slumbering. He hoped he hadn't made a mistake coming here.

And sure enough, Gryphon had laid up a big pile of firewood under the front porch and plenty inside the cabin so it would be at least a day before Wyatt needed to bring any in.

"So it's just me and you and Saffron?" Wyatt asked as Gryphon started the fire in the woodstove (doing even that for him; so nice).

"Well, for today anyway. And tonight. You'll have company tomorrow, though." Then before Wyatt could even begin to get concerned, Gryphon assured him that the other guest would be staying in North One, and since the shower house's water supply was shut off for the winter, there was a good chance Wyatt wouldn't even see him. The other guest was looking to be alone as well. "A lot of people come to Camp to heal." He hugged Wyatt again. "And I hope your time here does that. Or at least starts it."

"Thank you, Gryphon."

"Saffron wanted you to know you're invited for lunch. One good and for sure hot meal while you stay."

Wyatt declined. He wanted to start his Seclusion right away. Already he was giving the word a capital *S* in his mind.

So Gryphon went on his way.

Even though it was the same relative size as all the other cabins, it looked so much bigger inside. It was the only cabin in Camp that was one big room instead of two separate halves. He thought of Dr. Who's TARDIS and giggled, then set about making the cabin his own, at least for a few days, by draping sarongs over the lamps and making his bed—the only real bed, a double, in all of Camp—with old bedding and his bearskin rug. The Green Man and pentacle tapestries he used for bedding he'd bought from the guys who sold the sarongs he'd draped over the lamps, something they did each summer at Festival. He'd only considered using one of the bunks for a second, because even though the bed was big enough to remind him he was in it all by himself, somehow he thought one of the smaller beds would be worse. He set up his CD player and put Celia to playing. He loved her music, and she would surely set the magickal mood he hoped to capture while he was here.

He checked the wood cookstove on the front porch and saw it was ready as well. There was wood already inside—Gryphon was a wonderful man. Wyatt also moved the garden bear statue he'd brought along and left on the front porch *just* so, wanting it perfect. Bear Spirit now watched outside, and with the skin on the bed, Wyatt knew that same spirit watched inside as well.

Strangely he began to yawn at that point, even though it was only early afternoon. But then, in the last few days, he had made two long trips on the road, packed for Camp, unpacked and set up his cabin, and perfected bears inside and out.

Why not take a little nap?

So he lay down and promptly fell into a deep and long nap.

WYATT AWOKE a surprising three hours later, alarmed when he saw the time, relieved when he opened the door and saw it wasn't dark yet. It would be soon, though; it was that time of year. He had something he wanted to do.

So he bundled up in coat, gloves, hat, scarf, plus one more thing, and headed down the north path, which followed the main road up the steep hill to the camping plateau above. When he reached a major bend in the path, he crossed the road and entered one of his favorite places in all of Sanctuary—Pax Place. He hadn't been here since Sinthesis, a Faerie he'd known for years—and one of the first to make him feel welcome at Festival—had performed a handfasting here last summer for a young couple. It had gone long, longer than anyone had expected, but it was so beautiful that Wyatt had no room to complain. What could have been done to make it shorter? It was perfect, and if that young couple stayed together longer than the promised "year-and-a-day rule," then it would be a night they both would remember forever.

Imagine…. Forever….

Pax Place, like everything else at Camp, looked different; however, the branches over the path that led to one of Camp Sanctuary's sacred spaces were so tight and tangled, it was like traveling down a narrow hallway of some Tolkien Elvin dwelling. The illusion was only altered by the presence of gold-painted Egyptian statues placed along that path: first two human-looking guards and then a pair of Egyptian gods. What thrilled him, though, was when the path opened to the twenty-foot circular clearing. As on the path, the branches above were so intertwined it was like the trees had decided to lend themselves to building a church—but a church of nature rather than some man-made creation. Wyatt had always thought the place beautiful with its canopy of leaves. But this looked somehow divine.

Wyatt stood for the longest time, taking it all in, feeling the power and the peace of the place. He wished it were warmer and camping were allowed here. He could only imagine what sleeping in this sacred space would be like—what dreams might come.

But it was getting chilly as the sky darkened, and Wyatt still had things he wanted to do.

He went to the stone-walled fire pit and saw that this was the only place Gryphon had not stocked. Luckily there was a big pile of broken branches set off near where the path diverged from the main road, and in only about fifteen minutes, he managed to bring back enough wood for the fire he planned on starting in a few days. When he had arranged the wood to his satisfaction, he took the last item he'd brought to Pax Place and draped it over the pile. It was one of Howard's big flannel shirts. He'd snuck it away in one of his boxes the dreadful day he'd had to move from his home. Foolishly, he had planned then to sleep with it. So he could smell his lover—ex-lover—in his lonely nights.

But now he knew it was time to get rid of it.

He would burn it. He would burn it in this sacred place.

WHEN WYATT got back to the cabin, he found fried chicken and rolls on a foil-wrapped plate lying on the small dining table in the center of the room. There was a note.

> *Start your healing journey with a full stomach.*
> *Love,*
> *Saff*

Saffron. Wyatt smiled. He loved Saffron. She was as integral to Camp Sanctuary as anything. *As* sacred. Like some kind of pagan Mother Teresa. Both she and her husband were as important to everything that *was* Sanctuary as anything—Pax Place, Sunflower Ridge, Serenity Lake, Gaea's Haven, Green Man Grove.

It would be a perfect start for his time here. He'd had her food before. She was a wonderful cook.

So he sat and he ate and he read some *Eat, Pray, Love*, and he cried a little bit, but not much.

He listened to Celia and some Christine Kane and was hit once again by lyrics. Words that he knew he'd heard a hundred times, but today, now, meant so much more….

> *I'm in this church*
> *Running down the aisle*
> *My heart is broken*
> *My-my dress is torn….*
>
> *Seasons changing on me now*
> *Wait for the flowers to grow, yeah*
> *Seasons changing on me now*
> *Watch for the roses in the snow*

Like the Universe had made sure he would hear the right songs in the right time. Like a message of hope.

Snow was coming.
But it wouldn't last forever.
That's what he had to believe.
That the roses would bloom again.

CHAPTER TWENTY-ONE

WYATT WOKE up late in the morning feeling surprisingly good. Better than he had in months. As good as or better than the evening he'd done the Yule ritual with his friends. There was a touch of loneliness, but it was strangely okay. Like it was supposed to be. "Seclusion" was what he was after.

He got a tiny smile as he thought of something. It was like the first few times he got fucked. It hurt… but that was part of it. Like being born, somehow. And for some reason that was what this loneliness felt like. A little sad, but as if…. As if something was waiting for him. Waiting just around the bend.

For months now he'd hung on to the necks of close friends (and he'd had friends to hang on to *despite* what Howard said!), hung out with acquaintances (and he had far more of those than he'd ever realized), played his music so loud it made his ears hurt (but it drowned out Howard's mocking voice), worked extra hours (the money helped), and played endless hours of Netflix (comedies, because the few depressing horror movies where everyone died at the end turned out to be a mistake). It was time to spend some time alone and to have a little silence.

Or mostly silence.

Wyatt pushed the covers back, sat up, and gave a little shiver. The fire had burned down, leaving a chill in the air, and as he climbed out of bed, he was glad he was wearing socks. He usually slept naked. Wyatt grabbed a couple of logs, opened the little metal door on the old-fashioned wood-burning stove (his grandmother had once had one like it, only twice as big), and shoved them inside. With some coals still glowing within, he figured it wouldn't take long before the fire got going again.

Wyatt was hungry. And he wanted some coffee. A warm little tickle formed in his heart, and he realized it was desire. Not sexual, but a desire to *do* something. To take care of himself, even if it was only to make himself something to eat and start a pot of coffee.

So he put some water and a filter in his little coffee maker and opened his bag of coffee from The Shepherd's Bean and was startled to see beans gleaming oilily inside. Beans. Shit. How had he done that? He'd forgotten to grind them and left his grinder at home—and wasn't it fortunate that was one of the things he'd gotten in the divorce? Howard had only ever liked Maxwell House. Hell, when camping Howard liked Taster's Choice! But it was at home, which did Wyatt no good and meant a morning without coffee. Shit!

But he wasn't going to let that get to him, and no coffee didn't mean no caffeine. He grabbed a can of cola from his cooler. Then he plugged in his (ridiculously small) microwave—it really wasn't much bigger than a breadbox—got the half-dozen egg container from the same cooler where he'd gotten the soda, cracked a couple into a coffee cup (might as well use it for something), stirred them up, and placed the cup in the microwave. One minute and he stirred them again, hit them for one more minute, and with some shredded cheese, he had a decent little breakfast. Microwaving had been his secret way of making some of the fluffiest scrambled eggs ever. It was a trick his mother taught him.

Quite suddenly he realized he had to go to the bathroom, and this was no peeing-off-the-porch kind of thing. He dreaded using the probably near ice-cold porta potty down the road and wondered if the water to the dining hall was shut off like it was to the shower house. It wouldn't hurt to check. He knew he'd better hurry, though.

So he shrugged into his coat, scrambled down the steps, and dashed down the path. Just as he was passing the last cabin, the caretaker's cabin, which was across the road from the guest cabins, he heard laughter and veered off to see if Gryphon or Saffron were out. Sure enough, even in this cold, they were sitting on their miniature patio and drinking what smelled like coffee.

Coffee. Gods....

Not important right now!

"Hey, guys," he called, waving.

They both looked up to see him standing above them. "Hey, Wyatt!" said Saffron with a big grin.

"Morning, Little Bear," Gryphon replied.

Wyatt began to dance. "Ummm... ah... guys? Ah... I was wonder... wondering... is the bathroom in the dining hall working?"

Saffron nodded, stood, and gave a toss of her head. "Sure. But don't worry about that. Come on down." She had the door open before he got there, and he shot past her and straight to their little bathroom. He knew where it was, naturally. He'd gotten high with Gryphon at many a Men's Fest.

Five minutes later he returned to the patio to join his friends, now a very happy camper—literally. The gods really smiled on him.

"Would you like some coffee, Wyatt?" Saffron asked.

"Would I!" He did a second little dance—this one a happy dance. He loved Saff. Loved that she never wore makeup. Loved her big smiles and her dimples and her blue-green eyes and her Beatles haircut that seemed almost hacked into shape rather than done by any beautician. And her spirit, of course—her soul.

A moment later he was drinking some most excellent joe from a big old mug and forgetting all about being by himself. They had a fire pit going, and even though it was so small it was cute, it was kicking out a nice amount of heat.

"You have a nice night's sleep?" Gryphon asked.

Wyatt nodded happily and took another sip of deliciousness. "I did. I *really* did!"

"Glad to hear it," Saffron said. "You wouldn't be interested in something to eat, would you?"

"I already ate—"

"It's my homemade bread," she said. "With my blackberry jam."

Wyatt sat up straight. "Blackberries from up top?"

She grinned. "Of course. Why would I use any others?"

Wyatt nodded enthusiastically. "Yes, please!"

They were eating when Gryphon broke the news. "Oh! Guess what? Our other guest who's arriving today? He's a Men's Fest-er."

Wyatt looked at Gryphon, startled. "Huh? Really?" What the hell kind of coincidence was that?

"Don't worry," Gryphon assured him. "I told him you wanted to be left alone…."

"Who?" Wyatt asked. Yes, he wanted to be alone. But he couldn't help but be curious. Who would it be? Gods, please *not* Howard! Or Naked Ned. He shuddered.

"Hodor," Gryphon told him.

Wyatt's mouth dropped open. His eyebrows shot up.

Hodor? Had he said Hodor? Hodor, of all people?

Wyatt saw him then. Almost as clearly as if he were right here, standing over him. Looking down at him with shining brown eyes. The man who had come to him in a vision on Yule….

Except he didn't come to you on Yule.

Except he did.

Wyatt was sure of it.

"Wyatt?"

He looked back over at his friends.

"I really don't think he'll bother you."

Wyatt shrugged. "He's a nice guy," he said. And that was followed by another thought. *Hodor, what are you doing here?*

Quite suddenly he felt afraid, even though it didn't make a bit of sense. Why would he be afraid? He wasn't afraid of Hodor, was he? Why would he be afraid of the quiet gentle giant?

In the vision Hodor was about to kiss him. *Had* kissed him.

Wyatt shoved the last three bites worth of bread into his mouth all at once and stood. "I'm gonna go back to my cabin." Except it didn't sound like that with a mouth full of bread and blackberry jam. He didn't wait to finish chewing but nodded at his friends and walked away.

Quickly.

CHAPTER TWENTY-TWO

KEVIN GOT to Camp right around noon on Tuesday. He had tried to drive straight through but had gotten very tired sometime after midnight. The lights of the oncoming trucks had begun to hypnotize him, and he knew that driving into a ditch or dying was not the journey he was wanting to take.

Luckily he saw the little sign, pulled off the highway, and stayed at some pretty much nameless place—literally; the sign said only Motel in big sky-blue neon letters—and slept for about five hours. He took the time to get a mostly hot shower—it was nothing like his magic shower at home, but hey, a shower was a shower—and grabbed a breakfast burrito at that state's (he wasn't exactly sure which state he was in at that point) version of a convenience store. It was pretty bad, but at least he had something in his stomach.

And then he kept driving. He had a big bladder.

He did stop at the Walmart close to Camp and picked up some things he would need. Food, of course—he found a six-pack of small breakfast steaks, some precooked chicken wings at the deli, some sandwich makings, bread, and a few other things. He even picked up a couple of small propane canisters for his stove. While he was at it, he found a space heater. It wasn't very expensive, and since he wasn't sure how reliable the ones that had been in the basement of the camp's main hall would be, he figured it might be a good idea. On a whim he bought some big pillar candles. He liked the scent of fresh linen, and they had several of those. But then he saw there were some on sale. Christmas leftovers. Forest-green candles with a pine scent. They claimed to be "real" pine scent. He had no idea why, but the compulsion was too great. He grabbed a couple of those as well.

Gryphon greeted him in the parking lot with a big hug as soon as he got to Sanctuary and helped him get his stuff to the first cabin on the trail leading north from the main complex of the camp's buildings. Kevin couldn't help but look farther down that way. Around the bend was N2 and then N3, where Wyatt was staying.

His heart sped up.

Why am I feeling this way?

Why couldn't he get Wyatt out of his mind? He thought he might have dreamed about him last night.

Kevin had this image of big sweet brown eyes and the ghost of a feeling of soft full lips on his own. The sensation seemed so real, he reached up and touched his mouth as he stood there on the path outside his cabin.

Yes, he'd admired the little guy for years. Loved Wyatt's gregariousness. His hilarious acts during the Know Talent Show every year. His crazy antics and wild T-shirts. He'd envied Howard on more than one occasion, wondered what it would be like to have the little ball of energy and light in his life. Thought that energy was wasted on Howard. Wondered what it might be like to cuddle with Wyatt on the beach or even in his tent.

And yes, Kevin had even had the opportunity once. He remembered clearly one night when Wyatt, who was quite drunk, made a *huge* pass at him. Wyatt had walked up to him, a full head shorter or more, looked up at him, placed a hand on his chest (Kevin's heart had raced beneath that hand), and then stood up on tiptoes and tried to kiss him. It had taken a lot of willpower to turn the little bear—Little Bear—away. To resist the opportunity to see what it was like to kiss those lips, those eyes. To make love to him.

But Wyatt had been drunk. Kevin hadn't wanted a drunk Wyatt. He wanted Wyatt in his full faculties. He would have hated it if the object of his little fantasy woke up and didn't even remember their night. That would have hurt.

Yet it was more than that.

Wyatt belonged—or had belonged—to Howard. Kevin didn't fool around with "married" men. It didn't matter that the two of them had an open relationship, that it wouldn't be cheating as far as they were concerned. It *would* be cheating to Kevin. Even if the only person being "cheated" was Kevin himself. He knew that if he had one taste of Wyatt, he would want more. And more is what he *couldn't* have. It would hurt too much to make love with Wyatt and then have him get up and return to his husband's bed.

Howard was a fool for sharing Wyatt. Kevin never would. If the little bear was his, he would keep him close. Close in his arms and close in his heart. Make Wyatt his once and forever. He would treat Wyatt right. He would cherish him. He would make it so Wyatt didn't need anyone else. Or want anyone else. Or….

"You all right, Hodor?" Gryphon asked.

His words yanked Kevin from his thoughts—*foolish thoughts*—and he turned his face away from the path and what lay beyond.

"Fine," he said.

They went into the cabin. Unlike the few he'd been in for a cocktail party or late-night coffee klatch, this one was divided into two distinct halves. They entered a tiny foyer-like area, and there were sliding doors to either side. Gryphon led him through the one on the left, and Kevin was immediately and pleasantly surprised how warm the small room was. He spotted the two space heaters that were merrily doing their jobs.

"Good?" asked Gryphon, quickly closing the foyer door so as not to let out the heat.

"Awesome," he answered.

Gryphon laughed. "You know, it occurred to me the other day when I hung up with you that you had said more words in our little phone conversation than I've ever heard you use. And today, even though you haven't said '*Hodor*' even once, you're back to being a man of few words."

Kevin shrugged by way of an answer. He didn't even want to say that word he was so well known for at Camp. Because that was Men's Festival. This was something different.

He just wasn't sure what it was yet.

"Okay." Gryphon squeezed his shoulder. "I'm going to leave you now."

Kevin nodded. Because that's what he wanted, right? To be alone? To get away from the city? And Cauley's things. From responsibilities he hadn't asked for. And buildings that wanted to fall down on him.

Why had Cauley done it? Why had he given him the responsibility? He had enough on his plate just dealing with his ex's death.

Death!

God.

He trembled. What was the world going to be like without Cauley in it?

But then he caught himself looking out the window. The one that looked north. To where Wyatt was.

What the hell is going on with me? Thinking about Wyatt now? When he had other things he needed to deal with.

He closed his eyes and turned away.

I am here to get away.

And that's what I am going to do.

Stay away.

So Kevin set up the room, chose one of the four narrow beds—not much more than cots really; he'd heard they were hand-me-downs from a local prison—made it, put his food away, and made a quick little trip to the dining hall to check the ice-storage machine. He was in luck. Even though it was winter, there were a few bags of ice, and he grabbed one, stuck his dollar fifty in the "We Trust You" box (he actually put in two dollars, fifty cents for a good cause) and put it in his cooler back in the cabin. For the nonce he even placed that in the little foyer. Keep his food nice and cold. He'd bring it inside before he went to bed to make sure nothing froze solid.

He picked some soft music on his iPod, set it playing, and plopped down on the bed with his copy of *Leap and the Net Will Appear!* Every time he read it, he found something he hadn't seen before. It was the perfect book for this getaway. Get him inside his own mind instead of thinking about a little bear not far down the path....

Stop!

He turned the book over, looked at the back, read the brief description of the author. Kevin would never forget meeting him. He'd been surprised at how young Malcolm Kane was. For some reason Kevin had expected a much older man. The author had collected so much wisdom in a relatively short life. Standing there, waiting for his turn to get his book signed, he'd almost fled several times—might have if Theresa hadn't been there, arm looped through his. Luckily he'd had a great excuse not to say much. The line had been long, with plenty of people waiting their turn. Kevin had told the author his name so it could be included in the autograph (although that hadn't really mattered to him), and that was about it. Except for thanks. He kept it to that because he was afraid he might have started gushing otherwise.

Kevin turned the book back to the simple front cover and then decided to start from the beginning. He even loved the introduction. Kevin propped himself up on his elbows, opened the book, and began to read.

But then…

He looked over his shoulder and out the north-facing window as if he could see the cabin that was up the rise and around a bend in the trail.

Wyatt. So close. And yet so far.

God.

Malcolm would not approve.

But then another thought came.

Maybe he would.

Wasn't the whole point of the author's mission to get people to trust—to take a chance? To leap and believe the Universe would provide?

Should I?

It wouldn't hurt just to walk down the path, would it? Hey! Maybe he could stroll down to Pax Place.

So he did. He put the book down, shrugged back into his coat, left the cabin, and started up the path.

Kevin heard the music first. He wasn't sure how he'd missed it before. Here he was, hadn't even reached N2, the second cabin along the path, and he could hear it already. Loud.

That would be Wyatt all right. Kevin smiled.

Sweet little Wyatt.

He smiled, stopped, and imagined Wyatt dancing around his cabin—probably wearing pink—raising an imaginary glass, shaking his hips, singing at the top of his lungs about being wrong in all the right ways. And could Wyatt be anything *but* loud?

You don't have any business bothering him. None at all.

Right then he knew that if he headed up that path and did *whatever* the fuck he was planning on doing—or not planning—it would be wrong.

Wyatt had been with Howard for a long time. That man—that *turd*—had *hurt* Wyatt. Why else would he be here at Sanctuary? Why, Gryphon had told him, hadn't he? Wyatt wanted to be alone.

And alone is what Wyatt was going to be.

Which was for the best.

Because Kevin needed to be alone as well. He needed to think things through. Decide what was next in his life. Because he was alive, wasn't he? Cauley was the one who had died, not him.

Kevin nodded.

Yes. Being alone was what they both needed.

CHAPTER TWENTY-THREE

WYATT PLAYED his music. He played it loud. He played it so it would drown out the voices.

(*"Goddammit, Wy! Could you* be *a bigger faggot?"*

"Tell Him you are no longer a sodomite and fornicator. Tell Him you renounce your faggotry!"

"The only reason you get laid is because of me. I tell them they have *to have sex with you if they want me."*

"And you're never going to last! Two faggots can't make a home.... How can two men—two sodomites—make a nest?"

"Fuck you, Wyatt! You're nothing but a clingy, jealous little bitch!")

He turned the music up louder.... But the music, no matter how loud he played it, didn't drown out the *visions*.

Hodor standing over him... looking down at him with amazing brown eyes... touching him... bending down to kiss him!

Gods. Hodor? Coming here? Today?

What could it mean?

It had to mean something, didn't it? What were the odds? Hundreds of people came to Camp Sanctuary. Thousands. But how many showed up during the off-season? How many asked, other than on the Sabbats, if they could come stay at Camp while it was more or less closed?

It couldn't be a coincidence, could it?

His heart was racing.

Wyatt grabbed his bearskin and wrapped it around himself and stepped out onto the cabin's little porch. The second stove took up most of the space; it wasn't a sitting-down-in-a-rocking-chair kind of porch. There was enough room for him to stand there, though. Stand and look off to his left, southward down the path. To where Hodor might be, even now.

Such a sweet man. Quiet. Had he ever heard the man say anything but "Hodor"?

He seemed so lonely.

Could he be as lonely as me?

Quite suddenly, and with a small gasp, Wyatt realized something.

Wyatt realized that not only was he lonely, but…

…he'd been that way for a very long time.

A lot longer than the last several months.

He'd been lonely long before Howard had kicked him out of their home.

So lonely.

And gods, he needed to be *not* lonely. If for only one single night. To be held.

Wyatt was torn.

Should I go down there? Screw being alone? He had a deep feeling that Hodor would want him to come. Hadn't he seen it in his eyes?

He'd always thought Hodor was hot.

Of course, he'd thought a lot of men where hot. He'd been with a lot of men. Howard had seen to that. Encouraged it.

Howard….

Howard who had convinced him that his dreams of finding fairy-tale love were total bullshit. Convinced him that his dreams were silly. Talked him into doing things he hadn't wanted to do. Made him believe that it was fun.

But wasn't it?

"We're men, Wyatt. The only reason you want monogamy is that's what you've been taught. It's cultural brainwashing. That you're supposed to be with only one person. But that is so medieval. Monogamy was invented so a man would know his heir was his kid. But you and me? Gay men? We can't have kids. And when you see a guy who turns you on? And he's willing? You should be able to have sex with him. You should have that *right*. You should be able to go for it. All men are different. We like different things. We're shaped different. We have different-sized cocks. Some are cut, some are uncut. God! Think about it! You've got jocks and bears and cubs and chubs and pups and muscle men and leathermen and twinks and lumberjacks and otters, and that's not even counting black men and Asian men and men from the Middle East and Latinos. And there is all *they* like to do. Some men like to fuck. Some like to be fucked. There's role-playing and rough sex and spanking and watersports and sounding and *orgies* and…."

And somehow Howard had convinced him.

To be fair, he'd had a lot of fun. Done all kinds of things with all kinds of men. He'd had *real* adventures to make any homebound dreamer and writer of the stories at Men on the Net or Nifty Archives or Literotica green with envy. He happened to *know* for a fact that a lot of those men, many of them married, were way too terrified to ever have real gay sex. They were men who wrote about their dreams and fantasies when their wives were asleep or at work instead of actually living and experiencing the lives they would have liked.

And maybe I'm being too judgmental?

Maybe.

And maybe not.

How many people were miserable because they'd been too afraid to be who they really were? How lonely must that be?

Maybe Hodor could use a night of not being lonely.

Wyatt looked down the path again.

But then, out of nowhere, a memory filled Wyatt's mind, a memory of a drunken night hanging out at Domi's tent. A night he'd made a pass at Hodor. And gods....

Hodor had turned him down.

(*"I... I can't, Little Bear. I... I don't fool around with married men...."*)

He'd tried to convince Hodor. Tried to convince him that men couldn't get married (or they couldn't then) and so why should they bend to the rules of a society that hated them? Why shouldn't they fool around?

But Hodor had still turned him down.

(*"I'm going to regret this Little Bear... but I can't."*)

Gods.

He said that he was going to regret not having sex with me.

Wyatt swallowed hard.

Hodor wanted more than a one-night stand. He wanted more than sex. He turned me away because he wanted something more than a drunken night of sex.

Could Hodor want the fairy tale that Howard said didn't exist? Howard had laughed at his desire for happily ever after. And Wyatt had been so desperate to be *with* Howard—so afraid to lose him, to be on his own—he'd forsaken his dreams. Was Hodor holding out for the fairy-tale ending after all?

But then Wyatt remembered something else. Remembered a slowly growing conviction.

A real thought that had filled his mind more than once lately.

What if there really were some strange cosmic order at hand? What if the Universe only allowed so much love to go around? What if him having Howard all those years had somehow blocked his friends from finding love? What if their finally finding love—love they deserved to have—meant that he needed to be single? That the cosmic balance had shifted. What if his even walking down to Hodor's cabin somehow endangered his friends' happiness?

Wyatt thought about how lonely and hurt and grieving Sloan had been until he met Max. Had he ever seen Sloan so happy before? The image of Sloan and Max standing on his porch all flushed and happy not so long ago filled his mind. Imagine. Sloan having sex! He had finally gotten over his ridiculous crush on Asher and made a life.

How could I stand in the way of that?

And speaking of Asher, *he* had found love. Asher! The man who had more sex in one year than Wyatt had had in his whole life—and that was saying something. Asher who laughed at love. A man who could be so damned selfish and conceited had found love. *Sweet* love. Asher catered to Peni in a way that reminded him of the Harlequin Romances that Wyatt's mother had read by the truckload (until his father had forbade them). Books that Wyatt had smuggled and read and dreamed of a strong handsome lover who would take him away and love him forever.

What if even flirting with Hodor somehow jinxed Asher and Peni? Could he live with himself if that happened?

And Scott. *Goddess*. What about Scott? Wyatt had never known an angrier and more pessimistic man in his life. Sure, his parents had been horrible. Wyatt knew all about horrible parents. But Scott hadn't found someone to take care of him—even a "someone" who turned out to be a man who would later reject him (at least Wyatt had *had* love). Instead, Scott had transformed from a man who scoffed at anyone's religious beliefs to a tree-hugging believer in manifesting your own destiny and seeing the Divine in every blade of grass. And the love of a good man—Cedar—had helped.

What if Hodor tried to kiss Wyatt? Like in his vision? What if a kiss could send out some kind of shockwave into the Universe and Scott and Cedar broke up? How could he look at himself in the mirror if something like that happened?

No.

He couldn't.

His friends deserved some happiness. They'd been alone too long. Now it was his—Wyatt's—turn to be alone. And really, as long as he had this land, and friends like Gryphon and Saff, and of course best friends like the Fabulous Four plus three, he wouldn't be alone.

And yet that sense of loneliness threatened to settle over him. He thought of Hodor, so close. Would it hurt his mission to seek out a little company? But no. Wyatt sat up straight, thrust out his chest, stiffened his jaw, and made up his mind.

He would not go see Hodor. He would turn his back on that vision.

If the gods really had decreed that he should be single, then that's the way it would be. It was time he learned to love himself.

And hadn't he heard that was the greatest love of all?

If the gods had something else in mind—if the Queer Spirits had some other destiny planned for him—he doubted he would be able to change it.

You're being silly, an inner voice told him. *There's no such thing as a cosmic "love balance." People break up. You and Howard broke up. How many relationships have you seen come to an end? Plenty. Both gay and straight.*

For a moment Wyatt didn't say anything. Didn't even think anything. How did he answer himself? Because wasn't the idea that his and Howard's love had blocked anybody from finding love pretty crazy?

There was a sudden howl of cold wind through the trees. Wyatt's short hair ruffled nonetheless. He shivered. Then laughed. Answered the wind with a long raspberry.

Cosmic love balance.

Silly!

He took a deep breath. Looked southward down the path. Thought of Hodor. Shivered again.

With that came a tiny little flake of snow. It drifted down like an oversized piece of dandelion fluff, floating, floating…. Then came another. And another. One caught in his eyelashes, and he absently wiped it away.

The snow had begun.

Within moments the air was awhirl with it. Wyatt sighed in wonder. Lovely! He'd never seen it snow at Camp. He'd always been there in the warm months—dancing around barefoot (even naked)—and worshiping the sun. Literally.

But this!

This really did look like something out of a fairy tale. And as it fell thicker, he could almost imagine Snedronningen, the Snow Queen, walking out of the woods, surrounded by her great swirling swarms of snow bees, waving her arms and orchestrating this fall of snow with her magick.

Wyatt smiled. Stood until he was coated, like a sugar-powdered cake, with white. Then he shook himself off and went inside.

He had plenty of wood. He added some to the fire. The snow would be nice.

And hadn't Gryphon said there would only be a few inches?

He couldn't wait to wake up and see.

IN THE dream he got up from his bed and went to Hodor's cabin. He knew it was a dream because all he was wearing was his bearskin, and he didn't feel the cold of the falling flakes. He was even barefoot, and he was walking through the snow, and then… then he was… was dropping to his hands and knees and bounding down the path on all fours. He *was* a bear! He could see that his hands were covered in deep dark brown fur and they ended in large black claws.

It was wonderful! He wanted to laugh it felt so good, but what came out were strange noises that he imagined were those a bear would make.

He dashed down the path, flew past North 2, went around a bend, and saw North 1 down at the end. The windows facing him were lit up, and he could see Hodor. He wasn't wearing his shirt, and even from there Wyatt could see the flexing muscles and the hair on his chest. Desire filled him.

Then Hodor was looking out the window. He saw Wyatt. Saw him coming.

He left the room and came out onto the porch of his cabin and was naked, and he was holding out his arms.

With a mighty leap, Wyatt was on the porch and rising up and throwing his huge hairy arms around the man and then… then they weren't hairy. They were his own arms, and the bearskin was wrapping around them both and they pressed their bodies together and they kissed. They opened their mouths to each other, tongues plunging and lashing together.

Kevin picked Wyatt up, and somehow they were going through the cabin door, and when they went inside, it was Wyatt's cabin, although the stove was now a roaring fireplace. The bed—big, much bigger, with a huge headboard carved deep with the figures of two mighty bears—was covered in furs. Then they were on it, Hodor over him and taking him, and even though Wyatt knew it was a dream, it felt so real!

He came in his sleep, something he hadn't done since he was twelve, and it was powerful and it was good and he awoke and he smiled and then he fell gently back to sleep and if he dreamed again, he didn't remember.

CHAPTER TWENTY-FOUR

WYATT WOKE to darkness.

What time is it? he wondered.

He glanced in the direction of his alarm clock but couldn't see it. Where was it? He reached out and felt for it. It must have gotten turned around. But when he did find it, turned it this way and that, he saw that it wasn't working.

Had a circuit blown? Had he lost power?

He got up and stumbled around. It wasn't pitch-black. There was cool white light coming from around and under the shades he'd drawn. So it was morning, then. He found the chains that hung from the combination light and ceiling fan and pulled the one with the little plastic fairy attached to the end and… nothing. He pulled it again. Still nothing.

Had he turned the light off with the switch by the door?

Wyatt made his way there. His eyes were adjusting, and he could now make out the ghost images of the little table, chairs, the bunk beds against one wall, the two beds by the door. When he got to the door, he flicked the switch and again, nothing.

What?

He looked outside to see if the big yellow light over the porch was on. Flicked switches. Nothing.

That was when he saw the snow.

He gasped.

"*Goddess*," he whispered.

He opened the door.

"Oh!" he said with a little cry and thought once again of Snedronningen, the Snow Queen.

It was no two inches of snow.

No, what he was seeing was at least two *feet* of snow. Maybe three. Why, there was a foot piled like little white walls on the porch railing. He could hardly see the stove, even though it had been sheltered under

the porch awning. Snow was piled at least a foot against the screen door.
It was almost scary-looking.

He pushed at the screen door, trying to open it. The screen bowed,
making him worry it would break. It didn't. And he managed to get it
swung to the side enough for him to stand sock-footed on a pie wedge
of cleared porch and look down at the south-facing steps. It was a slope.
He couldn't see steps at all. The slope went about halfway down and
then leveled out into a vast plain of white. The bear he'd placed there
was only a slight hump. He couldn't see anything but trees and snow.
The chairs around the fire pit to the south of the cabin were only bigger
humps.

"Oh my....," he said to the early morning air, and his words turned
into a white fog about his face.

Wyatt glanced up at the porch light again.

"The power lines must be down," he said aloud and was once more
enveloped in white fog.

A sudden realization came to him then. The famous "ridge" everyone
at Camp talked about. The one south of Sanctuary. It had fucked with
the weather patterns before. He remembered a Memorial Day event at
Camp where it had rained nonstop for four days, the only letup being a
fine mist, but usually a constant downfall. The weathermen had forecast
a few hours of possibly severe thunderstorms on Friday. The so-called
"ridge" had trapped the weather formation and kept it raining the whole
holiday weekend. It had been miserable, saved only by the parties and
shows under the pavilion up top.

White, white, white, as far as he could see. There was not so much
as a bird hopping across the surface. No little paw prints of squirrels or
raccoons or other woodland creatures. It made him feel lonely again.
Surreal. For a moment he wondered if he was still asleep and dreaming
a new dream.

That made him remember his dream with Hodor, and it was then
he realized he had come in his sleep. He could feel where his semen had
dried on his belly and in his pubic hair, and he scratched at it. That was
when he heard the mild mechanical roar coming from the south. It was
either a snow blower or.... *A generator*, Wyatt thought. Gryphon and
Saff must have a generator. They would have lights and heat and...

Shit! I'm letting my heat out!

He went inside and closed the door, then fumbled to the stove and
put several logs inside. The very hot coals seemed to attack them with

hunger, and the wood caught while he watched. He left the door open long enough to find a candle and then made a makeshift match with a twig and lit it. He had no idea where his lighter was. That's what happened when you didn't smoke. You misplaced lighters.

He held the glass pillar candle high and walked around the room, trying to spot more candles. He found a few stubby votives, burned mostly up, and two half-used taper candles on a window ledge, and that was it.

I guess I should have paid attention to Other Person Lady, he thought. *And brought the candles that Ut-naps-ism—*

"*Utnapishtim!*" came the echo of the old lady's voice.

—the candles that Oot-nah-pish-tim told me to bring. Green candles and not the purple ones, of course. Because Utnapishtim said...

"*He says that* forest *green are best.*"

Right now he just wished he'd brought any color of candles.

Then he discovered that even with all the shades pulled, there really was quite a bit of light in the cabin. It wouldn't help tonight, but that was okay.

Wyatt's stomach rumbled. He was hungry.

But there was no power. So no microwaved eggs this morning.

His eyes went to the little wood-burning stove. Of course, he thought. And there were a few frying pans. Buried in the snow on the porch maybe, but…. But no, there they were hanging on the wall over the stove. Had he brought Pam? Yes. He knew he had. Butter flavored.

Hey. This could be fun if he let it! He fought back the feeling of loneliness and the sneaking wave of melancholy that threatened. No! What was Max always saying? It was okay to feel something, but he didn't have to let it control him. He would not let that feeling take him over. He would experience this to the full. Another adventure. After all, he wasn't in danger. He had heat. He had some light at least. He had food. He had food he didn't need to cook and a stove to cook the rest.

His iPod would last for hours, so he had music even if he couldn't blast his boom box. He had an emergency charger. Had bought one after Pride one year when his cell phone had run out. Howard hadn't remembered to ask about it, and Wyatt hadn't volunteered it for the Great Divide.

Wyatt smiled. It wasn't like he was trapped after all, right? Surely Gryphon would be using the Bobcat to clear the snow away. A day or so.

And hadn't he also said that when the lines had come down in the past, the longest Camp had been without power was a day or so?

No. He would make the best of it.

It really could be fun.

KEVIN WOKE up shivering. He sat up, the covers half falling off him, and shivered all the more. "Freezing!" he said aloud. He swung his big legs out of bed and reached for the light chain that he knew hung there, pulled it, and nothing happened. He tried again.

He knew right away what had happened.

"Fuck. No power!"

It didn't make any difference how good those space heaters were. Their ability to heat worked only as well as their access to electricity.

Maybe they had blown the circuit in the middle of the night? There was enough light coming in through the blinds that he could find his little LED flashlight. He always brought a flashlight to Camp and hadn't even thought about the fact that the cabins had electricity. Of course, they didn't now. His at least.

But there was the thought in his mind already, as he opened his door and went to the little closet in the foyer to check the fuse box, that this was no isolated thing. The camp's power lines must be down. And he was going to need heat.

Just as he confirmed his suspicion that the problem wasn't the fuse box and everything was in order there, there was a knock on the door that made him jump. When he peeked past the door-window's shade, he saw Gryphon standing there all bundled up. Gryphon waved a big gloved hand.

Kevin, conscious he was wearing only socks and his long underwear, opened the door partially. *I need to get dressed before I freeze!*

"Hey, Hodor…. Not sure if you've figured this out yet but—"

"—the power lines are down?" Kevin finished.

"Yup! And it is going to take me quite a while to deal with all this. We got somewhere over two feet last night. I'm thinking three."

"So much for the weather forecasters."

"Yeah, well, I've always thought the weatherman was a demon from the seventh pit of hell," Gryphon said with a laugh. "In the meantime I've cleared a path with my blower up to your cabin. I'm going to go as far as Wyatt's, because like it or not, he's going to have to share."

Kevin's stomach jumped. Share with Wyatt? But he wanted to be alone. "Didn't he want to be by himself? Maybe I should leave."

Gryphon shook his head. "No. You aren't getting it, are you? We are *snowed* in. At least for a couple days."

"Main road too," Kevin realized out loud. "Shit."

"Luckily some farmer will take care of it. He usually does. But for me to get the parking lot cleared and then a path down to the main road? That's going to take me most of the day at the very least. Luckily it stopped snowing. There's no call for more."

"Of course, there was no call for more than two or three inches," Kevin said with a smirk.

"Tell me about it!" Gryphon laughed. "But look, realistically I don't see you leaving before tomorrow. It's only thirty degrees out here. And Saff and I don't have room for you. Wyatt's going to have to share his cabin. He's got the wood-burning stove. I'm sure he can stay an extra day or two if he really needs to."

Kevin nodded. There really was no way for him to stay in this cabin. He nodded again. Looked north. *Wyatt.* His heart skipped a beat.

"Why don't you get ready," Gryphon said. "And I'll get back to work. I think I can clear us a path in under an hour. A narrow one anyway."

Which would be a lot of work. The man could be working on the hill out of Camp instead. "I can probably wade my way through," Kevin offered.

Gryphon shrugged. "But do you want to get your clothes covered in snow?"

"Not really," he admitted.

"Okay, then. I'll come back when I've got the path made."

"Thanks," said Kevin and then shut the door. *Now* he was freezing.

And as he got dressed he saw Wyatt in his mind's eye. Adorable little bear Wyatt.

Sorry, he thought. *I hope you don't mind too much.*

Especially because, as far as Kevin was concerned, *he* didn't mind one bit.

He could mourn Cauley another day.

CHAPTER TWENTY-FIVE

WYATT HEARD the snowblower getting closer and closer as he dressed and then made his breakfast. When the loud roaring shut off, he wasn't entirely surprised when he heard a knock on his door.

He looked through the window in the door to see Gryphon standing there. He'd had to open all the shades to let in light. It was a lovely light. The sun had risen in an amazingly blue sky.

Wyatt went to the door and opened it, then had to shield his eyes from all the light. The sun was reflecting off the snow, and he was momentarily blinded. There was a shadow in the shape of Gryphon floating before his eyes.

"Good morning, Wyatt."

"Morning, Gryph!" He grinned, blinking.

"I guess you've figured out the power lines are down."

"And we got a *little* bit more snow than we were supposed to get."

"*Supposed* to get!" Gryphon laughed. "I always get a chuckle out of *supposed* to get. Like someone ordered a specified amount and someone else messed up when what we get is different than what we're told."

Wyatt nodded, starting to get his vision back. "You think it was that ridge thing, whatever it is, that had something to do with it?"

"People call it 'the split,'" Gryphon said. "It used to be relied on more, but there is really little talk of it since a tornado went right through town in May of 2000. Since then even the locals brush off the term like an urban legend or something they read about in the *Onion*."

"Oh." He didn't even know what to say about that. So the ridge—*split*—was just an old wives' tale? Boy, did he feel dumb.

"And we're snowed in. Hope you've got some polar bear in you."

"As long as I have plenty of wood." Wyatt squinted and peeked over Gryphon's shoulder. "How snowed in are we?"

"I don't imagine anyone is getting out of here until at least tomorrow. That's if luck is with us."

Which wasn't bad. He had food. He had wood. He had at least some music, and it could last that long.

"But I have some possibly bad news for you."

Wyatt rubbed his eyes. "Bad news?" Bad news? As the wicked witch said in *The Wiz*, he didn't want "no bad news."

"You know that Kevin Owens is staying down in North One—"

"Who?" *Kevin Owens? Who the hell was that?*

Gryphon rolled his eyes. "Sorry. *Hodor*."

"*Hodor*." Wyatt's heart jumped. "Is he okay?"

"Mostly. But he's going to be a Hodorsicle soon."

"Oh…. *Oh!*" Of course. Gods. He hadn't even thought about the fact that Hodor wouldn't have heat. The poor man must be freezing. He couldn't stay in his cabin. For one second Wyatt's heart sank. There went his determination to stay secluded. But the feeling lasted only a second. "How stupid…."

"I'm sorry?" asked Gryphon, a strange look on his face.

"*Me!*" Wyatt sighed. "*I'm* stupid. Fuck! I didn't even think of what poor Hodor must be going through." Which wasn't entirely true, was it? He'd thought about him all night. And just now he was remembering the dream…. He closed his eyes for a second. Saw bear feet. Felt that mouth on his.

"Look, I know you reserved this cabin, and you were wanting to be alone, but Kevin can't stay in N1 without heat—"

Wyatt jerked and opened his eyes. "No, of course not." He glanced to his left. Out the window. Toward Hodor's cabin. His heart began to speed up. Hodor. Hodor needed to stay here? With him? How crazy! What were the odds that it would snow so heavily—when every weather forecaster had predicted mere inches of snow? That the power lines would go down, and they would be forced to share a cabin. He glanced at the double bed—the only *real* bed in Camp. All the others were those cot things. Narrow. Plastic-covered mats.

He pictured himself and Hodor in that bed. Snuggling would keep them warm.

"He doesn't have to sleep *with* you, if that's what you're worried about," Gryphon said.

Wyatt blushed.

"D-do you guys need help getting his stuff here?"

Gryphon smiled. "No, thanks, Wyatt. You don't need to do that. And Camp will make this cockup up to you. I'll give you a free weekend sometime. In fact, we're not charging you for this week."

Wyatt shook his head. "No. That's not fair. I'm using your wood and—"

Gryphon threw back his head and laughed. "Don't know if you noticed, but we live in a forest here, Wyatt. There's plenty of wood. It's decided. Don't argue with me. And"—he raised an eyebrow—"you can use our toilet anytime you want."

Wyatt smiled. "Thanks." *That* he wouldn't argue with. "Now, really. Could you guys use my help?"

Gryphon shrugged. "It couldn't hurt."

KEVIN WAS getting cold. He was surprised how fast. He was fully dressed, wearing a coat, and had a blanket wrapped around him. He needed to get warm. But the whole idea of how that was going to happen was making his stomach get all tied in knots. Getting warm meant staying with Wyatt. And what would that mean?

When he heard the knock on the door, he practically leapt to his feet, nearly getting tangled in the blankets and falling on his face in the process.

And who should be standing on his porch with Gryphon? Well, Wyatt. Looking adorable.

Stop acting like a teenager!

He opened the door.

"You ready?" Gryphon asked.

"S-sure," Kevin said, stumbling over that one word. He turned to Wyatt. "Hey, Little Bear. Thanks for this. I know you were on some kind of sabbatical or something…."

"Don't be silly," Wyatt said. "I can't let you freeze to death."

Wyatt was wearing a big thick coat that seemed almost ridiculously large on him, along with a big hat that was—yes! (Kevin smiled)—a teddy bear's head. Its eyes were just above Wyatt's own, the ears where Wyatt's would be, and it even included a scarf with big bear paws on the end. He couldn't help but smile. It was all so… *Wyatt.*

Quite suddenly he wanted to kiss him.

Don't be silly.

But he couldn't help it.

"So let's get your stuff over to my cabin," Wyatt said. "It's freezing *balls*."

Kevin laughed nervously. "Okay."

So they gathered his belongings. He'd gotten most of it ready except for the blankets, and between the three of them, they got it all in one trip. And oh, how nice and warm Wyatt's cabin was!

"You two going to be all right?" Gryphon asked.

"W-we'll be fine," Kevin replied.

"Okay, then." He smiled. "I'll check in on you both later."

"Sounds good," Wyatt said.

And then they were alone.

CHAPTER TWENTY-SIX

"WOULD YOU like some breakfast?" Wyatt asked Hodor, because he had to say *some*thing. For some reason he was incredibly nervous. "I just made some eggs a bit ago, and cleaning the pan is going to be a bitch without water, so why don't I just make a few more? I got 'em."

"Sure," Hodor said. "If it won't be any trouble."

"No trouble at all!" Wyatt turned around and practically dashed over to a big blue cooler in the corner of the room. He pulled out the half container of eggs and a plastic bag of preshredded cheese. "Want some cheese with yours?"

"Sounds good." Kevin sat down on the end of the big bed. Then jumped up. Moved over to one of the other cot-like beds. *Prison beds.* Then: "I-I can sleep on this one."

You could sleep with me, Wyatt almost said. He said, "Okay," instead and then turned to the stove.

Gods! His heart was pounding. Why? It wasn't like he'd never been alone with a man before. A gay man. A hulking, hot man. So why was he acting silly? Wearing that stupid hat! Offering to make breakfast. And what had he almost done? Told Hodor that there was room in the bed for both of them? He looked at Hodor again—all six foot something, and those huge arms and that giant chest and those sexy eyes (*oh those eyes*)—and he wondered if there *would* be room for the both of them. They would have to get *awfully* close.

Wyatt shivered.

Okay. Now you're being silly.

Why was he acting like this?

Then he looked up at Hodor, and he knew why.

Gods. He is so damned sexy. So sweet. And.... His eyes widened.

"Hodor! You talked."

Hodor smiled (was he blushing?).

"I *do* talk, Little Bear."

And then for some reason, Wyatt realized he didn't want to be called by his Faerie name. He wanted this man to use his real name. "Wyatt," he said. "That's my name."

Hodor nodded. "I know. I've always liked your real name."

You have? "You have?" *He likes my real name?*

"But your Faerie name is perfect too. *Such* a sweet little bear.... *Just* right."

Wyatt blushed. "Gosh, Hodor—"

"Kevin."

Huh? "What?"

"Kevin. My name. It's Kevin. Wyatt... I would really like it if you would call me Kevin."

Oh! "Of course. Gryphon told me. I never knew." Kevin. Gosh. He hoped in his airheadedness he didn't forget his real name. Kevin.

"It's on my registration," *Kevin* said. "You usually meet me at the gate at Festival. I figured you knew."

"I guess I didn't look at that part. The off-site registrar puts our camp names up on the top." He paused. "You're talking," Wyatt said. "I think I've heard you say more in the last few minutes than I've ever heard you say."

The big man shrugged. *Kevin.* His name was Kevin. Wyatt smiled foolishly. He *looked* like a Kevin, didn't he?

How does a Kevin look?

Big and tall and hunky. That's how. To Wyatt's surprise he felt a stirring in his jeans.

"I *do* talk. Just not much. To people I know. And I know you."

He has such a nice voice.

Do something. You're staring!

"I was going to make you breakfast." Wyatt went back to the half carton of eggs. "I only have two left. Is two okay?"

"You really don't have to make me breakfast."

His name is Kevin. This wasn't going to be easy. He'd called the man Hodor for as long as he could remember. Six years. Seven? Eight?

"Don't give me the last of your food."

Wyatt gave a little chuckle. "It's not the last of my food. Don't worry. Scrambled okay? I don't guarantee I won't break the yolks if you want them fried. Sit at the table."

"Scrambled is fine," Kevin told him. "I like scrambled eggs. This is awfully nice of you, Wyatt."

For some reason Wyatt trembled. It was the way Kevin said his name. The way it rolled off his tongue. Strong. "It-it's no trouble," he managed. "It's nice making breakfast for a man again. Although it's the first time I didn't sleep with him first." He cringed. What the fuck had made him say *that*? "Sorry."

"Sorry?" Kevin asked.

"Ah... sorry I don't have any coffee," he replied, hoping it was recovery enough. "But I can give you a cola. It's not Coke, only Sam's. But it's got caffeine."

"Sure. That's fine."

Wyatt got it for him and then went back to making the eggs. He grabbed the can of Pam and began spraying again. "I hope butter-flavored spray is enough. I didn't bring any butter or anything...."

"Wyatt, I appreciate anything. And I'll make dinner, okay?"

"It's a deal," Wyatt replied. "Now sit at the table."

Kevin did as bid, and Wyatt flipped a slice of bread in the pan. It didn't take long to brown, and a moment later Wyatt was placing a paper plate with steaming cheesy scrambled eggs and a piece of toast in front of his guest. "Want two pieces?"

"One slice is enough," Kevin answered and dug in. Suddenly he was wolfing the food down. "These are great."

He scraped up the last bites. Looked at Wyatt. Wyatt found himself smiling. "You really like?" he asked.

Kevin nodded enthusiastically. "The eggs really are delicious."

And then they were staring at each other for what seemed like forever. There were all kinds of things swimming in Kevin's eyes. Wyatt didn't know whether to be turned on or go racing out the door into the snow.

Then suddenly: "So, Wyatt.... What do you think about this snow? Is this a son of a bitch or not?"

Weather? They were going to talk about the weather? He glanced out the window and realized it really wasn't such a stupid thing to talk about. "Yeah. Pretty crazy. Although I don't think Snedronningen would appreciate being called a bitch."

"Who is... Snod-rah—"

"Snid-ronn-gen," Wyatt corrected. "I think. Hope *I* don't piss her off mispronouncing her name. She's the Snow Queen. From Hans Christian Andersen's story."

Kevin smiled. "You would know that, Wyatt."

Wyatt's face heated. Was Kevin making fun of him?

"It's part of what I like so much about you."

Now Wyatt smiled. He pulled out a chair and sat next to Kevin. "I like that kind of stuff."

"Me too," Kevin said.

"The movie… *Frozen*? It's nothing like the story. She's a pretty bad bi…. Oops." He laughed and blushed. "I almost said 'bitch.'"

"So she doesn't sing that song that was so popular a while back?" Kevin asked.

Wyatt shook his head. "But I have to admit, I like the Disney version. The original story is kind of dark."

"Unhappy ending?" Kevin rested his chin in his upraised palm. "Like 'The Little Mermaid'?"

Wyatt laughed. "Oh my gosh, no! There's a happy ending. But *you* know that 'The Little Mermaid' had an unhappy ending!"

"I like that kind of stuff," Kevin said.

Wyatt leaned his elbow on the table and dropped his chin in his own hand. It put their faces pretty close together. Close enough that he could see how beautiful Kevin's eyes really were. He'd thought they were brown. But up close? They were hazel. With a bit of amber and dark honey. Swirled. Gorgeous.

Gods! I'm staring!

He leaned back. "Yeah! What about that snow!"

"A whole hell of a lot more than we were supposed to get."

Which reminded Wyatt of something Gryphon had said. "Gryphon had something to say about that. He says he's always thought it was funny when we say we're *supposed* to get a certain kind of weather."

Kevin nodded. "Right! Like *who* is it who says we're *supposed* to get a kind of weather! Who really knows? Except maybe God."

"Or Snedronningen?" Wyatt offered.

"Or *her*." Kevin grinned. "Blessed be her name."

Wyatt laughed again.

"We don't want to piss her off," Kevin said, brow furrowed but eyes twinkling.

"*Never*," Wyatt replied and looked once more into Kevin's handsome face. Who knew the guy was so sweet? "I like talkie-Kevin."

"Talkie-Kevin?" his companion asked.

Wyatt nodded. Actually giggled. "*Talk*ie-Kevin. The one who says more than 'Hodor.'"

Kevin shrugged. "Like I said, I talk."

"Then why don't you do more of it?"

"I don't know. I've just never been comfortable talking around people."

"You're talking to me," Wyatt said.

"I guess I'm comfortable with you, Wyatt," Kevin said. And a blush crept over his cheeks.

Wyatt's heart skipped a beat.

He cleared his throat.

What did he say to that?

Kevin stood up and walked over to the door, pushed the lacy curtain aside and looked out. "Gryphon thinks we got close to three feet. That we won't be able to get out of here until at least tomorrow. I wonder if even then. If they had more than one Bobcat, I'd help him plow the snow."

Which quite suddenly reminded Wyatt of something else. He sighed. "Well, crap. It sure did mess up my plans...."

Kevin turned, a sad expression flashing across his face. At least Wyatt thought he'd seen it. "Because you wanted to be alone?"

"I wanted to work a ritual up at Pax Place. I had it all set up and everything. Now I can't get there."

"At least for a couple days," Kevin said.

Wyatt sighed again. It was part of why he'd come here. That and to be alone. He wasn't going to do either now.

"What kind of ritual?" Kevin asked.

"It doesn't matter," Wyatt replied. It wasn't something he was in the mood to answer right now.

"You sure?"

"Sure," Wyatt said with a nod.

Kevin looked around the room. "I think I'll make my bed."

For some reason that sent a little pang to Wyatt's heart. He glanced at his own bed. Big enough for the two of them? If they got close?

Kevin looked at the bunk beds on one wall and then the two by the door. "Think I'll take one of these. Last thing I want to do is wake up in the night to take a piss and bonk my head on the upper bunk."

Wyatt looked at the little beds. Could Kevin even fit? "They're awfully small. Won't your feet stick out off the end?"

"They're the same size as the bunk beds."

"We could switch," Wyatt said. "You can have my bed."

Kevin shook his head, a sharp expression on his face. "No. Absolutely not. I've already taken your cabin. I'm not taking your bed."

I could share, Wyatt thought. In fact, he knew he would like that. Sex or no sex, it had been a long time since a man had shared his bed. He missed it. A lot.

But he didn't offer. Kevin was already making the bed.

Wyatt did help, though. It was the least he could do.

It was while doing so that Wyatt kicked something under the bed. "What was that?" he wondered aloud.

Kevin crouched to look. "Well, look at this!" He pulled out some boxes and put them on the bed. "Games."

And games they were. Monopoly. Checkers. Scrabble. Uno. Yahtzee. Sorry! Even Chutes and Ladders.

"How cool is this? We won't get bored!"

Kevin was grinning like a kid. Wyatt, however, immediately felt himself begin to sweat. "I… I don't know."

Kevin looked up, and after a second his smile turned into a frown. He looked concerned. "Wyatt?"

Wyatt's mind was filled with memories of Howard and the board games they used to play. How seriously Howard took it. How competitive he was. How mean he could get. Slaughtering his opponents instead of just playing to win.

"Wyatt?"

The look of concern on Kevin's face!

"I—I'm not very good at games," he said, omitting the total truth of the situation. He'd loved games growing up. He and his sister and mother used to play by the hour. And every Christmas both he and Wendy each got a new game. For them it was for the fun, not the winning. He also suspected his mother let them win many a time.

"Who cares?" Kevin said. "It's not about winning. It's about having fun."

And just like that Wyatt's sudden fear evaporated. "Really?"

Kevin nodded. "Give it a try?"

"I—I guess so," Wyatt said, a long-lost tingle starting in his tummy. Of how much fun he used to have with games.

"Monopoly?"

"I'm probably more of a Candy Land kind of guy," Wyatt answered.

The smile that spread over Kevin's face was almost radiant. "Candy Land it is!"

Wyatt smiled. "R-really?"

"What game is more fun than that?"

To Wyatt's surprise, he saw that Kevin meant it.

And so play they did.

CHAPTER TWENTY-SEVEN

KEVIN COULDN'T remember when he'd last had so much fun. He'd had to brush up on the rules of Candy Land. It had been about a zillion years since he'd played it last. Wyatt knew the rules, though, which really shouldn't have been a surprise. And he was smiling. A smiling Wyatt was a simply adorable Wyatt.

Why would anyone want to see Wyatt do anything but smile?

What pleasure could Howard have gotten from making this sweet little man do anything else?

He was startled when he quite abruptly realized that this was the first real one-on-one time he'd ever had with the little bear. Getting signed in at the front gate at Camp during Men's Festival didn't count (especially when gatekeepers always had a partner), and that drunken pass Wyatt had made at him one night most certainly didn't either.

It did hurt Kevin's feelings a bit that Wyatt didn't remember the last time they'd played a game together. Of course, that was about seven years ago, and there had been a bunch of them sitting around that dining room table playing the card game Magic: The Gathering. And Wyatt was being the social butterfly and entertaining everyone with his jokes and antics, while Kevin had only had eyes for Wyatt. Thinking back on that day, Kevin wondered if that was when his little crush on him had begun.

I don't have a crush on Wyatt!

But he'd no sooner thought the denial when he understood he was lying to himself.

Wyatt had been adorable that day too. His face had grown dark with a thick shadow over the week, and he was wearing this big necklace of clunky carved bears and a sarong so short his balls were showing. Not that Kevin had been looking, per se, but a card dropped on the floor had to be picked up, after all. More than once even. Wyatt's thick brows had been all bunched together, the tip of his pink tongue peeking out from the corner of his mouth as he concentrated, trying to decide what card to play next. It had been fun that day too. Howard hadn't been playing, but then it all seemed to fall apart when the big man did join them.

For just a moment Kevin was brought up short as he semiremembered that day. He had to stifle a gasp. Had Wyatt's lover been rushing him? Pushing him? God! Yes. And he'd slaughtered Wyatt, hadn't he? He'd destroyed Wyatt's hand with about twenty points in Fireball damage when it would have only taken about three points to take him out of the game. Humiliating.

And then Kevin *was* remembering that day, even if he couldn't quite remember the rules of that game anymore or the exact sequence of cards played. Wyatt had been clearly shocked when Howard threw down the cards that inflicted the damage. For a moment Kevin thought Wyatt was going to cry and then—clear as a bell—he remembered what Howard, Wyatt's "lover," had said that day.

"Oh no! Is the wittle bear-wah gonna cwy?"

And then the expressions that had flashed across Wyatt's face— all very fast—panic and hurt and embarrassment and maybe anger but ending with the magnificent (if not completely believable) smile that he had chosen to let win.

Kevin remembered Howard's words, and he almost broke out into a cold sweat because *he'd* heard words like those himself once upon a time, hadn't he?

"Oh, are you going to cry now, Kevie?"

…and…

"For Christ's *sake, Kevin! Can't you fucking* shut up *for just* one *single solitary* goddamned *second?"*

…and of course…

"Children should be seen and not heard. And preferably not seen."

That moment, that day, sitting at that long table in the dining hall across from Wyatt, filled Kevin's mind.

That's when I fell in love with him.

What?

Fell in love?

Or at least got my crush.

Kevin came back to the real world then because Wyatt was asking Kevin if he was okay, and he found himself sitting across another table from Wyatt, Candy Land spread out between them.

"I'm fine," he said. "Sorry. Woolgathering."

And he understood clearly then why Wyatt hadn't wanted to play any games.

Those voices. Wyatt had heard voices asking him if he was going to cry. Or expecting Kevin to hit him with twenty points of Fireball damage—or whatever Candy Land's equivalent was.

But now?

Now Wyatt was smiling. It looked genuine. He seemed to be having fun.

And that made Kevin very happy.

But there was one thing Kevin *didn't* do. He didn't tell Wyatt, "I know *just* how you feel." Because he *didn't* know *just* how Wyatt felt. Was there anything worse than someone telling you they knew *just* how you felt?

Echoes from the memorial service….

"Oh, Kevin. I'm sorry about Cauley. Be strong."

"He's in a better place."

Except Cauley didn't believe in "other places."

"He did what he came here to do, and it was his time to go."

Maybe. But Cauley wouldn't have thought so.

"I understand just exactly what you're going through."

But they didn't!

And he really didn't know Wyatt at all, did he?

Wyatt won the first game, and Kevin could have easily beat him the second time, but instead he let the little bear win. Somehow he thought it was important. Wyatt gave him one or two suspicious looks, but Kevin did his best to return an expression of pure innocence.

They advanced to Chutes and Ladders after that, and just as Kevin was convincing Wyatt that they could progress to Sorry! there was a knock on the door.

It was Saffron, and she was inviting them both to lunch. And it was delicious. A big pot of soup. Chicken noodle. And of course it was homemade. Saffron didn't do anything else.

After that Kevin offered to take a shift with the plow, but Gryphon turned him down.

"It's my job, Hodor."

"Call me Kevin, okay? Please."

Gryphon smiled and Saffron gave a laugh and shook her head. "So different."

"Different?" Kevin asked.

"Most people who come here? They want to leave their 'real' names behind. It's not just you Men's Festival people with your Faerie names."

Kevin nodded. Yes. He knew that, didn't he?

"And how many of them want to be called Raven?" Wyatt asked.

Saffron gave a pursed smile. "As many as want to be," she said. "As well as Phoenix and Cat and—"

"Don't forget Griffon," Gryphon said. "Of course, I spell mine differently."

"Because *no*body does that either," Saffron said.

They all laughed.

"You know, it's almost always the new pagans," Wyatt said. "I wanted to go by Ursa! I had no idea there were *hundreds* of Ursas. I was so naïve. Thankfully a few people clued me in. What we need is someone in charge of all of that. Registering names, you know? Warning them that they're picking a name a thousand other people already chose."

Saffron leaned forward on the table and clasped her hands together. "But why? What difference does it make? So they want to be called Merlin or Morgan? Brigid or Morgana? Who cares? Don't you think those gods, those archetypes, are happy to inspire a thousand-thousand people? Look how many Jesúses there are. How many Marys. Marías. Johns. My family is Jewish, so I grew up knowing several boys named Moses, and there were some Jacobs and Isaacs as well. I knew at least two men named Ram when I was in college. How many Mohammads do you think are out there? There is a lady who comes here who kept her real name. It's Tara, and she was given that name by her Buddhist parents. I dated a man who went by Tenzin, the fourteenth Dalai Lama. So what's wrong with wanting to name yourself Thor or Athena? Why can't there be a hundred Phoenixes? Why not a thousand Ravens?"

It was food for thought indeed.

Wyatt had certainly gotten very quiet. A silent Wyatt wasn't anything Kevin was used to. In fact, he looked a little stung. He wanted to reach and lay his hand on Wyatt's, but balked at the idea. How would that look?

"How did you choose your name, Kevin?" Saffron asked then. "Your Hodor name that is. Isn't he a character from *Game of Thrones*? Big hulking man? Mentally challenged. Can't talk except to say his name? That doesn't seem like you."

"Somebody gave me the name," Kevin replied, trying to recall exactly who it was. "I don't remember. We were all sitting on the big raft in the lake one night and I was being quiet as usual, and they started talking about the books—this was before the series even started—and somebody said I reminded them of Hodor because I don't talk much…."

"But you're talking now," Gryphon said. "You have since you got here."

Kevin shrugged, suddenly self-conscious.

"Maybe you're comfortable here?" Saffron offered. "I hope you're comfortable here."

Kevin looked around the table. At Gryphon. Saffron. And… Wyatt, who finally seemed to have come back from wherever he went, eyes sparkling in the way only his could. "I guess I am." A smile tugged at the corners of Kevin's mouth. He nodded. "I know I am."

After lunch, Kevin insisted that he take at least an hour shift on the plow. He liked the work. In New York he didn't even have to shovel the sidewalk, of course. Keeping his condo clean, and his workouts at Club Fitness, were about the only physical exertion in his life.

The air was crisp but not terribly cold. It gave him a little alone time, and Wyatt too. Except for the muffled roar of the jenny that was providing Gryphon and Saffron with power, and the little Bobcat, there was no other noise at all. How many hundreds of hours had he used a snowplow like this to clear his parents' driveway? Most kids thought it was the worst chore in the world, but it got him away from the yelling. The silence had become his only true friend. Like in that song he loved so much.

When they stop fighting to turn out the lights
I pretend I'm already sleeping
After the violence alone in the silence
Just me and the secret I'm keeping

But then…

But then Kevin couldn't stop thinking about Wyatt. What was the little bear doing? What was he up to? He couldn't blast his music—not if he wanted his iPod to last.

Kevin finished the parking lot by the main hall and dining room. Gryphon had been focusing on the huge hill that went down to the main gate, and that was a good thing. The hill was mostly gravel and it was steep, and Kevin had no experience with anything like that. His grandparents' little farm (where he'd spent Christmas breaks when he was a boy, and the only reason he'd had any kind of traditional holiday) had been as flat as Kansas could be. He would leave the hill to more practiced hands.

And he wanted to see Wyatt.

He wanted to talk to Wyatt.

He wanted to see if he could get him to smile again because that made his pulse quicken (as well as a few other things, dammit!).

They could play Sorry! That was a fun game. Play some music. They both had their iPods after all, and he had a charger, and he was sure that Gryphon and Saffron would be happy to let them charge their devices. He could play Wyatt some of his favorite songs. He wouldn't blast them like Wyatt's boom box, but it would give them something to listen to and help calm his nerves. Wyatt gave him goose bumps. The good kind. And music would keep Kevin from blurting out something stupid. Fears of such occurrences were another reason he preferred to keep his talking to a minimum. But that wouldn't really work today, would it? With only the two of them? He couldn't just sit in the background and let others do the talking.

But then he got an idea. It would take some time, but it was something he wanted to at least start.

So he went to Saffron—Gryphon was halfway down the hill in the Bobcat—and asked if he could use the snowblower. Gryphon had made a path only a few feet north of "their" cabin and stopped. It would have to go a good bit farther. Of course she said yes. She even insisted on topping it off with fuel, despite his objections.

"I can do it."

"Posh," she'd said, and the deed was done before he could say much else.

So he took the blower to where Gryphon had stopped and started it up and began clearing the snow past North Four. He was worried that Wyatt might stick his head out the door and ask what he was doing, and he didn't want him to do that. Not yet.

He did grow more and more conscious of how long he was leaving Wyatt all by himself, though. And while he knew Wyatt had come here to be alone, mightn't he wonder what was taking Kevin so long? Or was he happy to have this time alone?

Kevin hoped not.

Because he was growing more and more anxious to be back with his little bear and...

Your little bear?

He is hardly your *little bear.*

Oh shut the fuck up!

At least parts of the path north were easier to handle. There were a lot of trees, of course, and their overhanging branches had helped some to deflect the depth of the snow. He was beginning to get really cold and longed for the warmth of the cabin, but he was so close to his goal. Just a little farther?

Kevin reached North Five (he'd often wondered why the cabin was so far from North Four. A cabin could have easily been built between them. Maybe there had been a cabin there once upon a time?) and glanced off to his left. It was hard to tell, but he was looking for where the road took a decided sharp turn to the right and—yes—he saw he had reached that bend he was looking for.

He was going to do it.

Kevin pushed the snowblower down the steep embankment to the road and then made his way to the little path that cut into the dense trees there. It was tougher going on the road—the snow there was the deepest yet—but when he finally got to where he was going, what he saw made him laugh with joy.

Perfect.

Absolutely perfect!

But now it was time to get the hell back to Wyatt. He would be wondering what was taking so long. Kevin had said he would be back in an hour, and he knew he'd been gone at least twice that long.

When he got back to the cabin, though, what he found stopped him in his tracks.

Wyatt looked terrible.

He pulled off his hat. "Wyatt?" he asked, concerned. "Are you okay?"

"Oh, Kevin!" Wyatt looked like he was going to cry. "Is Howard right? Am I a total turd? Was the only reason anyone had anything to do with me was because I was with him?"

Kevin jerked. What? What was he saying? Where had this come from?

"Wyatt, sweetheart. What are you talking about?" He pulled off his gloves and laid them on the table, stepped toward Wyatt. "What's wrong?"

"I can't get what Saffron said out of my head."

Kevin had to think. What Saffron said? What *hadn't* Saffron said? He took another step, rubbed his hands together, resisted the urge to lay them on Wyatt. "Wyatt? What… what did she say that's upset you?"

"The part about the names, Kevin. About how people should be able to go by any name they want."

Kevin shook his head. He wasn't sure what this was about. "What about it, Wyatt?"

"I was being so *negative*."

Negative? Wyatt? Negative?

"What do you mean?" he asked, unable to keep from placing his hands on Wyatt's shoulders.

"I was being so judgmental. Making fun of people for the Craft name they wanted to use…." Wyatt's eyes were glassy, wet. It was obvious he was trying to prevent himself from crying.

"Wyatt. Sweetness."

Sweetness? Did you just call him "sweetness"?

Kevin took a deep breath. "You weren't making fun. You were just pointing out something a little amusing in the pagan community. We have to laugh at ourselves."

"But I wasn't laughing at myself. I was laughing at other people."

Kevin shook his head. "I can't imagine you laughing at *any*one."

Wyatt pulled away, turned his back. "But I do. *I do*. Howard used to think it was funny, and I liked to make him laugh. It was better than the yelling. But what I was doing. I wasn't *thinking*…."

Kevin didn't know what to do. What to say. He never did. That's why he'd hired Theresa Nash to do the public and presentation speaking *for* him. And *this* not knowing what to say was another reason to remain silent and let others do that talking. But today there was no one else!

He took another deep breath. What would Malcolm Kane say?

"I don't know what you were thinking, Wyatt. But if there is anything I know about you, Little Bear, it's that there isn't a malicious bone in your body."

Wyatt spun around, his face quite wet now. His tears had been so silent! "Not thinking is my problem. Maybe if I *thought*—used my *brain*—Howard would never have left me."

Maybe if you had "thought," you would have left him years ago, Kevin wanted to say. But he didn't. Instead: "Wyatt, just because you were a little insensitive about the magic names people pick doesn't mean you are an unthinking person. I mean, we've all joked about—"

"It's not just that," Wyatt all but spat. "I say things all the fucking time without thinking about it! Like the day I found out Howard was HIV positive—"

Kevin's eyebrows shot up. He couldn't help it. *Howard was HIV positive? Dear God!* Did that mean…?

"—I was talking to Kitty, and she was saying that the guy who manages the gas station next to the store was a dickhead—"

Kevin couldn't even wonder who the hell "Kitty" was. All he heard was "HIV positive." Was Wyatt…?

"—and *I* said that she should say 'vagina' and not 'dickhead' because penises were *good* things, and then Katherine pulled me into her office and gave me this lecture about how I shouldn't use the word 'vagina' in a negative way and I said—"

"Wyatt!" Now Kevin did grab Wyatt's shoulders. Hard.

"Ow!" Wyatt looked up into Kevin's face. "I didn't mean anything bad when I said it, Kevin! I was just trying to be funny. People use the word 'dick' to be a *bad* thing! So why *isn't* it okay to—"

"Wyatt! My God! Howard is HIV positive?"

Wyatt stopped. Opened his mouth. Shut it. He gave a slight nod, and then the tears began to flow down his sweet, round, beard-shadowed face. "Y-yes."

No! No no no no no! Had that *bastard* infected Wyatt? "And you? God. You?"

"What about me?" Wyatt asked.

"Did he infect *you*?" God! Oh God! He wanted to scream. Could someone *else* he loved have HIV?

Wyatt's eyes were huge and round and so very dark. Eyes that had always struck Kevin as beautiful now looked like holes into the abyss.

"N-no. I'm okay."

Okay? Okay? Did he mean…?

Wyatt shook his head. "I'm okay. He—Howard—he didn't infect me."

The relief was immense. Like nothing Kevin could remember in years. He pulled Wyatt into his arms, trying to pull him into his bones, his soul, and he did everything he could not to cry himself. He didn't succeed. Crying. Him. What would Theresa think?

But all *he* could think was *Thank God, thank God, thank God!* Hadn't Wyatt been through enough? Hadn't Howard already put him through enough, then to give him a final "gift" of HIV? Thank *God* Wyatt was okay. But then the worry came rising back to the surface like a rocket launching from a hidden submarine.

"A-are you sure?" he asked, letting go of Wyatt just enough so he could see his face. HIV! *Fucking* HIV! Hadn't the virus done enough?

Wyatt nodded again, his lower lip trembling. "Yes. I was tested. The guy there… he said enough time had passed since I was last sexual with Howard and—"

Kevin pulled Wyatt tight against him once more. He couldn't remember feeling like this. Discovering that Google wanted to purchase the apps he'd created—a couple of them he'd even thought of as silly— and had been willing to pay a hell of a lot for them hadn't brought him this much joy.

"K-Kevin" came Wyatt's muffled voice. "I can hardly breathe."

Kevin jerked and stepped back, if only by inches. "I—I'm sorry, dear."

"Dear?" Wyatt asked, that lower lip trembling again.

It was all Kevin could do to keep from kissing Wyatt. Wyatt's beautiful sweet mouth.

"You scared me, Wyatt. I thought that Howard had given you—"

"No." Wyatt stepped back. "And how do you know it wasn't me that gave it to *Howard*? How do you know it was him?"

He looked angry, and that was not what Kevin would have expected.

How did he know? He just *knew*. But could he say that? "I'm sorry, Wyatt. I wasn't thinking. I was just so relieved."

Wyatt turned away, walked over to his bed, and sat on the edge of the mattress. "Seems to be a lot of that going on. Me making crass comments on the names people choose for themselves. Me using the word 'vagina' to be a *bad* thing."

Kevin winced. Wyatt's comment hadn't hit him the first time. All he had heard was "HIV positive."

Boy! What would Theresa say if she'd heard Wyatt call someone a vagina? They would all have heard a lecture.

"Katherine said that women are made to feel bad about their bodies. About their… female stuff. That their… girl parts… were nasty and dirty. I didn't know that! All I knew was that I've heard straight guys wax poetic about them. I had a friend in high school go on for days about how beautiful he thought they were. It was listening to him go on and on about them that made me realize I *was* gay. He wasn't fooling. He was *serious*. He really did think they were *beautiful*! And I knew right then that was how I felt about penises. That *they* were beautiful, and not just hot. I liked dick and he liked vaginas. I mean, don't a lot of people like them? Vaginas? Rita Mae Brown loved them so much she wrote a book about it and called them 'rubyfruit jungles.' And didn't Georgia O'Keeffe paint her flowers to look like vaginas?"

Kevin fought the abrupt urge to laugh. He couldn't help it. Even in distress Wyatt was adorable.

"I've heard that wasn't really intentional," Kevin said. He'd seen an exhibit of her work at the Whitney Museum several years back, and he was sure that was part of what he heard while he was there.

Wyatt rolled his eyes. "Yeah! Sure! What*ever*! I may've not seen too many vajayjays up close, but I know one when I see one. And that's just what those paintings are!"

Now Kevin did laugh. He couldn't help it. One minute Wyatt was in tears because he thought he was an unthinking "turd," and now he was going on about Georgia O'Keeffe and vaginas. "The point, Wyatt, was that you didn't realize you were doing anything wrong."

"But shouldn't I have? Known?" Quite suddenly he was looking desperate again.

Kevin moved over to the bed and sat down next to Wyatt. "You probably don't spend much time talking about vaginas, Wyatt."

"…and I was watching this recent Margaret Cho special and she was talking about 'pussy' and doing this routine about gay men having to eat them for the first time in order to save the world, and it was *sooooo* funny and I was laughing *so* hard, and now all I can think of is that I'm some kind of misogynist and—"

"*Wyatt*!"

Wyatt jerked and looked up at him. Oh, those eyes!

"You are not a misogynist. I can't imagine you hating women. I can't imagine you hating anything."

Wyatt slumped. "You don't know me very well."

Ah, but I want to.

Now how to make Wyatt feel better?

"Wyatt, we can't help what we've done. We can only try and help what we are about to do." He was drawing from Malcolm Kane now (and again). "We can only do our best from day to day. And that is going to change each day. Yesterday's best will be different than today's best and tomorrow's. Whatever we do, we must simply try our best. You didn't know that there were women who were made to feel bad about their genitals."

"Margaret Cho sure doesn't seem to feel bad about hers," Wyatt said with comically wide eyes.

Kevin almost laughed again. But not now. Later. They could laugh about it later.

"Nevertheless, now you know. So now you know never to use the word 'vagina' as a bad thing. It doesn't matter that people use 'dick' as a bad thing. We should always keep other people's feelings in mind whenever we can. We can't monitor every single word we say. We can't know how everyone feels."

Wyatt gave a little sigh and looked at him with those big brown eyes again. At least now they didn't look quite so sad.

"And people *shouldn't* use the word 'dick' as a bad thing either," Kevin said.

"That's what Katherine said. She said, 'You've never heard *me* use that word, have you?'"

"I'm glad she did. It sounds like she was trying to help you."

Wyatt nodded. "She's like my mom." There was a flash in Wyatt's dark eyes, but it was gone as fast as it was there. "I love her so much."

"Then I'm glad you have her in your life." In fact, Kevin found he was a little jealous about that. "You know, 'dick' isn't the only word we shouldn't use in a bad way. What about 'junk'? I hate that people use that word! Is that what they think of their genitals?"

"Yeah!" Wyatt cried. "I sure don't call my stuff 'junk'!"

"Me either. Even if I'm not all that big when—"

Wyatt's eyes went big. "Not big? Your cock and balls are *fabu*lous!"

Kevin felt his face heat up. Wyatt had been looking at his…?

"I mean, your balls are so big! And your dick, it might not be flopping around like Rat Bastard's, but it's so thick. And *that's* when it's *soft*. I can't tell you how many times I've wondered how big it—" He stopped, and then it was his turn to blush.

It only made Kevin blush all the harder. Wyatt had wondered about his hard-on?

Wyatt looked away. "I'm the one with the tiny dick," he whispered.

Tiny dick? "Wyatt…. You don't have a tiny dick."

Wyatt nodded. "Yes, I do. Howard said that was one of the reasons he needed to be with other men. That mine wasn't big enough to satisfy him."

"Howard is a fucking fool," Kevin said with distaste. God, he couldn't stand that man! Imagine, making your lover—your *lover*—feel bad about his most personal part. "Wyatt, I think your penis is perfect. Perfect for you. You're not a big guy."

Wyatt looked back. His cheeks, which had gone from red to pink, heated up again. "You think my penis is perfect?" His voice cracked at the end.

"I think all of you is perfect," Kevin replied, and once more his face grew hot. How had they gotten into this conversation? And he did think Wyatt's penis was perfect. His testicles weren't small by any means, one always riding up higher than the other, especially when he came out of the lake when the water was cold. His penis, stout and riding up over his balls, was cut, and he had seen Wyatt with an erection. In the shower house for one, when men were rousting about late at night, catcalling and tickling each other and playing grabass (and more). "And yes. You have a very nice penis."

"You've looked?" Wyatt's expression was unreadable. Was it sad? Happy? Hopeful? What?

Kevin nodded. "I've looked," he said very quietly.

"I've looked at yours too," Wyatt said, equally as quiet.

They gazed into each other's eyes, and Kevin found he was getting hard right then. But this wasn't the time or place. Or at least the time.

But what to do?

Then he remembered his plans for the snow. And what he'd done.

"Hey." He grinned. "Want to play in the snow? It's the best kind. Snowball weather!"

"But it's so deep!" Wyatt said. "How could we do anything?"

"At least two feet!" Kevin smiled all the wider. "But the parking lot is all cleared now. Want to?"

"You won't throw one in my face, will you?" Wyatt asked with a little pout.

"Well… I can't promise anything."

Wyatt laughed… then grew serious. "You just came in from two hours out there. Aren't you cold?"

Kevin shrugged. He'd warmed up. And how! "I'll be fine."

So they got all bundled up and went to the parking lot and had a wonderful time. It was so grand to hear Wyatt laughing. And they both got a few snowballs in the face.

It wasn't until they were returning to the cabin that Wyatt noticed the path that Kevin had cleared to the north, past their cabin.

"When did Gryphon do that?" he asked.

"I did it," Kevin said and felt himself blush once more.

"You did?" Wyatt looked down the path, then back. "Why?"

Kevin cleared his throat and was surrounded in a plume of frosted air. "You said you wanted to do a little ritual down at Pax Place. I cleared the way for you."

Wyatt's mouth fell open. "You did?"

Kevin nodded.

Then Wyatt did what Kevin absolutely loved. He smiled. Wyatt had the most wonderful smile in the world. Then he jumped into Kevin's arms.

"Oh, thank you, Kevin! Thank you! I just *love* you."

Kevin felt his heart leap.

If only you did, Little Bear. If only you did.

CHAPTER TWENTY-EIGHT

IT HAD been a most interesting day. Certainly not the day Wyatt had expected, not at all what he'd prepared for. No, he'd thought this day was going to be about being alone and meditating and then working his ritual to try to finally say good-bye to Howard. Put him away, as he knew Howard had put him away.

That's not what happened. Instead Kevin—a man he'd known as "Hodor" for as long as he could remember—had shown up out of the snow and spent the day with him. An emotional day, filled with highs and lows, games and tears… and snowball fights.

Was it silly that he was reminded of that scene in *Beauty and the Beast* when Belle and the enchanted prince were playing in the snow? Kevin was no beast, but he was a head taller than Wyatt. And Wyatt knew he was no petite Belle, no beauty, but still. He couldn't help it. It had felt good to play. And really good to have someone say sweet (and sexy) things to him. Was it any wonder that song had filled his mind? Lyrics about something being there that hadn't been before?

Was there something there that hadn't been before?

And should he even be thinking about things like that?

He hadn't even been apart from Howard for six months. What was he doing thinking romantic thoughts? And he *was* thinking romantic thoughts.

Wasn't sex a much better way to direct his thoughts? Sex was so much easier. He wasn't stupid enough to think anybody would want more from him than that, even though Howard had said he wasn't sexy. But Kevin seemed to think so. Kevin said he had a nice penis.

He certainly liked the idea of having sex with Kevin. A lot. The man kept giving him a boner. He'd liked the idea of crawling into bed with "Hodor" for a long time. And from what Kevin said, he might like the idea too!

Hadn't Howard taught him that it was only natural for men to want to have sex? They'd evolved that way? To fight it was ridiculous? Of course, Howard had said a lot of things, hadn't he? Including years of very hurtful things.

But still....

Wyatt watched Kevin make him dinner. Cutting up potatoes, adding them to the frying pan with the small steaks, seasoning them. It had been a long time since a man had made him dinner. It was nice. And the smells were heavenly.

The music was nice too. Songs he'd never heard before. He asked about them.

"I guess you would call them New Age," Kevin said and leaned back against the wall next to the woodstove, crossing his arms over his (very nice) chest. Nice even with clothes on. And he was used to seeing Kevin (or Hodor in those cases) without much clothing. Hodor wasn't a nudist. He didn't wander around naked except on the beach. But like most of the men at Festival, he usually wore little except for a sarong. Days could easily reach the upper nineties at the end of July—the dates for Heartland Queer Men's Festival—and there had been years when they'd reached 105 degrees. Wearing as little as possible was the best way to prevent sunstroke. That and hanging out in the lake. But heavy clothes—jeans and big winter sweaters—still did nothing to hide that body. Funny that he was finding Kevin sexier than he did when he saw him completely nude.

A strange idea for a man who collected nude photos of celebrities.

Wyatt swallowed hard. "You know, I work in a New Age store. But I've never heard any of these songs."

"I'll bet you focus more on pagan songs?" Kevin asked. "Songs like we sing around the bonfire at Camp. 'We All Come from the Goddess,' 'Dear Friends, Queer Friends,' 'Ancient Mother,' 'Purple God,' and that goddess song. I don't know the name of it. Where all the goddess names are chanted."

Wyatt nodded, then sang, "'Isis, Astarte, Diana, Hecate, Demeter, Kali, Inanna....' It's the only name for the song I know." It was a song he loved to sing even though he could hear Howard telling him not to give up his day job.

Kevin laughed. "I can never remember the order that they all go in until I've listened to everyone chant it a few times." He went to the frying pan sizzling away on the stove, did something, flipping and stirring.

Wyatt rolled his eyes. "I was like that forever. I don't know when I finally got it. There is a god version, but for some reason we hardly ever sing it at Festival. Oh! Have you heard the one about Kali?"

Kevin glanced over his shoulder, nodded, and sang the first line. "Kali loves the little children, all the children of the world...."

Wyatt: "Roasted, toasted, broiled, or fried, with a salad on the side...."

Both: "Kali loves the little children of the *woooooorld*...."

They both burst into laughter.

"I've also heard it with coleslaw on the side," Wyatt said. "Or french fries."

This set them off again, and it felt so good to laugh!

"Seriously, though," Wyatt said, "the 'New Age' music we have at Treasures of Terra is the more pagan stuff. Like Celia...." But thinking about that wasn't good because it reminded him that Howard had taken his autographed Celia CD when they were dividing all their stuff, and he didn't even like Celia.

"These songs...." Kevin checked the potatoes—ignorant of where Wyatt's thoughts were going and thank the gods—and then turned back to face him. "They are the essence of what I believe. Paganism isn't *exactly* my path—although it's pretty close. I've always been comfortable in a Circle at Men's Festival. But *these* songs—" He pointed at the iPod. "—always give me the chills. But in a *good* way. Make me feel closer to some 'Higher Power.' That probably doesn't make any sense."

Wyatt nodded quickly. "Yes! It *does* make sense. I understand. So much more than 'Onward Christian Soldiers,' or that horrible 'Amazing Grace' song that everyone loves." He shuddered. "I mean those lyrics! All about saving some poor 'wretch like me.' Well *I* don't think *I'm* a wretch. They even used it in one of the *Star Trek* movies! People *love* that song. And even when I was little, everything inside me rejected the whole idea. Imagine! Singing merrily about being a wretch. How can a little kid be a wretch? And I would look around me, and everyone in church would be crying. Taking *comfort* that God loved them even though they were a 'wretch'!" He looked away, his heart suddenly hurting. "That's what my father thinks. He thinks *I'm* wretched! Well, *fuck* him! I am *not* wretched! I'm *not*!"

Kevin turned to the frying pan, stirred quickly, then took it off the stove. He went to Wyatt and placed a hand on his shoulder. Nodded. Sighed. "I know what you mean. My parents...." He sighed again. "They weren't religious. Not really. They went to church on Easter Sunday and on Christmas. They thought that somehow they could claim they were Christians that way. All I could see was the hypocrisy."

"Yes!" Wyatt exclaimed, his heart rushing once again. "*Yes*! I felt that—although my parents always went to church. At least ever since my dad was struck by lightning."

Kevin's eyebrows shot up (of course they did, why wouldn't they?) and then slowly relaxed. A little half laugh escaped him, and he said, "I thought you meant that literally." He turned around and began dishing out steaks and potatoes onto paper plates.

He placed them on the table. Gods, it smelled wonderful. Like what Wyatt's mother always used to make for breakfast. Even during those times when they weren't flush. Because she grew potatoes and onions in their garden, and a friend from church gave her fresh eggs all the time. Kevin sat down on the side of the table next to Wyatt instead of across from him.

Wyatt debated whether to say anything about what happened to his father that fateful night and then, with a slight lift and drop of his shoulders, went ahead. "I did mean it literally." He cut into one of the small steaks. They were just the tiniest bit pink—perfect. "My dad *did* get struck by lightning." He took a bite, and damn, they *were* perfect. "This is delicious." He speared a couple slices of potatoes and popped them in his mouth. Oh! *Just* like Mom used to make!

"Oh, come on," Kevin said and laughed. It sounded uncomfortable. "He didn't *really* get—"

Wyatt nodded hard. "Yup. He sure did. Coming out of a bar." Wyatt felt the side of his face tick. He shouldn't be talking about this. He shouldn't be thinking about that day and all that came with it (because there was just too much). He should just enjoy his steak and potatoes. They really were terrific, especially considering they were cooked in a little frying pan on a small wood-burning stove with no other seasonings than salt and pepper that came from the little packets you got at a fast-food restaurant. But before he could stop them, memories of Sunday morning breakfasts when he was growing up filled his mind. And of course, that reminded him of…

"When me and my sister, Wendy, got up the next morning, our Aunt Sue was sitting at the kitchen table drinking coffee." He took another bite of steak with potatoes and talked with his mouth full, using his hand to block the view of his chewing. "She told us. Said he'd been hanging out with this woman, smashed drunk, and he got struck by a bolt of lightning right there in the parking lot. Mom was at the hospital. Wendy started crying, and I was trying not to, you know? To be brave for her? I didn't do a very good job." He swallowed. The bite went down like a small stone.

"My God," Kevin said with a little gasp. "Did he live?"

Wyatt didn't say anything for a moment, then nodded once, twice. "Yes. But he changed. Not for the better. He stopped drinking. Stopped hanging out wherever he used to hang out. He stopped losing his job. That part was good...."

Wyatt felt the slap then. *Felt* it. Could almost taste blood. He took a bite to try to taste something else, but it didn't work. He fought a gag. On Kevin's iPod a woman was singing about cats and dogs and how four legs were good, two bad.

"He didn't stop hitting us." Wyatt took a deep breath and somehow didn't choke on his food. "He just hit us for different reasons. Said he was doing what God wanted him to do." Wyatt gave a strangled half laugh. "Fuck! My dad hadn't given a shit about God before that night outside the bar. Mom used to take me and Wendy to church, but *he* never went. He said it was bullshit. I wasn't crazy about the sermons, but I liked Sunday school. Our teacher, Mrs. Karras, had this felt board. And she would put these cutout characters on it and tell us stories from the Bible. The baby Jesus born on Christmas day and the shepherds coming. And the wise men. Or *Joseph and the Amazing Technicolor Dreamcoat*." He laughed. "Of course, she didn't call it that. And there was the story about David and Goliath or Noah and his ark. We all got to put different animals on that big boat! Those stories.... They were nice. Never scary. She never talked about hell or anything like that. My favorite story was about Jesus and his flock—the little paper sheep had cotton glued on them—and how he went to look for the *one* lamb that got lost. It was so... comforting. To think about Jesus coming to look for *me* if *I* got lost.

"And then Dad had his... accident. He said it was God. And that God had spared his life, and he was now going to be a proper Christian man and father." Wyatt pushed his plate away, his food barely half eaten, and then winced when he saw Kevin's reaction. "I'm sorry, Kevin." He bit his lower lip to keep it from trembling.

Kevin shook his head. "They're just breakfast steaks, Wyatt. Cheap at twice the price. Don't worry about it."

Wyatt sighed and looked out the window. Anywhere except Kevin's kind face, his sympathetic expression. It was starting to get gloomy out there. It was winter after all, and the sun set early—even though the Oak King had recently beat the Holly King in battle. He should light some candles.

"Are you all right, Wyatt?" Kevin asked in that caring tone.

And then Wyatt went on, as if he'd never stopped.

"That was when Dad spilled the beans about Santa Claus and the Easter Bunny and all the rest. Wouldn't even let us go trick-or-treating because Halloween was an 'evil pagan holiday' where witches worshipped the devil.

"I think that was probably when I got my first sniggling interest in the Craft. Because I sure didn't like my *father's* god." A small smile took Wyatt's mouth. "And that led to me discovering a few years later that Dad was wrong about that whole devil-worshipping stuff because witches didn't even *believe* in Satan. They worshipped nature and earth spirits and fairies. And I remember getting all warm inside because anyone who did that couldn't be bad in my book. There was nothing I liked more than nature. When I was growing up, I would take these long walks in the woods—"

"My religion is nature?" Kevin asked, and it startled Wyatt.

Then Wyatt smiled all the more, although it felt funny on his face. "Exactly." He nodded. "I liked *that* church much better than the one where the pastor told us we were all in danger of going to hell. *And* I liked the Wiccan idea that there wasn't any hell at all. Especially when I finally accepted that I was gay. I'd been afraid of hell, you know? So when I started learning about Wicca, it was nice to find a religion that didn't teach that I was damned because of the way I was born. I mean, I *wanted* to be straight once. I *wanted* to fit in. Get married. Have kids. Have a house with a white picket fence and a dog, or a cat, or both. But gods. I saw a *picture* of a vagina in one of Dad's old *Hustler* magazines that I found in the garage. All pink and open and…." He shuddered. Then twitched as he remembered he wasn't supposed to feel that way. He could hear Katherine's lecture about how women were made to feel about their bodies. Was he a misogynist after all?

"I don't see how you can be," Kevin said. "I've heard you talk about your boss many times at Festival. You obviously love her a lot."

Wyatt looked at Kevin in surprise. Had Kevin read his mind, or had he said all that out loud?

Kevin's hazel-and-honey eyes. So filled with sympathy. Wyatt didn't know whether to run from the man or be grateful.

He certainly yearned for the latter.

Then hardly knowing he was doing it, he began to speak again. "Now I practically growl when I see a billboard with a picture of Jesus or some Christian rhetoric written on it. The idea of Jesus looking for me doesn't give me one tiny bit of the comfort it did when I was a little kid. And I want to jump someone's ass hard when they sprout that shit about how it was the devil that made them do something wrong. *Fuck that!* The devil didn't do *shit*. They did the wrong! *They* did." His voice was climbing and dammit, he couldn't stop. "They pass the responsibility on to some devil instead of taking it for themselves. Dad used to say shit like that all the time. He said that Satan was the one who made him drink and cheat on Mom. *No* way! *He* did it all on his own without any help from anyone—especially Satan!"

He saw his father in his mind then—sitting at that kitchen table, the tarot decks and Scott Cunningham books before him. Saw the fire in the man's eyes. Heard him.

"I knew you were a sodomite. I looked the other way. Prayed for you, in Jesus Christ's name. That you could be turned from the demon called Homosexuality. But I was wrong. So wrong. I should have confronted you! Look where it has led! You're a witch! And thou shalt not suffer a witch to live!"

And then there was the slap.

And the taste of blood.

"That's why my father kicked me out! Not because I was gay. But because I was pagan. Kicked me out! *Slapped* me out. And I didn't see him or my mother or my sister for ten years!" *Until a few days ago....*

And suddenly he was crying. Crying like a fool. A child. An idiot!

He couldn't stop!

Fuck! He had ruined everything. Just like Howard said he always did. Everything had been going so well. Everything had been so good. The games. Playing in the snow. Laughing. Seeing Belle and the Beast in his head, prancing around in the snow with Mrs. Potts singing that song in the window. And then Kevin making him dinner, whether it was good, cheap steaks or not.

And then I ruined everything.

But to his surprise, Kevin took him into his arms. Had scooted his chair next to Wyatt's and pulled him against his big chest, gently swaying, stroking his hair and more—not shushing him, *not* telling him that he shouldn't cry.

Just holding him. Rocking him.

The tears slowly went away, the hurt in his heart soothed by Kevin's strokes. He melted against the big man, pressed his face between those hard but padded pecs—listened to Kevin's heartbeat.

He could almost go to sleep.

Now Kevin was helping him quietly to his feet and over to the bed, laying him down, crawling next to him and holding him close in a powerful embrace.

Kevin was such a big man. Tall like Howard. But even though he was padded—there was no clearly defined six-pack—Kevin was more solid than Howard. His arms were muscular, his chest hard beneath that soft layer, and even his upper shoulders and neck were well-developed.

It felt wonderful.

It felt…

…safe.

Could there be a safer place?

Wyatt finally felt calm and snuggled in even closer. It had been so long since he'd been held—really held. Years, maybe.

And just as he was truly drifting off….

This is my room and it's robin's-egg blue
And it's got a few cracks in the ceiling
This is my street where the minutemen meet
And my dad says I'll never be leaving….

Wyatt started in Kevin's arms.

I'm ten years old but know how to smoke
And the drugs help to cure the bad feelings
This is my home and the sticks and the stones
Are made up of the darkest of things….

Those words! Wyatt jerked upright. *Those lyrics!*

But in my dreams I can fly
And I soar and my feet touch the sky
And it seems I can go
Anywhere if I try
And the world's not so dark
When the clouds make it white
If there's no hope tell me why
In my dreams I can fly

"Wyatt?" Kevin seemed to ask from miles away.

"*That song,*" Wyatt cried. "I heard that song just the other day and…."

Here come the tears and I cover my ears
And I swear I can hear my own heartbeat
When they stop fighting to turn out the lights
I pretend I'm already sleeping
After the violence alone in the silence
Just me and the secret I'm keeping
My dad tells me I'm not worth anything
And I've almost admitted defeat….

"Kevin…. Gods! That *song!*" And within a few words, Wyatt was quietly singing along with the man whose name he didn't know.

But in my dreams I can fly
And I soar and my feet touch the sky
And it seems I can go
Anywhere if I try

Then Kevin was joining him.

And the world's not so dark
When the clouds make it white
If there's no hope tell me why
In my dreams I can fly

Wyatt turned and saw that Kevin was sitting up, and he said, "Who is this? I heard this when I was in the car…" *driving home from my parent's house. And it touched me then, and gods, now that I hear all the words, it means even more!* "It hit me so hard."

"In a good way or a bad one?" Kevin asked in reply.

"Both?" Wyatt answered.

This is my room and it's robin's-egg blue
And it's got a few cracks in the ceiling
This is my home and the sticks and the stones
Are made up of the darkest of things

After the violence alone in the silence
Just me and the secret I'm keeping

"He's a young gay man named Joe Donovan," Kevin replied. "He's about your age. I saw him in concert once and fell in love with his music."

My dad tells me I'm not worth anything
And I've almost admitted it....

Those lyrics. Gods, they hurt. But... "But in my dreams I can fly," Wyatt sang, closing his eyes. "And I soar..."

...and my feet touch the sky
And it seems I can go
Anywhere if I try
And the world's not so dark
When the clouds make it white
If there's no hope, tell me why
In my dreams I can fly.

Then Kevin joined him again and they sang the repeating chorus until the very last, "In my dreams I can fly."

The music faded away, and Wyatt let out a long sigh. "Kevin," he whispered. "It's like that boy is singing about me. *My* room. The cracks in *my* ceiling." *The buffalo head. The river.* "My life. My parents. *My* secret.... Dad saying that I wasn't worth anything." *That I was an abomination.*

"Enough. Get out, sinner! Get out, thou evil one! Never cast your shadow on me again. I turn my back on you! I dust off the dirt from my feet. I disown you!"

Wyatt turned back to Kevin, looked into his handsome face, his beautiful hazel-and-amber eyes. He reached out and touched the man's furry cheek—a man's cheek. The beard was thick, but so soft. Wyatt felt a breathtaking tingle shiver through him.

Oh Dad, he thought. *I wish you could see that what I'm feeling isn't Satan inside of me. It's God. I'm just what I was made to be. How could a devil make me feel like...* "I can fly."

"Have I ever told you what a pretty voice you have, Wyatt?"

Wyatt quietly gasped. "Me?"

Kevin reached out and cupped *his* cheek.

"Howard always said that when I sing I sound like a cat in he—"

Kevin kissed him.

If he hadn't been sitting on the bed, his legs would have gone out from under him.

Another great shiver passed through him—*zinged* through him!

It was such a gentle and soft kiss—no pressure, no urgency, but *whoa!* There had never been one like it before.

Never.

Not even his *first* kiss. Even that had been nothing like this.

Just a long, lingering, gentle, sweet kiss. But gods….

Another round of goose bumps rippled down Wyatt's back and arms.

Whenever, ever, had a kiss been so precious?

Then Kevin was lying back down on the bed, ending the kiss, pulling Wyatt down with him, and just holding him, making gentle, comforting noises.

The kiss had simply been a kiss. Beautiful and wonderful. But not *leading* to anything else.

It left Wyatt dazed and confused. Nothing like this had ever happened to him. He couldn't help but feel a little bit of disappointment.

But then he thought of something he hadn't before.

Maybe….

Maybe this was better?

And as he puzzled over that, he realized something else.

He had once had feelings just like that. Feelings that… maybe you were supposed to wait? That what came after a kiss was supposed to be special.

Wyatt snuggled in closer, loving the feel of this man—his chest, his body, his comforting presence. It made Wyatt feel different. Two men so close, yet with no seeming ulterior motive. At least not an immediate one. No one had ever held him like this, or cuddled with him like this before, unless it was leading to something else.

He remembered, then, Kevin turning him down for sex that one drunken night.

Because I was still with Howard.

But I'm not with Howard anymore.

Was Kevin just being nice to him that starry night?

"I'm going to regret this Little Bear… but I can't."

But that was followed by…

"The only reason you get laid is because of me. I tell them they have *to have sex with you if they want me."*

It was two *very* different voices. And the second one could take him to all kinds of very dark places.

Then… in that moment…

Wyatt decided to let go of the second memory. The voice that said no one really liked him. That people only hung out with him or had sex with him because of Howard.

He remembered instead six friends who had helped make a Yule one of the most amazing nights of his life.

Wyatt closed his eyes and sighed. His lids felt heavy. He was tired. "Don't know why…," he muttered.

"Don't know why what?" Kevin said softly.

"Why I'm so tired." A comforting blanket seemed to settle over him as he snuggled even closer, moved a leg over one of Kevin's, and… drifted.

So nice.

"Don't worry about it" came Kevin's voice from far away. "Go to sleep, Little Bear."

Wyatt shivered, but not from the cold. After all, the room was more than toasty—the wood-burning stove was small but very efficient. Hey, the cabin was small.

No. This shiver was something completely different.

So nice….

He let himself fall deeper and deeper and thought how nice it would be if he dreamed he could fly.

CHAPTER TWENTY-NINE

WYATT WOKE, eyes wide, jolted by the fact that there was someone pressed up against him. A man.

Howard?

No!

Hodor….

He smiled. *Kevin.*

Sighed happily. *Gosh*, he thought. *Wow.*

How amazing that he was *relieved* it wasn't Howard after he had woken up so many mornings hurting because his lover was gone.

Wyatt's smile broadened. He almost laughed.

Then he became conscious that he was hard.

And not just him.

Kevin was too.

Wyatt had lifted a knee and settled it over Kevin when he'd curled into him and fallen asleep, and during his nap that knee had found its way directly over Kevin's crotch.

There was no denying it. Kevin was hard. And even moving his knee against the solid column of flesh Wyatt could tell it was big. *Really* big.

Wyatt considered doing just that, flexing his leg against Kevin's erection. But then he remembered this *was* Kevin, not some one-night stand he'd brought home from a bar. Some nameless pickup might enjoy something like that—the few he and Howard would have actually let spend the night would have, and had.

But somehow he knew that Kevin wouldn't appreciate it. Not in the end. Doing something like that would be like violating him. Especially since they hadn't had sex. And the way things were going, he couldn't figure out if that was even in the cards.

It was frustrating because he was like a fish out of water. This was so different. He was out of his element. He didn't know how to act. What to do.

Maybe he should do a tarot reading?

He caught the aroma of the steak and potatoes and very suddenly realized how hungry he was.

So as much as he might have loved taking things further with Kevin, he decided to go with instinct. The one that told him seducing Kevin might be a mistake.

Would be.

He carefully disentangled himself from the wonderfully sweet and sexy man and slipped out of bed. He went to the little table, took his plate, picked up the steak with a forefinger and thumb, and took a bite. And, no. It wasn't hot anymore. Was barely warm.

But gods, it was still good.

"Wyatt?"

Wyatt jumped and looked over his shoulder. Kevin was sitting there on the edge of the bed.

"You know, I can heat that up for you."

Wyatt shrugged. Grinned. "It's good, Kevin. Delicious. I like it just like this."

Kevin gave a shrug of his own and got up and joined Wyatt at the table. He speared one of the last two of the small breakfast steaks with a fork and took a big bite of his own. He grinned. "It is, isn't it?"

They sat and ate and nodded at each other and agreed that their simple little meal couldn't be better. In fact, it really was finger-licking good.

Still, Wyatt would have liked to lick Kevin's fingers.

Strangely, he felt a pang of guilt. But why? He'd licked men's fingers for years. And a lot of other things. Those men had loved it. Howard had loved it. *He* had loved it.

Hadn't he?

But maybe today wasn't the day.

Still…

It *would* be nice. It had been so long since he'd been with a man. The closest he'd come was that guy in the bar who had flirted with him. Then disappeared.

And that had made him feel like shit.

He didn't want to feel like shit.

He certainly didn't want to make a man as sweet as Kevin feel like shit.

So they would have to find something else to do.

After they ate, they played Sorry!.

THEY WERE listening to someone named Christine Kane—she was the one who had sung the song about cats and dogs and four legs and two legs, only this time she was singing about watching for roses in the snow—when Kevin asked the question.

Or asked if he could ask one.

"I was wondering if maybe… I could ask you something?"

Wyatt looked over at Kevin. Saw an expression that seemed guarded.

He nodded, abruptly nervous.

Kevin cleared his throat. "Is it possible you threw the baby out with the bathwater?"

Huh? Baby? Bathwater?

"Or in this case… the baby Jesus?"

Wyatt stiffened. "What?" *baby Jesus?* He looked at Kevin more carefully, feeling guarded himself now. What was this about?

He *saw* Kevin swallow. *Heard* him. "I was just wondering," Kevin said. "Maybe you're not reacting to *Jesus* when you see those billboards. Maybe it's something Pavlovian. Maybe instead of Jesus, it's what your father put you through that upsets you so much?"

Wyatt pushed back from the table. He couldn't help it. "What?" His heart was skipping a beat (or five), but not in a good way. Was Kevin going to give him the "*Jesus*-talk"? Had he "*found Jesus*"? Wyatt had to bite the insides of his cheeks to keep his mouth from falling open. Was that what was about to happen? This man had never struck him as a *Christian*.

Kevin was looking at him intently.

Christine sang on—

Seasons changing on me now
Wait for the flowers to grow, yeah
Watch for the roses in the snow

—and then Kevin let out a long sigh.

"Okay. Let me start again." He cleared his throat. "You know that every time the media covers something gay—like a Gay Pride parade for instance—all they show is leathermen wearing assless chaps, or a NAMBLA float, or men in jockstraps? Or the Sisters of Perpetual Indulgence—who I love by the way, although anyone who doesn't understand what they stand for will only see them as sacrilegious degenerates...." His voice almost turned into a mutter at the last.

Wyatt shook his head. He didn't know where all this was coming from. All of this was completely out of left field. One minute they were listening to Christine Kane sing about new chances and starting over and believing in yourself no matter what, and the next something about throwing the baby Jesus out with the bathwater?

"I don't know about you, Wyatt," Kevin went on, "but it *pisses* me off. It makes gay people look like nothing but sexual perverts. Me and Bobcat and Donald and Cedar talk about this at Festival all the time. The media never show the PFLAG groups or the gay churches—like the Metropolitan Community Church. They don't show the Front Runners. The Gay-Straight Student Alliances. The bands. The Gay Men's Choruses. The flaggers. The anti-violence GLBT groups...."

Wyatt blinked at him. Kevin talked about this stuff at Festival? Quite suddenly he remembered a conversation a lot like this, with the men Kevin mentioned, that had taken place this past summer. It had made him a bit uncomfortable, and he'd gotten gloriously cocktailed. How could he get away from such talk now?

Change the subject.

"It's getting dark," he blurted. And it was. It was rapidly growing darker in the cabin and getting harder to see.

"The media doesn't show any of that, so what do the typical Mr. and Mrs. America think of us?"

Stop, Wyatt wanted to say. *Stop.*

"That we all like to show off our bare asses or dress up as nuns or that we all want to have sex with boys. And it's *not* true."

Wyatt started to open his mouth to ask what was wrong with being a leatherman and showing off your ass or dressing up in a fun outfit when Kevin continued.

"Not that there is anything *wrong* with leathermen—"

No. There certainly wasn't....

"—and the Sisters have done so much for our community, especially in raising money to help in the AIDS crisis."

Wyatt relaxed, a very small amount.

"Of course, I can't say the same of NAMBLA."

No. Certainly *not*. An organization founded on advocating pederasty and pedophilia wasn't the kind of group he wanted anyone associating with gay men. He had to agree with Kevin there, but…. But what did all this have to do with the baby Jesus?

Kevin sighed, reached out, and touched Wyatt's hand. He almost flinched. But then Kevin was gently stroking the web between Wyatt's thumb and forefinger and, *gosh*…. Wyatt trembled, looked up into those lovely eyes. "The media shows the bad and rarely the good. It covers Gay Pride parades, but only shows the pederasts. And—" He paused, but didn't stop caressing Wyatt's hand. "—it covers Christians and shows the Kim Davises. People shooting doctors coming out of Planned Parenthood clinics. Wyatt. Those kind of people are only a *fraction* of the Christians out there."

Oh no. Don't even go there. "Like my *father*?" Wyatt snapped and yanked his hand away.

Kevin's right eye twitched, and then those eyes of his turned sad. He nodded once. "Yes," he said very quietly. "I'm sorry."

"He—kicked—me—*out*." Wyatt touched his cheek. "He hit me. *Hard*." He stood up and walked over to the door, parted the sheer curtain, and looked out the window. *Remembering.* "He found my tarot cards and my Scott Cunningham books. He called me a Satan worshipper. Said I shouldn't be suffered to live. *To live!* And that being a witch had turned me gay. Some 'loving' Christian, huh?"

Wyatt's heart was slamming in his chest now.

It's why he did his best not to ever think about his father.

Of course, recent circumstances had fucked that up good. How could he *not* think about the man? It was a big part of the reason why he'd come to Camp. To be alone to try to sort it out. But then that wasn't what happened, was it?

And here he had thought Camp Sanctuary was magick.

Yet what had it done?

It had not only refused to give him the solitude—the seclusion—he'd wanted, but it had dumped a mountain of snow on him besides.

"But not all Christians are like that," Kevin said, hands spread out before him.

"Okay, then," Wyatt said, turning from the view of the snow outside. "What about the Mormons who made sure that Prop 8 was passed?"

Kevin shrugged. "Well… yeah…." He went silent. Of course he did. How could he argue? Kevin let out a long sigh. "Oh, Wyatt. Don't you see? Their whole way of life was threatened. People were scared—"

"*Threatened*!" Wyatt almost growled. "*Them* threatened? *Fuck* their 'way of life'!"

"—of all the changes that were happening in the world. A lot has happened for gays, and it has happened *fast*. A lot of people just weren't prepared for how fast it happened."

Fast! Fast? How could he say that!

But then Kevin stood up, practically wringing his hands, and quite suddenly the winds were totally out of Wyatt's sails. He hated seeing the gentle giant this way.

"Wyatt, I know *lots* of wonderful, *amazing* Christians. People who are nothing like Kim Davis or Anita Bryant or Jerry Falwell or Pat Robertson. People who totally disagree with people like *that*. Christians who don't see anything wrong with anyone being gay. My best friend Theresa is Christian. She volunteers at the LGBT Youth Center."

Again Wyatt opened his mouth to argue and again, slowly shut it. He knew some Christians who were fine with him being gay as well, didn't he? Even thought it was interesting that he was pagan. At least that's what they said.

Kevin came to Wyatt then. "Lumping all gays as pederasts is the same as lumping all Christians as haters. It's just not true."

Wyatt looked up into Kevin's face, his eyes now all but lost in the darkening room. His heart hurt. He hadn't meant to upset Kevin. It wasn't so long ago they'd been cuddled in bed. Now the man was so distressed. But damn. Couldn't Kevin see how Christianity had harmed Wyatt? What did Kevin want? For him to just forgive all of that?

Dear gods...! Was Kevin a Christian? He wouldn't have been the only one that came to Men's Festival, after all.

"Are you trying to convert me or something?" Wyatt asked, the words bursting from his lips.

Kevin's eyes went wide. "Hell no!"

Now he was putting his hands on Wyatt again, taking hold of his upper arms firmly in those big hands of his.

"I would never want to change you, Little Bear. You're perfect just the way you are."

Wyatt tried to look into Kevin's darkened eyes. "Even the anti-vagina-talk part of me? The part that is upset with Christians?"

Kevin nodded. "Yes. *Just* the way you are. You must walk your path and not someone else's. And there are so many paths for us to walk. Or so many paths to God."

"What if I believe in 'gods' plural?" Wyatt shot back in quick response. "What do you think of that?"

Kevin shrugged and then said, "I think it's getting dark in here." He stepped back, patted his pockets, reached in one, and pulled out a matchbook.

They still make those? Wyatt wondered.

Kevin went to the table and lit the white candle and then went to his bed and pulled a couple of Walmart bags out from under it. Reaching into one, he removed two dark pillar candles and put them on the table beside the other one. Wyatt joined Kevin, and as they were lit, Wyatt noticed what color they were.

Dark green.

It took only a moment for the pine scent to reach Wyatt.

Forest green.

Just like Utnapishtim told him to get.

He shivered.

He looked at Kevin.

Saw the flicker of the candles dance in his eyes.

"What do you believe?" Wyatt asked.

"I think God," Kevin said, "is in creation and entropy and in re-creation. In every molecule and atom. In nature and in us—every part of us. In our flesh and our blood and our muscles and our cocks."

Cocks? God is in our cocks?

"I think God is in this cabin and the woods around us. In the turning of the stars and the earth and the seasons. Spring, summer, autumn, and winter.

"And in the snowflakes that catch in our eyelashes…."

Kevin made a strange little noise at his last words that Wyatt couldn't quite interpret. A gasp? A sob? What was it?

Just when Wyatt felt as if he should say something to fill the silence, Kevin went on. "I think God is Love. I think that is all that God is. I don't think 'It' hates or gets jealous or punishes and floods the Earth or sends anyone to hell. I don't even *believe* in hell, because how could a God that the Bible said is 'agape'—unconditional love—*have* any conditions?"

Wyatt suddenly felt the need to sit down. Before he fell down. Everything Kevin was saying…. The words. Wyatt trembled.

Who was this man?

"And I think God wants to be expressed not through fighting about who is right and who is wrong. Which religion is the correct one and which false. But through acts of love. That every time someone performs an act of love, then Jesus comes again, or the Lord of Light is born from the Lady, or Ganesha dances around the Universe in honor of his parents. All are acts of love."

The words stunned Wyatt. So much of his life had revolved around people arguing and fighting about which religion was the "right" one! Even amongst his pagan and Wiccan friends, people argued about which path was right, which pantheon was best, which tradition the purest and truest. There had been huge fights here at camp over which pantheon should be celebrated with the rituals during the Solstices or Equinoxes.

And here sat Kevin—the gently silent Hodor—saying such words.

Wyatt couldn't speak.

And neither spoke for the longest time.

Then, finally, Kevin smiled, let out a snort, and said, "*Listen* to me! Who do I *think* I *am*? Some kind of Faerie prophet?" He slapped his thigh. "Forgive me."

Wyatt couldn't speak.

"Whew," Kevin said. "The air is *thick* in here."

True, thought Wyatt. But did he want to spoil it? Why, he felt like he was on the razor's edge of something very important.

"We need to lighten things up. Wyatt! Please. A joke."

Wyatt sat up.

What? What did he say? A joke?

"You want to hear one of my jokes?"

Kevin sat forward and propped his chin up on an open palm. "Little Bear, I *love* your jokes."

"You do?" Wyatt squeaked.

Kevin smiled. "I *do*."

That smile! It made Wyatt's heart flutter. How could he refuse?

All right.

He squinted. Thought about it.

And remembered an old one.

"Okay. In honor of our conversation. Three friends—two straight guys, a gay guy—and their significant others all went on a cruise together. Sadly, not a gay cruise, but I digress...." He rolled his eyes. "*Any*way, the ship is hit by this huge tidal wave and everyone is drowned. Then, before they know it, there they all are, standing before the Pearly Gates and who should be there?"

"Saint Peter?" Kevin asked with a grin.

Wyatt nodded. "So the first straight guy and his wife walk up to Saint Peter, but oh no! Saint Peter shakes his head and says, 'Sorry, I can't let you in. You were too greedy. You loved money too much. So much that you even married a woman named Penny.'"

Kevin nodded as if he hadn't just delivered a soliloquy that could have brought the house down. Or the cabin in this case.

"Then the second straight guy walks up to Saint Peter. But to his regret, Saint Peter shakes his head. 'Sorry, my son. I can't let you in either. *Your* sin was gluttony. You loved food so much you even married a woman named Candy!'"

Wyatt grinned. "Then the gay guy turns to his boyfriend—" He paused.

"Don't tease me!" said Kevin.

"—and whispers to him…."

"*Yes?*"

"This doesn't look good, Dick."

There was another pause. And then Kevin was laughing like Wyatt had never seen him laugh. Finally, with a gasp, Kevin said, "That was great, Wyatt."

Well, maybe not *great*, Wyatt thought. But a teller of jokes was only as good as how much his audience laughed. And in this case his audience had definitely laughed.

Wyatt realized he hadn't felt this good in a long time.

"Oh, Wyatt," Kevin said. "I just love you."

Wyatt's heart stopped.

Then he sighed.

If only, he thought.

Imagine having a man like Kevin smile at him, laugh at his jokes, and love him every day.

If only….

CHAPTER THIRTY

W YATT LAY in the pitch-black and stared up at a ceiling totally lost in the dark. He truly couldn't see his hand in front of his face. The only light was an orange sliver that came from around the crack in the door of the stove.

And even with Kevin only a few feet away, he couldn't remember feeling so alone.

But why?

Except for one brief moment, this day—unplanned as it might have been—had been wonderful. He'd even enjoyed games for the first time since he was a kid playing with his sister and mother.

He'd had good company.

New music.

And he'd seen a side of Kevin he had no idea existed before.

Of course, he'd really only ever seen Kevin as a big quiet guy. A big quiet *sexy* guy.

Now?

Now he saw a lot more.

But that didn't mean he didn't want to have sex with him. It had been so long. And something told him that sex with Kevin might be very sweet indeed. Just a kiss had been magic!

"Kevin?"

No answer. Was that a snore?

"Kevin," he said a little louder, with a pang of guilt.

"Yes, Little Bear?"

"You know you don't need to sleep in that bed over there alone...."

"*Wyatt.*"

"I saw you. You can't even lay down straight in that cot. You're too big. You're having to curl up."

"I'm okay. I've slept many a night on a couch."

For some reason Wyatt felt crushed. "Wasn't it nice cuddling with me earlier?" he asked, fighting to keep the whine from his voice.

Long silence.

"It was very nice, Wyatt. But…."

But? "But?"

Long silence.

"You're going to want more than I can give."

More than you can give? "More than you can give?"

"I know what you want, Wyatt."

You do?

"You don't want me to come over there to cuddle. You want more."

And you don't? "And you don't." This second wasn't a question. It was a statement. Kevin didn't want him.

But what about that erection? Didn't that mean 'want'?

Silence.

"Of course I want you, Wyatt."

Wyatt froze.

"I've wanted you forever."

What? "What?" he asked, voice trembling.

KEVIN LAY curled up in his bunk and stared into the dark. There was no moon tonight. Nothing to reflect off the snow and give them any light at all. There was only the tiniest fraction of light coming from the stove.

And even with Wyatt so close, he might as well have been as far away from Wyatt as if he were back in New York.

You could go and get in bed with him.

But that would be a mistake, wouldn't it?

It was one thing to curl up with him, lying back on that bed, on that bearskin, holding Wyatt and taking a nap.

If he crawled into bed with the little bear now?

He knew what would happen.

And as wonderful as that could be, would be, the price was too high. He would feel so alone tomorrow—beyond alone. Lost tomorrow (or the next day) when Wyatt went back to his life, and he went back to New York.

"Kevin?"

He froze. His breath caught.

"Kevin," Wyatt said, a little louder this time.

"Yes, Little Bear?" he managed.

Don't say it, Wyatt. Please don't.

"You know you don't need to sleep in that bed over there alone…."

He stiffened. God. "*Wyatt*," he said, trying to keep the moan from his voice.

"I saw you" came Wyatt's voice. "You can't even lay down straight in that cot. You're too big. You're having to curl up."

True. But…. "I'm okay. I've slept many a night on a couch." And he had. On Cauley's couch on nights when he was afraid his ex might die. When he wanted to be there in case it was the last night.

"Wasn't it nice cuddling with me earlier?" There was almost a whimper in Wyatt's voice.

Please don't, Wyatt. Please.

Don't break my resolve.

But his voice!

Was that hurt?

Was he hurting Wyatt?

"It was very nice, Wyatt," he admitted. "But…."

"But?"

God! What did he say? *But if I crawl in that bed with you…* "You're going to want more than I can give."

"More than you can give?" came the response.

Don't play with me, Wyatt. I've heard you many a time. I know how you feel about sex. I can't be just another pastime. "I know what you want, Wyatt." *You want far more than cuddling.* "You don't want me to come over there to cuddle. You want more." *Much more.*

"And you don't." His voice! He wasn't asking. *He's telling me. He thinks I don't want him!*

"Of course I want you, Wyatt." He'd said it even without realizing it. Let it all out. His heart sank. *Fuck it.* And then at last, at last, he told him, "I've wanted you forever."

"What?" came Wyatt's response.

CHAPTER THIRTY-ONE

"I'VE WANTED you forever," Kevin said, throwing it all out to the Universe. Totally exposing himself. And so what if it took the pitch blackness to allow him to do it. So what if he was only truly admitting all of this now, even to himself. "Since the first time I saw you sitting at that registration table my very first Men's Festival. I was so nervous. It took everything in me to come. I almost turned around a dozen times and went back home to New York. I almost didn't get out of my truck, no matter how many hours I'd driven to get there. And then there was you."

"Me?" Wyatt said, the shock in his voice impossible to miss.

Yes, you!

"You were so damned cute, and you were so nice, and you made me feel so at home I knew I'd come to the right place." Kevin couldn't believe he was admitting this. In truth, he was finally and truly admitting it to himself.

"I did?" Wyatt asked. He couldn't believe what Kevin was saying.

"I went and found a place to camp, and I set up way off from everyone else. On the edge of Avalon." Being at Camp had taken enough out of him. He couldn't set up camp right there with a bunch of men he didn't know.

"Way off is right!" Avalon was at the extreme south end of Camp Sanctuary property. The exact opposite side of the plateau where everyone else camped.

"And then I saw you at dinner, and I so wanted to come sit by you. I was trying to build up the courage when I saw you kiss this big man…." *God*, Kevin thought. *I'm admitting this!*

"Howard," Wyatt whispered.

"And so I sat down at another table," Kevin said. "And that's when I met Lorax and Domi Dearest and Lead Foot, and they told me you and Howard were together." *Domi saw me staring. But that time he thought I was looking at Howard. He was wrong. I was interested in you, Wyatt.*

But I don't—"But I don't understand why you didn't come sit with us anyway," Wyatt said and then immediately realized he did know. *It was because I was with Howard and—*

"I don't go for guys who are in relationships." *And after that, I pretty much ignored you. Or tried to.*

"But when did that ever stop a gay man?" Wyatt asked. And then his heart started to pound.

"It stopped me," said Kevin. "And I don't mess with married men. I don't do that." *Because how could I ever have anything but a one-night stand, then?*

"But Howard and I were in an open relationship," Wyatt said. *Why did you let that stop you? We could have had so much fun!*

"Wyatt!" Kevin took a deep breath. *Don't yell at him*, he told himself. *Hasn't Wyatt been yelled at enough?* "I don't do married men. I've told you that. I want to be more than a fun night for some guy. More than that year's conquest."

"But there are guys who get together all the time. Zebra and Historical Heloise are both in relationships, but they're together every year at Festival." Their lovers didn't come to Heartland Queer Men's Festival. They hated camping.

"Do their lovers know?" Kevin asked. From what Kevin had been able to piece together, their lovers *didn't* know.

"I... I...." Wyatt swallowed hard. "I think they've said that they are in relationships that are 'don't ask, don't tell.'"

Kevin shook his head, even though Wyatt couldn't see him in the dark. "A summer lover isn't good enough for me, Wyatt. It's no better than a one-night stand. I can't do it. I want forever."

"Forever?" Wyatt asked. *He means this.* Wyatt's heart skipped.

"I don't care if monogamy isn't 'gay.' That's what I want." It was the only thing he could do. He'd tried having an open relationship. Tried it for Cauley's sake because he loved the man so, and Cauley said he needed more. It was all a part of his activism, Cauley claimed. All a part of proving that gay men were different from straight people, and activism meant more than equal rights or the ability to get married. It meant the right to be different. In fact, Cauley had stayed out of the whole same-sex marriage movement. "Cauley said the same thing. That gay men didn't need to be monogamous. But it killed me when I knew he was with another man. He didn't do it often." *Or at least that's what he claimed.*

"Don't you think that's ego?" Wyatt asked. "Howard said that wanting somebody all to yourself was ego. It was trying to own somebody, and no one had a right to own anyone."

Howard said that? wondered Kevin. "The Buddha talked about that," Kevin said aloud and then cursed himself for getting religious—spiritual—again. "He said that owning things made us feel real and that we needed to learn we were real without having a title or property or a relationship. But he also said we should be monogamous."

Why? wondered Wyatt. "Why?" he said aloud. "Isn't that about owning someone?" *Tell me I am wrong. Tell me Howard was wrong. Because goddammit, that's all I ever wanted. One man. Who wanted only me.*

"Because being with one person isn't about owning anyone." And it wasn't. Kevin saw that once he let Cauley have his way. Kevin hadn't held to his convictions. He let Cauley talk him into something he didn't want. *And in the end it destroyed me,* Kevin thought. *Over and over again.* "Monogamy is about holding yourself to an ideal. It's about commitment. There is power in monogamy. Ask any true celibate priest or monk who gives up sex for their beliefs. There is power in celibacy because all that energy is used for something higher. That's what I believe monogamy is, Wyatt. I don't think I'm losing out on anything by committing myself to one man. I think there is power in it."

"Oh my gods," Wyatt said with a gasp, heart pounding. *He means this. It's real. Just like with Sloan and Max. And Scott and Cedar. And Asher and Peni.*

The fairy tale.

"And that is why I won't come get in your bed, Wyatt. I'm not ever going to settle for less than what I want again."

Like I did, thought Wyatt.

And then out loud. "Gods. Like *I* did. I settled, Kevin."

God, I'm not judging you, little bear, Kevin thought to himself, and then said it out loud. "I'm not judging you, sweet little bear. *Little Bear.*" The second time using Wyatt's actual Faerie name. His magick name. And not just because he was a sweet little bear. "I am only telling you what *I* want."

"But it's what I always wanted," cried Wyatt. He all but shouted it. "And Howard convinced me, Kevin. He taught me that what I was wanting was all a fairy tale. That it wasn't real. That I had been fucking brainwashed. And it hurt!"

Oh God! Wyatt's heart was pounding so hard now that it hurt. *Am I having a heart attack or something?* he wondered. "It hurt that what I wanted couldn't be had!"

One more fucking way that Howard hurt you! Kevin thought. *He let you settle for less. And no one should ever settle for less than what they want.*

CHAPTER THIRTY–TWO

"HE WAS so good to me in the beginning," Wyatt cried. He thought of pizza at The Watering Hole when he was hungry. And seeing Howard's altar for the first time. Happily discovering that there were people out there who *really* did have personal altars, just like Scott Cunningham, the gay witch, said in his books! He thought about how kind Howard had been and the way he taught him to make love. He thought about how Howard had introduced him to the gay community—but even better, the pagan community. And even better! The Radical Faerie community—queer pagans and witches and just plain old worshippers of nature. He thought about how Howard was a big strong bear and how Wyatt had always thought bears were sexy— before he even knew what "bears" were. He thought about how good the sex was. He thought about them buying a house together and making it their own.

And how when Howard wouldn't give him the fairy tale, the monogamy, that seemed a small price to pay. He'd seen the desperate, lonely people who would do anything—*anything*—to have what he had with Howard. And so he had paid the price.

He told Kevin all of that. He sat up in the big bed—relatively big, at least compared to that small cot Kevin was curled up in.

Wyatt covered his face with his hands even though it was too dark to see anything.

And then he told Kevin all about his friends. He told Kevin about how in the last year they had all found lovers—it took him a long time, and Kevin never once stopped him except for an "uh-huh" or some other noise that let him know Kevin hadn't fallen asleep—about how they had all found lovers who wanted only them.

He told Kevin about how he thought that maybe the Universe only allowed so much love, and that maybe he needed to be single so that they could have love.

And then…

AND THEN Kevin couldn't stand it anymore.

He got out of that damned fucking cramped cot—how could anyone sleep in that thing?—and went to Wyatt's bed. He climbed into it, and he pulled the sweet injured gorgeous beautiful kind adorable perfect harmed delightful belittled bear into his arms.

Their bodies fit perfectly together.

Kevin was wearing his long underwear and Wyatt—surprise, surprise—Wyatt wasn't completely naked but wearing a big baggy T-shirt.

"Oh, sweet little one," Kevin said. "There is no Cosmic Universal Scale demanding that you be alone so your friends can have love. I don't know how they all 'suddenly' found love like that. But I know this…."

"Yes, Kevin?" Wyatt cried, trembling in Kevin's arms.

"The Universe *is* Love. That's what the Universe is! That's what God is. Beyond being a candle or fire or wood or this cabin and this bed and the sky and the snow—"

…and the snow on my eyelashes.

"—God *is* Love. Unlimited love. Love isn't an ocean—even as big as the ocean is, *it* has limits. But not love. *Love* is limitless. There is no 'amount' of love. It is endless, forever and ever and ever, and there is plenty for sweet little Wyatt. And it isn't your job to be alone. It's your job to open yourself for some man—"

Me! Make it me!

"—who will love you unconditionally and the way you *want* to be loved. Don't settle. Wait for just what you want."

Like I am going to wait for what I *want,* Kevin thought.

"Do not settle, Wyatt! Don't ever settle again!"

"Oh, Kevin," Wyatt cried. "Really? You believe this?"

"I do, Wyatt. I *have* to. Believe, Wyatt. Ask. Believe. Receive. It *will* happen."

"Oh, Kevin," Wyatt said.

And because telling someone else was reminding him to believe himself, he said, "Leap, my sweet little bear. Leap and the net will appear."

Then, knowing it could be a mistake, Kevin kissed Wyatt.

Really kissed him.

Kissed him in a way that his body responded to, and he could feel Wyatt's had too. He could feel Wyatt's hard cock pressed against his lower tummy, and his own erection was wedged beneath the shorter man's balls.

He opened his mouth, and Wyatt opened his, and their tongues came together in quiet desperation—neither gently and sweetly nor hard and rough. It was more like a dance than a duel, with each partner perfectly knowing their part.

And this is where I will do it. I will cast caution to the wind. We'll have sex now, and it will kill me when Wyatt goes home and I go back to New York and I am more alone than I've ever been in my life.

And then…

Wyatt snuggled closer. Shoved his erection against Kevin. A couple of times.

And then…

Pulled his mouth ever so gently from Kevin's.

And then…

He settled.

He stopped his little thrusts.

And said, "Okay. If it's real, then let's don't have sex."

Wait. What had Wyatt just said?

"I'm so hard my balls hurt, Kevin. But I want to believe what you say is real."

It's real, Kevin thought. And maybe…

"And I don't want to settle. And I don't know if I'm ready. And as good as you feel, Kevin, I don't want to be hurt again. And if we make love now and you decide you don't want me—"

Like that could happen.

"—it will kill me."

Wyatt kissed him then, again. But gently and lightly.

"I can't have you tell me something I don't want to hear a week from now, Kevin," Wyatt said.

Kevin suppressed a gasp. Wait. Those were his words. He was the one who always thought that way. Wyatt was always saying monogamy wasn't natural. What had happened?

"Not again," Wyatt went on. "And if you were some guy just wanting to fuck? I would probably be fucking with you right now. But you've made me believe that something more is possible. And that's what I want."

Kevin's heart was pounding, and he both heard and felt Wyatt sob against his chest. Wyatt was crying. His tears were wetting Kevin's chest where the buttons of his long johns were undone.

Oh God, Wyatt!

"I feel your cock, Kevin. God, I want it. But I want something more."

Oh God, Wyatt.

"I'm going to do it. What you say. I'm going to goddamn leap."

Oh, sweet Wyatt.... And then Kevin realized he was crying too.

"I'm asking, Kevin."

Kevin took a deep, long breath.

"I am believing, Kevin."

He knew the ache in his own balls would relax.

"Now wait and receive," Kevin told the love of his life.

And he knew then that's what Wyatt was. Wyatt was the love of his life.

Now all he had to do was believe.

Ask.

Believe.

And wait and see if this was what he was supposed to receive.

Then he heard Wyatt's gentle snores, and he pulled Wyatt even closer.

He waited.

CHAPTER THIRTY-THREE

WYATT WOKE to filtered light coming around and under the window shade and the sound of beautiful birdsong—a cardinal, he realized—and the big man beside him. His eyes widened, and he let out a tiny gasp.

Kevin.

He was in bed with Kevin.

Wyatt was using Kevin's chest, his big soft and hard left pectoral, as his pillow, and Kevin's arm was around him for support. Wyatt's left hand was resting on his tummy, right where the buttons of his snow-white long johns opened to reveal his navel and a V of torso covered with soft dark hair.

He was snuggled close to the big man, his left leg tossed over Kevin's legs, and—yes—he was hard with a morning erection.

Wyatt's first instinct was to take it in hand, stroke it gently, wake the man in such a way that more would follow. Perhaps them shifting so they could suck each other at the same time. Or maybe he would just crawl up onto Kevin, straddle him, take that big cock inside him, ride him. After all, Wyatt wasn't wearing anything besides his T-shirt and thick socks.

And it had been so long since he'd been fucked.

Then Wyatt's eyes went wide again as he realized that yes, he was naked below the waist, and that last night he and Kevin hadn't had sex. And that he, too, was hard and had been slowly grinding himself against Kevin's hip.

He froze.

Oh gods.

The blankets were mostly pulled up around them, and as Wyatt tried to move without disturbing Kevin, he saw that his feet were tangled in the sheet.

Gods!

Pants. Underwear. Something. He had to get something on.

Because they *hadn't* had sex.

Because that had been important.

And as he stopped moving and rested there against the big man for a moment, he remembered why.

Proof.

It was about waiting for proof.

That magic still happened.

"Oh sweet little one," Kevin had said. *"There is no* Cosmic Universal Scale *demanding you be alone so that your friends can have love. I don't know how they all 'suddenly' found love like that. But I know this...."*

"Yes, Kevin?"

"Love is limitless. There is no 'amount' of love. It is endless, forever and ever and ever and there is plenty for sweet little Wyatt. And it isn't your job to be alone. It's your job to open yourself for some man who will love you unconditionally and the way you want to be loved. Don't settle. Wait for just what you want."

And that's what he did.

He, Wyatt Dolan, had waited!

Of course, Kevin had already said he didn't want to have sex—not without something more. But Wyatt knew then and he knew now that it wouldn't have taken much persuasion, especially after Kevin had gotten into bed with him. Howard had taught him many ways to seduce a man. He'd gotten good at it. Was quite good at it. He'd gotten *straight* men into bed.

But he had chosen to wait.

Suddenly words had started coming out of his mouth, and he hadn't even known from where. He had said, *"Okay. If it's real, then let's don't have sex."*

He couldn't believe he'd said it then, and he lay here in awe realizing it now. His balls had ached from want and need, and how long had it been since he'd had sex last? He hadn't jerked off in days, and he usually came at least *twice* a day.

And then he'd said, *"...I want to believe what you say is real."*

Could it be?

"And I don't want to settle."

He was tired of settling. Hadn't he done that for ten years?

"And if we make love now...."

Make love! Had he actually used the words "make love"?

I did. I did use those words.

"...and you decide you don't want me, it will kill me."

Kill me?

Would it?

He remembered making a drunken pass at "Hodor" in the dark and being turned down. Turned down but being told, *"I'm going to regret this Little Bear… but I can't."*

Kevin had wanted him. He had just wanted more. And Wyatt couldn't give him more because he had been with Howard. And he'd been so frustrated because he didn't know why he and Hodor couldn't just fuck.

Hodor—Kevin—was the one who wanted more.

Not me.

I've been the fucking poster child for nonmonogamy for years!

So who possessed me last night and said the things I said?

Wyatt kissed Kevin then, again. But gently and lightly.

"I can't have you tell me something I don't want to hear a week from now, Kevin."

And gods…. It was true. Wyatt's breath caught.

"Not again."

Because there had been men. Men who had made him cheat. Not with his cock, but with something else entirely. Men who had treated him nice and made him feel like they wanted *him* and not just his body.

"And if you were some guy just wanting to fuck? I would probably be fucking you right now."

He would have. Because that is what he did. Have sex with men. But Kevin made him believe there could be more.

"…you've made me believe that something more is possible. And that's what I want."

And then he'd begun to cry.

But Kevin hadn't called him a crybaby. He'd held him tight.

Who possessed me to say those words?

And then Wyatt gasped.

Because he knew who it was. Who it was that possessed him. Who it was that had said those words.

Me! It was me! It was the Wyatt who'd read his mom's Harlequin Romances and dreamed that it could happen to him.

It was me!

He had done it, in no matter how small a way.

Because I want more than sex.

Echoes of the past came to visit him then….

"Monogamy is not normal."

He had said that. Many, many times. He'd preached it.

Preached Howard's message.

"We're men, Wyatt."

Howard had told him time and time again.

"The only reason you want monogamy is that's what you've been taught. It's cultural brainwashing. That you're supposed to be with only one person. But that is so medieval."

Howard had preached it as his life's mission as if he were on the pulpit of some kind of Carnal Crystal Cathedral.

"...when you see a guy that turns you on? And he's willing? You should be able to have sex with him. You should have that right. *You should be able to go for it. All men are different. We like different things. We're shaped different. We have different sized cocks. Some are cut, some are uncut. God! Think about it! You got jocks and bears and cubs and chubs and pups and muscle men and leathermen and twinks and lumberjacks and otters and that's not even counting black men and Asian men and men from the Middle East and Latinos! And there is all* they *like to do! Some men like to fuck. Some like to be fucked. There's role-playing and rough sex and spanking and watersports and sounding and* orgies *and...."*

And he had listened. He'd converted. Like the Christians converted the Pagans in ancient times.

Convert or die.

Or the way they'd converted the Hawaiians. "Saving" them. The Mormons converting the Samoans? Should he count the conversion of the Tibetans from Bon to Buddhism? At least that last became a marriage of two religions.

He'd converted. Convert or lose Howard, and he had desperately not wanted to lose Howard. Who had saved him and given him a gay life, and introduced him to the pagan community... and gods! To Men's Festival!

"You're young" came Howard's echo. *"You need to sow your wild oats, Wyatt! Try things. Try different men. Experience life. I mean, don't you ever want to try topping?"*

Of course he'd wanted to try it. A beauty of being gay was that you could do both! Howard sure wasn't going to let Wyatt fuck *him*.

(except he let big-dicked men fuck him over coffee tables found at little antique stores)

And Wyatt had liked topping. It was amazing. Two men joining that way! Spreading a *man's* legs and seeing that beautiful hole, and the permission to take it and join with him, man to man.

But it had never given Wyatt the joy of when Howard fucked him. Claiming him.

At least in the early days….

Wait. Claiming him? Or enslaving him?

Yes. I converted hook, line, and sinker.

Became a willing slave.

Became a "fucking" missionary.

"*Gays are forgetting who we are, Asher. Gay is becoming okay because we're becoming homogenized, no pun intended. Gay marriage, gay churches, even the pope—an enemy—is suddenly telling people not to judge us. But don't you see? The world is saying that 'homo' is okay as long as we act just like them. Find a man, get married, adopt two point five kids, buy a house with a white picket fence. We're okay—as long as we don't wear pink and don't kiss in public. And as long as we're monogamous.*"

Wyatt closed his eyes tight. *Gods. My words. I said that.*

No.

Not my words.

It killed me when Howard said we could never be monogamous!

And then came *Kevin's* words.

"*I don't care if monogamy isn't 'gay.' That's what I want. Cauley said the same thing. That gay men didn't need to be monogamous.*"

And gods… Kevin had been converted too. And he hadn't liked it.

But I did. I liked the sex. I liked the men. I liked the experiences. I can't fucking blame it all on Howard. I liked it.

"*I don't care if monogamy isn't 'gay.' That's what I want.*"

Maybe it's time, Wyatt thought. *To put that behind? I did have fun.*

He propped himself up on one elbow and looked down into Kevin's sleeping face. His heart skipped a beat, and he thought, *How wonderful would it be to wake up every single morning with a man like this? And only him. To only go to sleep with a man like him. To only have sex with one man.*

Wyatt looked down into Kevin's beautiful face—his heart raced now—and thought…

Kevin Owens….

Not a man like him.

Him.

Kevin.

Oh gods…. Would he ever want me?

More echoes. Kevin saying…

"*I've wanted you forever. Since the first time I saw you sitting at that registration table my very first Men's Festival. I was so nervous. It took everything in me to come. I almost turned around a dozen times. I almost didn't get out of my truck, no matter how many hours I'd driven to get there. And then there was you."*

Kevin had wanted him.

I think he still does!

Kevin stirred then, and Wyatt suddenly remembered he was still half-naked, and he quickly slipped from the bed and looked about for his underwear. Luckily he actually had a pair with him as he usually went commando, but he'd discovered a brand he liked called Bearwear and of course he'd had to buy the red-and-black lumberjack pattern. He spotted them half under the table, not sure how they got there, and dashed for them, scrambled into them and…

"God, what a nice thing to wake up to."

Wyatt jumped and nearly fell to the floor, one leg in his underwear, the other not. They dropped, still around one ankle, and he had no choice but to bend and pull them up. Get the other leg in the other hole and…

"That adorable round plump butt."

Wyatt stiffened upright in surprise, yanking his underwear up as far as they would go, nearly wracking himself. "What?" he squeaked.

"God, Wyatt. I think you have the nicest bottom on the planet."

He turned—face burning—and in that early morning sunlight saw the desire in Kevin's eyes.

He wants me.

Kevin wanted *him*.

He stretched out a big muscular arm, held open his big hand, motioned with his fingers. "Come here," he whispered. "Come back to bed."

Now? You want me now? With bad breath and no showers for days and bedhead and….

"Thank God you put those underwear back on because there is no way I would be able to resist you another moment if you hadn't. And call me a fucking fool, but I want to wait. I want to wait until it hurts."

Then in complete shock, tears stinging his eyes, Wyatt went to Kevin.

He wants to wait.

That was a good thing.

He climbed into the bed, and Kevin swept his arms around him and rolled him back to the spot where he'd slept all night. They kissed. They both got hard.

And somehow they waited.

CHAPTER THIRTY-FOUR

THEY HAD hot cereal for breakfast and then decided to head out into the snow. Because "There's something I want to see," Kevin told Wyatt.

They bundled up and found that it was snowing again, big heavy flakes, but when they walked past the caretaker's cabin, they saw Gryphon and Saffron sitting at their little table (under the roof overhang, of course) as usual (even in the snow). And they assured Kevin and Wyatt that this time they really weren't supposed to get more than another inch (they did have their fire pit going, and Kevin couldn't help but be reminded of Cauley's).

"I hope so," Wyatt called down to them. "Otherwise we might never get out of here."

"I don't think that would be so bad," Kevin said and was delighted when he saw his little bear blush. Wyatt was wearing that cute bear hat and scarf, furthering his little bearhood, and... *God. I'm falling, and I am falling hard.*

As if he hadn't been in love with Wyatt for a long time.

Since the parking lot was plowed—"Oh, look!" Kevin said as he pointed—doing what he wanted to do wasn't going to be as difficult as he'd imagined. Gryphon had actually used the snowblower to clear a path as far as the steps. Something most people who came to Camp Sanctuary almost universally came to think of as The Steps.

There were sixty of them.

And after a week, or even just a weekend, of walking up and down those fuckers, it seemed a hundred and sixty at least. But it was better than the old way one reached the upper plateau, where most people camped. That way had been "stairs" made from natural rocks and various-sized slabs of stone that crisscrossed up the slope and were scary as hell to climb in the middle of the night. The newer steps, all sixty of them, were steep, but better. Far better.

Today they were covered in snow, but not as much as Kevin might have expected. Again he'd been blessed. Somewhere he wanted (needed?) to go was located up top on the plateau. And the blessing was that between here and there were a lot of trees growing very closely together, many of them pines with wide, overreaching branches. Pine trees stayed green instead of turning skeletal, and they had blocked a lot of the snow. The steps really weren't nearly as bad as he had worried they might be. His mission might very well succeed.

"We can do this," Kevin said aloud.

"You want us to climb those in the snow?" Wyatt looked at him incredulously. "*Today*?"

"Wait here," Kevin said and dashed off and was soon back with an oversized push broom borrowed from Gryphon.

"I can do that," Gryphon had said. "I was going to anyway."

"I got this," Kevin replied. At least he thought he had it.

These were The Steps after all.

Sixty of them.

Covered in snow!

But sixty. Not a hundred and sixty. And not *all* that much snow.

Thank you, pine trees!

And then, together, he and Wyatt cleared them faster than they both had expected, and in less than an hour, they had reached the top.

What they saw before them was breathtaking.

What was normally a football-field-sized expanse of grass, surrounded by a wall of trees, was now white, white, and white. The trees, usually thick with green, looked like black-and-gray skeletal hands reaching for the sky at the far side of the snowy vastness.

This was the place they camped every year?

And it was cold. There was no protection from the wind that swept over that field of white, and their breath swirled around them in smoky plumes.

"Gosh," Wyatt whispered.

Kevin only nodded.

He looked down to his left, north, to the area where he'd camped the last few years. He no longer set up at Avalon, far to the south. Now his tent was among friends (although he did set up back into the trees a bit; he wanted *some* privacy).

He turned back to Wyatt. "I know you're cold, and the snow is deep, but is there any way you'd go with me down to the end?" He pointed the way he'd been looking. "I want to see what it looks like down where I camp."

Wyatt looked that way and his expression turned contemplative. Finally, he shrugged, looked up at Kevin, and said, "Okay."

Kevin could see Wyatt wasn't sure, and he determined then that if the going was even half as tough as it looked, they'd turn around and come back.

"After all," Wyatt said then, "we've come all this way, right?"

Kevin smiled. He took Wyatt's right hand so that the little bear would be to his left, walking closer to the tree line—what there was of it—and they waded into the snow. It was at least two feet deep here, and the going wasn't easy. He was afraid it really wasn't going to work, when Wyatt started laughing.

Kevin looked and saw Wyatt staggering around like a drunk man, a big grin on his face.

"Laughing, baby bear?"

Wyatt nodded. "What do you think?" Wyatt lifted his furry scarf to show his ears.

"What?" Kevin asked.

"My earrings. What do you think of my testicle earrings?" Wyatt weighed invisible testes with the palms of his hands. "Do you think they'll ever go back down to where they're supposed to go?"

"We'll get them down where they're supposed to be," Kevin said with a smile.

"We?" Wyatt asked.

Kevin nodded, and Wyatt grinned hugely, and then they really started to plow their way into the snow.

"Be careful, baby." Baby? Had he just called Wyatt "baby"?

Wyatt laughed more, despite the fact the snow was sometimes hitting his balls.

"Now what are you laughing at?" Kevin felt a little *zing*! With everything this man-boy or boy-man had gone through, he was laughing! Howard was such a fucking fool for letting him go.

Could I be lucky enough…?

"Thinking of another joke."

Kevin grinned. "Tell it, then."

"You sure?" Wyatt asked and spiraled an arm to keep from falling.

"Of course," Kevin said, lending his strength to help Wyatt stay on his feet.

"Okay! If you're sure." (*pant, pant*) "These three buddies all decide to go to a ski lodge for the weekend." (*pant, pant*) "But when they get there, there's been some kind of mix-up and there aren't enough rooms. Not only that, but they're going to have to share a bed. All *three* of them!"

Wyatt panted again. "Then right in the middle of the night, the guy on the right wakes up and says, 'Whoa! I had this *wild* dream that somebody gave me a hand job!' And the guy on the left wakes up and, unbelievably, *he* says, 'I had the same dream!' Then the guy in the middle wakes up and says, 'Wow! I just had this really vivid dream that I was skiing!'"

Kevin started to laugh. He couldn't help it. He realized he'd even heard it before, but with Wyatt telling it, it was just so silly adorable naughty funny. He looked at the little bear, and his expression was so sweet it melted Kevin's heart.

Just don't go getting ideas, he thought. *Because if I ever get you into* my *bed, it will only* ever *be the two of us.*

They didn't get much farther before Kevin saw something he hadn't expected. It was enough to bring him to a gasping stop.

This part of Camp had always been called the Plateau, but somehow he had never realized how apropos that was. He had always thought the protective circle of trees around the field where most people camped was set right in the middle of a forest.

No.

A ring of trees was exactly what it was. But not a forest.

The land dropped off in a very steep slope, and to his shock he could see for miles. He could see great vastnesses of farms and fields, usually covered in corn and wheat and soybeans, now buried in snow. He could see roads—thin black crisscrossing lines—cleared by plows, and here and there a moving car.

It looked so desolate, and yet at the same time—

"It's beautiful," Wyatt said with a gasp of his own.

They stood there for what seemed like a very long time until Kevin noticed Wyatt was shivering and realized his own feet were cold—wet and *very* cold.

"Let's go back," he said quietly.

Wyatt turned to him. "But didn't you want to go down to the end?"

"I've seen what I really came here to see," he said. How different would the view be down there?

So they went back, as quickly as they dared, and helped each other down the steps to the bottom and then past Main Hall and across the parking lot, and as they were passing the caretaker's cabin, he heard their names being called.

They both stopped and looked down the small slope and saw Saffron standing at the door to her cabin. "We've been watching for you. We have hot chocolate."

"Oh, yummy!" Wyatt exclaimed.

"We're wet and cold," Kevin called back. "We *need* to change."

"Take it with you!" She grinned and ducked inside and was out in a moment, all bundled up, and came up the little path and handed them a big Thermos. "Enjoy."

"You are a goddess," Wyatt said.

She bowed her head. "You honor me." Saffron looked back up, a sweet smile on her ageless face. "I but serve the goddess."

They all hugged, and then Kevin insisted they get back to the cabin before they get frostbite. He hadn't been able to feel his toes for a while.

The cabin was very warm, and they both saw the huge pile of wood next to the stove.

"Gryphon," Wyatt said.

"Must have been," Kevin agreed, because the wood had been nearly gone this morning. He'd meant to restock it with the stack next to the cabin's steps but had forgotten in his mission to get up top. He opened the stove's door, and sure enough, it blazed. Gryphon had even built up the fire.

He turned to Wyatt, who was rubbing at his arms despite the warmth of the room.

"Let's get out of these clothes and into something dry," he said.

They both stripped down to their underwear, and Kevin couldn't help but admire the flesh revealed—Wyatt's legs were sexily hairy, but not overly so—but that's about all he really saw. Their underwear, his own long johns and Wyatt's T-shirt and red-and-black boxer shorts, were dry. But their feet, on the other hand, were wet!

"Get on the bed!" he commanded, and Wyatt did as he was told. Kevin climbed onto the bearskin-covered mattress on the other side, took Wyatt's feet into his lap, and rubbed them rapidly.

"Gods, that hurts and feels good at the same time!" Wyatt cried.

Then to Kevin's surprise, Wyatt pulled one of Kevin's feet to him and began to rub it as well. Kevin immediately saw what Wyatt meant by the pain/pleasure, and soon he was really feeling his feet again.

It occurred to him then that what they were doing was very intimate. It wasn't like you held another man's feet every day. Or rubbed them. Especially in your lap.

He realized Wyatt had very sexy feet. Strong, with cute, almost stubby, toes with just a smattering of hair on top. And the smell was nice. Musk. Man. Clean. Or as clean as they could be when neither of them had been able to shower in a day or so.

God. He thought he might be getting an erection!

Wyatt was on Kevin's second foot when he stopped and simply cradled it. He looked up and met Kevin's eyes. "They're so big."

Kevin gulped. "Is that a bad thing?"

Wyatt shook his head slowly and then pulled Kevin's foot closer into his lap. Massaged it slowly. Deeply. "I like them." Then ever so quietly he added, "They smell good too."

"They do?" Kevin asked, and blushed, because that was just what he'd been thinking about Wyatt's feet.

"Oh, yes. They smell like man."

Yes.

Like man.

They locked eyes then for the longest time, holding each other's feet like two meditating Indians who had somehow gotten too close together.

And then Wyatt was tickling Kevin's feet, and Kevin laughed and tried to yank them away, but damn, that little bear was stronger than he looked. So he started tickling Wyatt's back, and Wyatt shrieked with laughter, and in no time they were rolling about tickling each other everywhere.

Finally: "Stop! Stop!" Wyatt was all but screaming. "Uncle! Uncle!"

They laughed and collapsed back onto the fur and gasped to catch their breath.

Then Kevin remembered the hot chocolate, and they put on some clothes, Kevin reluctantly (and by the furtive glances directed at him, he thought Wyatt felt the same way). He liked the way Wyatt looked in those black-and-red plaid underwear, the crotch full with what they contained and the way the soft fabric clung to his round butt. Dress they did though; blazing stove or not, they didn't want to catch their deaths of cold. And when Kevin saw Wyatt struggling to put on a second pair of socks, he gave the little bear a pair of his own. These slipped on much easier.

"Your big feet," Wyatt said with a sexy grunt.

"*You* like them," Kevin said, surprising himself.

Wyatt nodded. "A lot."

And then before they jumped each other's bones then and there, they had hot chocolate.

THEY HAD sandwiches for lunch. They'd each picked up meat and a loaf of bread on their way to Camp, so there was more than enough. That was when Kevin noticed Wyatt's book. It was sitting on the little table next to the bed. It had been turned in a way that he could just now see the title.

"*Eat, Pray, Love*?" he asked.

Wyatt immediately looked wary. "You're not going to make fun, are you?"

Make fun? "Why would I make fun of you?"

Wyatt shrugged. "There's a lot of jokes about that book. I don't know why either. People make fun. They even had an episode of *South Park* about it called 'Eat, Pray, Queef.'"

Kevin shrugged. "Huh?"

Wyatt gave him a most curious look back.

"I don't get it," Kevin said.

"You don't get what?" Wyatt asked.

"What's qweef?"

And he could see Wyatt was about to laugh but then shook his head instead. "Never mind."

Kevin went to the little table and picked the book up. "Actually I love this book," he said. "I've read it twice."

"Really?" Wyatt asked. He looked like a puppy, afraid it *might* be about to get hit.

Then Kevin realized what this was about. "Howard. He made fun of you about this book, didn't he?" He sat down at the table next to Wyatt.

Wyatt was looking away.

He reached out and touched Wyatt's hand. "*Fuck* Howard," Kevin said.

Wyatt jerked in his seat.

Oh, sweet baby bear. "Don't let him *own* you, Wyatt."

Wyatt yanked his hand away. "Just like that?" he cried, and snapped his fingers. "*Just like that*? I'm supposed to get over him? Just *leap* and the fucking net will appear? I'm supposed to believe it's *that* easy?"

Kevin pulled back.

"Like you're supposed to get over someone named Cauley? Just like *that*?"

What happened?

One minute they were laughing and flirting and rubbing feet—God! That had been sexy, and it was feet, just feet!—and eating sandwiches.

And then he noticed Wyatt's book.

And then there was something about "qweefs," whatever *that* meant.

And then he saw that Wyatt was hurting because of that fucker Howard.

And then he had simply offered some advice and...

God.

I am fortune's fool.

"I'm sorry," he said. "Wyatt, I'm sorry.

Wyatt looked away.

"I *really* am."

And, oh God. Please have that be forgiveness in his eyes. Please, please have that be forgiveness.

"I'm sorry, Kevin," Wyatt whispered.

"There is no reason for *you* to be sorry, Wyatt. It was *me*! I am so sorry!"

Oh, the look in those eyes!

And they're looking at me!

AND OH, the way Kevin was looking at him!

Wyatt felt ashamed. How could he be angry at this sweet man?

Explain! Explain, you fool!

Howard. "He was like—"

Like what? What was he like? What was the man who had been in his life for ten years like? Sweet? Mean? Funny? Scary? Thoughtful? Thoughtless? So good in the beginning and then for some reason, slowly and inevitably, changing into something, someone, else? Yes. Howard was all those things. And he was.... Oh gods! He was...

"—like a *cancer* in me, Kevin! Slowly killing me. And you think something is wrong, and you can't go to the doctor because if you *do*, then you will *know*. And you don't want to *know* because then what are you going to do? You'll *know* you're dying! Or that you'll have to go through the hell of treatment before you *might* survive."

Wyatt began to cry and cursed himself for it.

"He *saved* me, Kevin! Howard came to me on a very dark night, and he saved me. He gave me everything I had ever wanted... and then...."

Wyatt's throat seized up and a sob wracked his body. "And then Howard *took it away*!"

This time when Kevin reached out to take his hand, Wyatt let him. He let that big hand take his, swallow his, and it was warm and soft and made him feel safe, the way a big man's hands always did.

"I should have gone to the doctor, Kevin! I should have left him *years* ago. They all said it. All my friends. Some more softly than others. Some louder! Asher made it clear! He told me that I was too good for Howard, and I didn't believe it. He said I was better off without him. Sloan was nicer about it. Even Scott, who could be a Grade A asshole, was nicer about it!"

Wyatt shook his head. "I should have left him, but I believed him. I believed him when he said that if I left him, I wouldn't have any friends—"

But I do! I have such wonderful friends!

"—and that no one would want me—"

But gods, the look in Kevin's eyes! He wants me!

"—and I would be alone for the rest of my life."

"Oh, sweet Little Bear. Don't you see it? It is the other way around. *No* one likes Howard. No one can stand *him*! They only put up with him because they like *you—love* you! Not the other way around."

Wyatt sat bolt upright in his chair.

"What?"

"Oh, sweet Wyatt. *None* of us liked him. Not anyone that called you friend. They didn't put up with you. They put up with *him*."

Kevin took Wyatt's hands in both of his and gently stroked the web between his thumb and forefinger as he had done before. Once again it made Wyatt tremble.

"I think the only people who like Howard are the people who don't know him."

Kevin was saying these things about Howard? About Big Sir? It couldn't be true.

"Think about it, Wyatt. You were the one everyone cheered for onstage. Did Howard ever get onstage except for maybe to show off his big cock?"

The time Howard played Pan in my Queen song about wanting to break free.

The whole theme of the act was escaping the enforced rules of organized religion. He'd gotten several of the Men's Festival attendees to dress up as famous religious figures to be his backup dancers. And

Howard had pointed out that he'd been Pan for Halloween a few years ago, and it had shocked Wyatt that he wanted to actually be on the stage with him. That he would be Pan, and Wyatt's other friends would play Jesus and Moses and Mohammed and Buddha.

Then it hit him.

It had been Howard's idea that he pull his dick out—

"I mean," Howard had said, *"isn't Pan's big cock showing in every picture you've ever seen of him?"*

—and he had been so thrilled that Howard had actually, for once, wanted to be *in* one of his acts that he said okay, even though that meant he couldn't put it on YouTube (and he'd really wanted to put that act on YouTube because it was the best act he'd ever done).

Was the reason he wanted to be in the act to try to give Wyatt second billing to his cock? Wyatt gasped.

"Jesus, Wyatt! That is why Howard put you down all the time! He was *jealous*. He *knew* everyone loved you. And he hated it. Before you started coming to Festival, he thought he was king of the hill. But once he started bringing you, everyone started paying attention to you."

Could it be?

"B-but I thought they were just being nice," he said. "The way you should always be nice when someone you care about gets into a relationship. You welcome their new honey."

"That's what *you* do," Kevin said. "Because you are a dear, sweet person, and you always want people to feel welcome. But the reason everyone was nice to you was because they genuinely liked *you*. And within no time, *you* were the one people wanted to be around. And he couldn't stand it."

Wyatt shivered. He couldn't believe what he was hearing. "Me?" he somehow managed to say.

"You, Wyatt. You. Only you."

Then Kevin got up and pulled Wyatt to his feet and covered his face with kisses.

AND STILL they waited.

They started by reading to each other. Kevin was first. He opened Wyatt's copy of *Eat, Pray, Love* and read out loud the chapter he said was one of his favorites. It was all about the author making a contract with the Universe. How she had physically written up her request and then signed it, and her friend signed it, and then they sat and imagined everyone they knew who would sign it. Her mother and father and sister. Friends. The two of them *imagined* them actually signing it. *Felt* it. And then they got into it and thought of other people they didn't even know that they thought would sign it. Bill and Hillary Clinton. Saint Francis of Assisi. Abraham Lincoln. Nelson Mandela. Gandhi. Mother Teresa. Jimmy Carter. Eleanor Roosevelt. The Dalai Lama. And then, like a miracle, just a few hours later, what the author wanted came true.

"I remember that part now," Wyatt said. "And it's like that thing you said. Ask. Believe. Receive." He was trembling with the idea. Could it be that simple?

"It's just like that, Wyatt," Kevin said.

Then Wyatt took the book and leafed through it and found one of his favorite passages and shared it. They were back on the bed now, and they'd pulled the bearskin up around them. There was a little hot chocolate left, and they shared that from the big red Thermos lid. Wyatt read about how Elizabeth Gilbert—the author—fell away from a religious teaching. How she had a friend that said you shouldn't cherry-pick your religion but Elizabeth disagreed. "I think you have every right to cherry-pick when it comes to moving your spirit and finding peace in God." He read the whole chapter, and Kevin listened to every word, never faded away, never interrupted him to ask if he'd seen that e-mail about "how we can save big on life-extending vitamins."

Wyatt had Kevin's undivided attention.

And when he was done, Kevin enthusiastically said, "Yes! I especially love where she says that we have the right to find *any* metaphor we need as we cross the 'worldly divide' so that we can feel elated— ecstatic—or comforted."

After that, Kevin had more he wanted to share. But first he made sure that Wyatt didn't mind (when had Howard ever done that?). "Do you mind if I read one of my favorite sections in here?" Kevin asked. "It's about a page…."

Wyatt didn't mind at all. He loved hearing Kevin's rich, deep voice. "Go for it," Wyatt said. "Why stop now?"

So Kevin read from the book he said was one of his favorites. *Leap and the Net Will Appear!* by Malcolm Kane.

"In 1957," he began, "a huge plaster Buddha had to be moved from its temple to another location due to a highway being built through

Bangkok. When the crane began to lift it, to the horror of the monks, it started to crack. They had it lowered back to the ground and covered it with a tarp because it was going to rain. Later, when the head monk went to check on it with a flashlight, he was surprised when something shone back at him."

Kevin looked up from the page. Was Wyatt still listening?

He smiled when he saw he was. He was paying attention to every word!

"He went and got a hammer and chisel and began to chip away at the cement. And what did he find? To his astonishment he found that he had uncovered a golden statue over ten feet tall, two and a half tons in weight and estimated at a value of 196 million dollars!

"Historians believe that a few hundred years before, when Thailand (known as Siam at that time) was about to be invaded by the Burmese army, the monks who ran the monastery covered the Buddha with cement to keep it from being looted. It appears that sometime after that the army slaughtered them. And therefore there was no one left alive who knew about the Golden Buddha. So for years and years, the monks who gained possession of that statue had no idea their Buddha was golden!

"What this story tells us metaphysically is we are like that statue of the Buddha. We are golden. But we have covered ourselves with years and layers of muck. We came to believe that we are common, worthless, and undeserving. And that is most untrue!

"For years I let my stepfather mistreat me. He regaled me with tales of how lucky I was that he'd married my mother. That if it weren't for him, she and I would be on the streets. That we would have lost our home and our car and everything. My dad had died and left us with considerable debts. My stepfather told me I was worthless. That had it been left to me, we would have been lost. That he had saved us and that I had done nothing, and what was more, I was still doing nothing.

"And then I began to really think about what he'd said.

"First, I realized that there was nothing I could have done to help me and my mother out of the predicament we were in. I was little. I was a kid! What was I supposed to do?

"But to my surprise, the rest… rang true. As an adult I still wasn't doing anything with my life. And whose fault was that? Certainly not his. Unless I really was worthless. And I sat down in the park and thought about it more. What could I do?

"Then this… voice whispered in my ear. I heard it. Clear as crystal. And it said, 'Why not pursue your dreams?'

"And to my surprise, the only answer I could really give was, 'Yeah. Why not?'

"Of course, I didn't do it overnight. It took me a while to *un*believe my stepfather. But with friends and teachers and wonderful books, I did learn.

"What's more, I learned that under the muck I was golden!

"*We* are golden! Each and every one of us!

"I began to believe in myself. Take care of myself. I made mistakes. But I was chipping away those shards of cement.

"And soon the gold began to shine.

"It is important that we know that we are all gold.

"But sometimes we must first chip away the cement, so that at last, we can truly shine."

Kevin looked up from his book to see Wyatt watching him. He saw Wyatt swallow. Neither of them said anything for what seemed forever.

Then Wyatt said, "Wow…," and Kevin couldn't help but smile.

SOMEHOW THAT turned into them reading the new Stephen King book to each other for several hours until Wyatt's stomach growled rather fiercely and Kevin decided it was time for dinner.

Hamburgers.

Even though there were no buns, there was plenty of bread and there was cheese and chips, and Wyatt couldn't remember when he'd had such good burgers.

And it was right in the middle of dinner that the lights came on!

"Yippee," Wyatt shouted and jumped to his feet and did some twerking right there. To his surprise, Kevin joined him—and gods, it was hot to see the big muscular man bouncing that big muscular man-ass and being so damned silly—and they made a complete circuit around the table before bursting into laughter.

They finished their burgers—but not before Wyatt jumped up and plugged in anything and everything that he felt needed charging. Some things the world revolved around, and needing to listen to P!nk was one of them. Wyatt then pulled some pudding cups from one of his bags and declared, "Dessert! Butterscotch, and unlike Walter, I love butterscotch pudding!"

Kevin looked at him blankly.

Did he explain what that meant? Did he tell him about *Fringe*, one of his favorite shows of all time? "Never mind, it would take too long to explain."

Then to his surprise, Kevin's eyes widened ever so slightly. "Are you talking about Walter on *Fringe*?"

Wyatt grinned near to splitting. He knew. Kevin knew!

And to his surprise Kevin did a passable imitation of John Noble as *Fringe*'s elderly crazy man. "They have this *horrible* pudding here. Butterscotch pudding on Mondays; it's *dreadful*."

"It's Thursday," Wyatt responded gleefully, quoting the next line from the episode.

"Oh," Kevin responded. "That's *fantastic* news."

They both burst into laughter.

Wyatt pulled open his container, and realizing the spoons were half a room away—and feeling a tad lazy—he stuck his finger into the cup and pulled out a glob of golden-brown pudding and stuck it in his mouth. Did he suck it off sexily, or not? Uncharacteristically, he decided on "not" and then began happily blathering about one unimportant thing or another, most of it somehow revolving around how happy he was that Ben Franklin flew a kite in the rain and Thomas Edison invented light bulbs.

But then something hit him.

He sat bolt upright in his chair. "Oh, gosh."

Kevin looked up from his pudding. "What?"

Wyatt swallowed and wondered how to bring this up. Because he found himself not wanting the logical answer.

"What?" Kevin asked, with a growing expression of concern drawn on his face.

Well, shit on a stick. Wyatt sighed. "Now that the electricity is back on… will you be going back to your cabin?" He couldn't believe how much he wanted Kevin to say no.

A startled look came to Kevin's face. "Oh!"

So he hadn't thought about that either.

"I guess…."

Was that disappointment in his voice?

"I mean, you came here to be alone, right?"

"Yeah," Wyatt said reluctantly. "B-but…."

"But?" Kevin said, sitting up straighter in his seat.

"I…. That doesn't seem as important anymore. For me." But then, hadn't Kevin come to Camp to be alone as well? "But…."

"But?" Kevin repeated.

"Didn't you come here to be alone too?"

Kevin slumped ever so slightly. Pursed his lips. Looked away. "I guess I did."

There was a long pause.

Kevin looked back at him, eyes deep and unreadable.

Again, neither said anything for a long time. But wasn't this Kevin's turn?

Finally, unable to stand it any longer—*please say you don't want to leave, please say you don't want to leave*—Wyatt said, "If you need to…." *Please say you don't want to leave….*

Another pause as all kinds of things seemed to flash over Kevin's face. "I don't know, Wyatt. Because to tell you the truth, I'm not fully sure why I came."

"I… I don't understand."

"It was lots of things, Wyatt. It was this strange and deep calling of the Land."

Wyatt nodded. He understood that call. Luckily he was less than an hour's drive from Camp Sanctuary. There were a lot of people, like Kevin, for whom that wasn't the case.

"It was the fact that… someone died."

It was Wyatt's turn to sit up. "Died?" he asked. "Oh gosh, Kevin. You didn't say anything about someone dying." *Did you?* Had he, and Wyatt had been too self-absorbed to hear it? "Did you?"

Kevin shook his head. "I didn't."

Because I was going on and on and on about myself? Wyatt wondered.

"But not because of you."

Wyatt breathed an inward sigh of relief.

"I…. It was private. And you and I talked about so many other things."

"My things," Wyatt said. "I'm sorry."

Kevin's eyes flickered. "Why? I'm an adult. If I needed to talk about something, it's my responsibility to bring it up."

Really? Because you've asked me all kinds of questions about myself. From throwing baby Jesus out with the bathwater to whether the better version of P!nk's song "Perfect" included the word "fuck." Kevin, surprisingly, liked the cleaner version of the song.

"Really?" he asked.

"Really," Kevin stated.

Pause.

"So you don't want to talk about it, then? Like your… friend dying?"

"I don't know what to say, Wyatt."

Pause.

"Was this someone close to you? I mean… to make you drive to Camp. Don't you live out east? New York or something?"

There was a slight smile on Kevin's face. "Yes. New York City. Rosebank in Staten Island to be precise."

That didn't mean anything to Wyatt, but he nodded anyway.

"Cauley was my ex," Kevin said.

"Oh."

"We haven't been together in quite a while. But we stayed friends. I found out I could be friends with him when I wasn't worried what he was up to."

"Up to?" Did that mean what it meant when it came to Howard?

There was pain in Kevin's eyes now, and Wyatt wondered if he should have let this go.

"We were together for quite a while. I fell for him fast and heavy. We met at a birthday picnic for a mutual friend in Central Park." A flicker of a smile passed over Kevin's face. "He was funny and crazy and wild and did the silliest things." The smile grew a bit. "I was *hooked*." He looked at Wyatt. "I guess I—no, I know I lived vicariously through him. He was insane." Kevin laughed. "But in a good way. Dressed up in crazy outfits. And he was an activist. A really well-known one in New York. Did you know he once—with some cronies, of course—painted some closeted senator's house in the rainbow colors while the man was out of town? I don't know how the fuck he did it."

No, Wyatt didn't know that. It sounded cool, though, and he told Kevin so.

"No, of course you wouldn't. Why would you?"

The sadness came back and Wyatt immediately wished there was something he could do about it.

"The problem with Cauley is that he just burned too bright, do you know what I mean?"

Wyatt wasn't sure. But then a scene from a movie came to him. Rutger Hauer playing an android replicant about to murder his maker.

"It's like that line out of that movie *Blade Runner*," Kevin said as if reading his mind. "'The light that burns twice as bright burns half as long.' And Cauley burned really bright, Wyatt. People loved him too. Trouble is, he didn't believe it. This was a man who traveled all over doing education on safe sex and the dangers of meth. And what happens?" Kevin took a big shuddering breath. "He somehow got mixed up with a bunch of meth heads!" Kevin shook his head and then his voice dropped to a whisper. "He doesn't even know how he got HIV. Doesn't remember. He started doing drugs and cheating on me, and he got HIV and doesn't even remember how. He had no idea who gave it to him. And I couldn't deal with it. I think I could have forgiven a mistake or two. I could have helped him deal with the drugs. I did, in fact. I could have forgiven him for an infidelity. No one is perfect. But putting my life in danger and then lying about it?" He shook his head.

Wyatt shivered, struck by some of the similarities of their stories.

Kevin looked at him again. "And when you were sharing about Howard, I didn't want to steal anything from it by talking about my troubles. When someone is pouring out their heart, the last thing they want is for someone to one-up them."

And meth addiction and dying surely topped anything he'd dealt with, thought Wyatt. Gods! A sudden new perception hit him. Even shame.

"I don't know, Kevin." He got up and went to him and first laid a hand on his shoulder, and then cupped his cheek. "I mean, when we think we have it rough, sometimes it helps to get things put into their proper perspective. How did you stand listening to me go on about that man after what you've been through?" Wyatt went to one knee and gazed into the face of this beautiful man. "I am so sorry."

"For *what*?" Kevin asked.

"What I was blathering on about must have seemed so fucking petty!"

"No!" Kevin cried. "And see? This is why I didn't talk about Cauley. I didn't want you to feel that way. That's why I shouldn't have said anything just now."

"Isn't that what friends are for?" Wyatt said. "To talk to? My mom has this movie she loves. And the big line in that one is, 'In a cold world, you need your friends to keep you warm.'" He glanced out the window. "It's certainly cold out there. And Kevin, I haven't felt as warm as I have with you in a long time."

Kevin smiled. "Really?"

"Really," said Wyatt and he hugged Kevin, and gods, Kevin hugged him back. Hugged him fiercely.

"Oh, Wyatt, you are such a beautiful man," Kevin said into his shoulder.

They held each other for a long time.

AND IT was shortly after that when Wyatt very abruptly knew it was time.

Thinking about all he and Kevin had in common—who would have thought? And how he had come here to put things behind him. It was time.

He stood up straight, took a deep breath, squared his shoulders.

I'll be alone all my life without you, Howard? Really? No one would want to be my friend? I have three of the best friends on the planet. And their lovers are becoming best friends as well. I work in a magical place with magical coworkers and a boss who is a mom. I have Men's Festival and gods, I've been so afraid of what it's going to be like this summer and how I would be treated, but if what this beautiful man says is true, I'll be welcome. And Kevin likes me, he wants me. Why did you treat me so badly, Howard? Why? Kevin says you're jealous of me. But why hurt me? Why?

"It's time to stop asking," Wyatt said aloud.

Kevin placed his hands on Wyatt's hips and raised his eyebrows. "Stop asking what?"

Wyatt stood up even taller. "It's time to say good-bye."

Kevin's brows came together. "You're leaving? Wyatt, just because we've got the electricity back doesn't mean we can still get out of—"

Wyatt shook his head.

"It's time for me to go to Pax Place."

Kevin's mouth opened. Then shut. He nodded. But he didn't say anything.

"And I need to go now. Before it gets dark."

He shivered—not so much from the cold, but for what he was about to do.

"Yeah, you don't want to be there in the cold and the dark."

"I'll take my bearskin."

Kevin nodded. "I think that's good. You are a bear."

"Bear is one of my guides," Wyatt said, and Kevin didn't laugh. Of course he didn't, and that gave Wyatt a little more strength.

I'm glad I'm wearing two pairs of socks, Wyatt thought. *I'm glad one pair is Kevin's.*

Without thinking anymore—because gods, hadn't he done enough thinking?—he prepared himself for the cold and for the big good-bye. He tugged a sweatshirt out of his bag and wiggled into it and then climbed into a pair of sweatpants as well. Two layers. Good. He nodded. Then came gloves and his bear hat—which Kevin liked!—and everything he would need for the ritual. Not much, really. His wand that he'd carved himself out of hawthorn from right here at Camp—hawthorn because of its masculine properties and fairy magick—and his athame. He wouldn't need his chalice or pentacle plate. His fireplace lighter, of course; he'd need that. The tiny bottle of fuel in case the wood was wet, even though he'd prepared for that. Nothing else. It was all there.

Then he went to Kevin, and Kevin met him and kissed his furry cheeks and then his mouth, and the promise of more kisses made him tremble.

Kevin nodded and gave him an encouraging smile, and that was one more boost of strength.

Time.

It was time.

He turned and went to the bed, took up his bearskin, and swirled it around him with great ceremony, glanced one last time at his friend—because Kevin was that if nothing else—and then headed into the snow.

CHAPTER THIRTY-FIVE

GRYPHON AND Saffron had been right. It hadn't snowed much that morning. There was just a gentle fluff on the path and, Wyatt supposed, everything else, although it was hard to tell, especially with the growing shadows.

And Kevin was right. The way he'd cleared with the snowblower went right to the break in the trees across the road and when Wyatt looked, he saw the path into Pax Pace was all but snow-free. Down the path he went, and while the path itself was magically and practically clear, to the left and right the snow was quite thick. The trees were tall but thin, and somehow it was only the path that was clear and heavy with pine needles and mulch. It looked like he was walking down a corridor through Snedronningen's castle—gorgeous! Of course, the Egyptian statues painted a different picture from Hans Christian Andersen's, but by then the image was already in his mind and heart.

There were two of the gold-painted statues only a few feet down the path, and he was surprised when he saw the next pair ten feet or so down the way. Normally, with the trees laden with leaves, the guardians would suddenly appear among the green. But now he could see them clearly.

There were short torches along the way, and even though it wasn't dark yet, it would be soon. It was winter after all. One minute it was sunny, the next in shadow, the next it was dark. So to help on the way back, he bent to try to light one of the torches with his big lighter and was delighted when it lit almost immediately. Then—careful not to drag his bearskin through any of them—he lit each one as he went. He recalled and laughed at a line he remembered from one of Scott Cunningham's books on ritual garments, how you needed to be very careful because they were unintentionally designed to be just ready to burst into flames.

It was at the second pair of statues that Wyatt stopped in his tracks.

If the path through Pax Place had been a corridor through the Snow Queen's castle, what lay beyond was her throne room. He gasped at the beauty and wished he were a poet so he could describe what he was seeing to his friends later.

Only the other day, the open twenty-foot circular clearing had reminded him of a church. The intertwined branches of the trees had made a natural roof of the goddess's creation. Normally it was a canopy of green above, but today it was ice. Snow was all above him, and there were already dozens of icicles of every size, like crystal stalactites, hanging from that white roof.

It was like being in a stunning white and crystalline room, and try as he might, he could find no true words to accurately describe its divine beauty.

The walls were curved outward and mixed with branches and trunks, and the ground, like the path, was relatively snow-free. There was a carpet of golden brown pine needles before him. But what was important was the stone fire pit. It had only a sugarcoating of snow upon it… and on Howard's shirt.

He went to it straightaway and looked down at it.

Oh, he knew that shirt.

Howard had worn it until it got holes in the elbows and then he'd just torn the sleeves off. "What do you think, babe?" he'd said and popped those big wonderful biceps of his. "Think that'll make the pups weak in the knees?"

"Yes," Wyatt whispered to the cold air, his words turning to smoke.

He went to one knee and picked it up—it crackled slightly as the thin glaze of ice cracked—and unable to stop himself, brought it to his face and breathed it in.

It smelled like earth and wet and leaves and—gods—beneath it all… Howard. Still. How could that be? Was it just his imagination?

"You're hungry, aren't you?"

Wyatt turned to almost see the big man before him. Really big. When had he arrived?

He's never left.

Wow, he'd thought that day so long ago. *He's fucking hot!*

He could almost see Howard's eyes.

"And you can't really afford anything, can you?"

And all he said he wanted in return was *"…for you to take your shirt off."*

Wyatt shivered.

"You really want me to take my shirt off right here?" Wyatt said to the snowy room.

"Why not?" came the voice of memory.

Howard had told him that he liked his chest. Had he?

Yes.

He did.

Once.

Howard asked if he could touch me.... He was so gentle.

They'd talked and talked and talked. Wyatt had told him how the day had started—his father slapping him so hard he'd bled, and how he had kicked Wyatt out and called him an abomination. And Wyatt had just jumped in his piece-of-shit car and driven until it died—right outside The Watering Hole.

The first gay bar I ever went inside.

For one second Wyatt saw his mother, hysterical, in his rearview mirror.

Then it was Howard again.

In that first apartment.

Howard showing him his altar and Wyatt wondering how such a coincidence could happen that the man he met was both gay and pagan.

Howard reaching out and cupping his cheek and looking deeply into his eyes and then....

Then he kissed me.

And then he sucked my cock.

He swallowed.

Gods how important and magical that had seemed at the time.

"Is it going to hurt?" Wyatt had asked. Because Howard was going to fuck him.

"Yes. At first. But that's part of it, my little bear."

That was the first time Howard had ever called him that.

"But it gets better."

And it had hurt. It had hurt so much. He'd felt like he was being torn apart.

But then it did get better.

It was like magick.

Howard had told him he was beautiful, and he believed it, and he stayed for eleven years.

Wyatt was crying then. Openly weeping.

Remembering Howard when he was magick.

But then other voices came.

"The only reason you get laid is because of me. I tell them they have *to have sex with you if they want me."*

"Goddammit, Wy! Could you be *a bigger faggot?"*

"You are a fucking clingy, jealous little bitch!"

He felt Howard's slap. Like his father's slap. Tasted blood.

Howard said he would never hit me.

He was letting some man fuck him over our coffee table.

More echoes….

"I want you out. I am done with your shit! I want you out by the end of the month!"

And then…

You said you would take care of me forever.

You lied.

Why?

No. Wyatt pulled himself away from painful memories and questions that would never be answered.

It doesn't matter.

And then Wyatt wiped the tears from his eyes with Howard's shirt. He bent and checked the wood, and he thought it was all right, but he poured the little bottle of torch fluid on it anyway. He spread the shirt out over it and poured what fuel was left on top of it.

Wyatt stood.

He closed his eyes and took a deep breath.

Time to say good-bye.

Then he saw Kevin's eyes in his mind and saw him smile and felt his kiss and knew that even if what he saw there wasn't real… there would be other men who would want him.

He was not alone.

Wyatt opened his eyes and began to slowly walk around the circle of stones.

Love has teeth; they bite… but the wound will close.

He took his wand from his pocket and let it guide his way.

"Queer Ones," he said. "I ask that you attend to me today. Come to my Circle. Be with me. Join me. Join with me. Gilgamesh and Enkidu. Apollo and Hyacinth. Achilles and Patroclus. Heracles and Hylas. Zeus and Ganymede. Eros, Hermes, Dionysus, Ganesha, Odin…. Hadrian and deified Antinous. Akhenaten and deified Smenkhare. Men made gods, Alexander the Great and Hephaestion, he who is also you. Bagoas, too! I forget you not! And I don't forget you, Edward, and nor your love for

Piers Gaveston! All of you and more… I call on you to be witness, and if you will, my helpmates."

Wyatt slipped the wand into his pocket and removed his athame, his ceremonial dagger. He raised it high above him. "Gods and men and Queer Ones!" he cried. "The time has come. The time for me to stop asking questions and put a part of my life behind!"

He began to make great slashing movements through the air.

"I cut away the old! I cut it away! It is behind me now! The past is the past!"

Wyatt stopped, heart pounding, face wet with tears.

"What's done is done!"

He fell to his knees, placed his knife to the side, and took his lighter out at last.

"What's past is past. What's dead is dead. And to honor the good, I let it burn."

The lighter started with one click. He touched it to Howard's shirt, and it burst into flames. Then he took the lighter lower, lit the kindling beneath the wood, and instantly it too was aflame. Immediately Wyatt felt the heat, and he fell back on his haunches, barely missing going all the way onto his ass and back.

The flames went up with a huge *Whoosh!* and Wyatt had to scramble back or get burned. He marveled at the sight, a great twisting fire eating away at everything. The air was strong with the smell of citronella and wood and fabric and the sounds of popping and crackling wood, and it was almost as if he could hear the gods within.

What's done is done! they seemed to say. *Ashes to ashes! What's past is past!*

The music came to him then and Wyatt rose to his feet and began to sing.

Purple God, Queer God,
Green God, Fairy God,
Golden God, Faggot God,
I welcome You….

Purple God, Queer God,
Green God, Fairy God,
Golden God, Faggot God,
Come be with me….

Purple God, Queer God,
Green God, Fairy God,
Golden God, Faggot God,
I thank you…!

It began to rain then, and Wyatt looked up with a *How can that be?* And he saw how it could be. The snow! The heat of the flames! It was rising up and, trapped by the "roof," had begun to melt the snow.

And it was raining!

Wyatt laughed.

He stood back.

He felt clean. For the first time in forever, he felt clean.

Wyatt stood and watched.

Howard's shirt—*and my tears*—was all but gone, and the wood was burning as if it were some raging beast. Wyatt found that he had to step back and, in surprise, step back again.

Did that little bit of torch fluid do this? he wondered… forgetting all about the gods.

And then there was a mighty cracking sound. It filled the air, cracked again louder. Wyatt stepped back a third time and looked about him.

What? What?

Then a large branch, weary for days from the weight of snow, broke.

It fell down on Wyatt, knocking him facedown to the ground.

Then came the snow.

And buried Wyatt beneath it.

CHAPTER THIRTY-SIX

KEVIN WOKE with a start.

He'd been having a dream. He'd followed Wyatt to Pax Place. He had quite suddenly realized that he needed to go as well. It was a feverish need. A *must*! He would take something of Cauley's and put it to the flame so that he too could say good-bye to the lover who had hurt *him* so much.

But when he got there, Wyatt was naked, and there was no fire, but a huge four-poster bed fit for Historical Heloise himself—the Faerie who set up his tent and camp each year fit for a medieval king's army encampment.

Wyatt was waiting for him, sprawled upon that great bed, and he was hard, stroking himself. "Come here," Wyatt said.

And then Kevin knew he couldn't wait another day, another moment, and if he had to return to New York alone, then that was what would happen.

But then the canopy over the bed broke, and just as he was about to climb upon the bed, that canopy fell upon him, heavy—*heavy!*—and so cold, suffocating, and Kevin had awoken, clawing, flailing and....

What time was it?

He found his cell phone, and God, it had been over an hour, and it was dark outside.

And for some reason that made the hair on his arms rise up and move like wheat in the wind.

Kevin checked his phone again.

He didn't want to rush Wyatt, but really... it was cold outside. *Dark.*

Quite suddenly he knew he couldn't wait. There was something wrong. It was the tickle. The one he had learned not to ignore. Quick as he could, he dressed in coat and gloves and stocking hat and left the cabin.

It was dark. If not for the porch lights of the cabin, he would not have been able to see. Yet the porch lights of the next cabins were not on, and he couldn't see beyond that point, and fuck it all, if Wyatt was in trouble, he couldn't help him if he couldn't see!

Then he remembered the Coleman lantern he'd brought on a whim and dashed back inside and found it right there where he'd left it, under his cot. He nearly screamed when he couldn't find the matches—he'd had them earlier, by God!—and then there they were, next to the stove. He lit the lantern and rushed back out into the cold, cold world.

You're being silly.

There's nothing wrong.

He's going to be pissed when you go charging in and ruin the end of his ritual!

But none of that stopped him. He ran and slipped twice, then nearly fell on his ass on slick stones climbing down from the path to the road.

"Wyatt!" he cried, giving his love warning so that if he really might ruin everything, Wyatt would have time to ask him to wait.

But there was no response.

He plunged into the break in the woods and saw the small torches lighting the way, saw gleaming Egyptian gods, fire dancing on their golden skin, black kohl-lined eyes staring at him and…. *What?* Were they telling him to leave? Commanding him to hurry on?

"Wyatt!" he called out and saw nothing, no fire in the pit ahead, and shouldn't he see that? If Wyatt had lit a fire, wouldn't he see something? Could he be done already? Could he have put it out and… what? Gone to see Gryphon and Saffron to tell them what he'd done? *Why would he go there first? Why wouldn't he come to me?*

"Fuck it," he said aloud and stepped past the Egyptian guardians and into darkness once again. He held his lantern high and saw… nothing.

Nothing…?

Where's the fire pit?

Kevin stepped into the clearing that was not a clearing but was mounded with snow and…. *What is that?* Was that a rabbit? A *dead* rabbit?

He stepped closer and lowered the lantern to see that handspan of dark brown fur and—

"Christ!" he shouted. It was Wyatt's bearskin.

Kevin fell to his knees, put the lantern aside, and dug. He dug with clawed hands, for he had nothing else, not even a stick or piece of wood.

He dug and clawed and shoved and pushed and the "rabbit" turned into more and more, a blanket and—*fuck!*—a foot!

Wyatt's foot!

God oh God oh God oh God…!

Oh please, please, please be alive. Oh, Wyatt! Wyatt, my sweet little bear.

Kevin was moaning but not crying—there was no energy for that—and with all the desperation he had, he dug into the snow and unburied Wyatt from foot to leg to torso.

Face! I've got to find his face!

And then there were bear ears and rolling plastic eyes—*Wyatt's hat!*—and then his sweet face, and Kevin pulled Wyatt up into his arms and begged him to be alive.

In the light from the lantern, it was impossible to know anything but... but it seemed Wyatt wasn't breathing!

Kevin touched Wyatt's face and it was *so* cold, and he settled Wyatt back and, not really knowing for sure what he was doing, opened Wyatt's mouth and placed his own mouth against Wyatt's and *breathed*....

Wait.... Aren't I supposed to be pinching his nose closed?

He did so and *breathed* into Wyatt.

And thank every single god—Christian and Pagan and Jewish and Tibetan and any metaphor that would take him across the worldly divide—Wyatt began to cough!

His eyes opened, and they looked into Kevin's, and never—*never!*—had Kevin felt anything like this in his life.

I love you, Wyatt Dolan.

Wyatt coughed again and words came from his lips.

"C-c-cold, K-Kevin. I—I'm s-so c-cold."

Then with strength Kevin didn't know he had, he stood up and pulled Wyatt with him, into his arms, and leaving the lantern behind, ran. He ran past the little torches, ran across the road, leapt up slick stones that moments before had nearly set him on his ass. He climbed on hinds' feet, it seemed, and then down the path and up steps and burst into the cabin.

He would have drug the bed to the stove, or even the stove to the bed, if he could.

But instead he put Wyatt on the cot and stripped him of his cold, wet clothes—Wyatt was shaking so hard. Stripped him naked and then picked him up again and put him on the big bed. He was still shaking! Then he tore his own clothes off (a button really did fly off). He had never undressed so fast, everything, and he climbed onto the bed and pulled Wyatt tight—still shaking—and yanked covers over them both and wrapped himself around Wyatt like a cocoon around a caterpillar. He rubbed Wyatt's back and his ass and drew him even tighter.

And finally….

Bit by bit….

Wyatt stopped shaking.

Bit by bit.

Kevin's relief was total when he felt Wyatt respond. He wrapped his arms around Kevin and said something—*"I love you too"*—that couldn't have been what Kevin thought Wyatt had said.

They were so close it was as if they were one.

And bit by bit Wyatt stopped trembling.

God. Kevin could actually feel Wyatt's heart beating against his own.

Then: "Did you hear me?"

"Hear you?" Kevin asked.

"I said I love you, Kevin Owens."

Kevin thought his heart would leap out of his chest. God! Then he said it, said it out loud, said it clear, revealed his heart: "I love you too, Wyatt Dolan."

By God I do.

"More than life."

One last tremor, and then Wyatt was quiet.

"Baby Bear?" he asked softly.

There was no response, but he could hear Wyatt breathing.

And so he shifted so he could get Wyatt even closer to him and, exhausted, drifted off to sleep.

CHAPTER THIRTY-SEVEN

WYATT WOKE to light and warmth and man.

His head was resting against flesh, inviting and safe. Like home. Even the scent of him. Man.

Kevin.

The realization hit him, and it was like summer.

"...I love you, Kevin Owens."

"I love you too, Wyatt Dolan. More than life."

Oh gods, had Kevin meant it?

Did I?

And then that summer was inside him and he knew.

"More than life," he whispered.

They were naked, and so entangled he wasn't sure where he ended and Kevin began. Arms around each other, legs interlocked, cock-to-cock, Wyatt's face against Kevin's softly furred chest.

It was the most intimate experience of his life.

He began to get hard.

Gods, is that all right?

Did that make him a slut? Would it make Kevin mad? Did he need to pull away?

But gods, he did not want to pull away!

Oh.... Then he felt it. Kevin. Gods. He was getting hard too. He could feel Kevin's cock shifting against his own. Oh, yes. So sweet and sexy and....

Maybe he's just asleep?

Do I look?

Wyatt did. He looked up, and oh, Kevin was looking at him. Looking at him with beautiful, alert, shining hazel eyes.

And then Kevin kissed him.

Gentle only for a moment, and then there was a hunger in it that made Wyatt gasp. And when he did, Kevin's tongue was in his mouth and it was warm and demanding and man.

Their tongues lashed against each other, and Kevin was moaning and Wyatt was too.

But…. But is this all right?

Kevin pulled slightly away, breaking the kiss, and Wyatt whimpered in protest and opened his eyes and met Kevin's once again.

"I want to make love to you, Wyatt. Is that all right?"

Is it all right?

"Gods, yes," he said.

Kevin kissed him again, and Wyatt wanted to laugh and cry at the same time. The kiss was less urgent this time, lips against lips, and then Kevin was kissing Wyatt's eyes and his cheeks and his ears, sucking gently at his earlobes, and then his neck and Adam's apple, and as he was about to kiss Wyatt again, the memory of the snow hit Wyatt and he shivered.

Kevin stopped. "Are you okay?"

"You…." And now he was really trying not to cry. "You saved my life."

Kevin's smile was slight, but his cheeks actually pinked, and then he gave an almost imperceptible shrug. "Did I?"

Wyatt nodded and a tear rolled down the side of his face. "Yes. You saved me."

"I… I don't know what to say." Kevin looked embarrassed. But then a certain strength came into his eyes. "It was an honor."

"Thank you."

By way of a response, Kevin kissed him again, and the urgency was back.

They opened their mouths to each other, and their tongues danced. Wyatt thought he would pass out. He'd never waited before, and this… this was days, and he supposed it wasn't the months or year or more that some people waited, but he couldn't conceive of that.

He just knew this big, wonderful, beautiful man was holding him and kissing him, and it really was all he could do not to pass out.

Wyatt shivered again, but this time from total delight. Kevin shifted against him and rubbed his chest against Wyatt's, and the feeling of their hair mingling was so, so good. So wonderful.

And oh, this was so good, but gods, it had been so long. He hadn't made love since the last time with Howard, and that could hardly have been called loving. It felt like years since he'd been with a man. Had it only been months?

He shivered again.

Kevin stopped kissing him, and he wanted to demand that mouth back, so sweet and hot, but Kevin was looking at him, concern in those beautiful eyes.

"Are you okay, Wyatt?"

He nodded, but Kevin must have seen something in his eyes because he asked again.

"I think I'm a little scared," Wyatt said.

Now Kevin's eyes filled with apprehension, and no, that wasn't what he wanted Kevin to feel. "You don't think I'll hurt you, do you?"

"I hope not," Wyatt said. Because this was so different. *So* different. This wasn't just two rutting males. It was more. And what if it was only for one night? What if Kevin showed him a world he'd always wanted, then took it away?

He closed his eyes, then looked slowly up, feeling suddenly shy. "I feel like a virgin," he whispered and felt the heat of his blush.

Kevin smiled. "I'm scared too," he said softly.

Kevin? Scared? "You are?" he asked.

"I'm scared this is only one night. That I should get up and go get in my own bed, but I can't. I'm here now, and damn the consequences."

Wyatt nodded. "And this is your bed now, Kevin. It has been. Especially after you saving me. Keeping me warm. Oh gods, Kevin!"

Kevin let out a long moan and took his mouth again, and this time it was fierce. Kevin shifted again, and Wyatt felt Kevin's hard cock press up against and alongside his own—thought that he'd cum from it. He wanted it. Wanted to see it. Desperately wanted to touch it. Kiss it....

But dammit, Kevin was making him wait again!

Yes, the waiting was good. Was so good. Good being kissed and held and nibbled on and oh, sharp teeth against his collarbone! So good! So exciting. He felt so alive.

Kevin began to kiss down Wyatt's body, and once more Wyatt felt shy and unsure. What if Kevin was disappointed? What if he was too small?

Now Kevin was licking and sucking his nipples and giving him those little bites! Oh, so good. And then lower, and oh, it was so unfair, and...

"Oh God, Wyatt. It.... You.... So beautiful."

Wyatt looked down to see Kevin gazing at his cock, which ran freely with precum.

"These balls!" Kevin gave a little growl and took them in his hand, and Wyatt arched upward, not knowing anything could feel so good. Then Kevin dove in and took one of Wyatt's testicles into his wet, hot mouth, gently but passionately, and rolled it in his mouth, bathing it in saliva. Wyatt couldn't figure out how he didn't shoot right then, and it got worse (better!) when Kevin let it slip from his mouth and took the other one in. Wyatt's cock was pressed against Kevin's face, wetting it, and Wyatt wasn't sure he had ever seen anything so sexy (and beautiful) in his life.

Then Kevin let the second ball go and licked up the length of his cock, his big flat tongue running upward, tasting him and making Wyatt shout to the gods, and when Kevin reached the top, he sucked Wyatt in and took him deep, deep.

He let Wyatt's cock rest there, took it even deeper, then swallowed, his mouth and throat milking Wyatt in the most exquisite way.

Wyatt felt it then, knew if Kevin went one more second he might cum, and he so didn't want that. Not yet.

"Please!" he cried. "Please stop, Kevin!"

And oh thank God, Kevin did.

Kevin looked up at him with love in his eyes and smiled, and Wyatt said, "Please? My turn?"

Kevin gave him only the slightest nod and then climbed back up Wyatt's body and kissed him, and Wyatt could taste himself on Kevin's tongue and that almost made him shoot as well.

Wyatt tried to roll Kevin over, and of course there was no way he was going to be able to do that. The man was six feet of muscle. Wyatt made a little whining noise, and Kevin laughed quietly and rolled over for Wyatt, but took him with him so that he was lying full-length upon the man, chest-to-chest, but only partially cock-to-cock. Kevin was so much taller, and the upper half and the tip of his hardness was lodged against the root of Wyatt's hard-on, and once more, even that almost made Wyatt cum.

He lifted himself up, straddling Kevin, legs on either side, pressure off the base of his cock, and he scooted just a small amount back and looked down at his cock rearing up over Kevin's. His mouth fell open.

"Jesus," he said—and since when had he called upon that name?—and, "You're huge!"

And Kevin was. He had to be at least eight inches and thick and cut, the head a dark maroon, the shaft slightly darker than the surrounding skin, the circumcision scar slightly askew, slightly larger on one side than the other.

Their mixed scents rose up to Wyatt, and his mouth watered. He wanted that inside him. Wherever inside him, but could he? *So big!*

Wyatt took it in his hand with his own cock and pressed them tight, letting them rub slightly, the slickness of their mutual need making it so good and, damn, he couldn't get his hand around the both of them, they had so much cock together.

He glanced up at Kevin, who was blushing—blushing!—and Wyatt laughed in delight—so sweet and sexy!—and then scootched some more so that now his legs were up and over Kevin's thighs, or at least he tried to, but there was so much muscle! They were such big thighs.

So back a bit more to sit carefully now on Kevin's knees and then shifting so that one of them was lodged into the cleft of Wyatt's ass, and when Wyatt rearranged himself ever so subtly—gods!—his asshole was square against that knee, and who knew it could feel so good. *I'm not even being fingered. Not fucked.* It was just the pressure, and that pressure was so good!

Kevin was watching him intently, and it nearly drove Wyatt mad. He thought, *You want to watch, huh? Watch this!* And he shoved back down Kevin's legs and fell forward so that Kevin's hard cock was right in front of his face. Wyatt looked at it reverently. So beautiful! So big! *Huge!*

He knew he was up for the challenge.

Wyatt put his fist around it and lifted it as best he could, and then he took Kevin in his mouth, and he could barely stretch his lips wide enough. But oh, with a few practiced bobs and shifts, he had Kevin deep in his mouth, which it filled almost to overwhelming, and sucked it, tasting Kevin's fluids, moving, letting it slide in and out, and Kevin slapped the bed on either side of Wyatt and said it was "So good! *So good!*"

Oh, now his balls! And he let go of that great phallus and went down and saw that Kevin's balls were huge as well. They looked as big as eggs, and the scrotum was loose and, for such a hairy man, nearly hairless itself, with just enough that Wyatt knew Kevin didn't shave them like so many gay men.

He somehow managed to take one into his mouth, and he nursed it gently, made love to it, and his mouth was so full. So full of Kevin. Wyatt reluctantly let it go so he could take the other in as well, and it felt so good there, and Kevin smelled so good and tasted so good and…. Oh, he wanted to taste something else and surely Kevin would only let him go so far, but ask? Believe?

Wyatt released the testicle—the delightful satiny scrotum drew up—and stuck his tongue out far and let it travel down a bit, a bit more—he wanted to taste Kevin's most private place and would Kevin let him and—

"Oh, God! Wyatt, please!"

—Kevin lifted and spread his legs wide, and there it was, flawless, the folds spread out in a perfect star, slightly pink, and Wyatt had to have it.

Wyatt pressed his face into that wide cleft and laved it with his tongue, and Kevin shouted and cried out and—"Please! Please! Oh, Wyatt, my love!"—and the taste was exquisite. Skin and sweetness and that new-penny tang and the hair there unimaginably soft. He pointed his tongue and teased and pressed and licked and sucked and nibbled, and soon Kevin was opening up to him, the tiny folds smoothing out, his hole relaxing, and Wyatt pressed into him and it was like wet velvet.

He went on and on and couldn't stop, went until his jaw threatened to cramp, and dimly he was aware that Kevin was saying he didn't know how much he could stand, and what finally jolted him to reality was the cry, "Wyatt! Please. Please fuck me!"

Wyatt sat slowly back on his haunches and looked at Kevin in astonishment. The big man was holding his knees back with those big hands of his, and his eyes were filled, swirled with need and lust.

Kevin wanted Wyatt to fuck him?

It seemed impossible. When two men got together, did one so large and manly let someone as small and round as Wyatt top him?

But that look was clear, and Wyatt's cock grew so hard it hurt.

"Condoms?"

Kevin shook his head. "I believe in you, my love."

My love?

"I trust you. I know it will be fine with us. Do you trust me?"

My love!

Wyatt did trust him.

And trembling, he kneed himself closer, closer still, looked down at that hole, open slightly, seeming to wink in need, and he couldn't believe he was going to do this.

Wyatt spit into his palm and carefully lubed his straining cock, worried that even this might make him cum. His precum was flowing thick and free, a huge pearl forming at the slit, and he thought, *I think I can do this.*

He wiggled forward just a bit more and then guided his cock, and then it was kissing that place, and it opened and took the tip of his head, and Wyatt moaned and shifted again and watched in amazement as the full head of his erection slipped into that hot, tight sheath.

Wyatt cried out, and gods, nothing, nothing had prepared him for such a feeling! Kevin's large muscular legs wrapped around his waist and pulled him tight, and Wyatt couldn't help but impale his lover.

"Christ!" Kevin shouted, and Wyatt was buried balls deep, and he knew if he moved even a fraction of an inch it would be over. Kevin was so hot, so deep, so tight, so wet! He trembled, and Kevin reached out and took Wyatt in his arms and pulled him up and on top of him, and Wyatt's cock seemed to bury itself even deeper into Kevin.

Kevin strained his face forward and took Wyatt's mouth with his—as surely as Wyatt was taking Kevin's ass—and plunged his tongue inward, and Wyatt gasped and, without knowing it, started a motion as old as mankind. He fucked his lover.

To be fair, neither of them lasted very long. Wyatt tried, but it was just too much, all of it, the reality of what was happening and being in Kevin's arms and his hot depths, and suddenly he—without warning even to himself—was cumming hard, and it almost hurt it was so powerful. He felt like he was shooting his life into Kevin. They were both sweating profusely by then, and Wyatt's slick furry belly had been sliding against Kevin's cock and now it was shooting, firing great white jets of semen between them that fell upon Kevin's belly and chest and neck and once on his right cheek.

Wyatt's legs and knees gave out, and he collapsed atop Kevin. His vision went blurry, but somehow, miraculously, he didn't pass out. He lay gasping in Kevin's arms, his cheek against Kevin's drenched chest, listening to the pounding of his beautiful heart—or perhaps listening to his own in his ears.

After a long while, Kevin moved in such a way that Wyatt slid off him and to the side. Wyatt's cock had long since grown soft and left his man.

Still they held each other and looked into each other's eyes and kissed and kissed until they both, incredibly, began to harden again, and then Kevin had his turn.

Kevin turned Wyatt onto his belly and kissed him everywhere and then made love to his ass with his mouth and all but sobbed about the beauty of it—Wyatt's face blazed from the compliments; he could scarcely believe them—and Kevin, like Wyatt, took a long time at what he did.

He had to prepare Wyatt for something much bigger than what Wyatt had taken Kevin with.

Wyatt was afraid and not—afraid of the size, but not of Kevin—and when Kevin was finally inside him, he had never felt so incredible in his life. So big and so warm, and it filled Wyatt, claimed him, took him, made him Kevin's.

They lasted only slightly longer, with Kevin biting at Wyatt's shoulder and Wyatt pushing back into every hard thrust, and then they were both cumming, Kevin inside him—he could feel it!—and Wyatt against the mattress.

And then Wyatt really knew no more as he was pulled down into the most excellent bliss of dreams and love.

CHAPTER THIRTY-EIGHT

WYATT WOKE again, but this time to pain.

Gods. Pain.

Wait! What was this? What…?

His lower back…. It was…. "*Gods,*" he groaned. *Oh!* Like a knife to his lower back—left side? Right? He couldn't tell and…. "*Aaaarrgh*!"

Kevin jerked.

Oh, then more! Gods, it hurt! Wyatt cried out, and his arm flailed without control.

"Wyatt?"

Kevin was lifting up on one elbow and looking at him. "God, baby, are you all right?"

And no! He wasn't all right.

He bent one way—no, that was worse—bent another and—no! That was even worse!

"Kevin!" he cried. *Oh shit*…. "My back! It's… it's *killing* me!"

Kevin sat up, unlocking their legs. Sat up totally, and their eyes locked for only a second, and then the pain, it was just too much. Wyatt closed his eyes and tried shifting, tried anything…. Some new position. There had to be one to stop this!

So much pain! It was hurting. Gods, gods, gods…!

"Baby Bear, please" came Kevin's voice from very far away. "Roll onto your stomach."

Wyatt tried, but even that was not comfortable and—oh, oh, oh—Kevin's big hands were massaging his back and…

"Lower," Wyatt managed between gasps.

Those hands, flexing, fingers probing….

"Lower." He tried to point, tried to bend his arm in a way that would let him point his outthrust thumb where the pain was coming from, and gods—it, hurt, *so,* much!

Kevin's hands found the spot, and for one second there was *tremendous* relief, but then it was worse. "No! Stop!"

"Oh, Wyatt! Tell me how to help you. What's wrong?"

The branch? Had the branch hit him there? Was this some kind of delayed…? Then waves of pain radiated out and up and drowned his ability to speak.

Tears were streaming down his face, and for one instant Howard loomed over him to call him a crybaby, but Wyatt used the pain for strength and banished that face away.

He bent again, flipped over, bent another way and—*fuck!*—his back hurt so much! How could anything hurt so bad?

Kevin was up and out of bed and dressing. "I'm going to get help." Wyatt could hear the desperation in his voice, and it made him feel bad, but gods, he was hurting so very much it was drowning out everything. He could barely think.

"I'll be right back!" Kevin assured him and then was out the door. *Gone! He's gone?*

Wyatt tried do sit up, and nausea hit him immediately.

Throw up. I'm going to throw…. He swung his face over the edge of the bed and felt it hit, but nothing—nothing came up. Dry heaves wracked him, and he broke out into a sweat. Wrong. *Oh gods, there's something wrong with me…!*

The heaves hit him again, and he somehow made it to the edge of the bed and swung his feet to the floor and—*Oh fuck! Oh gods!*—he retched and retched again and nothing. Nothing came up. New sweat washed across his forehead, even above his lip, and he wiped both and retched again.

"Wr-wrong…." *Gods!* "S-some-th-thing's wrong with…."

The door opened and in came not only Kevin, but Saffron and Gryphon as well. She, in the lead, took one look and rushed to his side.

She touched Wyatt's forehead and her hand felt so cool, but….

"Only a slight fever," she said. "And that's a maybe. Wyatt? Tell me what's going on."

He shook his head. "I—I d-don't kn-know." The heaves hit once more, and he was sure he would throw up this time—fuck, right in front of everyone—and he saw the trash can and staggered to his feet, only to fall to the floor.

"Wyatt!" cried Kevin.

At least he was by the trash can, and he stuck his face over it and… no. Great heaves, but nothing.

Kevin was at his side, and he was so humiliated, acting like this in front of people!

Saffron was there as well, and she and Kevin, once she was sure he was done, helped him back to the bed. He shivered and his teeth chattered and—

"Gryf! Take the Bobcat. Didn't you say a plow went by a little while ago?"

"Yes," he answered swiftly. "But it threw snow at the gate and—"

"Exactly. Get the Bobcat down there fast and clear that up. Pronto!"

And Gryphon was out the door.

"Wyatt, can you tell me what you're feeling? Kevin said something about your back?"

Her voice came from miles and miles away, and Wyatt felt high, like he'd smoked some really great pot—which he rarely did, although he usually had one of Lorax's magic brownies ever year at Festival—and, oh no! The pain came back—*WHAM!*

"*Aaarrghh*"! He bent double, almost fell on the floor again, and tried to answer—"Oh yes it's my back and it's horrible, *horrible*!"—but nothing would come out of his mouth, not dinner and not words.

Some small part of him saw Kevin wringing his hands, his eyes—usually so beautiful, but now ghastly—open wide. "I have to *do* something!"

"And you're going to," Saffron said. "Your truck. Wyatt's Mini Coop. They're both still buried?"

Wyatt didn't hear an answer, only Saffron's next words. "You'll take the camp truck. It's a piece of shit in some ways, but the heat works like a motherfucker, and it's good in the snow for some magically crazy reason. The keys are under the sunscreen. Get it started."

"Want me to back it up?"

"Why? There's just snow along the road. We'd have to wade through it. We best get Wyatt up to—"

"I cleared a path from North Five down to the road."

"You did?" Saffron asked, the surprise clear in her voice.

"So Wyatt could go to Pax Place and work his rit—"

"In *this* snow? Mother!"

"That's how he got buried in the snow and—"

"Men!" cried Saffron. "What would you…? Oh, never the hell mind. Yes! Go! Get the truck! And whatever you do, don't drive it into the ditch along the road."

Like Gryphon before him, Kevin all but saluted and was out the door.

Saffron turned to Wyatt. Leaned so she could reach behind him and started doing something to his back. God, it hurt! How could anything hurt like this?

"No bruises," he heard her say from a million miles away. She touched his forehead. "Wyatt." When he didn't respond, she said it again. "*Wyatt*!"

He turned to her and her face was swimming in a sea of pain. He began to shiver again, and it was only then that he realized he was naked. He dropped his hands into his lap.

"Oh for the Goddess's sake, Wyatt. I've seen you naked on the beach before. I've seen more dick than a prostitute in King's Landing. Now *look* at me."

Wyatt did as commanded, as all men around here appeared to do.

She took him by the shoulders and *looked* at him. It felt like *into* him. She closed her eyes and ran a hand down his back—slowly, slowly, slowly—and stopped right where the pain was, exactly. Spread her fingers out. Flexed them. Pressed.

"Oh gods," Wyatt groaned.

"That's where the pain is," she said. It was not a question.

He tried to answer, and when words once more refused to issue forth, he nodded instead.

"Thank the Goddess this happened today instead of a few days ago. We're going to get you to the hospital."

"H-hospital?" he moaned.

"Yes. I think it's your gallbladder. I'm pretty certain of it, in fact."

"I don't want to go to the hospital," he whined, and she nodded and told him she knew that but he was going anyway.

"No insurance," he said.

"Well, the local hospital is one of those that starts with 'Saint,' and that means it's a charity hospital. You show them you don't have the means and they'll write tons off. Gryphon didn't have to pay a penny when he had his appendectomy year before last."

"Gryph-on had an app-app-app...." Another wave of pain—no, fuck that, agony—hit, and he couldn't finish his sentence.

"Appendectomy. Yes."

"D-didn't...." That was as far as he got.

"Yeah, well, we didn't broadcast it. Gryf's that way. Now let's get you dressed. I've seen your weenie a time or six, but you don't need to walk into the emergency room that way."

Wyatt's eyes went wide, and then he started to laugh and gods! Hurt!

She got up and looked at the scattered clothes, began to pick them up. "Which of these are yours? Crap. These are all wet."

"Th-there…." Wyatt pointed at his bag on one of the cots.

She went to it and started pulling things out willy-nilly. Settled on some sweats and a T-shirt—the one that read I Kicked Anorexia's Butt!—and went to him. "Underwear, chief?"

"R-red-and-b-black p-p-plah-plaid."

"Huh?" She looked around and then said, "Oh!" and fished them out from under the table.

How did they keep getting under there?

"Okay, now, let's get these on," she said and knelt in front of him and helped him get his feet through the leg holes.

He had time—in a strange, pain-riddled interval—to reflect that there was a woman on her knees in front of him, and *that* had never happened nor would likely happen ever again, and he started to laugh again and—*more pain!*—regretted it. She looked up and must have seen what he was thinking because she laughed too and said, "Yeah, well, to everything there is a season, yeah, yeah, yeah. Now can you stand up, Little Bear?"

Somehow he did, wishing slightly that it was Kevin doing this, but what the fuck. To everything there is a season, after all, a time to every purpose, and she pulled his underwear up and then helped him into his sweatpants. Next was his T-shirt, and that was a bitch and a half.

"This too," she said and picked up a sweatshirt. He tried to tell her that it was Kevin's, and she said, "Whatever. Isn't that part of what's so great about being a bum bandit, you can wear each other's clothes?"

Wyatt's mouth fell open, and then he saw she wasn't being cruel at all, just trying to lighten the mood, and that made him laugh, but the pain made him stagger. "S-stop m-ma-king me laugh!"

She smiled her Mother-Goddess smile and then said, "Well, it's better than crying." Then: "Arms up!" and she dressed him like a child, and suddenly he was glad it was her and not Kevin.

Speaking of whom, he came bursting through the door right then, while Saffron was sitting him down and putting him into two mismatching socks.

"Saffron!" Wyatt moaned and pointed and worried about what the ER people would think of him with one Hanes sock and one with a black W at the top—Kevin's?—and once again it was like she could read his mind, and she rolled her eyes and told him that she thought he was going to be all right.

"Now remember, tell them you think it's your gallbladder. It'll save a shit-ton of time and tests, okay?"

He nodded.

"Kevin—"

(he all but snapped to attention)

"—*you* tell them, okay? Tell them you think it's Wyatt's gallbladder."

"Gallbladder?" In his back? But your gallbladder is…. "It wasn't the tree?"

"I was a medic in Desert Storm, and I saw a lot."

Next it was shoes and coat—it was only damp—and gloves (Kevin's) and when they saw how wet his bear hat was, Saffron pulled off her own bright orange wool cap and put it on Wyatt's head, and Wyatt was still trying to process that Desert Storm thing. Saffron? Peace goddess who wouldn't let people kill copperheads? Saffron was in Desert Storm?

Then they both helped Wyatt out the door and down the steps (it was a procedure) and then up the path and down to the road and into the thrice (at least) beat-up Camp pickup.

"Good luck," she said and hugged Kevin and then leaned in the door and kissed Wyatt's cheek. "You're going to be fine in the end. Just remember you have people who love you to get you there, okay?"

Love me?

He nodded.

"Remember," she said again. "You will make it. We always do. We have to. And a year from now, you'll look back at this and remember only the good that happened here tonight."

"The good?" he managed.

Her eyes flashed. "The love," she said and then stood and slammed the door.

Kevin was already in the cab by then, and he drove them carefully down the road and then very, very carefully down the steep hill that went to the gate and to the main road. The Bobcat was pulled to the side, and Gryphon waved them through.

"He got it cleared!" Kevin cried, marvel in his voice, and he lifted one hand in a quick wave and then they were on the road.

CHAPTER THIRTY-NINE

FOR KEVIN it was a nightmare. Wyatt was in pain. All he wanted to do was make the little bear happy, and tonight, on a snowy road on a cold, cold night, there was nothing he could do to help.

But get him to the hospital.

How could this be happening? They were making love a few hours ago—at last—and God, it had been exquisite! And now Kevin was afraid Wyatt was dying.

Poor Wyatt. He couldn't find a single way to be comfortable. Kevin had insisted he wear a seat belt, but that intensified Wyatt's pain so much. The only way he seemed to get any relief was to push his feet down onto the floorboards and straighten himself out—and that meant no seat belt.

The GPS in Kevin's smartphone led them to the hospital, and they got there just as the sunlight was beginning to touch the horizon. There weren't many cars parked by the emergency room, thank God, but it wasn't like he was worried about that. Fuck parking! He pulled up near the glass doors, got out, and ran for Wyatt's side of the car. Pulling it open, he paled when he saw his love by the hospital lights. He looked blue. His lips looked blue!

He helped Wyatt out of the car—Wyatt crying out as Kevin did so—and they headed in, the doors sliding silently aside.

"Help!" Kevin called out, arm around Wyatt and practically carrying him. "We need help!"

A male nurse rushed out and helped them to the counter, but as soon as the lady in charge saw Wyatt's face, she took them back into the emergency room proper. There were only a few people in the waiting room.

She immediately started asking questions, and Kevin did the best he could to answer. Wyatt was hardly saying anything.

"G-g-gall...," Wyatt tried. "Saff... Saff... ron s-says... my-my... gallbladder...."

"Who's Ron?" the lady asked.

"Saffron," Kevin supplied. "She's…." What did he say? A caretaker at a witch camp? "She was a medic in the Army."

The woman gave him a look he couldn't identify, nodded, and began working on Wyatt. "You're in a lot of pain?" she asked.

Wyatt—who was lying on one of the ER beds by now—let out a long moan and a tear ran down his face, and Kevin's heart broke. *We were making love!*

"I've never seen him like this before," Kevin said, implying (he hoped) that he knew Wyatt well. Then, very quietly, "He's scaring the crap out of me."

The nurse nodded and asked Wyatt more questions: Where does it hurt? How long? When did you first feel it? On a scale of one to ten, with ten being the worst pain you've ever felt, how would you rate your pain?

"A thousand!" Wyatt cried.

"I'm going to get you an IV," she said, and Wyatt protested—

"I hate needles!"

—but Kevin calmed him enough to get it done.

"Thank Asclepius, she was good," Wyatt said tearfully afterward and then, "Gods, you must think I'm the biggest goddamned baby in the world."

Kevin told him, "No, no, not at all," and before he could help it, he kissed Wyatt, and then to his surprise the nurse got a whole lot nicer.

And then there were tests….

The hours went by, and whenever she could, she let Kevin be there, but of course there was only so much she could do. Blood work and CAT scans and EKGs and nothing…. They couldn't find a thing.

And Wyatt's pain did *not* abate, and it was only after they gave him one pain medication, and then another (was there a third?), and then (finally) morphine (twice), that Wyatt was finally able to doze off and get some rest.

And then there was the matter of Wyatt's friends.

Wyatt wanted him to call them, then didn't, then begged him to call Sloan, and then begged him not to, and it was while Wyatt was dozing that Kevin made the calls.

"No," he said, he didn't think they could help, but he wanted them to know, and there was the weather and all and still…

Each and every one of them showed up.

The tears pricked Kevin's eyes, and he had to fight to keep those tears in check—but oh, so wonderful that Wyatt had such friends. A cute redhead with a lot of freckles, who looked like he might be around thirty—his name was Sloan. Ah, the famous Sloan. His more rugged and hairy boyfriend, Max, was with him—obviously a protective type, and one of the lovers that were part of Wyatt's crazy idea that there was some cosmic balance and only so much love to go around in the world. Roman and Jockster, Kevin knew of course. They called him Hodor when they got there, and they all reintroduced themselves to each other with their non-Festival names. So Roman was Scott, but he knew that because he'd gone by that the whole time he'd been at Camp and hadn't taken on his Faerie name until the last night, and Kevin—well, Hodor—had been there for that. Jockster was Cedar in "real life," which was a Faerie name unto its own. Finally there was Asher and his lover, a lovely Samoan named Peni.

They all came, but they had to sit in the waiting room with nothing to do, and that's why Kevin had told them not to come. Still, Wyatt had been pleased to hear they were there.

"Tell them they should leave," he slurred and dozed off again, and Kevin went back and forth. The nurse lady—whose name he'd finally found out was Doris—told him to tell anyone who asked that he was Wyatt's husband.

Husband.

Imagine!

"It's not like we ask for marriage licenses," she said, "and what they don't know won't hurt them."

Eventually she told him that they could send Wyatt home now—the pain had finally stopped, really stopped at last and not just been temporarily covered up by morphine—but Kevin wanted to know one thing.

"Is it possible to have him stay? Because I'm telling you, there is something *wrong*. It's serious. I'd *like* to take him home, he *wants* to go home, but what if this weather gets worse? He needs to be somewhere where he can be helped. If this gets worse. And if it's the fact that he doesn't have any insurance, I'm good for it."

She looked him deep in the eyes, and then she peeked through the curtain one way and then the other and finally whispered, "I'll get him in a room."

And after that she did.

Now there was just the matter of telling Wyatt's family....

CHAPTER FORTY

LATER IT all sort of fused into a blur.

One day turned into two, which turned into three, which turned into….

Once the pain was gone, it was so much better. Wyatt wasn't happy to be in the hospital. It wasn't anything that had ever happened to him, and being away from home and hooked to an IV and the beeping machines and wake-ups in the middle of the night to get blood draws wasn't exactly his idea of heaven. But less pain? That was a blessing that drowned out almost everything. And of course Kevin was there.

Of course?

He couldn't believe how safe that made him feel.

It was all so strange….

With all the comings and goings of doctors and nurses, Wyatt managed to register some of what he heard and saw. It got confusing. Sometimes the morphine made him so foggy he would forget things that happened only moments before, and that could be disconcerting. Considering the alternative? That horrible, unbelievable pain? It seemed a small price to pay.

And it did make him feel silly sometimes, and that made it easy to be nice to the nurses, who were only doing their jobs. There was one who seemed like a giant. He referred to her as "Big Nurse," after the nurse from *One Flew Over the Cuckoo's Nest*, and he thought she was going to be a problem. She was pretty mean at first, and he thought she didn't approve of Kevin for one thing. But he made up his mind he'd win her over and flattered her outrageously.

"I love those earrings," he said on the first afternoon after she hadn't been very nice about a blood draw. In fact, she had kind of harpooned him, and he'd wanted to smack her. He'd already told her he hated needles, and he was practically in tears for having to get what felt like the 175th one already.

Her brows came together, and she reached up absentmindedly and seemed almost surprised to find them there.

"Are those blue topaz or sapphires?"

The corner of her mouth flickered. "Why…. Why, they're topaz."

Wyatt nodded happily and pressed the little button on the control in his hand to administer some morphine. He had to wait between doses and had just noticed on the clock that it had been enough time—not that he was clock-watching or anything.

"They really bring out your eyes."

She blushed then, the old battle-ax, and the corner of her mouth rose slightly despite herself. "Really?"

"Oh yeah." He turned to Kevin. "Don't you think?"

"I was just thinking that," Kevin replied.

Then she really was blushing. "I have some sapphire earrings that my mother gave me, but I'm afraid to wear them. Afraid of losing them."

"I find it hard to believe that you're afraid of anything," Wyatt told her very seriously. "And besides, how can you enjoy them tucked away in a drawer?" He tried to focus on her name tag, but the morphine had something to say about that. "Janet?"

"Janis," she said. "Pope. I'm the head RN on this floor."

"I love that name," he said. "Janis." And then tried to sing a little bit of "Piece of My Heart."

"That's who my mother named me after," she said. "She saw her at Woodstock."

"You're not old enough for your mom to have been at Woodstock, are you?"

Now Big Nurse, aka Janis Pope, head RN of the seventh floor, was smiling. "You're just pulling my leg now, Mr. Dolan—"

"Wyatt," he corrected.

She brushed at her hair with both hands. "I was born in 1970," she said. "The year after Woodstock, which was in 1969."

"Well, you're living right, then. I wouldn't have put you a day over forty. Thirty-eight even, right Kevin?" He snapped his attention back to the man who made his heart go pitter-pat and tried not to laugh at Kevin's deer-caught-in-the-headlights expression.

"Easy," he managed with much aplomb.

"You really do have beautiful eyes," Wyatt assured her. "But I hope you don't mind me saying this, they're second to my boyfriend's here." And he motioned to Kevin.

She bit her lower lip, looked back and forth between them, and then said, "No, of course not." Then shading even redder, she all but dashed from the room.

"You are incorrigible," Kevin said, laughing.

Wyatt shrugged and remembered the pain. He pressed his morphine dispenser, but nothing happened. He had to wait. He guessed that was a good thing. He'd always been terrified of the idea he might become a drug addict. "She does have pretty eyes," he said. "And the earrings are nice. I'd wear them."

"I'm sure you would," Kevin said and winked.

"We could wear matching ones," Wyatt ventured and then held his breath.

"Maybe," Kevin replied and Wyatt let his breath out. "Although they're a little flashy for me, don't you think?"

"I was thinking they were a little small," Wyatt said with a slight toss of his head.

Kevin's smile was beautiful. "I think, for you, they might be."

What are you doing here? Wyatt wondered then. *Why are you here with me?*

"We'd have to find matching stones," Kevin replied and wow. Really? Matching stones? "But different sizes, okay?"

"What are you doing here?" he asked aloud. And, "Why are you here with me?"

Kevin got up from his plastic chair—it looked hideously uncomfortable—and came to Wyatt's bed—which *was* pretty damned uncomfortable—and sat on its edge. "Did you want me to leave?" he asked quietly.

"No!" Wyatt said. *Gods, no. I don't know what I would do if you left.* In fact, one time he'd woken from one of his naps and the nurse who'd been on call thought he'd left. He'd almost panicked, when Kevin came in with two little cups of soft serve.

"You'll be thrilled, it's peanut butter!"

"How did you know I loved peanut butter?"

"Oh, Wyatt! Why do you ask such silly things?"

"No, I don't want you to leave. I…." And then he did panic and couldn't say, "I love you," because he was afraid it was all a pain-induced dream.

So then Kevin said it instead. "I'm here because I love you, Wyatt. I've loved you forever. I just finally realized it the last few days. I don't know how I *didn't* know."

"I love you," Wyatt said, glad of the drugs so that he said what he was feeling, and if it was stupid for him to have fallen in love in one weekend, why then he could blame them, couldn't he? "I do. And I don't know how I didn't fall in love with you the day you drove in the gate for your first Faerie festival—"

"You don't remember that day, Wyatt."

"—or the night you wouldn't take me to bed when I wanted you so much."

"Did you, Baby Bear? Want me? Or were you just—"

"I wanted you a lot…, Daddy Bear." His heart skipped when he called Kevin that, and he heard Kevin's breath catch, which made him hope that *he* liked it too. "And maybe for some of the 'wrong' reasons, whatever those are. Maybe because Howard made it okay for me to want. But I want you right now, and I wish we could. Right here. Right now."

Kevin kissed him then, long and hard, and Wyatt's head swam, and it was better than morphine.

Then, because he was feeling extraordinarily and uncharacteristically shy, as soon as Kevin sat back up he said, "And besides, it *pays* to be nice to nurses. They are underpaid and overworked and patients treat them like *shit*. You just have to make sure you *never* lie to them. Say what you mean because they will *know* if you lied, or they will find out, and then you're fucked and not like I was fucked by you the other night."

Now it was Kevin who was blushing, and Wyatt liked making Kevin blush.

THERE WERE no masses in the CAT scan, so if the pain was because of a stone, he'd passed it already—although Wyatt couldn't imagine *when*. He hadn't peed in a toilet in at least twenty-four hours. They wouldn't let him, so he had to piss in this odd bottle-like thing with a handle that they called a urinal—which was not a urinal at all. They were measuring his pee flow, and it had taken everything out of him not to ask what kind of watersports they were into. He hadn't. And if he had passed some kind of stone, wouldn't he know? Wasn't it supposed to be one of the most painful things a man could experience? Wyatt knew he was dreading it like a sentence in prison—because he knew what that would be like for a little fag like him, and it wouldn't be at all like the hot gay porn movies from Raging Stallion or Titan or Steam Engine.

So with Kevin asking the questions he'd been too afraid (or too confused) to ask, he discovered that the clear CAT scan meant that he didn't have cancer, which he'd worried about until his boss, Katherine, got there and ordered him to get "that worry" right out of his mind.

"Remember," she said. "Don't think about how you *don't* want to be here—"

(and how was he supposed to do that?)

"—because the Universe only hears 'hospital' and gives you more of what you're thinking about. Think about being healthy. Think about already being well. Think of yourself bathed in golden healing light."

Which wasn't easy, but her words had impressed Kevin, and he'd held Wyatt's hand and said soothing things and petted his forehead or hand or arm when the pain got bad—in other words, whenever the morphine wore off and he couldn't yet get any more.

"Your boss," Kevin said. "She believes what I believe."

"I guess she does," Wyatt said. "But she's a witch, you know. And I've been thinking a lot about what you've been saying. When I kind of float away? And I've been thinking that your 'ask, believe, receive' was really exactly like spell work. That's what I do, isn't it? I draw my Circle and call on my gods, and use my herbs and crystals and wand and blade, and isn't all I'm *really* doing asking and believing and waiting to receive?"

"Yes," Kevin said, his beautiful hazel-and-amber eyes flashing. "That's exactly what I think. It's why I'm just as comfortable in a Catholic High Mass as a Queer Gods Ritual at Festival."

Wyatt found out that everything going on had been wonderful and confusing and mystifying—how the heck had all this happened, so much and so fast?—and he wasn't sure how he would have done it without Kevin.

A man who said he loved him.

Could it be?

Could it be true?

Wyatt woke up over and over again to find Kevin there. He could hardly believe it.

When he woke up in his room that first time to find all his friends there, Wyatt had been amazed. Not just the FAB-ulous Four but their mates. And Kevin, thank Anubis.

Thank you. Thank you, thank you, thank you....

He introduced them all but found that had already been done while he'd been off in La La Land. And there were lots of curious looks and a mouthed, "Good going, *dude*!" from Jockster (which made him blush and laugh and… shit, that made him hurt!).

It had all been like some corny but wonderful scene from a movie like *The Broken Hearts Club*, where Benji wakes up in the hospital after his overdose to find all his buddies there. Except Wyatt didn't get scolded or asked why he'd done such a stupid thing because he hadn't—*thank the Goddess!*—done *anything* wrong. Or *Peggy Sue Got Married* or even the end of *The Wizard of Oz*—and wouldn't that be nice? If all this turned out to be a dream?

But that didn't seem to be the case—*alas*!

Wait! No! Not a dream. He didn't want Kevin to be only a dream.

Oh, it had been good to see them and know that they loved him and that Howard…. Was. Fucking. Wrong! People *did* care about him, and not just those "stupid fags" Howard said he liked to get drunk with. Their spouses liked him too. And his boss. And according to Kevin, just about everyone at Men's Festival.

They asked what had happened and hugged him and asked him for jokes and told him a couple he could use later and wrote down lists and entertained him until he couldn't keep his eyes open.

And Kevin stayed.

Kevin sat with him and helped him sort through things. Remember things. Decisions to make. There was stuff he kept… losing. Stuff he lost between pain and then pain's end through the morphine.

Kevin explained that the hospital people hadn't found any blood in his urine in the emergency room, and all that had something to do with him either passing or not passing a stone (he wasn't clear on that), nor had they found any evidence of pancreatitis, which was the area in his body where he seemed to be feeling the most pain. The CAT scan definitely didn't show any stones, although he guessed from what he could remember through the fog of morphine that he might have passed it partially already.

"Does that mean the little fucker is sitting in my bladder," Wyatt asked Kevin, "and I have the pain of pissing that out to look forward to?"

"If you do, baby, I'll hold your hand. Hell," and Kevin turned bright pink, "I'll hold your dick for you, Baby Bear."

Baby Bear.

He was hearing Kevin use that name more and more.

Wyatt blushed, and he didn't even know why—because the dick holding didn't bother him one bit, even if he was peeing at the time.

Because, well, it would mean that big wonderful man was behind him and holding him up and not letting him fall.

He sighed.

"No comment?" Kevin asked. "I can't believe you let that one go."

"Later," Wyatt mumbled and faded into morphine land—with a bit of *He said he loved me!* traveling down into that faraway place with him.

Thank the goddess he had drugs!

Then, later….

It seemed the doctors found some blood in his urine after all. Was this from another urinalysis? That report said "plus 2," whatever that meant.

They were now sure something internal was going on—*oh, really? Really?* He could have fucking told them that and he never went to medical school!—and it had nothing to do with his back. They were wondering about prostatitis now. Prostatitis? Wasn't that something old men got? Kevin told him the doctors said that while he was a bit young for prostate problems, it happened.

But how would that account for all his stomach pain?

He felt as if he were forgetting something. That there was something he should be asking about, but if so, he couldn't remember what it was.

A very cute doctor named Clay concluded that he had, in fact, passed a stone.

"The worst part is passing a stone through the kidney, but if you're lucky and it's small and not jagged, it can pass through the penis and not even be felt." But then he described the worst parts of it all as being a man's introduction to how it feels to have a baby.

Wyatt had no idea if he was right or not, or if the doctor—a man, after all—could even know if he was right. But Wyatt did know one thing. He certainly wouldn't have more than one child if it was true! How women had two or three or six he would never know.

Kevin explained that the CAT scan showed an enlarged prostate, but nothing cancerous.

The relief was beyond words.

Dr. Clay did do a prostate examination, though, and Wyatt was amazed he didn't even think of flirting with the guy. Dr. Clay was more than cute; he was hot. He reminded Wyatt of Spencer-*fucking*-Morrison, and he told the man that too.

"I've been told that," Dr. Clay said and then told Wyatt he was going to stick his finger up his ass. He didn't say it in those words, of course, but that's what Wyatt heard, and he wasn't happy about it. Not in these circumstances at least. He was too busy wondering if Dr. Clay could tell that he'd been fucked recently. If he could tell, he didn't say a word. It all seemed so funny, but gods, it had just been so embarrassing.

Then he placed orders for *another* urinalysis and *more* blood work. *Gods!*

Again and again Wyatt could only be thankful that Kevin was with him.

He quickly lost track of time and what happened when. Days fused all together. They did a test that he was glad he could only partially remember. They hooked him up to some machine that used a radioactive dye so they could do a nuclear medicine photo-op. But they had a lot of problems getting a picture of his gallbladder. They even used several extra tricks to do it, but had no luck. Wasn't his gallbladder what Saffron told him to ask about? And he remembered that was what had been bugging him. What he'd forgotten. No. No, he hadn't forgotten. He was sure he had tried to tell them, but no one really noticed. She had been so insistent that it was his gallbladder, and if they knew that, it would "save a shit-ton of time and tests." At least that very test seemed to point out that it wasn't his gallbladder, thank all the gods that ever were, because that meant he wasn't going to have to have surgery! Surgery would mean a scar, and he did *not* want a scar!

One day—after some distasteful news about a procedure he was going to have to endure later that afternoon—Scott and Cedar showed up (how was everybody getting off of work?), and they brought a few things Wyatt had really wanted. Two small statues for the side of his bed. The first was of Asclepius, a bearded man—a god—in a rather revealing toga-like garment, holding a snake-entwined staff. The second was about half its size and was a stone rabbit—Tu Er Shen—the Chinese god of homosexuality. Two very good gods to have watching over him in the hospital.

Oh. And candles. Green. Forest green. Utnapishtim would be happy, although Wyatt wasn't sure they would let him light them in the hospital. He could always sneak it here and there. Wasn't Kevin good for keeping watch?

Wyatt was sure that he was.

"And socks," said Cedar and pulled out three pair from a deep jacket pocket.

"Oh, thank you!" Wyatt flexed his feet under the mismatched socks. He'd been so embarrassed every time someone saw his socks.

"*And*"—from Cedar's other pocket came—"*underwear*! I was going to bring those hot jocks of yours I found in the bottom drawer."

"And I reminded him," Scott said, "that the point was you didn't want anyone to see your ass."

"Although you've got a nice ass," Cedar remarked.

"Hey," cried Kevin, while Cedar laughed and Wyatt blushed.

Cedar slapped Scott's ass. "Relax, Hodor… ah, Kevin. I've got all the sweet butt I can handle right here."

"Cedar!" Scott spun around and glared at him.

"Thank you, Scott." Somehow just seeing them there gave Wyatt a lot of comfort. "You too, Cedar."

Scott shook his head. "I'll do anything for you."

"I mean it," Wyatt said.

"Yeah, I know you do." Scott bent and kissed Wyatt's cheek, surprising the hell out of him. "I was worried I got the wrong one. You've got a bunch of statues of guys in togas. But he was the only one with snakes."

"You got the right one," Wyatt said. "He's the god of medicine and healing."

"Ah!" Scott shook his head. "Good one to have around, then."

The new Scott never ceased to amaze Wyatt. He really had changed. It was a wonder what a week out at "witchy-woo-woo" camp and meeting a hot motherfucking jockstrap-wearing guy could do to a man. He glanced at Cedar, who had an arm slung casually and perhaps a little territorially around Scott's shoulder. He winked as if he'd read Wyatt's mind.

"I thought so," Wyatt said.

"Whatever makes you feel good, my man," Cedar said. "*Whatever* makes you feel good." And then he used his eyes to motion toward Kevin.

Wyatt blushed.

They talked for an hour or so and watched a couple of episodes of *Adam-12* (what a surprise that show was on repeats), and it was about then that they came for Wyatt to go do the "awful thing" he was decidedly not looking forward to.

"Can I go with?" Kevin asked.

"I am sorry, Mr…?"

"Owens-Dolan," Kevin said. "I'm his husband."

That startled Wyatt and then made him feel warm, and maybe a little braver.

"Well, I'm sorry, Mr. Owens-Dolan, that's not possible," said the very adorable Indian man. Was there a requirement that the men who worked in this hospital all look good? Wyatt wondered. Or was the administrator of the hospital just a dirty old fruit? "You can wait for him in recovery, but it would be mighty boring. This will take a couple of hours, and we will be bringing him back here as long as there's no trouble, and I can't imagine there will be. We do these every day."

"Kevin, Cedar and I thought we could take you to Camp," Scott offered. "Then we can get your cars."

"Oh, wow!" Wyatt said. Saffron had called to let them know that she and Gryphon had dug them out.

"One of us can get Wyatt's Mini Coop back to his place, and you can get your truck. You could have it with you and then you wouldn't be trapped here."

"I don't know," Kevin said, shaking his head. "I don't like the idea of being away in case anything…."

"Nothing's going to happen," Scott told Kevin and then used his eyeballs to bounce a few ixnay-ixnays in Wyatt's direction.

"I *saw* that," Wyatt said as a cute African American hospital person—Wyatt wasn't sure what he was: Nurse? Resident? Medical assistant? What?—helped him into a wheelchair, the back of his hospital gown flopping open as usual. Thank Arachne he had underwear!

Then it hit him.

"I really think you should come with us, Hodor," Cedar was saying. "Hell! What if it snows again? Let's get the cars where they're safe."

They were taking him down for that test—oh gods!

"I would just like to be right here in case."

He didn't want to do this. And they were going to knock him out!

"I understand," Scott said. "But we have *this* afternoon off, Hodor. This is your best opportunity."

"It's Kevin," Wyatt cried. They were wheeling him toward the door, rolling his IV behind him.

"Shit!" Kevin cursed and then, "Oh, shit! Wyatt, do you want me to go down with you?"

Wyatt held out his hand to the guy pushing him. Then he turned to Kevin. "I want you to tell me it's going to be all right. I want to know it's going to be so all right that you can leave here with all the confidence in the world and take care of our cars. And make sure you get all our stuff from the cabin. I want my iPod. I want my books. I want Scott and Cedar to take my bearskin home so it's safe. I want you to kiss me!"

Then Kevin was on his knees and kissing him. And when he finally broke that kiss, he sat back on his haunches and assured Wyatt of everything he'd said.

"You're going to be all right, Baby Bear. And I will go take care of the cars. And we'll get all your stuff, and I will bring you your iPod, and Scott and Cedar will take your bearskin home. And I love you. I love you so much." He claimed Wyatt's mouth—Wyatt felt the *claiming*—and it took his breath away, and he suddenly knew that this *was* going to be all right in the end.

That Kevin would be waiting for him.

"And it's Dolan-Owens," he called over his shoulder as he was taken from the room.

"Wow," said the cute black guy pushing his wheelchair quickly down the hall. "You are one lucky dude. If I had a man like that kiss me, I'd cream my panties."

Wyatt laughed.

And for a few minutes, at least, he felt a little better.

CHAPTER FORTY-ONE

THEY HAD him lie on the table and explained again what they were going to do.

It really sounded horrible.

It was something called an endoscopy. They were going to run a tube down his throat with an itty-bitty camera attached to scope out what was going on someplace inside him. The anesthesia was to make sure he didn't gag at having something pushed down his throat. He wanted to make a joke, but he just couldn't.

The gadget they were going to put in his mouth was terrifying.

It looked like something for a Dom/sub game—something to force and keep someone's mouth wide open so that his Dom could facefuck him. But this wasn't a dick going down his throat, and the scary-looking guy who was going to do it proved that his theory that only hot guys could work at the hospital was wrong.

I won't remember this, was his mantra. *I won't remember this.* That's what the anesthesiologist told him. Whatever they were giving him would make it so that he didn't remember any of this.

But then that thing was being put in his mouth, and it wasn't fun, and then they were bringing the tube and his eyes went wide and he made the noises he could.

The second medical guy looked at him in surprise and asked, "Don't you feel the meds?" and he shook his head no and then…

…nothing.

THEY CLIMBED into Scott's absolutely lovely cream Lexus ES 350. It wasn't quite what Kevin was expecting. But then, cars weren't important to Kevin. And besides, everyone parked their cars up top and far to the south of the plateau at Festival. People walked. They didn't drive around. So he didn't know what kind of car Scott had. It just wasn't what he expected.

He went to climb in the back, but Cedar insisted he get up front. "You're nine feet tall."

Kevin laughed. "I'm six foot. Not that much taller than you."

"So let me be nice," Cedar said and ran fingers through his fauxhawk. "I'm not nice very often."

"Don't let him fool you," said Scott. "He is love personified."

"You're prejudiced," Cedar said, and while they debated this, Kevin got in back. He wanted the two of them together. Like he wanted to be together with Wyatt.

I want that.

I need that.

So he didn't even want to keep them from being in the front seat together.

They weren't on the road long when they asked. He knew it was coming. How could they not ask?

"So, Hodor," Cedar asked, turning and looking into the back seat, "you and Wyatt, huh?"

"I hope so," Kevin replied and gave Cedar a single nod.

"Ahhhh…." This was Scott. "When did this happen?"

"This?" Kevin asked, knowing exactly what Scott was wanting to know.

"Are…. Well, are you and Wyatt…?"

Scott paused and Kevin waited for him to finish.

"Are you two fucking?" Cedar finished for him.

"Cedar!" Scott cried. "For God's sake!"

"Well, that's what you wanted to know, right?" Cedar looked back at Kevin but cocked a thumb at his lover. "That's what he wants to know. I mean, I want to know too, but that's what he's beating around the bush about."

"Cedar! Please!"

Kevin didn't know how to answer. It's none of your business? Since just the other night? He found himself freezing up, his old tongue-tied ways returning. It really wasn't any of their business. And yet he wanted to declare his love for Wyatt from the mountaintops. Maybe if Cedar hadn't said "fucking"?

"Forgive Mr. Unsubtle here," Scott said. "It's just that…. Well, Wyatt is very important to us."

"He's very important to me too," Kevin replied.

"We all feel protective of our bear."

Kevin nodded. "It's hard not to want to protect Wyatt. He brings that out in people. I know I want to protect him."

"You sure as shit got him to the hospital," said Cedar, bobbing his head in the affirmative.

"Wyatt's been hurt," Scott continued. "*Bad.*"

"By that motherfucker Howard."

There was a pause.

"Yeah," Scott said. "By that motherfucker Howard. I fucking hate him. We all do."

"He's a pretty despicable person," Kevin said.

"None of us have been able to figure out why Wyatt was with him in the first place."

"It's because Wyatt is a pretty wounded guy," Kevin said. "And for some reason he felt he deserved whatever Howard did to him. He told me that Howard rescued him and gave him all his dreams. And then took them away." Was he betraying a confidence by saying this? He didn't think so. "He didn't think he deserved any better. But I hope to show him different. If he'll let me."

Another pause.

"You really do care for our Wyatt?" came Scott's cautious question.

"I do. I love him, Scott. I think I have for a long time." *A long time.* "And it makes me happy that you guys have been taking care of him. Wyatt told me that. He said he wouldn't have made it without you guys. The Fabulous Four."

"Plus three now," Cedar said.

"Well I hope it can be four now," said Kevin.

Another pause.

"I know that none of you know me—"

"I know you," Cedar said. "I've always thought you were a nice guy."

"But you don't *know* me. Nobody at Festival does because I keep mostly to myself. I want to try and change that, but it's not easy for me. But Wyatt helps. He gives me… confidence. He makes me want to be more outgoing, you know? And I want to be there for him. Protect him. And I am glad you're suspicious of me—"

"Not suspicious, really," Scott interjected then. "We're just…. We don't want him to get hurt again and—well—suddenly you've appeared out of nowhere, and we're all pretty surprised. Wyatt isn't exactly secretive about his life, and it was a shock to see you and to realize that something has happened with you two. And we're worried and—"

"And I'm glad. I'm glad that you worry about him. And I am sure I'm a surprise. Hell! I'm as surprised as you guys. More! I've harbored a crush for years and—"

"Really?" Scott asked.

"Yeah." Cedar nodded. "I believe it. I've watched you give Wyatt puppy-dog eyes for a long time."

"You *have*?" Scott looked at his lover, agog.

"—and I don't know how it happened, and frankly I'm worried to fucking hell that I'm his rebound, but I'm praying I'm not."

And fuck! I just said all that out loud!

"Wow," Cedar said with a very sweet smile, eyes alight. "I can't believe *you* just said all that out loud!"

"God, you guys," Kevin said, and apparently his spewing of the mouth wasn't over! "I love him. I really do. I love him *so* much."

Another pause. This one went on for about a million years.

Then Scott said, "Well, good, then."

And they drove to Camp and picked up the cars. Not only had Gryphon and Saffron dug them out, but they'd even packed them.

"You guys…," Kevin said and then didn't know what to say. What was there to say?

"It's okay," Gryphon replied. "We only want to help."

They asked how Wyatt was doing, and Kevin explained as best he could and then told them he needed to leave. He *had* to get back to the hospital.

"Of course you do," Saffron said. "Get back to him. But I've got something…." She dashed down the little path to her home and then was back, running. She was carrying the Thermos that she'd lent them earlier. "Hot chocolate," she said, pressing it into his hands. "And it'll stay hot for a while. This is a damned old Thermos. It was my parents'. Made when a Thermos really kept things the right temperature for damned near ever. Just get it back to me, okay?"

"I will," he said, and then he hugged and kissed them both because Gryphon wasn't settling for anything else. And then Kevin climbed into his big F-150 and with Scott in his Lexus and Cedar in Wyatt's Mini Coop, they hit the road.

Because Kevin knew something was up.

He had to get back to Wyatt.

WYATT AWOKE surrounded by the ugliest curtains he had ever seen in his life.

"Geez," he said. "It's obvious *no* gay man ever picked *these* out!"

He said it just as a nurse appeared at the one side the ugly curtains weren't hanging.

He swore she almost hurt herself laughing.

Then something wondrous happened.

She brought Kevin.

"Hey, Baby Bear," he said, taking Wyatt's hand.

"*Keeeee*-vin," he said—he felt himself drifting off again. "You were supposed to help get the cars."

"I did, Wyatt. You were out for quite a while."

Wyatt smiled.

"That's a good thing, right?" he asked.

"Yes." He squeezed Wyatt's hand. "But don't ask me to do it again." The look on Kevin's face was very serious.

"I won't. You've got your car and—"

"Don't ask me to leave you again." To Wyatt's shock Kevin got down on his knees, held his hand even tighter, and kissed him ever so lightly. "It was horrible being away from you. And I don't want that again."

Wyatt could hardly breathe. His heart was pounding.

"Okay," he said.

And then Kevin kissed him again.

Before they took him back to his room, the nurse bent nearly as close as Kevin had. "I'd hold on to him, sugar."

Wyatt smiled. "*Giiiirrrrrrlllll*," he said.

WYATT HAD a late lunch and it wasn't much—a sandwich of sorts because he'd missed lunch, and he was pretty pissed about it. He was starved. Kevin let him know he'd have a good dinner, and he even brought him a piece of so-so pizza (he consumed it anyway) from the cafeteria and some soft serve. It wasn't peanut butter, but it wasn't bad. Cheesecake. And of course there was hot chocolate. And it really was hot.

The menu actually had some pretty good options. He ordered the roast and mashed potatoes and candied carrots. And ice cream for dessert.

But then, right before dinner, they came in to let him know.

"It's your gallbladder, Mr. Dolan-Owens."

"Huh?" he asked, looking away from Kevin, who was reading to him from what he'd come to think of as "their" Stephen King novel.

The surgeon—at least that was how he introduced himself—was a very big, very heavyset bear of a man with a beard streaked with gray, and he told them that they had figured out what was wrong. It was Wyatt's gallbladder. "It needs to come out. Pronto."

"Pronto?" squeaked Wyatt, and his voice broke besides.

Gallbladder. That was what Saffron had said. Then "pronto" hit him again, and he asked when that was.

"First thing in the morning," Dr. Lyons (who should have been named Bear) said. "We thought it might have to wait until day after, but a patient had to be bumped, so the slot is open and we've put you right in it."

"But tomorrow?" A fear so great it made Wyatt want to burst into tears began to mount upon his shoulders. But then Kevin sat on the edge of his bed and laid a hand on his chest and kept the dark thing at least partially at bay.

And then there was some explanation about how it was no big deal, that he'd done hundreds of such procedures, it was done laparoscopically, and if everything went as well as he expected, Wyatt could be home day after tomorrow, and didn't that sound good?

The going home sounded wonderful and now there was a big warm presence helping fight off the dark fear, but he had no idea what lap-ro-scop-ick-ly meant.

So then Dr. Lyons said that meant that instead of an incision, his gallbladder could be taken out through a very small hole, and that in six months he wouldn't even be able to tell where it had been done.

"Really?" Wyatt said, his vanity joining the brawl. "Because I don't want a scar."

"Oh, scars can be sexy," Kevin assured him, but for once Wyatt ignored him.

"I mean it." The very idea of surgery terrified Wyatt, and not for the first time did he reflect that his father was far away in a hospital of his own facing who knew what? But the idea of no scar? Or at least one that would go away fast? That was good. "My chest is my best feature," he said proudly, although it came out as a whine.

"Hardly," Kevin said and squeezed his shoulder.

"We'll have some paperwork for you to sign, and no eating after midnight. In fact, let's make it nine." He consulted with the two people standing with him, then said, "I'll see you tomorrow, then, Mr. Dolan."

"Dolan-Owens," he called after the big man, and as soon as he was out of the room, Wyatt burst into tears.

KEVIN, ALL six feet of him and all those muscles, somehow climbed into bed with him and held him close. He assured Wyatt that all would be well, that everything would be okay, and he so wanted to believe it. Then he asked once again if Wyatt wanted him to call his parents.

"No!" Wyatt said adamantly. "Do. Not. Call them. I mean it!"

Kevin didn't like the idea, but he told Wyatt that he wouldn't.

He hated the fact that Wyatt had to go through all this, and he hated that he didn't want his family to know what was going on, but it wasn't like Kevin's own family would have jumped aboard a plane. Yeah, right! So he hated instead that both their parents were missing out.

And then he decided—remembered—to just accept and know that the Universe was unfolding as it should.

"I'll be here," he told Wyatt. "I will be waiting right here. I'll keep the bed warm for you."

"You will?" Wyatt asked him, eyes filled with tears and fear and something else. "You promise?"

Promise? Was that it? Was Wyatt somehow assured that it would be okay because Kevin would keep the bed warm for him?

"Yes, Baby Bear. I promise."

So he held Wyatt close, and asked him if he wanted Kevin to read to him, but Wyatt decided he wasn't in the mood to hear Stephen King. So Kevin read him a romance story by someone named Jude Parks, and that made Wyatt happy—or if not happy, at least a little happier.

It was a funny book, and sweet as well, and that was what Wyatt needed.

Then some nurse or other came in and needed a blood draw, and Wyatt bore it, and Kevin was glad he didn't get upset again, because he surely hated getting poked by needles. He even complimented the nurse on her haircut, and she laughed and patted at it as if she were trying to remember what she'd done with it that day. Kevin marveled once again at what Wyatt did to people.

His little bear—and God, he prayed that Wyatt was *his* little bear—nodded off a while after, and Kevin climbed carefully out of bed. His left arm had gone to sleep, but he hadn't wanted to upset Wyatt by getting up.

Kevin read a little from *Leap and the Net Will Appear!* And then it quite suddenly hit him that he hadn't talked to Theresa in days.

He went out into the hall and stood in a place where he could watch Wyatt while he made his call. Theresa answered right away and asked how gay camp had gone, and he told her just how it had gone.

She was pretty stunned, to say the least. By all of it. She let him know she couldn't pick out what surprised her the most.

"Who is Wyatt?"

"I've told you about him."

"Never," she swore.

And looking at Wyatt's sweet face, jaw shadowed by days of not shaving, through the open door, Kevin couldn't imagine how that could be true. How could that be? How could he have not talked about Wyatt? At least since he'd broken up with Cauley.

"Little guy," he said. "Was in a relationship with a total turd. A cub."

"A *what*?"

"A young bear."

"Wait a minute…." Her voice faded. "Maybe…. Maybe something about a little cute bear…. Sings crazy songs onstage?"

"Yes!" cried Kevin and then ducked his head at the annoyed look from a passing nurse.

"Wait…. You're telling me that you—Kevin Owens—are in love?"

"Yes," he said and could almost see her face.

"Well, hot dog," she said. Then: "Wait. Crazy. Songs. On. Stage. You're not getting involved with another—" And thank goodness she had the good grace not to finish her sentence. *Another Cauley.* Some respect to the dead at least.

"No," he said. "Wyatt doesn't have a tenth of the ego."

"Which could send him right to the same me—"

"Theresa! Enough. Stick with the 'hot dog' and be happy for me. And I am happy."

"Except for the part where he's in the hospital," she replied.

"Yeah. Except for that."

"I'll pray for him," Theresa said. "And I'll light a candle too."

"Thank you." He smiled and felt some warmth in the midst of the worry that was so hard not to feel.

"Do you need me to fly out?" she offered. Of course she did.

"There's nothing you can do," he said. "But I'll keep you informed."

"Any idea when you'll be coming home?"

The question made his stomach turn into lead. Home. Away from Wyatt. "At this moment I have no idea. And it's not like I have a nine-to-five job."

"Nope. That's mine. Speaking of which, I have some work to do here."

"Okay," he replied.

"Love you," she said.

"Me too."

They switched off and he went back to Wyatt's room, and just as he did, Wyatt's cell phone began to vibrate on his tray table. He picked it up, not wanting even that much noise to wake Wyatt up. He needed his rest.

He looked at the screen and his eyes went wide. Shit.

Mom flashed in blue.

God.

He answered without thinking about it. "Hello?"

"Hello?" came a strained response. And was that... a sob? "Who is this?" It was a woman's voice. Of course it was. "Mom."

"My name is Kevin. I'm... a friend of Wyatt's."

"I see."

"This is Wyatt's mother?" he asked.

"Yes," she replied. "Can I speak to Wyatt?"

"Ma'am, he's asleep."

"Well, can you wake him? This is—" And then she did sob. "—important."

In that moment Kevin decided to lie. Partially. Because he was having a bad premonition about this call. "Ma'am. He's in the hospital."

He heard her breath catch. "*What?*"

"He's sedated. He's having his gallbladder out tomorrow morning early."

"Oh, my precious Lord," she said with a gasp. "Why? *Why?*"

Was she asking him? "Because he needs to have it out. I don't know why—"

"Why does the Lord sometimes choose to put so much on our plates?"

He had no clue. Not one single one. "Ma'am, is there something I can tell him?"

There was a long pause. "Wait until tomorrow to tell him," she said then.

My plans exactly, he thought, and then told her precisely that.

"It's his father," she said, and that time he did hear the hitch in her voice. And a strangled sob.

"Ma'am?"

"He's dead. Wyatt's father died a half hour ago."

CHAPTER FORTY-TWO

WHEN WYATT woke it was hard not to tell him. But Kevin knew when Wyatt was too nervous to eat even ice cream that he had made the right decision. Wyatt had "enough on his plate" simply dealing with the fact that he was going into surgery the next morning. It was taking all of Kevin's comforting skills just to keep him calm. Add his father's death onto that?

No way.

Kevin got Big Nurse to give him something to help him sleep—simple Benadryl because she didn't want any kind of added narcotic in his system, not when he was going into surgery.

"What if they have to cut me open?" Wyatt asked Kevin.

"They're not going to have to do that. Right"—and Kevin was glad when he suddenly remembered her name—"Janis? Tell him."

She came over to the other side of Wyatt's bed and, to Kevin's surprise, reached out and took Wyatt's hand. "Sweetie, it's a laparoscopic surgery. Three tiny little holes."

"But they said there was a *possibility* that they'll have to cut me open," Wyatt said and it was clear to Kevin he was trying very hard not to whine. "And if they have to, I *have* to have a pretty scar."

Her eyebrows shot up, and she laughed and told him that he needed to stop worrying and that with a laparoscopy, a "pretty scar" was a given.

"You don't understand," Wyatt said. "I'm going to Men's Festival in less than six months, and I'll be running around in nothing but a sarong, and I have to have a pretty scar. I can't have people pointing or being grossed out. My chest is my best feature and…."

She squeezed his hand. "It's all going to work out in the end, dear. I know. One way or another, you're going to be fine."

So Kevin read *All Alone in a Sea of Romance*—apparently it was a true story, he remembered now that the guy who wrote it had been on *Ellen*—and wasn't fifteen minutes along when Wyatt began to snore.

Then he went to his recliner—Big Nurse had found it for him so he could spend the nights—and somehow fell asleep, the worrying he'd made Wyatt swear not to do following him into his dreams.

WYATT DECIDED when he woke up that he was not going to fret. He wasn't sure how, but he made up his mind. He checked his phone to see if there were any messages, but it had died in the night. Kevin apologized profusely for that, but before they could do anything, the transport orderly arrived, and thank the gods, he was another hottie.

Kevin rolled his eyes and Wyatt could only say, "I'm only noticing, Kevin. It's like that line from *The Color Purple*. You know the one?"

"The one about how Shug is just like honey. 'And now I'm just like a bee'? Because that is what it is with you and me, Baby Bear. You're the honey, and I'm like a bee. I can't stay away from you."

Wyatt blushed and his heart skipped at least two beats, and the orderly went on doing whatever he was doing, oblivious. "The one I meant," Wyatt said, "is the one where Shug says that she thinks it pisses God off when you walk by the color purple in a field and don't notice it."

"And what's that got to do with him?" Kevin bobbed his head in the orderly's direction. The orderly who was now telling Wyatt he needed to get off his bed and into the wheelchair.

"Never mind," Wyatt said. Because seeing Kevin looking at him the way he was, Wyatt wasn't sure he would ever want to notice another man again in his life. Even if it only meant he was wanting to appreciate what the gods had made.

Then he said his good-byes with Kevin, and the orderly pushed him out the door.

As they headed down, Wyatt once again mentioned his "pretty scar" worries, only to have the guy say, "Don't worry, dude. Chicks dig scars."

"Like that's gonna help me!" And then he was amused that it was obvious the orderly guy didn't get what he was implying.

Once arrived and settled in pre-op, Wyatt decided to make "pretty scar" a joke and entertained the nurses there with the story of orderly guy not getting why he wasn't excited about chicks digging his scars.

A pretty redhead giggled and said, "Yep, that sounds like Jesse."

The consensus of Wyatt and nurses alike was Jesse was "a hottie, but not too bright."

That's when he reminded the nurses that they had to ensure him he'd have a pretty scar, even though they, too, assured him that with laparoscopic surgery, he wouldn't have to worry about that.

"Now, before I see you on the other side of this," the cute redhead said, "is there anything else I can get you?"

Wyatt looked thoughtful for a moment and then couldn't resist.

"Why, yes! Yes, there is!"

"What's that, Mr. Dolan?"

"You know that stuff they sprayed down my throat the other day during the endoscopy to suppress my gag reflex?"

Redhead looked at him curiously. "Why… yes…."

"Is there any way you could get me a couple of cans of that for me to take home?"

Her brows came together in confusion. "Why would you need that?" she asked.

Wyatt didn't say a word.

Waited for it….

Waited….

Then her red brows shot up under her bangs, and she cried, "Mister *Dolan*!" and turned a brighter shade of red than her hair. She rolled her eyes. "Sorry, I don't think I can do that."

Wyatt pouted.

Dr. Lyons showed up a few minutes after that. Once more he was sort of pompous and had a severe lack of personality.

And a total lack of humor.

"Mr. Dolan, I am here to make sure you are healthy and well and possibly save your life. A pretty scar is not part of my job description."

And then Wyatt surprised even himself.

"Doctor," he said in all sincerity and found himself once more fighting off a rush of fear and wishing Kevin were here. "You don't understand." And he told him all about skinny-dipping at Camp and taking his shirt off at bars. "Please? My chest is the only thing about me I like. I can't have an ugly scar. Please? Pretty scar?"

Dr. Lyons was clearly startled by Wyatt's speech and assured him once more that there really wouldn't be a bad scar with the type of surgery he was performing.

"Pretty scar," Wyatt repeated one more time, and Dr. Lyons was gone.

The nurses, each and every one, made sure he knew that Dr. Lyons was a great surgeon and that before Wyatt knew it, he would be going home. And then Wyatt was wafted away on a wave of anesthesia.

CHAPTER FORTY-THREE

WYATT CAME slowly awake in the recovery room, and the first thing he thought was that at least these curtains weren't as hideous as the last.

After moments of hearing only muffled voices and being confused by the strange feeling all down his chest—everything was so numb—he called out for a nurse.

It was the cute redheaded girl, he was happy to see, but when he saw her nervous smile, he felt a jolt of worry.

And then he knew.

He knew before she said it.

"I'm sorry, Mr. Dolan—"

Owens-Dolan, he thought.

"—there was a complication."

"Can I see Kevin?" he said, tears stinging his eyes, and then his throat closed for a moment, preventing him from saying more.

She sighed. "They did have to open you up after all."

Gods! No! No, no, no, no....

And he began to cry.

"Oh, Mr. Dolan," she said and took his hand. "It'll be all right. I promise."

"Owens-Dolan," he managed through his tears.

And then he drifted off.

HE WOKE in his room, and Kevin was there, and his eyes were red, so Wyatt knew he'd cried too.

"I'm going to be ugly now," he said, and the tears welled up again.

"You'll never be ugly to me," Kevin said and bent and carefully kissed his chest, but lower, down a bit and on the left. Such careful kisses. "And when these bandages are off, I promise to kiss your scar every single day."

Wyatt tried hard to believe him.

It turned out that when they began the laparoscopic procedure, the surgical team pretty quickly saw why the nuclear procedure hadn't worked.

Finally Dr. Lyons and his fourth-year medical student (resident? Intern? He wasn't sure of the correct terminology) came to talk to him. They explained what had happened. The surgeon even brought photographs from the operation to illustrate, and Wyatt surprised himself by being able to get past his usual squeamishness to look at them.

Wyatt's gallbladder was bright red (when it apparently should have been a robin's-egg blue) and swollen and filled with gallstones. Lots and *lots* of gallstones. Dr. Lyons had to switch from the planned laparoscopy to full-out abdominal surgery, which meant a bigger incision—and gods!—a longer recovery time.

The thing that had interfered with the nuclear medicine test?

A gallstone "the size of a shooter marble" had blocked what was essentially the intake valve of his gallbladder—that's how Kevin helped him understand it more fully later—and that had prevented the radioactive stuff from going into his gallbladder. The big problem, though, was that this gallstone had been blocking its intake for quite a while.

Long enough that it had atrophied and then died from disuse.

His gallbladder had been rotting inside of him. It had actually been gangrenous!

Wyatt shuddered at that.

When Dr. Lyons had lifted his gallbladder to remove it, it shredded. He and his team had to use a tremendous amount of sterile water to flush his abdominal cavity and make sure they'd gotten rid of all the necrotic tissue. Otherwise, it would be even more icky, although later Wyatt doubted that anyone had used the word "icky." But by then he was getting so grossed out that he had actually grown faint. Something about how there could have been further infection and decay, a possibility of sepsis and more.

Not good stuff.

Dr. Lyons left after that, but to Wyatt's surprise, the medical student lingered behind.

"I just wanted to tell you that I've worked with Dr. Lyons for a year now," she said, "and he really is a brilliant surgeon even if he... well, even if his bedside manner is a bit lacking."

She went on to say that it was the worst gallbladder she'd ever seen, that it had felt so large and hard and there were so many stones in it....

Wyatt paled at that and decided he'd really heard far more of this icky stuff than he wanted to hear.

Then she told Wyatt something else. "It's just that…. What I wanted you to know is that I've never seen him take as much time and care during a closing."

Wyatt could only blink.

"Mr. Owens-Dolan—"

And confused or not, that made him smile, even if it was only the smallest one.

"—he usually has me or someone else close for him. But he did it this time, and he put in so very many teeny, *tiny* stitches."

Wyatt shook his head, and she explained that he usually put in bigger stitches and didn't even worry if they were 100 percent even.

"I don't understand what you're saying," Wyatt confessed.

Then she gave him a truly lovely smile, leaned in, and said very clearly…

"In other words, 'pretty scar'!"

Wyatt had to laugh at that. He couldn't help it.

But he cried again after she left.

Only this time the tears weren't so bad.

As Kevin held him as best as he could, Wyatt found he was feeling a little bit of hope.

KEVIN CALLED Wyatt's mother after Wyatt slipped off to sleep once more. He was dreading it. Dreading telling her that he still hadn't told Wyatt about his father, but what could he do?

He couldn't tell Wyatt the night before his surgery.

And now? After the trauma of today?

What was he *supposed* to do?

And more, how did he drop all this in the woman's lap? She had just lost her husband. Did she need to know how serious the surgery had been? How Wyatt might have quite easily died?

Thank God that lady in the ER—Doris, he remembered—had found a room for Wyatt and gotten him admitted. Wyatt's gallbladder had been *rotten*! Kevin knew without a shadow of a doubt that Wyatt could have died.

So make the call he did.

He thought about calling on his own cell, but thought that in a time like this, it was pretty damned likely that she wouldn't answer the phone if she didn't recognize the number.

"Wyatt?" she cried into the phone on the second ring.

"No, Mrs. Dolan. It's Kevin again."

"Wyatt's… friend."

"Yes, Mrs. Dolan," he said. "Wyatt does have friends. Lots of them." He immediately regretted his tone—*This is why I have Theresa do all my talking for me*—but *not* what he'd said.

"So you're not *that* kind of friend." There was no question in her tone. She wasn't asking. "Because I know that Howard is finally out of his life and—"

"And thank God for that," he replied. "Howard is a—" He almost said "motherfucker" but changed his tack. "—a despicable person."

"I… I…. How is my son? How did the operation turn out?"

So Kevin told her. His tone softened a bit, but not much. He didn't tell her how Wyatt's gallbladder shredded and dumped necrotic tissue into his abdominal cavity or the possibility of sepsis and more. Or stones the size of shooter marbles. But that was about all he left out. Her husband had just died, after all.

"But he's okay?"

"He'll be in here at least another three days or so. I don't think he's going to make the funeral."

"Who gives a da—*dang* about that?" she said, surprising him. "I might have to miss it myself."

Kevin's eyes went wide in more than surprise. In shock, even.

"My son is *alive*. My husband is dead. Charles has had his entire funeral planned out for years. Everything is taken care of. He doesn't need me. But Wyatt? Maybe *he* does."

Kevin could have dropped the phone. Wyatt hadn't talked much about his mother in their days trapped in the snow, but from what he had said, Kevin hadn't been prepared to hear the woman talking that way.

"Hello? Are you still there, Mr.—"

"Kevin. Just call me Kevin."

"Can I talk to my boy?"

Kevin opened his mouth, shut it, opened it, and shut it again. Geez. "He's out again, ma'am. Like I said, this took a lot out of him. A whole lot."

"Oh my." Pause. "And you think he'll be there for at least three days?"

"Yes."

"All right, then. Please tell me which hospital."

Kevin told her.

She took a long breath. "I'm coming, then, Mr.... Kevin. The funeral isn't for five days. I'm coming."

"But—"

"I'm *coming*. I'm his mother and I have the right.... Well...." Her voice hitched. "I guess I don't know if I do have the right. But I'm coming."

"Mrs. Dolan," Kevin said then. "I haven't told him about his father. I don't even know how. With all he's going through...."

"Then don't. I will. Maybe that's best."

"I...." Kevin didn't know what to say. "I don't... I don't know what to s-say."

"I'll figure that part out. Don't tell him I'm coming either. It might upset him. No, it probably will. Especially given what happened the last time we saw each other. Better the upset of me showing up unannounced than him fretting while waiting for me to arrive."

"You realize...," Kevin said, then swallowed hard. He heard the click in his throat. "You realize you're putting me in quite a predicament. He told me not to call you."

"Well, the first time you didn't. I called, now didn't I? And now you're in this either way. So let's just see where the cards fall."

Kevin didn't like the idea.

But then, what else was there really to do?

CHAPTER FORTY-FOUR

WYATT WOKE to pain. Some of the worst pain yet. He couldn't believe the pain and dammit, with his fucking gallbladder out, shouldn't this be done with?

And he was hungry. So hungry.

How could he be both?

But Kevin was there, thank the gods—all of them. Kevin was there and holding his hand and telling him he'd get the nurse.

Then he dashed out of the room even though Wyatt was struggling to find the damned call button. Where the fuck was it? Morphine! Oh gods, he was afraid of the stuff—he'd heard so many tales of people getting addicted to the shit—but this was terrible. This pain was enough to make him scream, and it was all he could do not to do exactly that.

Only then did he realize that the morphine administrator was at his wrist. Kevin had attached it to his ID bracelet with a little clip, the kind that always reminded Wyatt of a little black leather purse for Barbie.

He was crying then, crying that it hurt so damned much, and Kevin was back—

"Oh Kevin, it *hurts*!"

—and how could anything hurt this much? He thought he had experienced the worst pain on the planet, but it was nothing compared to this!

Big Nurse came in, was at his side in a flash touching him, and he swatted at her and then burst into tears and apologized and told her, "It hurts so bad, Big Nurse! It hurts!" Through the fog of pain, he realized what he'd called her and tried to apologize, but she was acting as if she hadn't noticed.

She took his hand again and said, "Mr. Dolan."

He opened his mouth, but nothing came out but a half-strangled shout.

"Mr. Dolan-Owens."

He shook his head, and it wasn't to correct her. He was trying to beam it to her. Beam to her how—much—this—*hurt*!

"*Wyatt*!" she shouted. And she did shout, and his eyes flew wide, and she took his hands, pulled one right out of Kevin's, and she *squeezed*—squeezed *hard*—and said, "Look at me!"

He tried. He did. But everything was blurry and was that fucking morphine *ever* going to kick the fuck in?

"*Look at me*!" This time as loud as her previous shout and his eyes went wide and he *saw* her.

"*Aaarrghhh…*," he groaned.

"Look at me," she said again.

"It's *killing* me, Big… Janis. *Janis*." Tears were running down his face and into his ears, and he thought he just might—lose—his—*mind*!

She squeezed his hands again. He could feel her nails in the heels of his palms, and Christ on a crystal crucifix, *that* hurt.

But he could see and hear her now—and he could hardly believe *that* was an accepted medical procedure!

"The morphine will kick in, honey. It will."

"Why does it hurt this bad?" he somehow managed to get out.

She shook her head. "I don't know, sweetheart, but I am going to call someone. But I want you to look at your husband here. Look into his eyes."

Husband?

"Kevin, take his hand and tell him you love him and get him to listen and calm down, and I'll be right back."

And he did. Kevin came around and took his hand, and he got right on the edge of the bed and leaned over so his face was very close to Wyatt's and told him he was there for him. "I love you, Wyatt. I love you so much. I'm here for you, baby. I'm here. Look in my eyes."

Wyatt did and they were so big and so beautiful and oh, it still hurt so bad, but at least this way it seemed to be bearable and then—*ooooohhhhh*—was… was that… the morphine at last?

"Only six inches," he sighed.

"What?" Kevin asked and gave him a comical look.

Oh! Wyatt laughed. "M-my scar. They said only… o-only s-six inches. Could h-have been twelve, they said."

"Pretty scar," Kevin said, and he smiled, but oh, oh, Wyatt could see the tears in his eyes.

"S'all riiiight," he muttered and then fell into the night.

WYATT WOKE again to pain, pain, pain… and this time Kevin was there, and he was holding his hand and telling him to look in his eyes, and he promised that he would push the damned dispenser from now on and for him not to worry about it.

Because that was a part of it, they said just a little while later. When he fell asleep, he wasn't able to press the button fast enough to make sure the pain didn't come back and, "Please, please, please, can something be done?" He tried not to cry—what was Kevin thinking about him? That he was the silly little faggot that Howard always said he was?

"Oh no! Is the wittle bear-wah gonna cwy?"

No! Wyatt shouted back to the voice in his mind. *You're done! I've put you behind me. I will not listen to you.* And the voice went away, thank Morpheus.

After that he was afraid to sleep because what if the pain came back?

But Kevin assured him that wouldn't happen.

"I'm here for you, lover," Kevin said, and *Oh, that sounded nice. Lover.* And, *I'm here for you.*

And Wyatt trusted him.

THEY WOULDN'T let him eat.

Nothing.

Because all the pain might be because he had another infection.

And no eating if they had to do another procedure….

How long would this last?

How long?

CHAPTER FORTY-FIVE

W HEN W YATT woke the next time, Katherine was there.

Oh, thank you, Goddess, he thought. "Thank you, Kath—"

But then with a shock he saw it wasn't her.

It was his mother.

A chill swept over him.

She came to the edge of the bed and reached out, and he flinched and then so did she.

"Oh, my boy, my sweet boy…."

"M-Mom?" he asked, wondering if this was some kind of morphine-induced illusion.

"Yes, Son. It's me. Kevin?" She looked away. "Can you get me a chair, please?"

Kevin. She knew Kevin's name?

They met while he was out, Wyatt realized.

"You can have this one."

She shook her head, her graying hair swaying at her shoulders. "No. I want to be able to get close. And my back hurts. That drive. It was a long one."

"Mom?" Was this real?

"Of course, Mrs. Dolan."

Kevin moved as fast as he always did, and he helped her sit in one of those awful plastic chairs, but his mother only told him how grateful she was.

Then she laid her hand on one of Wyatt's. "Oh, my poor sweet Wyatt."

"What—what are you doing here?" He pushed at the morphine button. If this was real, he couldn't face it sober.

"I called. And Kevin answered. And he told me what happened. Don't be mad. I'm a mother. I made him."

Wyatt flashed a look at Kevin—who looked miserable—and of course he couldn't be mad, even though a part of him really, *really* wanted to be.

I love him too much.

For a moment Wyatt found himself swept up in the marvel of it all.

I love him!

A week ago he had been alone. Well, not alone. But without love. No! Not without love. But without a special love.

And now he's here.

It was unbelievable.

It was magick.

"Wyatt?"

He turned slowly back to his mother. She looked even bigger than he remembered when he'd seen her back home. Could she really be bigger or was it the drugs?

Her eyes were red, and there were dark shadows the color of bruises under them.

She looks like Kathleen Turner, he thought quite suddenly. *An older, heavier Kathleen Turner.*

"Son, I am so sorry. Sorry for so many things. I know you probably can't forgive me, but I am saying it, and I will say it a million-million more times. I can't say it enough. I can't say it as many times as you deserve for me to."

Wyatt tried to shake his head, but it was too heavy and he was just too tired. "Mom?" was all he could manage.

"I wanted to do more. I wanted to be better. But your father...." She closed her eyes and when she opened them, they were full of raw pain. "I couldn't...." She swallowed hard. "A woman must obey her husband."

"What?" he asked, his voice cracking.

"For the husband is the head of the wife, even as Christ is the head of the church." It was her quoting voice. Wyatt recognized it, even though it had been a long, long time. He'd heard it enough. "And he is the savior of the body. Therefore, as the church is subject unto Christ, so let the wives be to their own husbands in everything." She closed her eyes again, tightly, pursed her mouth, her lips turning into a thin line. "*Everything,*" she whispered.

A rage rose in Wyatt then that was huge and red and hot and violent, and he thought his head might explode—erupt like a volcano. Fucking blow to the sky like Mount Vesuvius.

She was going to let her fucking Bible make it okay for her to let his evil bastard father kick him out of the house and his family?

Then she opened her eyes again, and they were so red and the tears ran freely down her round cheeks.

And Wyatt was just… too… *tired* to be angry.

"Evil" tumbled out of his mouth, unbidden. And, "Lightning should have killed him." And that was all he had left.

He watched her draw in a deep, long breath, her shoulders lifting, and he was sure she was about to tell him some bullshit like how he shouldn't say such things, but then she surprised him more than even her sudden appearance had done.

"Maybe so," she said so quietly he wasn't sure he'd actually heard her.

He sucked in a breath. What had she just said?

"Maybe you're right."

"Yes, I'm right," he hissed and then once again was just too tired to rage on.

Another tear, impossibly big, spilled from her left eye and landed with an actual sound on the white sheet over his mattress. "Things would have been different had the finger of God killed him rather than changed him into… what it changed him into."

Wyatt willed the energy to shake his head. Shake it vehemently. "*No,*" he said with surprising strength. "*Not* God."

"I think God is Love. I think that is all that God is. I don't think 'It' hates or gets jealous or punishes and floods the Earth or sends anyone to hell. I don't even believe in hell because how could a God that the Bible said is 'agape'—unconditional love—have any conditions?"

"God is love," he told her firmly. Marveled that he was saying it. "That's all God is."

From the corner of his eye, he saw Kevin and felt his strong hand rest on his right shoulder and give a gentle squeeze.

"Dad made his choice. He chose to be a vile, mean old man. God didn't have anything to do with it." And in a flash of insight: "And he was always a *fucking* bastard—" Wyatt ignored her wince. "—and after what happened he let 'God' be his excuse."

Then she said it, and it was like a punch to the gut, knocking the wind from his lungs.

"Maybe so," she said. "But please, Son. Do not speak ill of the dead."

Dead? Did she just say…?

She nodded. "He died yesterday morning, Wyatt. He had another stroke, and he was gone before anyone even knew."

The tears began to flow again.

Wyatt tried to get a breath. Tried again. Gasped. Kevin's hand squeezed again. Wyatt struggled for a breath. Finally got it. "He—he's dead?"

"Listen, you old bastard! You touch her again and I don't care that you're on your fucking death bed, I'll beat the shit *out of you!"*

His mother nodded once.

"Daddy's dead?"

"You are a vile evil old man! That lightning should have killed you. I wish it had!"

"Yes, Wyatt."

Wyatt looked to Kevin, eyes wild. "Did you know?"

Pain filled Kevin's face, his beautiful eyes going dark like storm clouds. "I'm sorry, Baby Bear. I couldn't—wouldn't—tell you the night before your operation."

Wyatt sighed and was just too fucking worn out and pain-wracked to be mad at his big, beautiful loving man.

He didn't tell me because he loves me.

But he should have told me.

Wyatt shook his head slowly back and forth, once.

"I'm sorry, Wyatt."

He did the right thing.

Somehow Wyatt reached up and touched that big hand that lay still upon his shoulder.

"No need," he whispered.

Wyatt looked back at his mother. She was still crying. Crying for that hideous old fuck. And even though there were shadows of guilt waiting around the edges for him—guilt for the last words he'd ever said to his sire—

"Fine! And I *have no father!"*

—with a mighty, exhausting thought, he banished them.

I don't have a father….

"Are you okay, Mom?"

And then she did something that surprised him most of all.

She smiled.

It was weak and it was small. But she smiled, and a flicker of light came to her eyes.

"Yes, Wyatt. Because I'm free. At long, long last. I'm *free.*"

CHAPTER FORTY-SIX

HE HIT her. Wyatt's father. He hit his mother.

But never anywhere anyone could see.

The rage at that nearly overswept Wyatt, but she took a hand and laid it on his heart and told him what was past was past—although gloriously so.

"I think Norman hits Wendy," she said.

Wyatt's eyes flew wide again, and once more came his mother's hand. "I shouldn't have told you," she said. "At least not yet."

"Mom. We have to do something."

His mother let out a long sigh. Then finally, "I think maybe you're right. Although I am not sure what we *can* do. I let your father treat me the way he did for over twenty years." She closed her eyes again. When she opened them, they were wet once more. "I let him do the same to you. Oh, Wyatt…."

A different kind of pain hit Wyatt then. Something different than medical. Something deeper than that. Something that had been opened when she walked into his room.

"And the kids," Wyatt said. "Mary? Norman Jr.?"

"*That* she won't put up with," his mother said. "And that was when I pretty much knew what was happening. And I blame myself for that too."

"Why?" he asked.

"Because our children learn more from their parents than we might want." She took a deep breath and let it out slowly. "I taught her that it's all right to let her husband treat her any way he wants. *My* parents taught *me* that. They so ingrained the Bible in me, it's automatic. Still. After all this time."

"Mom." He reached out to her.

"I would dream about leaving your father… but I just couldn't. It was like asking a fish to fly." She shook her head. "I couldn't."

"Mom. It's not like that at all."

She caught him with a steady gaze. "No. Not entirely." She looked away, then back. "I did things your father didn't know about. And I hid my books a lot better than you did."

The comment startled Wyatt.

His Scott Cunningham books. *The Spiral Dance*, by Starhawk. His small collection of tarot cards. He thought he'd hid them well. Nothing as silly as a box under the bed or a high shelf in his closet. He'd found a loose board in the floor by his bed. It was like something out of a movie. And it had worked for years.

"I kept mine with my… female things."

Female things? *Oh!* He blushed.

"Your father didn't even know I didn't still need them. He actually had no idea I'd stopped using them years ago. No idea what menopause really *meant*. At least that's what I thought." She shrugged. "He must have figured it out finally. I came home one day a few weeks ago and he was sitting at the same table, right there in the kitchen, with my books in front of him."

Wyatt shuddered. The image was too real, one he figured he might never forget.

But then…. "What books?" he asked.

Their eyes found each other again. What was that he saw in hers?

"A book by the Reverend Troy Perry."

Wyatt's mouth fell open.

"You've heard of him?" she asked.

"Yes."

"He's a Christian," she said in an offhand tone.

Wyatt nodded. "But a hero."

She tilted her head. "Really?"

"Mom. He started the *gay* church. He founded an entire denomination! For all those people out there who thought they were going to hell because they weren't straight, because of lifetimes of being told they were abominations."

His mother raised a hand. "I know. I read it."

The world seemed to go off skew. His mother read a book about…. Wait….

"But I wasn't sure if you would have heard of him since you don't believe in God." A pained expression came to her face.

"But I *do*, Mom," he said, and the other hurt came back.

She held up her hand. "I know…. But it's been… *hard*. It has been a heck of a journey." She shook her head. "A lifetime of being told there is only one way."

Wyatt sighed. "If only you knew *why* I believe what I do."

"Wyatt. The book by Rev. Troy Perry wasn't the only book that was lying on that table the day I got home from grocery shopping."

Wyatt clenched his jaw, then sighed.

"Actually it all started one day when your dad was out of town. I was watching TV, and this movie came on called *Prayers for Bobby*. Gosh. That was six or more years ago? It starred that wonderful Sigourney Weaver, and it was all about—"

Wyatt knew what it was all about, but the world skewed off even more at the thought *she* knew what it was about.

"—this woman who loses her son because he kills himself because he's gay. I was frozen, baby. I couldn't *move*. And I cried! Oh, how I cried. That sweet boy killing himself, and the mother…. Thinking over and over again that he did it because she told him it would be better that he was dead than be gay." Right then more tears started down her face. "But then she did this search, tried to understand, and how she was led to believe it was all right to be homosexual. That God didn't hate gay people." She trembled. "I bought the book and read it and read it and read it. It's a true story. And the mother—Mary Griffith? She became a gay rights activist. And she came to Little Rock, and I wanted to go meet her." She let out a very long sigh. "Of course, it wasn't going to happen." She looked up at Wyatt. "But it started me on my inner journey, Wyatt. I had come to believe it was possible you could be gay and be a Christian—"

"But not *pagan*."

There was a long pause, then she continued. "A lifetime of being told there is only one way, Wyatt. It was a pretty huge thing for a woman like me, growing up where I did, a country girl, to accept you were gay, honey. But the pagan thing? The *witch* thing? All those verses in the Bible about not suffering a witch to live! And not to seek out mediums and necromancers. How sorcerers were lumped right in there with murderers and idolaters and the sexually immoral. Which took me right back to the gay thing!" She raised her hands, spread them wide.

She took another long breath. Then looked him in the eyes again.

"So I did what I did before. If I could read that book about Mary Griffith and that one by Troy Perry. Or this really amazing book called

Stranger at the Gate by a man named Mel White. Oh! And—" She trembled. "—the one by Matthew Shepard's mother! And this wasn't easy, honey. I couldn't just order them from Amazon because then your father would want to know what I was buying! I used the cash tips from the diner, and even then I had to be careful because your dad knew how much I usually *made* in tips."

"Mom?" Wyatt couldn't believe what he was hearing. His mother read all those books? And went through so much trouble to buy them. For what?

For me?

"So if I could read those books, why not see if there was a different truth about your whole pagan thing? And I bought a book called *Gay Witchcraft* by Christopher—"

"Penczak," Wyatt finished. "You read *that* book?"

She nodded. "I did. Heart pounding the whole time, I might say. Scared me to order it. Scared me when I first started reading it. I was afraid I'd be struck dead."

This was a dream. Had to be. This couldn't be real. *Couldn't.*

"And then when I didn't die—when God didn't strike me dead—"

"You mean with a bolt of lightning?" Wyatt asked.

Again they just looked at each other for the longest time.

"Did you know Christopher Penczak converted his mother to his religion?"

Wyatt had to clench his jaw to keep his mouth from falling open.

What was she saying?

She was looking out the window. It was not a very good view. She could see the sky at least, but the rest was the roof of part of the building. Dull and not very uplifting. Not that he'd seen much of it. He had to get out of bed to do that, and it took a lot of effort, and thank the gods for Kevin there as well.

"Your father had the stroke when I told him," his mother said quietly.

"What?"

"I came home and saw him sitting there. Wendy and Mary and Norman Jr. were with me, and my stomach dropped down through the floor and then…. Then he said, 'So like son, like mother?' and I didn't know what to say. Then he said, 'What the *hell* is this, Rebecca?' Using my full name. And then…. Then I saw him hit you. In my head. I wondered, *Is he going to hit me now? Right in front of Wendy and the kids?*" She turned back, and the faraway look was *gone.* Her eyes flashed instead. "And… and I saw *red*." She nodded, once, twice. "So I says, 'What the *hell* were you doing in my maxi pads, Charles?' and you should have seen the look he gave me! I thought his eyes were going to pop right out of his head."

Wyatt all but gasped. This had happened? His mother had talked back to his father? She had said *hell*?

Her eyes flashed again. "Then before he could do anything more, I lifted my shoulders high and I thrust my big old breasts out—"

Wyatt did gasp then.

"—and I walked straight up to him and started to grab my books, and his hand came down on them and I shot him *such* a look and I yelled. I told him. I said, 'What'cha gonna do, Charles? *Hit* me? Like you did our boy? You gonna hit me right in front of your daughter and your grandkids?' And I thrust my chin out and I said—no, no, it was more like I hissed it—I said, 'Go on. I dare you. But you better not sleep in this house tonight, Charles Dolan, or you might just find yourself wakin' up in hell!'"

Wyatt's mouth fell open.

"Wendy was crying out about how we needed to calm down, and Mary started crying and he—the lord and master of his domain—jumps up, then his eyes go even more buggy, and he just falls on the floor. Had a stroke. And that's how it happened."

"H-he died?"

"No, this was the first time. Scared the crap out of me, Wyatt. I even had me a little setback. I felt terrible. But darn it, I wasn't going to let him hit me. I was tired of it. Tired of *all* of him. And bless me, Lord, there was a part of me that wished he *had* just died."

For the longest time neither of them said anything. Then finally Wyatt broke the silence. "Mom, what did you *ever* see in him? *Why* did you marry him?"

She let out a long breath and then seemed to almost melt into the chair. "Oh, baby. He was different once upon a time. I was working in the school lieberry—"

She pronounced it just like that, and it used to drive Wyatt insane, it was so small-town, and he hated "small-town" with a passion, but today it didn't seem to matter anymore.

"—and he would come in and get books on sports and such. And he was so darned handsome, and all the girls were head over heels about him. He always made sure I was at the desk when he checked out the books, and then one day he just asked me out. And of course I said yes. He picked me up and opened the car door for me and took me to dinner and then a show, and he was the *perfect* gentleman. And there I was, living in my house with three brothers and four sisters in a tiny town and knowing my grades weren't good enough to get any scholarships, and I thought I'd be trapped with my bastard of a father for the rest of my life. I'm hardly the pretty sister."

"Oh, Mom," Wyatt said, because he thought she was beautiful. Kathleen Turner beautiful, even older as she was now. "You're gorgeous."

She shushed him and went on. "He made me feel wonderful. He made me feel special. I felt like he'd saved my life. He went to church in those days, or started to so he could take me, and he did really well there and joined and went to Sunday school even. He learned his Bible verses and impressed everybody, and that whole year we was going steady, he never tried anything sexual. Or not too much anyway. We kissed, of course, and he would sneak in little squeezes of my bottom when we danced—"

"Mom!"

"—but that was it. So when he asked me to marry him, of course I said yes. And things were grand at first. But then they changed. He changed. Bit by bit. He started belittling me and telling me I was fat."

Gods, he thought. He felt a rush of goose bumps. *Just like me.*

"And then one day he hit me. I would blame it on the booze, which he had started to drink, but only a few beers at first, on Fridays after his week at work. But then he was drinking every night, and then it was the heavier stuff, and I thought about leaving him, but you just don't do that in Damview, Arkansas, population 700-some. And we were Christian, although he'd stopped going to church by then. Saturday night was his big drinking night, and he was always too hung over on Sunday to go. And you two were in the world by then, and how was I supposed to take care of you? I couldn't move back *home*. Lord, no."

The faraway look was back and she stared out the window, but Wyatt couldn't help but think she was looking somewhere else. Back through the years, perhaps?

"And then he got struck by the lightning. And he did change. For the better."

Wyatt didn't remember that. He remembered it for the worse. And he opened his mouth to tell her so, but she cut him off before he could start.

"No. I lie. It was better for a few weeks, maybe. At least the hitting stopped. Well, for a while. And I don't know why I didn't leave. Sometimes you just get stuck. Because I was afraid to leave him. Because I didn't know what I would do. And he told me that if I left him no one would ever want a fat old cow like me."

"Sometimes love has teeth...." Wyatt's eyes went wide. And the dark echoes threatened to come back.

No! No, you won't! he shouted inwardly at those voices. *Done with you.*

She turned back to him. "This Kevin...."

That startled him. Kevin.

"Is he a good man?"

A warmth came deep out of him and spread out in waves, and the echoes were gone. "Oh, Mom. He's wonderful."

"He seems nice." She smiled. "He sure is a handsome fellow."

Wyatt blushed.

"Does he treat you right?"

"Mom...." He started to feel giddy. "Yes, Mom. Like I'm made of gold."

She nodded. "Good. That's good." Then: "I need some water. How about you?"

She got up and told him she was getting some ice, and when she came back and poured them each a glass of water, she sat down and reached in her bag and pulled out another book. "I want to read to you from this. And no eye-rolling! I love this book, and I want to share it with you."

She held it up. *Wish You Well*, by David Baldacci, was the title and author. He'd never heard of either.

"Mister Baldacci usually writes these action thrillers, like *Last Man Standing*. But this is my favorite, and it's all about this precocious twelve-year-old girl who lived in New York City but then has to move with her family to live on her great-grandmother's farm in Virginia...."

Wyatt really did start to roll his eyes—*gods, this sounded saccharine*—but his mother narrowed hers, and he bit his lip and then smiled.

She nodded. "All right, then!" She settled the recliner back a bit, shuffled in her seat, opened the book, turned a page or two, and began to read. "The air was moist, the coming rain telegraphed by plump, gray clouds, and the blue sky was fading fast...."

CHAPTER FORTY-SEVEN

IN THE coming days, Kevin was more grateful than he could have believed for Wyatt's mother.

She helped. She helped so much.

Together they took shifts, except for the two days when she did go home for her husband's funeral.

"For Wendy," she said. "And Mary and Norman Jr."

He understood, even if it pissed Wyatt off. Thankfully only a little bit.

Kevin didn't know what he would have done without the woman.

The days turned into a week, and the week into nearly two. One trouble after another, and Kevin wasn't sure how Wyatt was making it. Kevin was exhausted. His mother was. His friends were—friends who took turns making the nearly hour-long drive to come every evening and try to help.

Words and more words and speeches and doctors' promises and possibilities all ran together.

Wyatt would go home in a few days.

No, it would be three-to-six days. Three-to-six weeks before he could go back to work.

"Kevin! I'm the store manager! I can't be gone for that long."

And thank God for Katherine Grimsley arriving and assuring him his job was his forever—if he wanted it.

Of course he did. He was the manager of one of the most successful New Age stores in the country. There were shops in New York and New Orleans and San Francisco and Chicago that had not lasted as long. And Wyatt had helped put the store online—with Katherine's help and guidance, and sometimes his ideas instead.

Wyatt's simple surgery had turned into a major one.

He worried and worried about the medical costs, and Kevin told him over and over not to, but it wasn't until he shocked his Baby Bear by telling him—*sort of*—how much he was worth that his words had an effect. He told Wyatt that Google had been very happy to pay a lot of money for some apps he'd created—an app that gently woke you up instead of jolting you up (one he hadn't needed but came up with listening to Cauley complain), another that immediately sent a message to your closest friends that your phone was dying and you wouldn't be available, and the one called Pack that offered templates that could be adjusted for the type and length of trips or vacations to help make sure you remembered everything you'd need. And they kept him on retainer for tech support on his apps and for any new ideas he came up with. That's when Wyatt finally, eyes wide, accepted that Kevin could afford to help him.

Wyatt loathed the drain they put into him. He couldn't look at all, not at all. A bulb at the end of a tube that came right out his side and filled with some kind of bodily fluids.

But oh, the visitors!

How could Wyatt ever have doubted he was loved?

It made Kevin's heart swell to near bursting at all the love.

And know he was lucky to have Wyatt in his life.

God, he hoped that was true.

Please let it be true! He would worry and then remember what the Universe heard. No worries that Wyatt might leave because then that would be what he thought about and could therefore manifest. No. Gratitude instead.

But real.

Real gratitude with only Wyatt's best interests at the center of his mind.

It wasn't just the Fabulous Four that came to see Wyatt. It was more than that.

Customers came!

Local Faeries—attendees of Queer Men's Festival. Gentle Ben and his lover—a man nearly as shy as Kevin himself. Bunny and Kirk and Kirk's lover, Michael. Historical Heloise came by and gave him a lovely necklace of amber that had driven Wyatt nearly mad with appreciation.

And some not so local.

Domi Dearest drove all the way from Eureka Springs, and Greg from Springfield—bartender extraordinaire—stayed the night at the hotel where Kevin had put Wyatt's mother up. He wasn't the only one. Lorax had come. And more.

Rat Bastard had called from China, where he worked when he wasn't at Festival every other year (although the call had been short, after all).

There were so many more, and oh, Kevin knew it had all helped.

There was a Porch Night at the hospital as well, since Wyatt's hospital stay coincided with Asher's turn as host. He brought virgin cocktails. It turned out that he'd decided to put alcohol on vacation—the duration of which remained undecided. And he brought a rough cut of his movie, *Drunks*, and they'd watched it right there in the room together and clapped when it was over. Kevin saw the movie was a little too much for Wyatt—a little too long in his physical state—but he wouldn't hear of not watching it. Kevin thought in the end it was worth the strain (although it did give him a pretty ugly nightmare of giant bottles of wine and beer and whisky chasing him across a great and endless field).

And the nurses. With their twelve-hour shifts, they would then have three and four days off, and almost to a man and woman, they would stop by if they thought they might not see Wyatt again and love on him—all declaring that they wished all their patients were at least half as sweet as he was—and tell him how wonderful he was.

Sadly, many of them did see Wyatt again.

It all helped, and Wyatt needed it all, because it seemed every time he took two steps forward, something would happen to set him at least one step back.

There was the night that his morphine stopped helping with the pain, and finally the nurses discovered that his intravenous shunt wasn't working correctly, so they put in a new one. Only, one nurse tried for twenty minutes and couldn't find a vein—and God, how terrified Wyatt was of needles and how this could set him back a decade on that—but then they called down to someone in the ER to come help. Who should arrive but Doris, and Wyatt had wept in gratitude.

After a while they—whoever *they* were—decided it was time to take him off his meds button and convert him to oral ones instead, and of course that didn't work as fast.

There were more tears, and this killed Kevin, especially when he could see how hard his Baby Bear was trying to be brave.

But at least he was getting out of bed and moving around. The ubiquitous "they" were pleased with his progress.

Through and through it all, there was Becca, Wyatt's mother, and soon she was fawning over not only her son, but Kevin as well.

She read to Wyatt too, from a book called *Wish You Well*, by David Baldacci, a book that Wyatt admitted "would have made me stick my finger down my throat a few short weeks ago."

But he'd changed his mind.

"I'm enjoying it so much," Wyatt said. "I feel like a little boy again when Mom was reading me all about one fish, two fish, red fish, and blue fish or that book I was crazy about, *The Enormous Egg*, which was all about the farm boy whose chicken lays a triceratops egg and…."

And oh, to see what was happening between Wyatt and his mother made Kevin's heart swell with joy. All that love.

If only….

But no, Kevin decided not to even go there. He knew his own mother cared not one whit, or maybe she might have called him once in the last six years.

God, and then Wyatt had a relapse.

More pain.

Another endoscopy.

But no jokes, Wyatt confessed, about wanting the spray to help with his gag reflex—"Although I could use it with you!" he'd said while muddled on the returned morphine drip, embarrassing the hell out of him in front of Becca.

She only blushed a tad herself and said something like, "Well! And I thought it was just your sweetness my boy liked!"

Kevin nearly thought he would die.

The infamous "they" thought Wyatt's problem might be due to his liver leaking bile into his abdominal cavity, and he could very well need yet another operation.

Wyatt had wept helplessly in Kevin's arms, and all he could do was hold his Baby Bear and love him and tell him that all this would end, he promised. Promised with all of his heart and soul and mind.

Pain.

And more pain.

Terrible dreams.

An evening of total amnesia after he'd been given too much anesthesia during the second endoscopy.

It all ripped Kevin apart.

There was simply nothing he could do.

He finally broke down crying while Wyatt was off at some test or another, and to his shock, Becca had comforted him.

"You're right, you know," she told him. "This will end. Wyatt—all of us—will get through the tunnel and into the light on the other side."

"You sure that light won't be an oncoming train?" Kevin asked, and then she hugged him and held him tight—her head resting even lower than Wyatt's on his torso—and let him know that there were no more oncoming trains.

He was almost done.

She knew it. "A mother knows things," she said.

And then, as if she really had somehow known—and why would he really doubt it?—there came good news.

The procedure "they" decided on was something called an ERCP, or an endoscopic retrograde cholangiopancreatography. No incision. A scope was sent down his throat and into his abdomen. And the surgeon had decided the leakage was actually very small, and there would be no need to install a "stent." He might be going home soon.

It all seemed impossible.

The last problem was that he was still draining, more than he should've been, and they couldn't figure out why.

Finally his doctor came by and sat with him. He asked for privacy and asked Wyatt just that. "You tell me, Wyatt. What's going on? Don't you want to go home?"

Kevin knew he should have gone out into the hall, but he couldn't. Neither could Wyatt's mother. They both stood there, on the other side of that curtain, listening.

"Of course I do," Wyatt said in a voice so weak it made Kevin want to cry again.

"I'm not sure that you do. Nearly two weeks not enough?"

"Yes. I hate it here."

"Wyatt, then show us. We've done all we can do. You're healing… but you're not. It's like you're preventing yourself from going the last step. Like you're afraid to go on. Afraid to go home. Like you're holding on to something."

Wyatt insisted that the doctor was wrong and sent him away, and when Kevin and his mother went back in, he refused to talk about it.

Oh my sweet lover, Kevin moaned inwardly. *If there was only something I could do.*

And that was when possibly the worst thing that could happen, did.

Howard showed up at the hospital.

CHAPTER FORTY-EIGHT

WYATT WOKE to some commotion on the other side of the curtain that kept him from being viewed by people walking past his room. He didn't like that, being observed when he didn't know about it.

But now it kept him from seeing what was going on.

"Just what the hell are you doing here?"

"I have a right—"

"*What* right? What right do you have to be anywhere near him after what you've done?"

"This is important."

Wait! That voice! Gods… it was….

"And unless you're going to call security or something, Hodor, I'm going to see him."

And with that, Howard stepped from behind the curtain.

It was a complete shock. Wyatt froze. He could all but feel the color drain from his face.

Howard didn't look good. It wasn't that he looked sick exactly. But his color was off. There was the strange, almost jaundiced, shade to his skin. And bruises under the eyes. He'd shaved his beard—*Howard*—but then it had started to grow back, and, gods, had there always been gray in it? Wyatt didn't remember if there had been. And his eyes, that dark slate of them that Wyatt had always found so gorgeous, looked faded—washed out.

Wyatt had to fight to keep from shaking.

"Howard," he said, and cursed himself for the tremble he heard in his voice. "What are you doing here?"

Howard took a step and Wyatt could see there was some kind of smudge on his sweatshirt. Ketchup, maybe. Or spaghetti sauce.

"Oh God, Wyatt…." Howard's voice faded away as if someone had slowly turned down the volume of his voice. Kevin, maybe? But then he began again. "I heard… I'm so sorry…."

Wyatt blinked at him. Sorry?

"This is all my fault. Christ, Wyatt! What have I done?"

Huh? "What did you do, Howard?" *Beside try to destroy me, that is,* Wyatt thought.

Howard's eyes were a bit wild. "You being here. I couldn't believe it when I heard. You're this sick already? Oh, Wyatt, I did this to you."

Wyatt blinked again. "I don't understand. How did you do this?"

Now Howard looked confused. "The HIV. You're here because of that, aren't you?"

It hit Wyatt. Howard thought he had HIV. They'd never talked after that day at the store. Howard thought he was in the hospital because he had AIDS.

Then, in some strange mockery of Howard's words that day, Wyatt said, "I don't have it, Howard."

Howard froze. Shook for a second. Took a step back. Stopped. Then took three forward. "You don't?"

Wyatt shrank back for a second. *He's mad. He's mad I don't have it.*

Howard staggered, fell into the ugly orange chair. "You don't have it," he said, a whispered statement and not a question. "My God." Then louder and eyes growing wet—

Am I really seeing that?

—"You don't have it! Oh my God! You don't have it?" A question at last.

Wyatt shook his head.

"How is that possible?"

Wyatt shrugged.

"I… I don't believe it. Wyatt…. You just don't know the *relief*!" And then, to Wyatt's astonishment, a tear fell down Howard's face. Howard's face. Howard's! Somehow, Wyatt, in dim nightmares, had imagined this conversation ending with Howard being furious. Shouting. Screaming it wasn't fair. That he—Wyatt, a stupid little faggot—*should* have it. That he—Howard—should be free of it and Wyatt forever. Instead, this?

Howard was shaking his head. "I don't believe it. For weeks I've been trying to decide whether to come to you and tell you something, and then I heard on the *Faerie Grapevine* that you were here…." *The Faerie Grapevine*—the official e-mail newsgroup for Heartland Queer Men's Festival. "I just assumed that my HIV—"

His HIV….

"—had hit you harder than me. I've just known I gave it to you. I never thought for a moment I couldn't have. I seroconverted months before I found out. I fucked you so many times during that time. I assumed…. Oh, Wyatt!"

And he jumped from the chair and dashed forward to the bed, and Wyatt saw that he was going to hug him and cringed back into the pillows, and that stopped Howard short. Oh, and the sorrow that took over Howard's face.

"I'm sorry…. Of course. You don't want me to touch you."

Tears suddenly welled up in Wyatt's eyes. "It's not that I don't want you to touch me, Howard. But I don't want you to *hug* me." Never again.

Howard stepped back, hit the chair with the backs of his legs, and then slowly settled back in it. The pain was raw on Howard's face, but Wyatt knew then that he couldn't concern himself overmuch with that. He didn't wish him ill. But there was a line. "You said you've been wanting to tell me something, Howard. What was it?"

"I—I…. That I'm leaving."

Leaving?

"I asked for a transfer with the company. And I'm going to put the house up for sale."

"I see," Wyatt managed through his shock.

"Unless you want it…?"

His voice. So hesitant. Unsure. What the hell was going on?

"The house?" Wyatt asked, dumbfounded.

"Yes. I know you love it—loved it."

I did. Once upon a time. But now? With what it represented? "I… I… I'm sure I couldn't afford what you're wanting for it."

"No!" Howard shook his head back and forth, almost violently. "I'd just let you take over the house payment. We'd work out something later."

Take over the house payment?

Move back into his…. But no. He quite clearly realized he didn't want to live there. Not at all. Because it wasn't *his* anymore. It was only a symbol of something that had never really been. Wyatt sighed, but then somehow felt something… stir upon his shoulders. "No, Howard. I don't want it."

Was that a flash of pain in Howard's eyes?

"I… I guess I can't blame you." Howard cleared his throat and then set his shoulders. "All right, then. Okay, so, so then you should know I'm going to give you half of what I get for it."

Wyatt would have fallen if he hadn't been lying down.

"I'm moving to Birmingham—"

Birmingham? Alabama?

"—which isn't like I'm moving to San Francisco after all, where you could pay a million dollars for a house half the size of ours."

Ours.

"The HIV care there is really good. I want that. I understand they have the biggest HIV research hospital in the country."

Treatments. Gods. Well good, then. Everyone deserves quality care. And he knew then, to his surprise, that he meant that. And that strange… stirring on his shoulders continued. So: "Good, Howard. That's good."

"It's not a death sentence anymore, right?" Howard asked, looking like a child instead of the huge strong man he'd always been.

Was Howard asking him or was this a rhetorical question?

"There are people that say it's no harder to deal with than diabetes these days. Of course, my mother just had her right foot removed because of her diabetes, so I think she might argue with the whole 'easy' thing, you know?"

Howard's mother had to have her foot removed? Wyatt felt a surge of compassion for the woman he'd never met. The poor lady. "I'm so sorry, Howard."

"Not that I ever gave you the opportunity to meet her." Howard sighed. "I'm sorry about that, but—"

But you were so angry with her.

"—I was so damned mad at her, you know? For the way she treated me. Put me down."

She put you down? "I knew she didn't take your coming out very well."

Howard laughed. "Did I say that?" He laughed again. "She didn't really care. She just thought it was one more way I let her down."

"Oh gods, Howard." Oh, the look on his face!

Howard held up a hand. "It's okay. In fact, things are… well… better there. I've gone to see her. Last week, in fact. I helped her get home after the operation. And we had a lot of time to talk." There was sorrow on Howard's face. But…. Something else. Was it hope? "Wyatt, we're talking. Mom and I are talking."

Wyatt felt a little skip in his heart. He couldn't help it, dammit. After all, he'd been with the man for ten years, eleven really. And he knew how it was to have a mother that didn't talk to you.

"That's really good news, Howard."

Wait. The full impact of what Howard said earlier hit him. Howard was going to give him half of what the house sold for?

"I thought so." Howard gave him a smile that reminded him somewhat of the one that had won him over a thousand years ago.

He scooted the chair closer to the bed.

"Anyway, the house…." A terrible look crossed his face and then Howard seemed to shake it off. "I did you wrong there. Your name wasn't on the mortgage, but it was yours too. And I want you to have half. You could put a hefty down payment on the place you're staying at now or pay off totally a new, smaller house. Better setup."

Wyatt had to fight to keep his mouth from falling open. He clenched his hands into fists and hoped Howard didn't notice. He shook his head. "Why are you doing this, Howard?"

"And I want you to have more of what's *in* it. There were a few things I took… well… it was just wrong." Then to Wyatt's surprise, another tear dropped from Howard's eyes. "There were a lot of ways I did you wrong."

Was… was this happening?

Howard stood up.

"And I don't know why. I've asked myself that a million times the last few weeks. But not just then. Even when I was doing it all… I would say… I would say to myself, *Why did you do that?* You were my little bear, Wyatt. And I've never been able to answer. Except…." He wiped at his eyes with the back of a hand. "I was jealous?"

Howard made a move to sit on the edge of the bed and then checked himself. He sat back down on the chair instead.

"Everyone liked you, Wy. No, they fucking *loved* you! Every time I went somewhere without you everyone would say, 'Where's Wyatt?' And for some reason I would get so fucking mad. Or they would go on and on and on about your act at Festival or your Halloween costume or your jokes—as freaking bad as they've always been, sorry, baby—or how funny your T-shirts were or… God. Before I met you, I got the attention. But not long after we got together, it was you."

Another tear formed, and this one began to roll slowly down Howard's face.

"Then I realized something else. It was never *me* they liked. It was my cock. They wanted me to fuck them or let them suck it, and so they would be really nice to me so that would happen. But once they were bored, they were gone."

"Howard." Wyatt reached to touch him, then became conscious that he wasn't even ready for that. He pulled his hand back. "That's not true. *I* wanted you, and I didn't even know about your penis. In fact, you scared the shit out of me when you showed it to me."

Howard went on as if he hadn't heard Wyatt. "But with you, they wanted you no matter what. Guys would stop me on the street and ask me about you."

They would? Wyatt wondered. "Really?"

Howard nodded. "And they still do. Every single day it seems. It's part of the reason I need to get away. So I can have a chance to be *just* Howard."

Wyatt nodded. He understood that feeling. Needing to be just Wyatt and not Wyatt and Howard.

"A Howard with no past and hopefully some kind of fucking future."

And then Wyatt did reach out to him. And Howard did the same. But only their fingers intertwined, only for a second, before Howard pulled his hand back.

Howard swallowed. His Adam's apple bobbed from the force of it. And then he said, "I wanted you to know that I *did* love you. I really did." Another tear joined the others. "I still do, *dammit*. And I've lost you."

Wyatt sucked in a deep breath, let it out in a shuddering sigh, and felt tears of his own begin to gather.

"I *have* lost you, right?"

Wyatt closed his eyes, and when he finally opened them again, those tears slipped out freely. He nodded. "Yes, Howard. You have."

Howard closed *his* eyes. Clenched his jaw. Opened his eyes again. "Hodor?"

"Kevin," Wyatt corrected. "His name is *Kevin*. But he's only a part of it. I wouldn't take you back now for anything in the world. Not for *anything*."

Howard flinched, and Wyatt was sorry for it. Mostly.

"I don't mean to hurt you, but it's true. Not for a million dollars. Not for a million-million. I'm free of you, Howard." And with a startled mental gasp, Wyatt quite *suddenly* realized it was true. The weight that was stirring and shifting on his shoulders *lifted*. He *felt* it. That was exactly what it felt like. Like tons and tons and tons and tons of huge stones had just raised up right off not only his shoulders, but his heart and mind and soul.

I'm free of you.

There was open pain on Howard's face now, but alas, there was nothing Wyatt could do about that. That was Howard's load to bear.

After a long moment, Howard stood up.

"I'm sorry, Wyatt. I wanted you to know that too. That I am truly, *deeply* sorry. I know that probably doesn't mean shit to you. You can tell me to fuck off."

I haven't yet.

"But I am. Sorry. It's not just words. I am sorry to my bones. To the marrow of my bones. And…."

Howard shook, then put his arms around himself as if to calm it. "And I am so thankful that I didn't give you HIV. I gave you enough without giving you that too."

Howard turned then and started to walk out.

"Howard?"

The man who had been his lover for so long, the man that was truly walking away forever, stopped. He turned slowly.

Do it, Wyatt thought. *Go on. Truly free yourself forever.*

"I forgive you." And with those three words, all the weight in the world simply disappeared and was gone, gone, and gone. Something swept over him. A freedom so deep and complete Wyatt almost lost his breath.

Howard surged forward and then stopped, and with a sigh, Wyatt opened his arms.

His ex-lover carefully pulled him into his arms, watching cuffs and wires and IVs, gave him a hug—for Howard, a huge one—and Wyatt hugged him back. He did it the way Katherine had taught him so long ago. With heart. Because it was easy to say you forgave someone, but meaning it was something different. And this startling freedom meant hugging with heart.

Then Howard pulled away. "I'll always love you, Wyatt," he said quietly, and then he walked away.

HOWARD STOPPED on the other side of the curtain. Kevin was standing there.

"You heard, huh?"

Kevin nodded. He didn't say anything.

"Didn't take you long to step in."

"It took me years," Kevin said.

Howard nodded himself. "Fair enough. You'd be stupid not to."

"And I'm not stupid," Kevin assured him.

Howard shook his head. Then, "I truly did love him. And a big part of it was jealousy. My God. We would go somewhere and Wyatt would be wearing pink from his Converse sneakers to his camo baseball cap, even one of those canvas belts with the metal sliding buckle like I wore in the Boy Scouts—only *pink*. And I would think, *Really? You're going to wear that?* And I'd say something... mean. Really mean. And the son of a gun would stick out his chin and defy me and wear it anyway, and what would happen? Everyone would go apeshit telling him how great he looked. And there I would be in my thousand dollar or more leathers, and I was lucky if a half-dozen people said a word." He shook his head.

"That's Wyatt," Kevin said, and he couldn't help but smile. Because that *was* Wyatt. And he would have been proud to be seen with his Baby Bear in such an outfit and glowed with every praising remark Wyatt got.

"Take care of him, Hodor."

Kevin nodded and didn't correct him. What the hell difference did it make?

Howard took a few steps and then stopped.

He turned around. "There was one more thing," he said in a voice so light Kevin could barely hear him. "I thought about telling him... and then I couldn't. You tell him if you want."

Kevin geared himself up for it. What would Howard say?

"I was the one that did it." A tear, huge, rolled down Howard's wet cheek. "I'm the one who scratched 'faggot' on his car."

"What?" And then his eyes went wide. Last year, of course. When Wyatt had come to Camp. The word "*FAGGOT*"—in big capital letters—had been scratched across the right passenger quarter panel of Wyatt's beloved Mini Coop.

"He didn't even notice for two or three days. I kept waiting and waiting, and finally I had to point it out, and Wyatt was upset for what looked like about a minute, and then he said it was kinda cool. Like out of *Queer as Folk*. I was furious."

Oh, that's what he pretended, Kevin thought, remembering. *But Wyatt cared.*

"And you're dropping this in my lap?" Kevin said, fighting a rising anger.

"No. I just thought now wasn't the time for him to know." He looked toward the curtain. "I thought it was a bad one, in fact. But I thought someone should know. And I think you'll know if there is a right time."

I think that time will probably be never, Kevin thought.

"Good-bye, Hodor," Howard said, and turned and almost walked into Wyatt's mother, who was just returning from the cafeteria with three cups of soft serve.

"Good-bye, Big Sir," Kevin said, letting the man have it one last time.

Howard froze for an instant. And then left.

And was gone.

"Who was that?" Wyatt's mother asked.

"I'll let Wyatt tell you. But only if he wants, okay?"

Their eyes met and there were questions there and then... understanding.

"All right," she said.

And then they went to Wyatt's side of the curtain.

"Piña colada, anyone?" she asked.

"Oh, yummy!" Wyatt cried in delight. "I hope it has rum in it. *Lots.* I could use it."

"Somehow I doubt it," his mother said and took the terrible chair and with sharp eyes indicated Kevin should take the recliner. He didn't argue. "You know I've never had rum before. What's it like?"

"Oh, *delish*!" Wyatt exclaimed happily. "But mostly only *in* something?"

"Something like this?" she asked, and took a taste. "Oh, that is yummy, isn't it?"

"I'll make you a real piña colada when we get home," Wyatt said.

And there was something different about him. His shoulders were higher. Wyatt was no longer slumped with the pain and wear of days upon days upon days.

He looked... happy.

Kevin smiled.

And felt blessed.

THE NEXT day Wyatt astonished everyone when his drainage bulb was empty except for only the tiniest amount. It hadn't been emptied since about an hour after Howard's visit.

"They" all picked and pecked amongst themselves like biddy hens, wondering what had changed.

But Kevin knew.

They released Wyatt that afternoon.

CHAPTER FORTY-NINE

KEVIN TOOK Wyatt home and was glad of it. It was a fairly big house, and he had to figure out how to set his cub up. There was only one bathroom in the house, and it was upstairs. And getting him up there was a bit of a deal—the staircase was narrow, and he wasn't excited about Wyatt trying it himself, at least for a few days. An older lady several doors down offered to loan them her portable commode, and Wyatt paled at the idea.

"Poop in *that*?" Wyatt pointed at it, horrified, when Kevin brought it into the house. "I dar'st not!" he exclaimed dramatically, spreading fingers across his chest. "And then I would have to drag it upstairs by myself anyway, because there is *no* way I'd let you!"

"I don't mind," Kevin said. "It's just p—"

"*Tch*! *Tch*! *Tch*!" Wyatt *tch*'ed, raising a finger imperiously. "I have spoken! The plastic urinal thing I'll use. It's almost fun. Sticking my dick in there and all. I can't remember who it was—it should have been me—who said one of the best things about being a man is making the world your urinal! But I will not—" He pointed at the plastic and metal cheap-man's throne and shuddered. "—use *that*. I'll wear Depends first. Or stay upstairs."

"Okay, okay," Kevin said, laughing hard enough that he had to wipe tears from his eyes. Then, changing the subject: "By the way, your front yard. Is that a *garden*?"

Wyatt nodded. "It sure is. Spectacular too. You should see the daffodils! It was Sloan's mother's garden, and he's afraid to sell this place because he's afraid the new owner will just rototill it over and roll out some sod."

Kevin gasped—his turn to be horrified. "That would be terrible!"

Wyatt nodded and shrugged, somehow at the same time. "But it's a lot of work, and I think that Sloan was hoping maybe I'd take care of it, but gods. All that dirt under my nails? I pay to get these done."

"There are gloves, you know," Kevin said, laughing again, and then reflected on how often he'd wished he had a garden, but living in the big city—especially in a condo—made that pretty difficult.

Wyatt didn't respond right away, but there was a twinkling in his eyes.

All of Wyatt's friends had been there the day Wyatt got home, even Asher, who luckily had finished his pickup shots in LA just a few days before.

There was tons of food, and Wyatt had even gotten Asher to make piña coladas for his mother, and of course the bartender par excellence had come through, even finding a pineapple vodka to sweeten the alcoholic deal. He himself only had a sip, though. "They're for your mother, after all," he said, and then had not so much as a beer.

But of course Wyatt wouldn't let his mother so much as taste them until he had sung the infamous piña colada song.

"Whew!" Wyatt's mother cried after one sip. "So *that's* rum!" She switched to water partially through her second drink when she found herself plopping down in an easy chair and unwilling to get up. "I don't know how you boys put these away like you do!"

Wyatt was in high spirits and had even tried to dance to the famously corny song, but by the time he'd reached the first chorus—about liking piña coladas and hating yoga and having half a brain—it was clear to all, even him, that he had to sit down.

The doctors had warned Wyatt that he might never get back to the way he was—what had happened to his gallbladder and what it did was very traumatic to his body—but Kevin wasn't about to remind him of that. Thoughts became things after all.

And he had thanked that emergency room nurse named Doris who had gotten Wyatt a room and might have saved his love's life.

No one stayed late, much to Wyatt's objections, but all could see even he didn't totally mean it.

They didn't make love that night, even though they both wanted to. Wyatt's spirit was willing but his body wasn't, and Kevin was afraid he'd hurt him. There were a hell of a lot of stitches involved in the creation of a "pretty scar" and while Wyatt refused to even peek under the bandages, Kevin had and saw it was healing beautifully. One day—and he could almost see Wyatt in his mind's eye—he was sure his lover would be proud of his life's battle scar.

Two weeks passed, and each day Wyatt got a little stronger. It would be weeks before he could go back to work, but his boss made sure he knew his job would be waiting for him. There had even been a collection by his coworkers of food and necessities to stock his cupboard. It had made Wyatt cry and made Kevin proud that so many people cared so much for his lover.

Lover.

The word made his skin tingle.

And any fears he might have had that he was just some rebound were eased not only by the way that Wyatt looked at him, those gorgeous deep brown eyes aglow, but by friends and Katherine, Wyatt's boss, and even Wyatt's mother.

"Don't you hurt my boy, or you'll hear about it from me," she warned him, but one time only. One time was all he needed—not that he ever planned on doing anything of the sort.

They grew closer every day, sharing stories and experience and laughter and pain and music and passages from books.

Wyatt's mother stayed for only a few days—long enough to finish reading *Wish You Well*—and after reading enough to catch up while Wyatt took one of his frequent naps, Kevin found himself loving to be read to by the woman as well.

"You are wonderful," he told her many times through his days of getting to know her from hospital to home. "Wyatt is so lucky to have a mother like you."

She shook her head. "I'm trying to make up for a lot of lost time," she replied, looking at her son thoughtfully. "And so grateful Wyatt's letting me. I'm so sorry your mother doesn't know what she has in *you*."

Kevin didn't know what to say about that. "They never really treated me badly," he said, banishing memories of being asked if he couldn't please shut up for just one single solitary goddamned second. "I think they just didn't know what to make of me."

Wyatt's eyes cracked open.

"I was like a changeling or something to them. I just plopped down in front of their eyes. I was a total mistake—"

"You're *no* mistake," Wyatt said, and the way he said it made Kevin's knees go weak.

"I was not expected," Kevin said. "I was that 1 percent chance that the pill didn't work. My mom and dad had never planned on being parents. I think they would have put me up for adoption if they hadn't been such prominent members of their community. They were both professors at Columbia University in New York. So they didn't really have a choice, not and keep their standing with their peers. They never beat me or anything like that. They were just *really* bad parents." And sometimes that made him really sad.

"Oh, darlin'," Wyatt's mother said and reached out and touched his hand.

But today?

"Then I'll be your mother."

Today not so much.

"If you'll let me call you son."

Kevin's breath caught. "That…. That would be really nice."

"But you have to stop calling me Mrs. Dolan. I want you to call me Mom."

Today not so much at all.

"I will," he told her. Then he sighed. Returned to his story. "You know, in point of fact, they weren't even good at being married. My dad cheated all the time, and I mean a lot." He closed his eyes and clenched his jaw and remembered his mother crying in the early years. "And then after a while, she just didn't care anymore." And sometimes that made him sad too.

Wyatt sat up and reached out for him.

"Which is why," Kevin said, "I decided I could never be in a relationship like that. My way or the highway. Monogamy or nothing."

Wyatt dropped his hands, pain sparking in his eyes.

"Total love, or nothing."

KEVIN WENT with Wyatt when it came time to take care of the stitches, which were actually staples. Tiny ones. The stitches were all internal.

He held Wyatt's hand, and Wyatt tried really hard not to whimper, but he was Wyatt, after all, and there were a lot of them.

But when all was done, he was finally willing to look, and red as it was….

"Pretty scar?" asked Dr. Lyons, who had insisted on doing the work himself instead of letting one of his students do it.

"Pretty scar," Wyatt agreed with a weak little smile.

And then the days turned into even more weeks, and time seemed to have frozen.

Until Kevin got the phone call.

Wyatt was shocked when Kevin told him about it.

Somehow Wyatt had just let himself pretend that forever was going to be about him recovering and Kevin being there to help.

"I've got to go to New York," Kevin said. "I've got to take care of Cauley's estate. I've just totally ignored it. And SAFE wants to take it over. I've put them off too long."

"You're going?" *But what am I going to do?* he wondered, filled with dread and sorrow.

"And I was wondering, Wyatt. Would you go with me?"

What? What had he said? "Go with?" he asked.

"Oh yes, Wyatt. Because I can't stand the idea of being without you for a single day."

Gosh! Go to New York?

"For how long?" he asked, glancing around the room. A room—a house—he'd actually begun to think of as his.

"Well, I was thinking of to live," Kevin said. He came to Wyatt then and got down on the floor next to the couch where Wyatt was resting. "And I was wondering—and God I know this is *not* romantic and you deserve romantic—if… if you'd marry me."

Wyatt gasped. "Marry you?" Marry him?

"I thought what a good idea it would be. If you married me, I could carry you under my insurance and really be able to take care of you."

Wyatt could hardly believe what he was hearing. Marry him? Marry Kevin?

"We've only been together for weeks," Wyatt said. "What if you change your mind? What if I fuck up? What if it doesn't work out? What if I *fuck* up? I mean, what if…." He gulped. "I've been around the block quite a few times, Kevin. What if I get cocktailed up at Festival and find myself in somebody's tent?"

"Then we'll deal with it," Kevin said.

"But you said total monogamy or nothing."

"I didn't say that I'd throw away the love of my life for a mistake, though. Working through things is what being married is all about."

Wyatt gave another little gasp.

And Kevin said he wasn't being romantic?

"You know that I love you, right?"

"You do?"

Kevin looked at him sternly. "Surely you do, right? After all we've been through? I wouldn't do all that for just anyone." But then his firm look melted. "Oh God, Wyatt. You're giving me your Bambi eyes. I can't deal with those sweet Bambi eyes!"

Wyatt sighed happily.

"I love you so much, Wyatt. I wish I could tell you how much."

Wyatt's heart began to pound and the words flew out before he knew it. "I love you too, Kevin."

And by Eros, Venus, and Clíodhna, he did.

"So will you?" Kevin asked.

"I will," Wyatt said.

And what do you know. There was no cosmic scale keeping him from getting love, was there?

After all, he was going to be the first of the Fabulous Four to get married.

CHAPTER FIFTY

WYATT AND Kevin threw some things together—with the idea that they would be back for what they needed—and flew to New York the next morning. And hey, Howard had been serious about letting Wyatt have more of the things he'd kept. They would need that too, although once Wyatt saw Kevin's condo, he wasn't sure where it would all go. The condo was a stark black and white, but it wouldn't be that way long with Wyatt's stuff added in.

Kevin assured Wyatt he didn't mind at all.

They had a civil service before a judge right away, and almost no one could make it, of course. Theresa was Kevin's witness, and he flew Sloan in to be Wyatt's, which was fitting because Sloan was Wyatt's best friend after all. He couldn't even stay that night because something huge was happening at his work. When it became apparent that, with Sloan leaving, dinner would be either two or them or three, Theresa begged off, even though both of them assured her she was welcome.

"Not this time," she said with a radiant smile. Then nodding at Wyatt: "I'll get to know you better soon."

So Kevin took Wyatt to a small, quiet, out-of-the-way almost-hole-in-the-wall for a sweet and romantic dinner.

That night they made careful love. Wyatt wasn't quite healed yet, but he rode Kevin admirably, marveling out loud that he couldn't believe what was happening and how thrilling it was.

The next day was business and the basement of Cauley's house. It was hard for Kevin not to fall into despair. This was Cauley's life they were going through.

But during it all, Wyatt not only didn't complain, but was incredibly efficient. Kevin did most of the box moving, but Wyatt was able to quickly figure out what to do with everything and made piles and helped Kevin make objective calls on what should be kept, what should be donated to the GLBT archive, and what should be thrown away. And he helped, too, when Kevin couldn't be objective.

Then Wyatt did something that made Kevin love him more than he could have ever imagined. He was near despondent over the fact that what was being given to the archive could simply disappear forever when Wyatt made a suggestion.

"You know, if we could do it—I mean you'd have to make the final decision, and it might not be easy—we should pick out about a dozen things—they'd have to be flat, like an article or a photograph or a magazine cover—and frame them. Then we could hang them in a room. No, better yet, the staircase. Make it a memorial to Cauley. Even insist on it to SAFE. The staircase would be a remembrance to all who stay here of who Cauley was."

Kevin rocked back on his haunches, stunned by the idea.

And instantly won over by it.

He went to Wyatt and kissed him, and then they—astonishingly—quickly picked out a baker's dozen items and set them aside, and somehow, through some miracle, got through everything over the weekend. Wyatt had to take a few naps, but that was understandable. He did it on the ugly couch instead of the bed. Most of the rest of the furniture was gone by then. Kevin had let Cauley's mother send a lot of it to local secondhand stores—the charity ones. He'd reminded her not to tell the shops how Cauley had died. The times were indeed a-changing but he knew the word AIDS would scare a lot of them. Let them wonder all they wanted about how Cauley had died.

It was with a heavy but happy heart that Kevin gave the president of SAFE the keys. The house would provide a place to live for those in need—for their final weeks of life for many, and for others, a new start—but it would never again be Cauley's house. Back at the condo, it was Wyatt who held Kevin this time while he cried.

Then Kevin quite suddenly had another issue to deal with. There was a problem with one of his new apps Google had bought that wasn't coming together the way it should. With it a customer could create an account and make a list of friends who also had accounts. Then they could take a picture and send to one or more friends. The "friends" could view the picture once or twice, but then it went away. The customer could send a message along with the picture, or just send a message without a picture. Same rules applied, but there was a limited life on the messages.

Kevin figured out what the problem was within a few days, and Theresa dropped in on Wyatt to make sure he was okay.

It embarrassed Wyatt because he really was doing better every day—he wanted to show Kevin he could be a man—but he just got winded quite easily.

Kevin took him places, and he soon got caught up in the magic of the City That Never Sleeps. Kevin took him to some Broadway shows— oh, that had been thrilling!—*Wicked* and *Kinky Boots* and *The Book of Mormon*. And that had caused one of those embarrassing days. The first show had been *The Book of Mormon*, and he was falling asleep in it and was unable to get comfortable, and Kevin insisted on them leaving during the first intermission, but not because he was mad (which Wyatt had thought at first). The tickets weren't cheap, after all, but then he was stunned once again by the love in Kevin's lovely eyes and the assurances that it was just a show—imagine! *The Book of Mormon* being *just* a show!—and that they could go again.

And they did.

Kevin took Wyatt to the Empire State Building, and he knew the off days when there were almost no crowds at all, and they went almost immediately to the top. The view was spectacular, but Wyatt did get scared. He knew he couldn't fall, but the way the walkway was built, with only that storm fence there to keep people safe, it *looked* like he could fall. He'd had to sit down right there, which sent a young guard into a tizzy telling him he *had* to get up, and *no* amount of Wyatt's insisting that he *couldn't* stand up would calm the man down, and then what should happen? Kevin scooped him up as if he were a child and carried him inside.

And Kevin said he wasn't romantic!

But….

Wyatt fell in love with Times Square, and Kevin promised him that he'd take him to see the ball drop come New Year's Eve. They'd get a room right there so they wouldn't have to fight hours of traffic to get home, and boy, that sounded nice.

But….

He fell in love with Theresa in no time, and he liked that she had been so cautious the first time or two they met. That meant that Kevin's best friend truly loved him and wasn't at all the type who was secretly holding a candle for her gay best friend.

But….

Kevin took him to art museums, where he saw Dali's famous melting clocks and Frida Kahlo's *Self-portrait with Cropped Hair* and Andy

Warhol's *Gold Marilyn Monroe* and Pablo Picasso's *Les Demoiselles d'Avignon* and Willem de Kooning's *Woman I*, but….

Except for maybe the clock one, Wyatt found them to be pretty fucking hideous.

"These are the most famous pieces in New York?" he asked, not thinking, as he was prone to do. "I mean, we have that gorgeous Saint John the Baptist by Caravaggio for the gods' sake, and what has got to be one of the world's best known Kwan Yin! I mean, I knew we wouldn't see the *Mona Lisa* or Michelangelo's *David*, but golly…."

But….

But Wyatt wasn't sure just what it was that made him feel so…. So…. So he didn't know what!

February Porch Night came, and he wasn't there. It was Scott's turn to host, and he made his margaritas, of course, but now he had graduated to real ones made with top-shelf tequila and in a blender and everything. The whole gang was hooting and hollering over the phone about how good they were and gods…. Gods, it sounded so fun.

And that sweetheart Kevin even ran downstairs and across the street and got mixings and made them for the two of them, and it was so sweet and fun and they were even able to dance to Harry Nilsson's "Put the Lime in the Coconut" song, just like the Fabulous Four (plus three) were doing while they all watched *Practical Magic*. Kevin and Cedar got the movie timed so eight men separated by thousands of miles could watch (and dance) at the very same time.

KEVIN WOKE up one morning and found Wyatt on the balcony, looking out at the city. A view that Kevin loved so much. A view that Wyatt told him he loved as well.

But….

The look on Wyatt's face.

He'd seen it more and more.

Wyatt wasn't happy. Not really.

It was the old familiar tickle that made him sure. The one that started at the base of his skull. The one that traveled over his scalp. The one that happened more and more lately. That now traveled even over his shoulders and down his arms.

The "knowing" that no matter how brave his face, Wyatt was *not* happy.

He left Wyatt alone for a bit, went and made coffee—the Sweetleaf bean he loved, but even he had to admit it wasn't as good as the coffee from The Shepherd's Bean (Wyatt's favorite coffee).

When it was done, he brought two mugs out onto the balcony and handed one to his sweet Baby Bear. Wyatt was wearing his flannel pajamas and his big bear slippers and his matching bear hat and nothing else, and Kevin had brought the quilt that Wyatt's mother had given them and they kept over the black suede couch.

"You must be freezing," he said.

Wyatt shrugged and said it wasn't so bad. "Hey, you're talking about the guy who was buried in snow. Nothing is cold after that!" He even managed to laugh about it.

Maybe. Maybe not. But there was still snow about, and it was too cold for Wyatt not to be wearing a coat.

"I love you," said Wyatt and sipped at his coffee.

"Do you?" Kevin asked, heart in his throat. He didn't know what he'd do if Wyatt said otherwise.

The look that came through Wyatt's eyes then was as immense as Manhattan itself.

"Oh gods, Kevin. I never knew what love was before you." He smiled and his entire face lit up, and any fraction of unhappiness that Kevin had seen growing in Wyatt over the past couple of weeks vanished. "I'm so in love with you. My heart… it swells until I think it will burst. I want to be a poet so I can tell you how much. I wake up in the mornings and just look at you sleeping next to me, and I can't believe I ever thought there was some cosmic balance keeping me from love."

Kevin felt the rush come over his own heart. He knew what it was like to wake up and just look at his lover and be amazed. The unattainable dream there in his bed and in his life. "I don't know, Wyatt. That sounded pretty poetic to me."

Wyatt took a bigger drink of his coffee, looked down the street and the look—for one second—came back to his face. He turned back, the smile returned, and he said, "You're right. Too cold for pajamas. Let's go in. And maybe you can warm me up." He growled.

And the loving had been sweet. They'd had to be so careful in their lovemakings at first, but it had been getting easier as the weeks passed. And having to be careful at first had somehow made the sex all the better. Had made them make love instead of passionate rutting. And while Kevin looked forward to some wildness again, right now what they were doing was perfection. It was building a foundation. At least he hoped so. It's what he felt.

But....

"You hungry?" Kevin asked and Wyatt said, oh yes, he was, and sat down on the couch and pulled Kevin to him and dragged his very full (by now) Calvin Klein underwear—red—down under his balls and took Kevin into his mouth and—*God, God, God! What Wyatt did with his mouth!*—and way too fast he was cumming, and Wyatt was moaning and greedily drinking him down. When he was done swimming in the aftereffects of Wyatt's brilliant talent, he pulled his lover to his feet and picked him up—*God*, Wyatt loved it when he did that, and so he loved to do it—and carried him to the bedroom and ate that adorable round plump butt, and it was so sweet, delighting his tongue, and then when Wyatt was begging him to fuck him, he rolled his lover onto his back instead and straddled him and took that thick cock inside him with only a bit of spit— he wanted, *needed* to feel this—and rocked and lifted and dropped himself until Wyatt was shouting and cumming inside him—Kevin could *feel* the rod of flesh thrumming, feel it like water rushing through a hose, feel the heat of his seed, and it was glorious—and Kevin was fisting his own cock and then shooting a second time, his cum landing all over Wyatt's sexy hairy chest in what seemed like endless pearlescent ropes.

And it was all the best positions so that Wyatt wasn't hurt, and Kevin made sure he didn't collapse upon the smaller man—they both loved it that Wyatt was smaller (in almost every way)—and let himself fall to the side instead, and they went naturally together in each other's arms, and—*oh!*—the loving was so good.

But when he roused himself he saw that Wyatt was awake and looking out the window.

And Kevin knew.

Wyatt *wasn't* happy.

THEY WERE looking at adoptable dogs online—they both agreed that rescuing was the best—because Wyatt needed something to mother—

"I wish we could get a dog from Four Footed Friends," Wyatt said. "It's right around the corner from The Shepherd's Bean. Bean himself got his dog there, you know, and he loves her so much."

—and then Kevin *knew*.

Knew more than he knew anything.

Knew more than he knew computers and phones and applications.

Knew that he loved the Land.

Knew that he was monogamous.

Knew more than how much he loved Wyatt.

Wyatt, the love of his life (his very existence), was *not* happy. No matter what he said.

Kevin let loose of the mouse he'd been using to find them a dog looking for a forever home and swiveled his chair about so that he was facing Wyatt, and he said it. He said, "You're not happy."

Bless him, Wyatt looked shocked. "How can you say that?"

Kevin shook his head. "You're not."

Wyatt looked at him in confusion. And yet.... Kevin saw the flicker of not-confused. Of—*No, I'm not!*—and loved him all the more for it. For trying to hide it.

"I've never been more happy, Kevin! What could I want more than what I have right now?"

"To live in Terra's Gate," Kevin said right away. "To live in that house you were living in. To be around your friends."

Wyatt shook his head. "You're all I want!"

"No, I'm not," Kevin said.

"Yes! I never thought I could have this and—"

"You want it all," Kevin said.

Wyatt looked at him in confusion. "I... I what?"

"You want it all."

Dawning came to Wyatt's eyes. He rolled them in that hilarious way of his. "Oh, Kevin! I know what I've *got*. Believe me. I'm happy."

"You're forgetting something, Baby Bear."

Wyatt smiled. "And what is that?"

"That the Universe gives us what we want, as big as we are willing to dream. That we are the only ones who believe that there are *small* dreams or *big* dreams or—the worst curse yet—acceptable, reasonable dreams. You *can* have it all. You can have whatever you want. As long as you are willing to *want* it."

"Kevin?"

"Ask, baby."

"Ask?"

"And then believe."

"Believe?"

Kevin smiled, his heart turned to golden light, and he said, "And receive."

"Receive…." Wyatt sighed.

For a long moment, they lay there together. Then Kevin said, "I've checked."

"Checked?" Wyatt asked.

"Sloan would love to sell us his mother's house. More than love."

Wyatt's eyes widened. "What?"

"And my bosses? I've told them, and they're okay with me not being available at a moment's notice. Theresa actually got them to admit I've spoiled them. And that they can live with me being a plane flight away."

"What?" Wyatt pulled back in shock. What was Kevin saying?

"It's not like I work nine to five," Kevin said.

"What?"

"I called Katherine, too, and guess what? Kitty was a miserable failure. She quit. Treasures of Terra needs a manager. One that has to be there at a moment's notice."

Wyatt couldn't believe what he was hearing.

"And how can there be a Fabulous Four without you? I mean, God, Asher is thinking about moving to Los Angeles. Even he says it all doesn't make sense without you."

Was Kevin suggesting what he thought he was suggesting?

"I think I should put the condo up for sale."

At that Wyatt actually had to sit up in bed. "What?" he asked again.

"I mean, with the money I'll make, we can buy Sloan's house with cash. The difference in the cost of living is pretty astonishing."

"What are you saying?" Wyatt asked.

"I want you to be happy."

This couldn't be happening.

"And you are not happy here."

"Yes, I am. I love New York," Wyatt lied, and didn't realize he was lying until he said it.

"No you don't. And you're not happy. But you're going to be. And so am I…."

EPILOGUE

Five Months Later

SO IT was the first Saturday of the month, and that meant it was Porch Night, the must-not-miss evening for the FF, aka the Fabulous Four.

Except they weren't the Fabulous Four anymore, were they?

They still hadn't decided on a new name.

The original foursome sat around one of the tables that had been set up in Max's backyard—now Max and Sloan's since Kevin and Wyatt had bought the house next door. On the table sat a huge vase of flowers that Kevin had grown in the garden that had once been so carefully maintained by Sloan's mother. It made Sloan so happy that Kevin had taken the garden to heart, and with some help from Max, it had won a neighborhood award. It even contained some stalks of Bells of Ireland, to honor Cauley. It was very special.

But special or not, the vase had been pushed from the table's center. The Fabulous Four were debating their name.

"The Extravagant Eight?" Wyatt suggested, sure that he should be the one to name them—he had dubbed them the *Fab*-ulous Four, after all.

"That sounds too much like it's about money," Scott argued—of course.

"How about the Remarkable Eight," Sloan offered.

"'Remarkable' doesn't start with the letter *E*."

"So the fuck what?" Asher said. "It doesn't need to!"

"Tell Marvel Comics that," Wyatt snapped. "How about Exalted Eight?"

"I'm not sure," Sloan said. "That sounds awfully godlike. I'm not sure I'm comfortable with that."

"We're all gods," Wyatt returned with a confident toss of his shoulders.

Scott shook his head. "I think we should say frig Marvel Comics—"

Wyatt gasped.

"—and just go with what we like. How about Marvelous Eight."

"You know, we don't need a damned name," Asher interjected.

Wyatt gasped even louder. "*Heresy!*"

"What is?" asked Kevin, bringing them a tray of refills on their Bloody Marys. All except Asher, who grabbed one of the two meanest, tastiest "virgin Marys" he'd been able to come up with (and oh, how Wyatt had howled at that!).

Asher took it and sipped and nodded his approval. "We're still trying to come up with a new name for our group."

Kevin shrugged. "Why not just the Fabulous Four Plus."

Wyatt stuck a finger down his throat—

"Okay!" Kevin laughed.

—and went on. "The Excellent Eight?"

Scott, Sloan, and Asher nodded.

"Not bad," Asher said with a raise of an eyebrow. "Not bad at all."

Peni, Cedar, and Max joined them and grabbed their Bloody Marys, Peni taking one of the other two "unleaded" tomato cocktails. Cedar had just finished a set on his guitar and was done for the day, or at least the afternoon. This party, which had begun at noon instead of the traditional evening and was in a backyard instead of a porch, was going to go all day, so he didn't even entertain the idea that he might have at least one more time at bat.

An adorable guy was sitting on the high stool now, tuning his own guitar.

"*What's* not bad?" Max asked. "The Bloody Marys? I think Kevin did a remarkable job."

"No," Wyatt said.

"They're still trying to come up with a new name for the Fabulous Four," Peni said.

Max shrugged. "I still don't see the need—"

"No!" declared Wyatt. "We have to have a name for all eight of us!"

Max ducked his head. "Okay. Sorry!"

"What about The Stupendous Eight," Cedar recommended.

"No," Asher said with a moan. "Wyatt says it has to start with the letter *E*."

"I don't know," Peni replied. "I think you're missing out on some cool names. The Greatest Eight. The Incredible Eight. The Awesome Eight."

"*No!*" bellowed Wyatt, and Peni too ducked his head.

"How about The Super Eight," Asher said with a Cheshire-sized grin.

"We are not naming ourselves after a string of hotels! We might as well call ourselves the Top-Drawer Eight."

"What about the Extraordinary Eight?" Peni offered.

They all froze.

"I like that," Sloan said with a nod—he who had never liked Fabulous Four in the first place.

"I *love* it," Asher said. "After all, we're all pretty frigging extraordinary."

Cedar grinned.

Scott nodded. "I like it, Peni."

Peni smiled. "Really?"

"Oh, wow!" Wyatt said in delight. "Oh. My. Gods! Peni! I love it!"

Peni beamed.

"Everybody? Everybody?" asked Wyatt. "What do you think?"

And when everyone—everyone—admitted they liked the idea, the Fabulous Four "Plus Four" had a new name.

TODAY BOASTED quite a turnout. They'd broken the rules—and they'd done a lot of that since love interests had begun to join the quartet—and invited a lot of people. It was a stunningly gorgeous day, the sun high but not too hot, temperature in the upper seventies—surprising when August could reach into the upper nineties and even lower hundreds in Missouri.

Max's brother Dennis was there with his lover, Armel. Correction! Husband. They'd gotten married while Wyatt was in the hospital. Max's son was there of course, but sadly on his own. Apparently he and Devin had drifted apart. He was depressed, but Wyatt had hugged him tight and assured him that anything could happen. And he forwarded some wise advice a good friend had given him once. "You'll make it through this, Logan. A year from now, you'll look back at this and remember only the good times. And I bet you'll have a boyfriend who will make you wonder how you could be so lucky."

Logan hugged him tight at that and thanked him. "I hope you're right."

"I am," he assured Logan. "I know I am. Trust me!"

Earl Beebe, the owner of Café Namasté, had come with a huge tray of vegan food.

A wonderful coincidence had brought Kit Jeffries, the young artist who had grown up a few doors down and made it big and now lived in New York with his husband, Nick St. George (along with a host of brothers and sisters as well as his parents).

"I'm so glad you finally came out," Kit said to Sloan, eyeing Max. "I always knew you were gay."

"You did?" Sloan had asked, surprised.

"But I sure didn't know about Max. I mean—" He raised his eyebrows up and down. "—good way to come out!"

"Hey, hey," said his handsome bespectacled spouse and put a claiming arm around Kit's shoulders. "Watch it!"

There were others as well. Bean from The Shepherd's Bean, along with his dreadlocked lover, H.D. And of course Mara, who worked for Bean, and her lover Elaine, who owned Four Footed Friends with H.D. (who had found Wyatt and Kevin a wonderful rescue dog named Oliver, a dachshund-Yorkie mix who was barking heartily and scoldingly from the other side of the fence for being left out).

"You might as well go get him," Kevin said. "I know that you want to. He'll be good."

And Wyatt grinned and dashed next door.

There were a lot more. Asher's very good friend Rabbi Dov Kushner, and some of the original cast of the Kansas City production of *Drunks*, as well as Guy, the director, and his lover, Austin. Austin's best friend Todd was there with his fiancé Gabe. Todd had brought food as well. He was one of the two top chefs at Izar's Jatetxea, a Basque restaurant in the city, and said the food was most unusual but utterly delicious.

There were several local Faeries from Men's Festival—all of whom had visited Wyatt in the hospital. Bunny and Kirk and Michael and Historical Heloise and Gentle Ben and his lover (they were also apparently married now!).

And yes, Gryphon (with a ton of his famous smoked meat) and Saffron with loaves of the most wonderful breads.

Wyatt's mother (who was wearing a lovely goddess necklace) and Wyatt's sister—sans kids—had come. But before Wyatt could think of being sad about his missing niece and nephew and the likely reason they were not there, he found out through his mother's whispers that Wendy had found a lawyer and was about to spring quite the surprise on her husband.

Peni's mother was there, and a virtual legion of his brothers and sisters, and of course—being Samoan—they brought food as well. Platters of it. Turkey tails and corned beef and Samoan chop suey and boiled bananas (which surprised more than one guest for their lack of sweetness and their much more potato-like flavor and texture).

There was a feast of food, and that wasn't counting Max's grilled hamburgers and hot dogs!

Everyone was simply stunned when Cedar's mother, world-famous rock star Cyan Carrington, arrived. It had caused quite a buzz.

And Sloan's boss Gary, and then—*holy shit!*—Peter Wagner as well? The owner of the company Sloan worked for and one of the richest men in the world?

"You know," said Wyatt. "Something's up."

"What do you mean?" asked Scott, who had switched over to rum and Cokes and was busy with one at the moment.

Wyatt waved at the crowd. "I mean, these people!" He gazed at Cyan, grace personified and looking ethereal in her shawls and flowing lavender and aqua and purple skirts.

"She is Cedar's mother," Scott said.

"Yeah. *But.*"

"You don't think it's pretty cool?" Scott asked.

"Sure I do." His brows came together suspiciously. "But still…."

"I think you're making a big deal out of a pretty damned cool one," Asher said. "And after all, we're the Extraordinary Eight. We bring about such commotion wherever we go!"

Scott grinned. "Yeah! We're magick, right?"

"But look," Wyatt said, and pointed to where the four friends' lovers were huddled together. "Look at our men! Something is going on, I tell you!"

With that the huddle broke.

And the four men turned and started their way.

They came and the gathering parted like the Red Sea before Moses's staff.

Each of their lovers came to them—Wyatt's husband, of course—and without a word took their hands and led them to the center of the yard. They took them by the shoulders and gently pushed them together in a square, arms touching, backs to each other, each facing out at the crowd.

Cedar cleared his throat. "Okay," he said aloud. "This was originally Kevin's idea. But then the rest of us, the 'Plus,' said, 'Hey wait, you've already done this. Not fair!'"

"But I pointed out that what I had done hadn't been at all romantic," Kevin declared.

Wyatt raised an eyebrow (because he thought Kevin had turned out to be one of the most romantic people he'd ever met).

"Doesn't matter," Max said and ran his fingers over his beard thoughtfully. "I mean, if this were all in order and proper, I should have been doing this today before you, especially Kevin." He pointed. "Because Sloan and I met first, and you went and upstaged us all."

"Well, there was the practicality," Kevin said.

"Nonsense," called out Peni. "Love isn't, nor ever has been, practical!"

"Amen," cried his mother, as accompanied by some hoots and hollers and "tell me about it!"

"The thing is," Max said, "the four of us got to talking, and we decided there was really only one way to do this. One way that no one would be upstaged. And no feelings hurt."

The other three nodded their agreement.

"And so…," Cedar said.

Then as one, the four men went down on one knee before their loves.

Sloan staggered. "Wh-what?" he said.

Asher's eyebrows shot up. "Peni?"

Scott's mouth fell open comically.

Wyatt looked around him and then down at Kevin. "Daddy Bear?" he asked—his new name for Kevin.

Then each of the kneeling men pulled small boxes from their pockets. Boxes that everyone present recognized for what they were.

They opened their boxes simultaneously, as if perfectly choreographed, and four wedding bands sparkled in the afternoon sunlight.

Sloan's was a lovely simple gold band with a line of diamonds.

Scott's was white gold with a red-and-steel-blue stone.

Asher's was gold with silver Hebrew writing.

Wyatt's was a tangle of rose and silver and gold Celtic knotwork.

"Sloan, Scott, Asher, Wyatt," their names were chorused. "Would you marry us?"

Then came that silence, the hush through the crowd, the wondering—what would happen next? And God! What if the answer was no? What if there was even a single no?

And with this, the tension was times four!

The answers came next.

"Oh my God, Max." Sloan trembled and went down on one knee with his lover. "Yes."

Scott was next. He followed suit and dropped to the ground—and he never told if it was to imitate Sloan or to keep himself from falling. "You mean it, Cedar? You? The gypsy?"

"Come gypsy with me," Cedar said. "Forever."

"Oh, yes! Yes, I will!"

Then Asher. He pulled Peni to his feet and kissed him. Kissed him hard and then lifted him high and told him not only "Yes," but "Hell yes!"

Wyatt put his hands on his hips, threw back his head, and cried out, "Now *that's* romantic." He looked at the crowd. "Does he make up for it, or does he make up for it?" Then he took Kevin's hand and guided him to his feet. "Eye-to-eye," he said. "Forever."

And still there was not a noise. Wyatt looked at the expectant people around him. He rolled his eyes. Then smiled beatifically at Kevin. "Of course, Daddy Bear. Yes, I will marry you. As many times as you'll have me!"

The crowd roared and clapped and stomped and cheered and Kevin lifted Wyatt even higher than Peni and Wyatt cried, "And that's what I call magick!"

And it was.

THE TORCHES still burned but most of the crowd had gone.

It had been a hell of a party.

The bearded young man had played and shocked Wyatt when he realized that he was *the* Joe Donovan. And yes, he sang "Fly," and some jubilant happy-themed songs as well. The lines of one in particular stood out for him....

Of all the people, you coulda won
Despite the craziest things I've done
Billions of hearts beating under the sun
You chose mine....

So, through every problem, take me along
Set with my suns and break with my dawns
We could go on the run or you could just sit on the lawn
By my side....

Oh, so let me be crystal, let me be clear
I want you with me for all of my years
So put on your nice clothes
We're gonna walk down the aisle...!

The crowd had gone wild at that point. They liked the sentiment too!

Peni and his brothers leapt and spun and wove in their brightly colored sarongs to powerful drum beats in traditional Samoan dances.

Cyan Carrington put on a concert that brought neighbors from blocks away—

"My God, is that...?"

"Holy shit! That's Cyan Carrington!"

"Oh! I hope she sings 'Dark Witch.'"

"How the heck did they get her here?"

—and yes, Cedar sang a song or two with her.

There were fireworks. Of course there were. Peter Wagner was there, by God, and he was famous for his fireworks (although these were a bit more contained than his giant annual Fourth of July party).

And so much more.

Dancing and music (Michael DJ'd well into the night and nary a cop showed up—Peter Wagner was there, of course) and hugs and kisses and congratulations and lives changed and prayers given and blessing made.

Taxis took those who were too drunk to drive to local hotels.

Oliver barked.

A lot.

And then four best friends, tired and overjoyed and loved, came together and held each other and marveled at how much their lives had changed in a year and a half.

They cried.

They hugged.

And finally they vowed.

The Extraordinary Eight was born this day.

But at the heart of them, the Fabulous Four ruled and were blood-bonded forever.

AND THEN....

"Okay, guys," Wyatt said. "Stop me if you've heard this one before...."

"Oh no," Scott cried.

"Are you sure?" Sloan asked.

"Because this has got to be a good one," Asher advised.

Wyatt paused. Then pouted.

"Gosh, guys. I like it. But it's not like it's great."

They all sighed.

They all smiled.

And then they told him to go on.

Wyatt grinned. "Okay," he said. "If there are two green balls in your hand, what do you have?"

They all admitted that they didn't know.

Except for one guess about tennis.

"Nope," said Wyatt. "You've got Kermit the Frog's undivided attention."

And after a few groans—deserved—their laughter filled the night.

A NOTE FROM THE AUTHOR

EVERY NOW and then a book comes along that makes an author bleed. For me, this was that book.

An author is often asked which character of theirs is most "them," or did any part of a particular book happen to you?

Well, not exactly.

But wow, does this one come close.

I was with a man for many years who treated me very badly and hurt my heart, and I did stay with him long, long after I should have. I didn't think I was worth more. But I finally learned that I was. I finally learned to love myself, and I came to see that I would rather live in a cardboard box in an alley in the snow than be with him one more day. I left him despite the fact that he had pretty much convinced me I would be alone for the rest of my life.

That was in July, and I met Raymond, my future husband, in November of that same year. As I write this, we've been together over fifteen years. Love does come. Love worthy of any of us.

And yes, out of all my characters, Wyatt is the most me, although a bit crazier and more flamboyant—the inner me, my inner Little Bear.

There were also some very rough hospital stays…. And more….

It took me about three to four months each to write the first three books in this series. It took me over a year to write *Winter Heart*. For that I deeply apologize. I know you were waiting, but I hope it was worth the wait. It's a big book! I think even longer than *Summer Lover*.

My next few novels are going to be much shorter with much less hardship and angst, I promise.

(Although there will be *some* angst of course—after all, how could it be one of my books otherwise?)

As for those plot threads that you might feel I should have addressed and didn't, I apologize for that as well. This tome already weighed in at well over 130,000 words. I had to stop somewhere!

And know this! There are always more books! I am never going to stop writing.

Meanwhile, remember…. Never let anyone tell you that you can't. You *can*. You're worth it. You're golden!

And it's never too late to pursue your dreams. Leap! The net will appear!

Namasté,
B.G. Thomas

ONE LAST THING!

I WANTED you to know that Joe Donovan is patterned after Bobby Jo Valentine, who is a very real person. A sweet, adorable, supremely talented, kind young man. He very graciously allowed me to use some of his lyrics in this book.

I met him last year and got to hear him perform and then talked to him afterward.

See, the lyrics to "Fly" blew me away.

I *knew* it was Wyatt Dolan's song.

So I asked Bobby if I could use it, and he said yes!

(He even called me "handsome man," which startled me and made me blush. I mean, he's gorgeous!)

"Fly" became intrinsic to this story.

Ifyouwant(andIhopeyoudo)youcanfindhissong"Fly"onYouTubeat: https://www.youtube.com/watch?v=2DUWHlblEm0&nohtml5=False And tell me he's not gorgeous and heart-stoppingly talented! I dare you!

Then please check out his work at:

http://www.bobbyjovalentine.com/

Remember to support artists! It's their livelihood.

Again, Namasté,
B.G.

B.G. THOMAS lives in Kansas City with his husband of more than a decade and their fabulous little dog. He is lucky enough to have a lovely daughter as well as many extraordinary friends. He has a great passion for life.

B.G. loves romance, comedies, fantasy, science fiction, and even horror—as far as he is concerned, as long as the stories are character driven and entertaining, it doesn't matter the genre. He has gone to literature conventions his entire adult life where he's been lucky enough to meet many of his favorite writers. He has made up stories since he was a child; it is where he finds his joy.

In the nineties, he wrote for gay magazines but stopped because the editors wanted all sex without plot. "The sex is never as important as the characters," he says. "Who cares what they are doing if we don't care about them?" Excited about the growing male/male romance market, he began writing again. Gay men are what he knows best, after all—since he grew out of being a "practicing" homosexual long ago. He submitted a story and was thrilled when it was accepted in four days. Since then the stories have poured out of him. "It's like I'm somehow making up for a lifetime's worth of stories!"

"Leap, and the net will appear" is his personal philosophy and his message to all. "It is never too late," he states. "Pursue your dreams. They will come true!"

Website/blog: bthomaswriter.wordpress.com

Seasons of Love: Book One

Sloan McKenna is going through a tough time. His beloved mother has recently passed away, leaving him her house and beautiful garden. But should he keep the house? Sell it? To make matters worse, he's in love with one of his best friends, Asher, a man who can't (or won't) love him back.

Sloan's neighbor, Max Turner, is married to an ambitious woman with far-reaching dreams, including moving the family to France. But Max is happy teaching at the local college and living in their nice, quiet town. Then he discovers his fourteen-year-old son is not only gay, but out and proud as well. That throws him into complete disarray, for more than one reason….

When Max's wife leaves on a two-month business trip to Paris, circumstances throw the two men together. As they become friends, Sloan finds himself falling in love with Max, who is completely unavailable… just like Asher. As for Max, he is discovering that both his son's coming out and his new friendship with Sloan are stirring up feelings he thought buried long ago. Spring is a time for rebirth—Is there any way the two men can find happiness and a new beginning?

www.dreamspinnerpress.com

Seasons of Love: Book Two

Scott Aberdeen doesn't believe in Santa Claus, the Easter Bunny, or God. Or love—at least, he knows no one will ever love him. After all, he has carried a torch for his best friend Sloan for a decade, hoping his feelings will be returned one day. But when Sloan finds springtime love with another man, Scott's fantasies are crushed and his skepticism confirmed.

Cedar Carrington, raised by rock star parents, leads a free-spirited, nomadic life, never staying in one place for long. Due to a dark past he refuses to share or even think about, he is willing to let men into his bed for sex, but never for the night.

When Scott finds himself camping in the middle of nowhere with over a hundred men who all believe in love—and faeries and a magickal gay brotherhood—he's pretty sure he's in the wrong place. And when Cedar connects with cynical, critical Scott, he wonders how he could be falling in for this man of all men. But hearts and lives have been transformed at the Heartland Men's Festival before, and it might be just the place where two very different men can release their pain and find true love at last.

www.dreamspinnerpress.com

Autumn Changes

Seasons of LOVE

B.G. Thomas

Seasons of Love: Book Three

Asher Eisenberg is a brilliant actor, destined for fame and fortune. But a traumatic incident in his past has caused him to reject his Jewish heritage and hide from everyone behind walls of arrogance and selfishness, and he blurs his loneliness with a lot of sex and alcohol. When he meets Peniamina Faamausili, however, he strangely can't stop thinking about the young man.

Peni is struggling with his sexuality, the Mormonism he was raised in, and the Samoan heritage that calls to him. He longs to receive the pe'a—the traditional Samoan tattoos-- and learn more of his people's ways. He has no interest in a man like Asher, who appears to use men and put them aside and whose drinking can't help but remind him of the drunk driver who killed his father. But he can't deny his attraction to Asher and finally agrees to a date if Asher can go thirty days without a drink.

Asher is about to go on a journey that will awaken him to his friends, his past, his future, and even to love. But that awakening could well demand the sacrifice of the dream he holds most dear.

www.dreamspinnerpress.com

B.G. Thomas
J. Scott Coatsworth
Jamie Fessenden
Michael Murphy

A MORE
PERFECT
UNION

On June 26, 2015, the Supreme Court of the United States made a monumental decision, and marriage equality became the law of the land.

That ruling made history—but what about the gay men who waited and wondered if the day would ever come when they could stand beside the person they love and say "I do"?

Here, four accomplished authors—gay married men—offer their take on that question as they explore same-sex relationships, love, and matrimony. Men who thought legal marriage was a right they would never have. Men who now stand legally joined with the men they love. With this book, they share the magic of dreams that came true—in tales of fantasy and romance with a dose of personal experience in the mix.

To commemorate the anniversary of full marriage equality in the US, this anthology celebrates the idea of marriage itself--and the universal truth of it that applies to us all, gay or straight.

www.dreamspinnerpress.com